# The Love of a Lawman

# The Love of
# a Lawman

Anna Jeffrey

A SIGNET BOOK

SIGNET ECLIPSE
Published by New American Library, a division of
Penguin Group (USA) Inc., 375 Hudson Street,
New York, New York 10014, USA
Penguin Group (Canada), 10 Alcorn Avenue, Toronto,
Ontario M4V 3B2, Canada (a division of Pearson Penguin Canada Inc.)
Penguin Books Ltd., 80 Strand, London WC2R 0RL, England
Penguin Ireland, 25 St. Stephen's Green, Dublin 2,
Ireland (a division of Penguin Books Ltd.)
Penguin Group (Australia), 250 Camberwell Road, Camberwell, Victoria 3124,
Australia (a division of Pearson Australia Group Pty. Ltd.)
Penguin Books India Pvt. Ltd., 11 Community Centre, Panchsheel Park,
New Delhi - 110 017, India
Penguin Group (NZ), cnr Airborne and Rosedale Roads, Albany,
Auckland 1310, New Zealand (a division of Pearson New Zealand Ltd.)
Penguin Books (South Africa) (Pty.) Ltd., 24 Sturdee Avenue,
Rosebank, Johannesburg 2196, South Africa

Penguin Books Ltd., Registered Offices:
80 Strand, London WC2R 0RL, England

First published by Signet Eclipse, an imprint of New American Library,
a division of Penguin Group (USA) Inc.

ISBN 0-7394-4841-2

## ACKNOWLEDGMENTS

During the research I did for this story, I was lucky to meet Tammy Bradbury, horse trainer and Aussie girl. Tammy's a storybook person if I ever met one. Except for red hair, she looks like the character Isabelle might look. Tammy patiently showed me around a superb cutting horse operation, showed me some outstanding horses, and answered every one of my dumb questions about breeding, foaling, and training these smart, magnificent animals. Through e-mail, she faithfully enlightened me with far more information than I was able to put into this book. She may recognize here and there a smidgen of Isabelle Rondeau's dialogue as being similar to conversations she and I had about horses. Thank you, Tammy.

I appreciate my cousin Kevin who, too, is a trainer and cutting horse owner. He allowed me to tramp around his barns and corrals, answered my questions, and showed me a number of potential champions, including one of his own.

From the law enforcement community, I thank Sheriff Mike Hawley of Island County, Washington, for his input on what it's like to be a sheriff in a sparsely populated county in a northwestern state. I also thank Idaho State Police public relations officer Rick Ohnsman, who answered my questions about criminal pursuit in Idaho. If law enforcement mistakes show up in the story, they are my own.

I have to acknowledge my husband, George, and our neighbor Mike Vardeman who helped me brainstorm John Bradshaw's adventure in the mountains. With both of them being gnarly old cowboys, their contribution made the last couple of chapters more interesting. They would be disappointed if I ignored them.

I had two great critique partners who spotted my flaws and helped me enrich my story, Mary Jane Meier and Elaine Margarette. Nor can I give short shrift to the suggestions from my agent, Annelise Robey, and my editor, Laura Cifelli.

As always, I thank my biggest cheerleaders, my husband, my daughter Adrienne, and my family.

*The Love of a Lawman* is the last book in a trilogy set in the fictitious town of Callister, Idaho. Though the books stand alone, some characters do cross over from novel to novel. The two previous books, *The Love of a Cowboy* and *The Love of a Stranger*, should still be on store shelves or they can be found at the online bookstores.

Thanks for reading,
Anna Jeffrey

# Chapter 1

*Crack!* A rifle shot pierced the morning stillness.

"Mamaaa!"

Isabelle Rondeau's heart streaked up her throat. A plastic bottle of dishwashing soap slipped from her hand and hit the kitchen floor with a *thud*.

She tore from the kitchen, out the back door. Stumbling off the stoop, she sprinted across the yard and through the wooden gate that led to the driveway.

Her ten-year-old daughter, Ava, ran toward her from the pasture left wet by last night's storm. "Mama! Mama! Something happened to Jack!"

Jack, their four-year-old border collie. Isabelle thought he was penned in the backyard. She caught her daughter in her arms. Heart pounding, she dropped to her knees on the wet grass and grabbed the girl's narrow shoulders. She looked her up and down, yaned open her puffy nylon coat and searched for injury, but saw nothing wrong.

"He ran off . . . next door and—" The child began to wail.

"Ava, Ava, don't cry. You're all right." Isabelle rushed her hands over her daughter's long russet braid. "Show me," she said in as calm a voice as she could manage.

"Over there." The small voice hitched as she pointed toward the hillside some three hundred feet away, on the other side of two barbed wire fences.

Isabelle strained to see through the gray veil of morning fog. A tiny dim image of black and white stood out against winter's beige grass. A sick feeling grew in her stomach. Burning tears rushed to her eyes. She pulled Ava's thin body close and enclosed her in an embrace. "Shh-shh. Mama's here."

Instinct urged her to race to their fallen pet's side, but the same instinct told her it was too late and Ava needed her presence more than the dog did.

Swallowing hard, she shot a look past her daughter's shoulder, her eyes panning the fenced fifty-acre pasture that lay between her house and the county road. Two of her three most valuable possessions grazed down by the road. Cutting horses. A six-year-old sorrel mare named Trixie and a ten-year-old blood bay named Polly. Her gaze zoomed over to the smaller side pasture that held her stallion. All the horses appeared to be fine. One sliver of anxiety quelled.

She swung her focus back to the black-and-white spot, then on up the hill to a massive log house that looked as if it had been hewn from the vast mountainside against which it stood. A lazy trail of smoke drifted from a wide rock chimney.

Tears welled again. To compound her anguish, the cold fog turned into a heavy mist and stabbed her face with prickles of chill. Her body began to quake from the cold.

With one last glance at the black-and-white spot, she put her arm around Ava and walked her toward the old house where they had taken up residence, the house of her own miserable childhood.

Ava tried to look back, but Isabelle held her shoulders firmly and steered her straight ahead. "But—but, Mama—"

"Shhh. Let's go inside."

She guided Ava through the gate in the hogwire fence that enclosed their large backyard, through the screened-in porch with its painted plywood floor, to the long mudroom where heavy coats hung on iron hooks made of used horseshoes. A row of assorted boots lined up beneath them. Still shaking, Isabelle stopped and stripped off her daughter's rubber boots. "Honey, your socks are soaking."

"Is Jack gonna be okay, Mama?"

Isabelle peeled off Ava's wet socks and hung them on the side of the deep fiberglass laundry sink. "Go stand in front of the fire. I'll be there soon as I take off my boots."

Ava continued to weep as she left for the living room. Isabelle tugged off her own boots and followed.

A low fire burned in the brick fireplace. The gloom of a cold, foggy day forced itself through a pair of curtainless two-over-two windows, but the fire and rustic furnishings made the room feel cozy. She knelt in front of Ava as she worked the wet coat off her daughter's spindly arms. Ava sobbed and shivered.

"We have to get you warm," Isabella said.

She grabbed a thick knitted afghan from the back of the sofa and wrapped it around her, then urged her to a seat in front of the fireplace. Isabelle sat back on her heels and rubbed the slender bare feet between her hands. "Your feet are ice-cold." Her own shearling-lined slippers sat on the hearth and she grabbed them up and slid them onto Ava's feet.

"He isn't going to be okay, is he?" Ava's voice began to hitch again.

The ten-year-old was too wise to be fooled by an unrealistic white lie and the dog meant too much to raise false hope. Isabelle hugged her close. "I don't think so, but I'll have to go see."

"Go now, Mama. Go now."

Isabelle's heart kept up a rapid tattoo. Anger seethed within her, but she held it in check and pushed back a tendril straying from the braid that hung down Ava's back. "First, we need to put a log on the fire. Want to help me?"

Ava's sobs abated to weeping and sniffling. She wiped her nose with the back of her hand. "No."

"Okay. You get warm. It'll only take me a minute."

By the time Isabelle stoked the embers to a roaring blaze, Ava had ceased crying and was staring into the orange flames. "I hate it here," she said. "I don't know why we had to come."

*Oh, Ava, please don't hate it.*

They had been in Callister three weeks and Isabelle was uneasy enough about the move without Ava hating it. "This is where our family is, sweetie, and family's important." She removed Ava's wire-rimmed glasses and wiped them clean on the tail of her flannel shirt. "While you get warm, I'll go next door and see what happened."

"I want to go, too."

"No, sweetheart. You need to stay where it's dry and warm." She set the glasses back on Ava's nose. The lenses magnified her dark brown eyes to where they looked huge and owllike. "You watch the fire."

Her daughter didn't agree or disagree. She only stared with accusing eyes. But she was calmer now. Being given a task, a responsibility, had always settled her. *Too old for her ten years.* The thought sent a stab of guilt all the way through Isabelle's heart. "Please, Ava. I need you to stay right here until I get back."

Ava stared at her, her eyes red, her rosebud mouth turned down at the corners.

Isabelle rose and walked to the mudroom, keeping her steps light, careful not to bring more tension to the brittle moment. She picked a clean, dry shirt from the laundry line that stretched wall to wall above the antiquated washing machine, pushed her feet into rubber Sorels and yanked her heavy coat off its hook. Tears still hovered near the surface. She stamped toward her pickup, shoving her arms into the coat sleeves and zipping up as she went.

The Sierra fired on demand and she drove down the long driveway, through potholes and puddles, sending muddy water flying. At the county road, she made a sharp right turn, drove a few hundred feet and made another, then sped up the smooth gravel road that went to the log house of the neighbor who had never been a friend, Art Karadimos.

On the left, just below Art's house, Jack lay uphill from a huddled band of grimy sheep, their fleece turned gray by the wet conditions. She halted the Sierra and sprang out, climbed through the strands of a barbed wire fence and dashed to the border collie that had been with her and Ava since puppyhood.

She dropped to her knees and ran her hand over his hair, now wet and stained dark. She had no trouble spotting where a bullet had pierced his small chest. Art had always been a crack shot. A sob burst from her throat. "Dammit, Jack. Why didn't you stay home?"

Wiping her tears with her sleeve, she tried to think. Jack couldn't be left here in the sodden pasture, but how could she take him home, knowing Ava would see him shot and bloody? Even now, her grief-stricken daughter would be watching out the window.

On a hard swallow, Isabelle lifted the dog's limp body and carried it to the Sierra's bed. "Friggin' sheep," she mumbled, slamming the tailgate shut. She climbed behind the wheel and plowed up the road toward the log house.

Nearing the front deck, she spotted the owner standing there, his shoulder leaned against a thick log porch support, his face a scowl behind a drooping mustache. Eighteen years ago she had thought he looked grizzled and withered. He still did. Apparently age hadn't changed his personality. Her dead dog was testimony to that much.

She lurched to a stop, leaped out and stomped to the edge of the deck that struck her at chin level. "That's my daughter's dog you shot!"

He glared down at her and threw a fist in the air. "I warned you yesterday. I won't have him running my sheep."

"You didn't have to shoot him. You could have called me."

He huffed, turned his back, walked into the house and slammed the door.

"You're a mean bastard, Art Karadimos," she shouted at his front door. "You always have been. You were mean to my mom and dad. You were mean to me and my brother."

Silence.

She picked up a baseball-sized rock and hurled it with all her strength against the side of the house. It clunked against the thick log wall and bounced off. "I'm back, damn you! I'm gonna live here and there's nothing you can do about it! I'm gonna call the sheriff! You can't just shoot somebody's dog!"

Stamping back to the Sierra, she dug in her coat pocket for her cell phone and came up empty-handed. She had left the phone on the kitchen counter back at the house. "Shit!"

She roared back down the long driveway to the sagging lodgepole entrance to her own place and stopped to collect herself. She had to get a grip. She was all Ava had. A daughter shouldn't see her mother fall apart.

"Calm down, Isabelle," she muttered and eased up the driveway.

Sheriff John Thomas Bradshaw, Jr., listened to a breathless female voice on the phone, pretty sure the woman was crying.

"...shot...my little girl's dog....He..."

"Where are you, ma'am, and who shot him?"

"I'm at...home...in my barn. My neighbor..."

John groaned mentally. In the three months he had been sheriff of Callister County, Idaho, he hadn't been called on to investigate much and he couldn't recall from the Idaho State Police's two weeks of sheriff's school he had attended in Boise if dog-shooting incidents had been addressed. "Tell me who you are and where you live, ma'am."

When he heard her name, his mental groan grew louder. Izzy Rondeau. He remembered her from high school. Pretty, sweet-natured, sort of quiet. Had a long mop of curly red hair that flew wild and free as a windstorm. In school, she had been labeled Frizzy Izzy, among other teenage sobriquets. Hearing her name surprised him. She had left town before he graduated and he hadn't heard of her since.

She was calling from her folks' house, so the neighbor would be Art Karadimos, a gnarly geezer who raised sheep and damn sure had it in him to shoot her dog. Or even her, with the right provocation. He was one of John's dad's good friends.

"Just stay where you are. I'll be out there." John hung up and got to his feet. He grabbed his battered Stetson off the top of the nearest filing cabinet behind his desk and his down coat off the oak coat tree in the corner.

In the reception area outside his office sat Callister County's one deputy, Rooster Gilley, and Dana Mason, the department's receptionist, clerk, secretary and dispatcher. Setting his hat on his head, John stopped at Rooster's desk. "When did Izzy Rondeau come back?"

Rooster glanced up from a Solitaire game on his computer screen, his face set in its usual dolorous expression.

The deputy's face made John think of a basset hound. "Maybe three weeks now," Rooster said. "Why?"

After several months associating with Rooster, John had ceased questioning the deputy's knowledge of Callister County and its population. The older native knew all thirty-five hundred citizens and somehow knew the county's every happening, no matter how trivial. He had been the deputy sheriff for over ten years. He was a little puny in the thinking department and this was the best job he had ever had. He was loyal and steady.

John shrugged into his coat. "Art 'Dimos shot her dog."

"Ooohh, shit. You going out there?"

"Have to."

"Billy ain't with her," Dana put in, without looking away from her computer screen. Her hands flew over the keyboard keys. She wasn't playing Solitaire. Having done a hitch in the army where she was some kind of clerk, she maintained the record-keeping end of the sheriff's office with ruthless efficiency. "Izzy's cousin said he ran off with another woman."

No big surprise there. Billy Bledsoe had always been a prick, even as a kid. Izzy and he had left Callister together.

"The hell. I'll be in the Blazer if you need me."

John clumped up the steep wooden stairs leading out of the courthouse basement that housed the sheriff's office and jail. Outside, he drew into his lungs a big helping of chilled air, thick with moisture. Spring had to be just around the corner.

The sheriff's department's aged Blazer with its encircled gold star logo on the front door waited for him like a faithful, if broken-down, steed. He thought again about asking the county commissioners for a new rig. Travel on the mostly unpaved county roads wore out a vehicle in a hurry.

He scooted behind the wheel, looking around as he plugged the key into the ignition. Through the silver mist, he could see the entire town strung along two sides of the high-way that passed through. Except for automobiles and the paved highway, John suspected the town didn't look much different from when it began in 1840, when a Bradshaw had been one of the founding fathers. John's roots ran deep.

Things looked quiet this morning. Still, he could almost feel the town's pulse elevating to a steady drum as the weekenders anticipated the evening. Typical for a Saturday.

The radio, which he kept tuned to a country-western station, came on when he switched on the ignition. John shifted gears and nosed east as George Strait crooned "Amarillo by Morning." The lyrics told a story of a rodeo cowboy, broke and down on his luck. John had heard the song many times, but it still had special meaning to him, for he himself was a broke, down-on-his-luck rodeo cowboy.

The Karadimos and Rondeau places were about fifteen miles out of town. Because they were the only two dwellings at the end of Stony Creek Road, Callister County's four-man maintenance crew kept the gravel passage in only fair shape. The Blazer furrowed through mud ruts and rattled over wet potholes, making poor time and giving John's mind an opportunity to dwell on Izzy.

In school they had been in 4-H together; both had raised steers. A couple of years older than he, she'd had a woman's body when a lot of the girls his age looked more like boys than girls. He spent his whole sophomore year at Callister High School sporting a hard-on, watching her heart-shaped butt twitch up and down the hallways in tight jeans. And dreading the day when she would graduate and take that vision away from him.

He invited her to a rodeo once to watch him rope, but his being the only Callister High School kid ever to be a steer-roping champion at the national level hadn't impressed her. She'd had eyes only for Billy, who wasn't a champion at anything.

John reached the weathered Rondeau gate, slowed just past the cattle guard and looked at two horses grazing on his right. Their images were blurry in the fog, but they looked like mares. Izzy fooled with horses when they were teenagers, probably would have competed in rodeo if she'd had some support.

A white frame house of no particular style hunkered at the end of a half mile of driveway. John couldn't guess its age, but he was sure it was older than he. Its most obvious distinctive feature was wood siding badly in need of paint. A huge barn in need of more than paint and a couple of out-buildings with attached corrals lay to the left and slightly back from the house. John ground his way uphill toward the complex.

Near the house a lone horse grazed in a separate pasture adjacent to a small barn on his left. Had to be a stallion. With springtime being peak breeding season, poor old studs got stuck out in a pasture all by themselves until needed for what they were most good for. Some people liked stallions, but he didn't trust them. Most were unruly and unpredictable. All the horses John had owned had been geldings.

He pulled to a stop in the tire tracks worn into the grass in front of the house. A woman zipped up in a bright blue parka stood at the front gate, obviously waiting for him. Izzy. John recognized her, even with a hood covering her hair. One arm was wrapped around a little kid who seemed to be all coat and boots.

He scooted out of the Blazer and walked over. Unable to tell if she recognized him, he lifted his hat, offered his right hand and introduced himself.

"Oh, yeah," she said, shaking hands and looking up at him with eyes dark as coffee. Even when they were kids, John had wondered what deep secrets those midnight eyes hid. There had always been a lot of talk about the Rondeaus. "I recall, sort of," she said. "You were in Paul's class in school. Well, that is, when Paul was *in* school."

Paul Rondeau. Izzy's badass little brother. He had been in trouble from the first grade forward and not much in that regard had changed. He had already tested the law's author-ity once by arguing when John confiscated his truck keys and kept him from driving drunk. "That's right. I was."

"This is my daughter, Ava."

The kid frowned up at him from behind glasses sheened with moisture. She had dark brown eyes, freckles and rosy cheeks, and full, ruby lips—just like her mother. She also had red, swollen eyes. The dog was probably here.

"Ava." He touched his hat to her, but she didn't move a muscle or change her sour expression.

"I didn't know you were the sheriff," Izzy said. "Last I heard, you were rodeoing."

John chuckled. "I quit. Slim pickings if you don't hit the good money."

What he didn't say was when he had reached the brink of the good money, his life had caved in and he had lost his concentration. "I'm filling out Jim Higgins' term. You probably heard, he went to jail. The county commissioners appointed me. Let's see, you left town, what, around fifteen or sixteen years ago? With Billy Bledsoe, as I remember."

"Eighteen," she said curtly.

John waited for more, to add to the information Dana had volunteered, but all that came was an awkward pause. "Okay," he said finally, "where's your dog?"

She tilted her head toward a fairly new, mud-spattered GMC truck parked beside the barn.

"Let's have a look."

"Go in the house, Ava," she told the girl.

A defiant little chin thrust forward.

He dug a stick of chewing gum from his shirt pocket. "Tell you what, Ava—"

"You can't bribe me with gum," the little girl said, not changing her expression or removing her hands from her pockets.

"Ava, go," Izzy ordered, her tone firmer.

The kid stomped into the house and slammed the door. John followed Izzy toward the pickup, glancing back at the door to see if the glass pane fell out. "How old is she?"

"Ten. Please try to overlook her rudeness. She's headstrong. And mature for her age . . . She's upset."

"Yeah, I guess she would be." John pondered if his ten-year-old son knew what a bribe was.

At the truck, Izzy opened the tailgate and John saw a pretty, but very dead, little border collie on the truck bed. It had probably been shot with a .22, the varmint gun of choice. The sight hurt John's heart. He loved animals and he especially loved working dogs. Growing up on a ranch, he had always been around two or three. Anger leaped into him. "What happened?"

"I don't know. I was in the house."

A little flutter danced through John's stomach. Art was a grouchy old codger, but surely he had more sense than to fire a gun onto a neighbor's property. "Where was he when he got shot?"

She pushed her hands into her coat pockets and stared at the ground, pausing a few seconds before she answered. "Over there on the hillside, just below Art's house."

John threw a glance at the grazing herd of a hundred or so sheep. *Uh-oh.* It didn't take a genius to see what had happened. "Tell you what. I'll go up and have a talk with him. See if we can get to the bottom of this."

"What good's that going to do? I want the sonofabitch arrested."

So much for the quiet, sweet-natured girl from high school. "Ma'am, er, Izzy—"

"No one's called me Izzy in years." Those warm brown eyes gave him a glare cold enough to freeze ice cubes. "The name I use is Isabelle."

John hesitated a few seconds, unable to interpret the vibes coming off her in waves. One of the many things he remembered about her as a teenager was she had been a puzzle. It appeared that much hadn't changed. He ducked her piercing eyes and shook his head. "Look, just hang on here 'til I get back, okay?"

# Chapter 2

As the county's white Blazer bounced down her rugged driveway, Isabelle watched until the mist swallowed it up and she could see it only as a filmy object.

*The county commissioners appointed me.*

Had they lost their minds? She knew rodeo cowboys. Most of them should be *in* the jail, not minding it. John Bradshaw couldn't be any different. Well . . . maybe he was a *little* different; he was better-looking than most.

The discussion of when they last saw each other rekindled memories as ugly as a bad scar. *Eighteen years.* In all that time she had come back to Callister only once.

She had traveled a circuitous path since leaving this town. In the glare of the bright lights she had seen, high school days had dimmed, but she recalled John asking her for a date once. She remembered that particular instance because it had infuriated Billy. Crazy, how thrilled she had been all those years ago when handsome Billy Bledsoe showed jealousy over *her*, the redheaded, freckled daughter of the town's worst drunk.

As a teenager, John had been tall and skinny and baby-faced. Cute. Now, he appeared to have filled out, but it was hard to tell a man's build when he was wearing a padded down coat. What she *could* see was that the soft face of a boy had turned into the chiseled features, lean cheeks and square jaw of a man. He would be around thirty-two now, Paul's age. People looked so different when they grew up. Just like horses and cows. And dogs.

*Dogs.* The day she had brought Jack home flashed behind her eyes. Ava had fallen in love with him at once and Isabelle could still see him as a bouncy puppy and hear her daughter's bubbling laughter as the two of them played in the grassy yard of their home in Texas. The memories brought a new urge to break into tears.

Without a doubt, the feisty border collie had loved driving Art's sheep uphill and down. She caught him doing it twice last week and again as recently as yesterday. She thought he was secure in the backyard, but either he escaped or, she suspected, Ava, who didn't know the strength of the border collie's instinct to herd or the years-long bitter history of the Rondeaus and Art Karadimos, had taken him outside the fence.

She could blame no one but herself for this latest catastrophe in their lives. She should have trained Jack. Or better yet, never brought him, or herself and Ava, to Callister.

And she shouldn't have contacted the sheriff's office, shouldn't have brought attention to herself. The Rondeaus had never cozied up to the law. The phone call had been spurred by grief and frustration. All it had accomplished was to set her up as grist for Callister's gossip mill. The wheel still turned, no doubt, as ceaselessly as it did eighteen years ago when some member of her family had often been its subject.

She drove the pickup inside the barn so Ava would be less apt to view Jack's carcass in the bed. A blue plastic tarp used for covering hay hung over a stall door. She spread it on the pickup's tailgate, lifted the dog onto it, wrapped him and tucked the corners. She was all but sobbing by the time she finished. "Dammit, Jack, I wish you'd stayed home."

Tonight, after Ava went to bed, she would come back to the barn and bury their beloved pet.

She tugged her coat hood over her hair and trudged toward the house, rehearsing words to allay her daughter's grief. How could she explain away yet another loss in Ava's young life? Opening the back door with no dialogue formed, she grabbed onto her emotions and schooled her face. After having failed her child in so many ways, she had to be strong for her now.

She removed her soaked coat and muddy boots in the mudroom, then walked into the living room. Ava, wrapped in the Navajo-patterned afghan, was hunched on the edge of the sofa staring into the fire. Isabelle drew a deep breath, took a seat beside her and rested her elbows on her knees. "Want pizza for lunch? We've got one in the freezer."

Ava's head slowly shook.

Isabelle put an arm around her and drew her into an embrace, placed a cheek against her hair. "We'll get a kitty. We could get two or three to keep the horses company. Kittens would be fun."

Ava pushed away, now dry-eyed, her mouth pursed and rigid. She had always worn anger like a miniature suit of armor. "I don't want any cats," she said. "It's your fault. If you hadn't run Billy off, we wouldn't be here."

"Ava, I didn't run—"

An engine hummed out front, then stopped. Isabelle looked out the window and saw the sheriff on his way to the front door. "Stay here, Ava. I'll be right back."

She rose and left her daughter, opened the door before the sheriff could knock and met him outside on the porch, out of Ava's hearing range.

"Not much I can do," he said soberly. A drop of water fell from his hat brim onto the concrete porch.

She pulled her loose flannel shirt tightly around her and crossed her arms against the damp chill. "That's one of life's little problems, isn't it? No one ever does anything about the Art Karadimoses of the world."

His shoulder lifted in a shrug. "He says your dog was running his sheep."

"Jack lived around livestock all his life." Then, as if the devil himself had jumped into her mouth, a lie spilled out. "He wouldn't chase sheep."

The truth was, the dog had been around horses and cows. In the ten years they had lived in Texas horse country, she couldn't recall seeing a single sheep and if the dog had seen one, she didn't know it.

John looked at her a few beats, his brow arched. Of course, he didn't believe her. "If Art bothered *you*," he said, "I *can* do something about that."

"What, give him a lecture?"

"Listen," John said, his tone turning sharp, like he meant business. "I never said I was an expert, but I don't have to be to see what went on here. You should've kept your dog at home. I'll tell you again—if Art threatened you personally, *that* I can do something about."

"Art Karadimos better hadn't dare threaten me," she said, equally sharp. "I've got a .22 rifle in the living room and a 9 mm under the edge of my bed that says so."

"Izzy—Isabelle—"

"Even if he did threaten me, nothing would happen." She walked to the edge of the porch and looked out at the awful weather, planting a fist on her hip. "I remember how it always was around here. He'd get a slap on the wrist, then come back here and fight with me over everything that comes along. Just like he always did with my mom and dad." A memory came back of how Art had accused Paul of theft or vandalism, no matter how unreasonable, every time the old bastard found something out of place. "And my brother," she added.

She gazed across the pasture. The mist had turned into a steady drizzle, blurring sharp lines and erasing color from the scene. Her two mares ambled toward the shed connected to one side of the big barn. She should have put them in the barn hours ago. They weren't accustomed to the cold. She would be lucky if they didn't come down with flu or something worse.

"Next thing I know, he'll be taking potshots at my horses. And I can tell you this much, *Sheriff* Bradshaw—if he does that, I'll take care of the problem myself. Those are cutting horses down there. Worth big bucks. He'd better not harass them or harm them."

"I'm gonna pretend I didn't hear any of this, Izzy—Isabelle. You can't say stuff like that to me. I represent the law. Just cool it with the threats."

She huffed. "Some law. The county must have been desperate when they hired you."

"Look," John said—gently, she had to admit—"I know you're upset. I understand. I like dogs as much as any man, but it's not against the law for Art to protect his herd. Any sheep grower in Callister would do the same. A person's dog can't pester his neighbor's livestock. That's just the way it is."

She turned her head and stared across her shoulder into his unsmiling eyes, into irises as clear and green as emeralds. What was a *man* doing with eyes that looked like jewels? In the face of his direct look, for some reason, she couldn't admit aloud her dog had escaped her control and done something that got him killed. "Art Karadimos used to be friends with your dad. I'll bet he still is."

And she couldn't keep the accusing edge from her voice. Wasn't offense supposed to be the best defense? Hadn't she seen that tactic work often enough, living with Billy for seventeen years?

"That doesn't mean anything. If I could fix this, I would." John peeked out at the weather, his brow creased. "You got anybody to help you bury him?"

"I don't need any help."

His hand came out and touched her forearm. "Isabelle, let me help you. I know your little girl's torn up. I'm—"

"What, sorry? A lot of good that'll do. Her heart's broken. Jack was her friend, her companion. We've had him since he was a puppy. She gave him his name."

He nodded and stared at the porch floor.

"And I liked him, too," she threw in for good measure, glad to have someone to rail at and unable to let the incident drop.

He nodded again. "I'm sorry."

Oh, hell, he probably *was* sorry. Why was she being such a bitch? More conversation would be useless and as painful as punching the barn door with her fist. "Okay, yeah. Whatever." She crossed in front of him, speaking as she walked. "Listen, thanks for coming all the way out here in such crappy weather."

She opened the door and went back into the house.

\* \* \*

John stood on the porch staring at the front door she had closed in his face. *Okay, fine, dammit. Just fine.*

"Women," he muttered, stepping off the porch and tramping through the wet grass toward the Blazer. He wanted to reach the end of this whole sorry experience, and soon.

His coat was soaked. He jerked the Blazer door open, yanked off the coat and threw it in the cab before climbing behind the wheel. Shuddering, he fired the engine and turned the heat on high, waiting for comfort before driving away.

While he shivered and waited, he scanned the nearest pasture, wanting to take a closer look at the stallion. He was nowhere in sight.

Backing in an arc, he saw a long horse trailer parked at the side of the barn and held his foot on the brake for a few seconds while he studied the sleek newer model. It had room for four or five head, had tack and feed storage in the front end and a bunk area. Maybe climate control, too. Art had told him Izzy came with a pickup truck and horse trailer worth more than Frenchie Rondeau's whole house and that wasn't far from wrong. The only people who owned horse trailers as fancy as that one were in the horse business big time.

As he eased down her rough driveway, he peered over at the mares again. Their rumps were turned to the storm, so he couldn't see them clearly. That horse trailer told him they were performance horses of some kind. Maybe they really *were* cutting horses worth big bucks.

Art Karadimos' words echoed in his ears. *Them three horses she brought in here ain't canners. If she's like her old man, she probably stole 'em.*

John didn't believe the neighbor's spiteful remark, but he couldn't deny his curiosity as to why anybody would bring highbred horses to Callister.

As he navigated the muddy county road, he thought about cutting horses. On his mom and dad's ranch they were simply called cow horses. Smart, quick animals able to isolate a cow or calf from a herd, then maneuver left and right to block its attempts to return. They had been around since the birth of the ranching industry. Every cattle operation with a fair-sized herd had a few trained for the task. Branding cattle and administering medical treatment would be harder without a good cow horse.

He had been in a few rodeos where cutting was an exhibition event, but cutting-horse people weren't usually rodeo people. The cutters had their own organization, their own shows.

Big bucks? Big deal. Oh, sure, there were cutting horses worth big bucks, just like there were rope horses, racehorses, et cetera, et cetera. In Texas, maybe, but Texas wasn't Callister, Idaho.

His thoughts veered to the dog. He was sure it had been over in Art's pasture, harassing the sheep just like the old fart said. Border collies were busy little critters. Why had Izzy lied? Why hadn't she just admitted what happened and been done with the whole thing?

Of the things John had learned since pinning on the sheriff's badge, one of the eye-openers that stunned him the most was almost everybody told him lies. Sometimes huge whoppers, sometimes little fibs, but untruths all the same.

Ah, well. He guessed fibbing to the law was human nature. He had done it himself a few times. . . . *I didn't see that speed limit sign, honest. . . . I didn't know that trailer taillight was out. . . . Hey, I only had one beer.*

He didn't know if he would ever be comfortable as the man behind a badge. Even after three months, the lawdog end of the peace officer/citizen relationship felt like a shirt that didn't fit. It was a good thing filling out the sheriff's term was only temporary. A little over six months to go and this chapter of his life would end. The county would hold an election for a real sheriff and he would go out and look for a job in the real world. A world hugely different from Callister.

Back in his office, he found a phone message from his dad. A phone call from the man he wanted to hear from the least put the crowning touch on a day that had already turned shitty.

He delayed returning the call by hanging his damp coat on a chair back and placing it near a space heater, just so. He sorted papers on his desk, read over the faxes that came in daily passing on data about wanted suspects. He kept feeling Rooster's and Dana's eyes watching him expectantly, so he faced the unavoidable and on a sigh shut his office door and punched in his dad's number.

An answer came on the first ring. "How's Callister's fine sheriff today?"

John could never tell if such remarks from John Thomas Bradshaw, Sr., came in jest or in judgment. His dad had thought John wearing a sheriff's badge a joke all along. Dad wasn't the only one who held that opinion. John himself sometimes thought the situation humorous. "Going okay, Dad. What's up?"

"Your mother's worried. You haven't called her in weeks."

Shit, what could he say? That he neglected calling his mother because he hated the possibility of talking to his dad? He closed his eyes, picturing the Bradshaw patriarch standing tall and straight in the office just to the right of the ranch house's front door. The receiver was at his left ear, the four fingers of his right hand were tucked just inside the edge of the pocket of his starched and pressed Wranglers. "Put her on," John said.

"She's not here. Went down to the mall in Boise to do some shopping. I expect you forgot her birthday's coming up. It'd be decent for you to show up out here. And it wouldn't hurt if you brought her a present."

John couldn't imagine his mom, a horsewoman who could ride and rope with the best of them, strolling through a mall, shopping. He glanced at the wall calendar, which still showed January, though the date was March 1. "I didn't forget. I'm planning on coming out."

"Fine. I'll let her know. Now, don't disappoint her. 'Cause if she's expecting you, you know she'll spend two days cooking."

Besides being colorful and full of fun, Katie Bradshaw had to be the most loving, selfless woman alive. If a dozen people went to the ranch to help celebrate *her* birthday, she would spend the day cooking up a big feed for them.

Long blond-laced-with-gray hair, pulled back and

banded at her nape, jeans covered by a ruffly apron, cowboy boots and sometimes spurs clumping and clinking around the kitchen—that was John's mother. He braced his elbow on the desk and propped his jaw on his hand, thinking of the similarities in personality between his father and Art Karadimos. And feeling sorry for his mother. "Okay, Dad."

"I heard the schoolkids are soon having what they call that spring break," his dad said. "I was thinking, if you wanted to bring Trey and Cody up for a week, I'd pay for some plane tickets. It'd mean a lot to your mother to spend some time with her grandsons."

Spending time with his boys would mean a lot to John, too, but he didn't know how he could remedy the present circumstances. When Julie and he divorced, the court had given her full custody, with him allowed only two weekends a month. Then she remarried and moved to California. Before going, she petitioned for a new visitation schedule and the judge had gone along. The alteration denied him the company of his sons during the entire winter, including Christmas. All he could look forward to now was a month in the summer—or two months, if he begged her. He tried to have a phone conversation with them every week just to stay in touch with their lives, but Julie's and her new husband's schedules made doing even that difficult.

His dad didn't understand that buying the tickets was only a tiny part of the problem. "Julie won't let 'em fly alone, Dad. Even if I went down there to pick them up, I don't know if that would work either. Hell, I don't even know if they're gonna come for their scheduled visit this summer. I talked to 'em just a couple of days ago. Julie's husband's already made plans."

"That's a damn shame, son. It's one thing to let rodeos and whiskey ruin your marriage, but I don't know how you managed to screw up custody of those kids. When a woman does what your ex-wife did—"

"Cut it out, Dad." To this day, John didn't know how his parents had learned he had caught his ex-wife with another man. He had never discussed it with them himself and didn't intend to.

"You should've fought her for those kids. Right now, you oughtta be—"

"Just tell Mom I'll see her on her birthday, okay?" John hung up. The incident out at Rondeau's place had left him a little short in the temper. He didn't need to hear all he had done wrong or what he ought to do in the future. He leaned both elbows on his desk, massaging his eyes with his fingertips. Jesus, would he ever do anything in his whole life that would earn his dad's respect?

When he opened his eyes, the calendar still loomed before him. Saturday. If he were still rodeoing, he would probably be at the winter show in Tucson, psyching himself up for the finals. After the show, he would probably hook up with some sweet thing and they would go to the dance. Or they might skip the dance, pick up a bottle of Crown and just go to the motel. That is, if he had enough money in his pocket to pay for a room.

The thing he would *not* be doing was readying to go out and patrol the streets and the three bars of a small town, prepared to arrest somebody for drunk and disorderly conduct.

Sometimes it was hard to be glad he had changed his ways. Sometimes, though he had been off the rodeo circuit for more than a year, when he thought about different shows in which he had competed, he still felt as if he was missing something by not being there.

# Chapter 3

Covered by the thick afghan, Isabelle lay back on the sofa, her head resting on the arm, her arms enclosing her distraught daughter. The orange flames in the fireplace threw warmth and soft glimmers into the dim living room light. At last she was warm and Ava had stopped crying and dropped off to sleep.

Her neck was twisted at a cockeyed angle, but Isabelle didn't move, lest she wake Ava and start a new cycle of tears. She lay with her cheek resting against her daughter's hair, breathing the soft perfume of strawberry-scented shampoo and thinking on why and how had she come back to this place.

Three years ago her father had been found frozen to death in the alley behind the Eights & Aces Saloon. No one knew exactly what had happened, but the speculation was that he fell on the way to his car and couldn't get back on his feet.

At that fateful moment, she and her brother, Paul, had become the heirs of this old house, two barns, a loafing shed, a storage building and some miscellaneous ranch equipment. And three hundred prime acres that backed up to Callister Valley's tallest mountain. Years back, their parents had been offered an insulting price for the land by Art Karadimos. When their father refused to sell, Art diligently tried to steal the place, setting off enmity between neighbors that existed to this day.

After Frenchie Rondeau's death, with her living in Texas and her brother owning a home in town where he lived with his family, logic would have dictated they sell the homeplace for a premium price. Buyers from out of state were crawling all over Idaho towns like Callister looking for land and homes, both for investment and for relocating from urban areas like Los Angeles and San Francisco. And Hollywood.

She hadn't even been tempted to sell and Paul hadn't mentioned it once, as if they both knew she would return someday.

Her conscious self hadn't made such a plan, at least not immediately after their father's death. She hadn't even returned to Callister for his burial. Her brother's wife had handled the details.

God knew, she had no scrapbooks of happy memories of growing up here, but much had happened in Texas in the past three years. The allure of an unmortgaged roof over her head and the opportunity to build a secure nest near her only family had finally drawn her home.

Now, looking back, she supposed she had been simply homesick. In the humid summer heat of North Texas, her body began to long for nights cool enough for a blanket, sleeping with a window open, escaping the constantly blowing air from an air-conditioning unit. Her eyes began to hunger for the sight of pastures breaking into spring with brilliant green and for the dark forests that rose like regiments of monoliths, dwarfing all around them. In the non-winter of the southern latitude, she missed banks of snow and a fire roaring in the fireplace and on a cold morning warming her hands on a cup filled with hot coffee. Most of all, she missed the electric blue of the Idaho sky.

Home, sweet home. Nowhere could ever replace Callister in her heart.

Oddly enough, Billy's leaving hadn't been the trigger that drove her to sell out, pick up and move back home. The idea had formed in her subconscious before that, when she learned her only brother's wife had left him and taken his two kids to live in Boise. On hearing that news Isabelle looked at her life and her surroundings and knew she was a misplaced transient. Her north country roots reached out and wrapped themselves around her ankle. On that day, in her mind, she left Texas.

Almost without a second thought, she put the Weatherford property—a house and barns and two hundred sixty acres—on the market and began scaling back her activities, making plans for the move. She sold what she couldn't conveniently haul. She said good-byes. Though she went through the motions for weeks, not until she actually hooked her horse trailer onto the Sierra's bumper, loaded Polly, Trixie and Dancer and headed northwest, did she actually believe she was doing it.

Her brother, her aunt and her cousin met her and Ava in a joyful reunion her first day back. The euphoria lasted a week.

Now, three weeks later, reality had set in, bringing a torrent of doubt and insecurity. Returning to Callister appeared to be the biggest mistake she had ever made.

With her neck pain growing worse, she eased from beneath Ava's body, arranged her daughter's sleeping form on the sofa in front of the fire and spread the afghan over her. Conscience urged her to go outside and bury Jack, but she didn't want to make the ten-year-old a part of the process, nor did she want her to wake up and wonder where her mother was.

Instead of going outside, Isabelle went to the kitchen and downed two aspirins for the neck pain and the dull headache that throbbed behind her eyes. Then she pulled a muffin tin, a bowl, and a box of chocolate cake mix from the cupboard. Why sweet food would be a balm to a child's wounded heart she didn't know, but the offer of kittens had fallen flat and she had to do *something*. She would be the first to admit that a mother-of-the-year prize would never share the mantel with her many horse show trophies.

She had just dumped the powdery mix, water and cooking oil into a bowl when she heard Ava's voice. "Mama?"

Isabelle turned and saw her standing in the doorway, her thin face set in a grim expression, a too-big green sweater hanging halfway to her knees. "Oh, hi, sweetie. I thought you were napping. I'm making some cupcakes." Lousy cook that she was, Isabelle could muddle through making cupcakes from a cake mix. The directions were shown in pictures. "Chocolate. Want to help?"

Ava came and stood beside her, ducked her chin and pressed fingertips on the counter edge, watching as Isabelle cracked eggs. "I let Jack out the gate," she said in a small voice.

A mix of sorrow and love piled onto guilt and pierced Isabelle's heart. It had never been necessary to punish Ava for a misdeed. The child had always punished herself. Isabelle wiped her hands on her jeans and hugged her. "Oh, Ava—"

"He was crying, Mama. He didn't like being locked up. I was going to let him loose for just a minute, but he ran off and he wouldn't come back."

"I know, I know." Isabelle sank to her knees in front of her daughter, looked into the troubled eyes and took the small hands into her own. "Listen to me. What happened to Jack, if it hadn't been today, it would have been another day. I don't know how we would ever have made him stop going over to those sheep. He wanted to do it. We couldn't have kept him penned up forever."

"Do you think he'll forgive me?"

"Yes. He will. He's in doggie heaven and he knows you loved him. It's my fault. I should have taught him better."

She began to cry again. "But I wasn't supposed—you told me not to—"

"Sweetheart, it was just one of those bad things that happens." Isabelle hugged her daughter fiercely, feeling the trembling in her slight body and fighting back tears of her own. When she could speak with a strong voice, she set her daughter away. "Now. You know your mama's not the best cook. These cupcakes will turn out a lot better if you help."

The corners of Ava's mouth quirked ever so slightly. "Okay," she said, sniffling.

Isabelle handed her the muffin tins and paper liners. "Here, you do this while I stir up everything. Let's don't cry anymore, okay?"

Later, they cooked pizza and ate cupcakes for dessert. They talked about Jack and how sometimes events, despite everyone's best efforts, spiraled out of control. Then they watched the video of *Harry Potter and the Chamber of Secrets* again. By now, Isabelle knew some of the dialogue by heart. Ava fell asleep before the end of the movie, exhausted by the emotional upheaval of the day. Truth be told, Isabelle was worn out, too.

After tucking Ava into bed, Isabelle donned a slicker and rubber boots and made her way to the ramshackle barn. The night was dark as a mine shaft and the drizzle had developed into a cold, steady rain drumming on the barn roof. Missing shingles made for a leak here and there, but one of the lights worked and gave dull amber illumination.

She lit her Coleman, picked up a shovel and went outside. Around the corner, she found a place for Jack's grave where the horses wouldn't trample. She began to dig.

Busy hands didn't keep her mind from repeating the recrimination she had heaped on herself for two weeks over the foolishness of coming back here. Losing Jack only added an exclamation point. If she spent every dime in her savings account, it wouldn't be enough to put this tumbledown place in good shape. And she owned only half of it.

The sad truth was, except for her clothes and a few pieces of furniture, she didn't own *anything* that was hers alone, not her horses or her truck and trailer. When Billy walked out, neither she nor he did anything about the legalities of dividing assets. She had been too devastated to deal with it and he had been too eager to follow his girlfriend to Oklahoma.

With a knee-deep hole finished, she retrieved Jack's tarp-wrapped body from the pickup bed and placed it in the grave. Being unable to see him made the burial easier. She began to shovel mud, covering the tarp.

Forcing thought away from the hurtful task only replaced it with nagging fear. Could she develop a horse-training business without Billy? How long would it take in an out-of-the-way place like Callister? How much of her nest egg would be eaten by living expenses while she tried? And if the venture didn't succeed and her money ran out, what would she do then? A woman's opportunities for making a living in Callister were few and far between, especially a woman with limited ability at basic skills, like reading and writing.

She *had* to sell the horses. That hadn't been her intention in the beginning, but now she could think of no other solution. As much as she loved them and wanted to keep them, their maintenance would consume her money even faster.

She knew a few potential buyers, but to sell them she had to get in touch with Billy. Though it had always been understood between them that the horses were hers, his name was on their registration papers as half owner. She had to get him to sign off his interest. Making that call to Oklahoma hung over her head as black and endless as the stormy night sky.

By the time she shoveled the last bit of dirt and mud onto Jack's grave, the slicker had slid down. Her thick hair was soaked and hanging heavy on her neck. For the second time today, she was wet and shaking with cold.

All three horses had ambled to the sheds and waited for their supper. Nine o'clock and they hadn't been fed.

She returned to the big barn and went to the grain bin at the far end where, last week, she had hauled in and stacked some sacks of oats. A little treat to warm bellies when nighttime temperatures still dropped below freezing. She scooped a coffee can full twice for each horse and dumped the oats into a gallon bucket on the barn floor. Then she lugged the bucket to the best of the falling-apart stalls and poured two one-third rations into wooden troughs on the ground.

That done, she pulled several thick slabs from a hay bale, stuffed them into mangers mounted on the sides of the stalls and opened the barn door to allow the mares to enter. They clomped in, snuffling and blowing. After being outside in the storm, they were drenched. Poor babies. She should curry them dry, but she was exhausted, so she shut them inside the stalls and moved on.

The tears held in check since morning puddled in the corners of her eyes and burned her nose. Through watery vision, she piled more slabs of hay into the wheelbarrow and set the bucket holding the remaining oats on top. She had used her only tarp to bury Jack, so she threw a plastic trash bag over the hay and oats in the wheelbarrow and rolled it over to the smaller barn a few hundred feet away.

Her stallion, Dancer, stood under the shed roof waiting for her. She wheeled his supper to a low feeding trough and dumped in the hay and oats. He nuzzled her hair and gave her kisses.

"You're spoiled," she said, sniffling and stroking his wet face, "but you're better than all the other men I know."

He yanked his head free and snorted, then turned his attention to the feeding trough.

Without warning, a sob burst from deep in her chest. Losing Jack in such a tragic way had been enough to bring tears, but now the thought of selling the animals she had sacrificed to own and protect was too much.

Dancer raised his head in her direction and snorted. She pulled a currycomb from a wooden box hanging on the side of the barn and began to brush him dry. "I don't know what made me think coming back here was an answer to anything," she mumbled.

Now that she had made the move, now that she had done something almost impossible to undo, the facts were obvious and disappointment assailed her. "This place hasn't changed since I left here eighteen years ago," she said, moving to Dancer's opposite side. The horse's muscles rippled under her currycomb.

Indeed, Callister seemed to exist in a time warp. The same small businesses still struggled along the main street. She hadn't been in contact with many of the natives since her return, but she sensed that a siege mentality still thrived among them.

Even the same bars still operated. When she was a kid, double-digit percentages of alcoholism and unemployment ran neck and neck. She suspected that was true today.

"I just haven't been thinking straight since Billy left," she muttered. "I've made one bad decision after another. You know I'm a mess, don't you?"

The horse's head sawed up and down. Even he knew her failures. She sank to a wooden bench against the wall, leaned back and gave in to a new spate of tears.

Dancer lowered his head, gave her a gentle head bump.

She rubbed his cheek, his velvety muzzle. "How can I sell you?" She looked into his beautiful dark eyes with their spidery lashes. "What would I do without you? Who would I talk to?"

# Chapter 4

Sunday morning, John came to consciousness with the previous day's incident at Rondeau's place replaying in his mind. He could still see the border collie's corpse lying in the bed of Izzy's truck and the little girl's face, swollen and red from crying, could still hear the tightly controlled anguish in Izzy's voice.

He could still feel a little tear in his heart.

It had been hard to remain objective in the meeting with Art 'Dimos. John had found himself sympathizing with Izzy. He had heard a distinct snarl in Art's words when he talked about Izzy and her family. What could the old fucker have against her? She had been out of the state for years. John made a mental note to ask his mother when he saw her on her birthday.

The dog shooting was another one of those uncomfortable raw edges that came with the territory of being sheriff. He had always respected a person's privacy, had ruthlessly guarded his own, but now he had a front-row seat to the disorder in people's lives. Half the time, when duty called for him to intervene in a dispute or interfere with a citizen's determination to break the law, he felt like an interloper.

He snugged a little tighter into the covers and tried to return to sleep. He slept late if possible on Sunday mornings and delayed going into the office 'til after lunch. He took the night patrol on Fridays and Saturdays. Rooster had a family to go home to, but all John had was an empty apartment.

Last night he hadn't gotten home until after the bars closed at two a.m. A band from out of town played at the Eights & Aces Saloon. The rain and chill hadn't inhibited revelers, either local or from out of town. With Callister full of partying drunks, it had been up to him alone to see that order prevailed.

So far, he'd had few problems with drunks. When he told them to pack it in and go home, they cooperated. Not only was he bigger and in better physical shape than most of them, he had known them and their families all his life and they knew him and his. A few remembered him as a rodeo champion, which, strangely enough, seemed to carry more weight than the badge on his chest.

Outside, the cold rain continued, forecasted to last through Sunday. The town would be moving at a snail's pace today. Most people in Callister went to church on Sunday, even the ones who had partied hard on Saturday night.

Unable to drift back to sleep, he got up and pulled on sweatpants, brushed his teeth and put coffee on to drip. Then he went to the second bedroom, where he kept a Band Flex home gym he had bought used and cheap through eBay. Since moving back to Callister he had resumed an exercise regimen.

During his rodeo days, he had always worked out. Stamina and strength were important to a good performance. They made the steer-roping event safer for the roper, the horse and the calf. When he and Julie split, his equipment went on sale along with everything else and he broke the strength-building habit.

He straddled the narrow bench and began a series of reps, stretching his arms and upper body, the exercise bringing back a memory of how devoted he had once been to his rodeo career. He didn't often talk about the end of that phase of his life, but if he somehow got trapped into a conversation about it, he said aloud that the day his exercise equipment went down the road was the beginning of the end of his career.

A haunting inner voice told him the end had begun long before that, like when he and Julie began quarreling over his traveling, the cost of hauling and maintaining his rope horses, the lack of time he spent at home with her and the kids.

He could admit now to the quiet four walls of his apartment just how hard a wife with two small children on her hands must have found his traveling and rodeoing. Most of their married life, if he hadn't been gone, he had been readying to leave or returning from somewhere, racing to catch up with what had been neglected in his absence and constantly working out and practicing. Practice, practice and more practice—the foundation of a champion.

He also had to admit that even if he had been underfoot every day, the marriage probably still would have fallen apart. Julie hadn't loved him any more than he had loved her. They had little in common except two kids. Living like a monk, as he had done since he returned to Callister, had given him opportunity for introspection and he had come to terms with some truths, including who he was beyond being a relentless competitor for an elusive prize.

The sheriff's job had saved him from himself. On the whole, Callister was a good little town. Churches outnumbered bars and honest, hardworking people outnumbered drunks, just as they had when he was growing up. Being their protector was an experience he wouldn't forget. He finished his workout ready to face the job, not unhappy with the choice he had made.

After spending the weekend in a funk of grief, worry and indecision, and at the same time nursing a fever and a cold, Isabelle awoke Monday determined to take charge of her circumstances and press toward her goal—providing a livelihood for herself and her daughter with a horse-training business. The storm that had kept her confined for several days had moved east and left behind bright, if chilly, sun and blue skies and a promise of spring. After she delivered Ava to the school bus, she had called her younger brother, Paul, and he soon arrived. Now she stood with him in front of the tall barn, studying the weathered wooden exterior.

"Lord God, Izzy. Where we gonna get the money for all this?"

From his perspective, the question might have been valid, but she had no intention of divulging her bank balance, even to the brother she loved. It was all the money she had in the world. "I'll pay for it. All I want is for you to do some of the work."

She had just ticked off the list of repairs needed to the barn's siding and the lodgepole corrals.

Paul's gaze traveled up to the barn roof, where dozens of missing shingles left gaping holes. "And where'd *you* get the money?"

"Don't worry about it, okay? Let's go inside. I want to show you what I want done to the stalls."

As they trekked through fledgling pasture grass toward the barn, Paul groused, "We shoulda sold this ol' piece-o'-shit place."

The house had sat vacant since their father's death. Her brother would have camped under a pine tree before living here in the old family home. She was grateful he hadn't made an issue of selling it. Though her childhood here had been wretched, the rolling pastures were rich with good soil and ideally fenced and cross-fenced for animals. Her mom and dad may have fallen down as parents, but they had been good stewards of the land.

"I'm going back to work in June," Paul said. "I may be going up on the Clearwater, which means I won't be around to help you."

Her brother worked as a contract sawyer for logging companies around the state. Cutting down trees paid him well but, in Idaho, put him in a state of idleness half the year. She gave him a wicked-sister grin. "Hmm. Then you'll have to hammer fast, won't you?"

Paul grinned and gave the back of her hair a yank, like he used to do when they were kids. "I'll get it done for you, Izzy. You know I will."

"I know." She smiled back at him and patted his shoulder. "Because as much as you try to be a shiftless clod, I know you really aren't."

A few feet from the barn her brother stopped and stared into the dark doorway. Isabelle stopped, too, knowing cruel memories haunted him—memories of beatings with a riding crop or a belt. Fists. Anything that caused pain. The instrument depended on their father's state of drunkenness. She had been lucky. Their mother's hysterics spared her from the physical abuse of a brutal man, but a mother's outcry hadn't protected Paul. Some adult should have come to his defense, but no one ever did. "He's gone, Paul. There's nothing in there now that'll hurt you."

He shoved his hands into his pockets and strode forward in the cocky way he always assumed to hide his vulnerabilities. "Hell, I know that. I was just taking a look, that's all."

They walked through the barn's shady interior, with her pointing out repair work needed—doors to be replaced on the three stalls, reinforcement of the roof, three new stalls added opposite the three existing ones. Rusted tools of various uses and dried-to-brittle leather bridles hung on the buckled plank walls of what had been a tack room. Isabelle couldn't keep from wondering if these very objects had torn and bruised her brother's flesh. She intended to trash all of them.

She had buried most memories of her youth in the deepest part of her brain, had worked for years to accomplish the task. Now what she remembered of Paul in those years was he never cried, but he sometimes disappeared into the mountainside forest behind their home for days at a time. Neither of their parents ever went into the woods to look for him. Mom would pace the kitchen, her face drawn with worry, or sit at the kitchen table, her hands clenched into chapped and neglected knots. But she never left the house in search of her son.

At times Isabelle had gone into the forest herself, seeking out her battered little brother, carrying a cheese sandwich in a paper sack in case he was hungry. Ironic to be seeking him out again all these years later.

"If I'm going to board other people's horses," she said, "this has to be a safe place."

"You're dreaming, Izzy. Who's gonna bring horses to train in a place like Callister?"

"I'm counting on my reputation. I'm hoping when I put out some ads and get involved with the horse clubs around Boise, people will want me to work with their animals. Billy and I always had winners. Most serious horse people know our names."

"Billy. There's an asshole for you." Paul lifted his greasy bill cap and ran a hand through his unkempt dark hair. "Bledsoes been over to see your kid since you got back?"

"They called once. I'm sure they're embarrassed by what Billy did."

"Fuckers. Bledsoes is all assholes. I never did know what you saw in one of 'em."

She knew. As a teenager she had seen Billy as her salvation.

Paul lifted a stall door lying on the ground near their feet and leaned it against a support post. "I'm glad to help you out with the barn for a little while. Just don't ask me to do nothin' with horses."

"Carpenter work is all I want. I know you're good at it." She tugged at his forearm. "Now, come on up to the house and I'll cook you breakfast. You smell like a brewery, so I'm thinking you could use some food." They walked side by side toward the house. "You were out drinking last night?"

"A little. Me and Merle was at the Eights & Aces."

*More than a little,* Isabelle thought, from the yeasty smell of him and the tremor in his hands. Merle Keeton was older, but he was Paul's lifelong friend. The man was even more of a maverick than Paul and had a mean streak that made Isabelle uneasy. She hated his influence on her brother, who didn't seem to have a mind of his own. "You could come out and visit with Ava and me instead of hanging out in the bar all the time. Ava would be thrilled to get acquainted with her uncle."

"Why would your kid want to be around me when my own kids don't even like me?" He gave a sarcastic grunt. "Neither does my wife."

Isabelle looked at her brother's strong profile, so much like her own and their father's. Unlike her, Paul had their father's black-as-coal hair. Cleaned up, he was handsome. On the surface he appeared to be easygoing, but she knew him to be as edgy and reckless as a knot-headed horse that would bolt and run through a barbed wire fence to escape. She had always worried about him, more so after his wife left him. "Sherry used to worship you. I imagine she got tired of living with a thirty-two-year-old man who acts like a kid."

"Bull. She got highfalutin ideas about living in Boise. Wanted a career and all that shit."

"Paul, cashiering in a grocery store isn't a career. But it *is* a steady job. You ran her off."

The mares, Trixie and Polly, came over and clomped along beside them, interrupting her lecture. "You guys are just big babies," she said when Trixie snorted near her shoulder.

Paul snorted, too. "Big pains in the butt, if you ask me. They act more like dogs than horses."

In the small kitchen, Paul shrugged out of his ragged nylon jacket that showed the lining through tears at the elbows. He hung it on the back of a chair at the oak pedestal table that had sat at the same spot on the end of the kitchen for as long as Isabelle could remember.

"You been to see Aunt Margie yet? Or Nan?"

Their mother's younger sister and her daughter, Nan Gilbert, were Isabelle and Paul's closest extended family. When Isabelle had decided to return to Callister, she had called her cousin and told her. Without Isabelle's request or knowledge and before her and Ava's arrival, Paul and Nan's husband, Roger, had come out to their parents' vacant house and checked the well, the septic tank and the oil furnace. Nan had even ordered a delivery of stove oil. Roger, though he scarcely knew Isabelle, had helped Paul cut and split a cord of wood for the fireplace. Their work had made settling in much easier and confirmed in Isabelle's mind the importance of living near family. In Texas she would have had to pay someone to do all of that work. "A couple of times. They're both so busy, it's hard to catch them. And I've been busy, too."

Paul poured himself a cup of coffee, then sat down, watching as she set a cast-iron skillet on a burner of the worn-out cookstove and put bacon on to fry. Isabelle had been around Ava's age when the stove was bought. She had enough trouble cooking in a modern kitchen where everything worked, but with an old, unpredictable stove she didn't have a fighting chance. "Who'll you be working for come summer?" she asked her brother.

"Miller Logging."

"But I thought they convicted Kenny Miller of murder." The only murder that had occurred in Callister County in over half a century had been committed by the most successful citizen in the county, who also employed her brother.

"His two sisters is running his company. Good thing, 'cause there ain't nobody else in this county to work for."

"I wish you could get a job that lasts year-round." She poured coffee for herself and sat down opposite him at the table. "You've been off, what, four months?"

He sprawled in his chair. One leg thrust forward, his foot shod with a well-worn lace-up work boot, the footwear worn by loggers and tree-fallers. "Since Thanksgiving."

Isabelle shook her head, frustrated at the lack of opportunity in a town of six hundred thirty-five people. Another fact to remind her that returning to Callister was supreme folly. "See? That's exactly what I mean."

She watched as he sipped coffee, noted his dirty black work pants, his faded and stretched waffle-knit shirt. Her brother needed some care. If she could make a difference in his life, perhaps that alone would turn out to be a good enough reason for coming back. "I'm going to Boise in a few days and buy a new washer and dryer. Then you can bring your laundry out here and I'll do it for you."

"You don't need to be washing my clothes. It ain't no big deal. When everything gets dirty, I throw it all in a trash sack and take it to that coin-op joint downtown and—"

"Paul, I want to do your laundry. Just bring it out here."

He shrugged.

"While I'm down in Boise, I'm going to try to see Sherry. When summer gets here, maybe she'll bring your girls up to spend some time with us. Ava doesn't know any of our family."

He didn't look at her, but studied the contents of his mug. He hadn't said how the breakup of his family had affected him, but Isabelle knew losing his wife and two daughters

would be a never-healing wound. "You're really hung up on
this family crap, ain'tcha?" he said.

"You and your kids are part of the reason I came back
here. That's why I want you to straighten up. I want you to be
a brother I can be proud of and the father your kids can be
proud of. It'd kill me to see you end up like Pa."

Paul huddled over his coffee mug. "On my worst days,
sis, I couldn't be as bad as that old sumbitch, but I don't think
anybody's gonna be proud of me anytime soon."

That could be true, Isabelle thought, but she said, "*I* will,
if you let me." She rose, put her cheek against his and hugged
him. Then, before they had time to break into tears, she returned to the stove.

She lifted the crispy bacon strips from the hot grease
onto a plate and broke three eggs into the skillet. They sizzled and spit as the edges of the whites crisped and curled.
*Damn. Lacy eggs.* She turned down the heat and reached for
the bread. "Will two toasts be enough?"

"Yeah. Listen, I heard in town Art shot your dog."

A mix of sadness and anger still burned inside her over
how the border collie had died. Isabelle dropped the bread
slices into the toaster. "Jack was chasing his sheep."

"Humph. Art 'Dimos and our old man. Now there's a
pair. Somebody shoulda killed 'em both a long time ago. I
can prob'ly find you another dog. What kind you want?"

Isabelle carefully turned the eggs, proud of herself for not
breaking the yolks. "I don't know if Ava's ready for another
pet. We'll just let it go for a while, until she says she wants
one. I've got my hands full with other things right now."

When the toast popped up, she removed it and began to
spread butter on it. "Paul, how long has John Bradshaw been
sheriff?"

She hadn't been able to put the altogether too appealing
sheriff out of her mind. To her continued dismay, the image
of his tight Wranglers hugging his muscled haunches as he
stalked across her yard kept coming back at unexpected
moments.

"I dunno. Since before Christmas, I guess. Why?"

"He came out about Jack. I was surprised to see him back

in Callister. Remember when he was in high school? He was a good enough roper to be on the Wrangler team. If someone had asked me what happened to him, I would've said he became a rodeo star."

"He tried, but he ain't no different from the rest of us Callisterites, sis. Born losers, ever' last one of us."

"Don't say that. I don't consider myself a loser. And you aren't one either unless you make it so."

"The busybodies say ol' John spent too much time on the road. Neglected his homework."

Her brother sniggered, as she had heard other men do when they talked about sex. Having worked all of her adulthood around more men than women, she had no trouble recognizing it as the male equivalent of a giggle. Isabelle rolled her eyes. "You men are all alike."

"Well?" Paul returned a wide-eyed look as if he were innocent. "What else would you call it? While John was off chasing rodeos, his wife fell into some college professor's bed down in Boise, then took off with him to California. If ol' John had been spending his nights at home, that prob'ly wouldn't of happened. It must've got to him pretty bad 'cause afterwards was when he took up whiskey."

Isabelle lifted the eggs from the skillet and slid them onto the plate with the bacon and toast. "That's too bad, but that's how it is with a lot of rodeoers who try to be married and have families. It's a hard life filled with temptations." She set the steaming breakfast in front of her brother, then returned to her chair at the table and her coffee. "He's divorced now?"

Why she asked, she didn't know.

Paul dug into the food like he hadn't eaten in a month. "That's what they say. She cleaned him out. They had some kids. She took them, too."

"I don't understand how he got to be sheriff if he drinks too much."

"He don't drink no more. Nobody else would take the job, Izzy. It went empty for weeks after they arrested Jim Higgins. You remember Luke McRae? He's a county commissioner now. He ran into John down in Boise and hired him to do it."

She scarcely remembered Luke, with him a senior and her a sophomore. The hard-up Rondeaus and the well-off McRaes had nothing in common. "How nice to be rich enough to just pick out the man you want to be the sheriff."

"Things ain't changed much around here, Izzy. Same ol' people running things and scratching each other's backs— the McRaes, the Flaggs, the Fielders ... the Bradshaws. Nobody was even surprised when all of a sudden a Bradshaw got to be the sheriff."

"Well, fortunately there isn't much crime here." *Unless you count murdered dogs.* "So when can you start work on the barn?"

"No time like now, I guess. Soon's I eat." He popped a bacon slice into his mouth and chewed, then washed it down with coffee. He gave her a mischievous grin. "I 'spect you ain't gonna pay me, but I hope to hell you're gonna keep feeding me. You're almost as good a cook as Ma was."

# Chapter 5

Barking dogs?

As John reached the bottom of the stairs in the sheriff's reception room, he saw Rooster and Dana huddled over a big cardboard box, playing with two blond puppies. So his ears hadn't deceived him. "Where'd they come from?"

"I found them this morning," Dana answered. "Someone left them in this box by the door last night. Bless their hearts." She picked one up and cuddled it at her breast. It wriggled free and climbed over her shoulder, letting out a whine. "Aren't they just the cutest things?"

"You taking them home?"

"Cliff'll skin me if I bring home one more animal."

John knelt on one knee, put his hand into the box and let the remaining pup lick his fingers. "You taking them to your house, Rooster?"

"Lord, no. I got two dogs already. Looks like they belong to you, John T."

"Me? I live in an apartment, remember?"

"If you want a doghouse, I've got one o' them fiberglass things you can have."

"Where'll I put it, in the living room? They male or female?" He picked the pup in the box up and peered at its belly.

"One of each, I think," Dana said.

"So what'll we do with them?"

"Maybe somebody'll come in today who'll want them," Rooster said.

"Maybe you could use your charm, John, and sweet-talk Morticia into taking them." Dana guffawed.

The receptionist was joking about Rita Mitchell, the exotic-looking brunette from Boise who had opened a coffee shop in town. She delivered free lattes to the sheriff's office and made it so obvious that more than free coffee was available that Dana and Rooster teased him at every opportunity.

Ignoring the receptionist's jab, John said to Rooster, "Since we don't have an animal control department, I suppose the sheriff gets stuck with that job, too, huh?"

Rooster laughed. "That's about the size of it."

John put both puppies back into the box and carried them to one of the two empty jail cells. Rooster and Dana followed and spread newspaper on the cell's concrete floor. Then Dana left for the grocery store to buy dog food and chew toys.

By six o'clock they'd had no more success at finding the puppies a home than they'd had at keeping them jailed. The dozen people who had come and gone in the sheriff's office had viewed the cell's occupants, but no one volunteered to adopt them. John had gone back to the cell to pet them and play with them several times and grown more attached with each passing hour, but he couldn't figure out how he could keep them. Dana ducked out for home before six, leaving the puppies' future to him and Rooster.

"What do you want me to do with 'em when I lock up tonight?" Rooster asked. "We can't leave 'em here overnight."

John's shift had ended, but Rooster would be keeping the office open until nine. "I'm not sure," he said. "My back-yard's barely big enough for my porch." The minute the words left his mouth, Ava Bledsoe's unhappy little face popped into his mind. "Wait a minute. I know just what to do with these guys."

An hour later he was standing on Izzy's front porch, the box of puppies under one arm. Hanging on the other was the plastic grocery sack of chew toys and the bag of Puppy

Chow that Dana had bought. A gray igloo-shaped doghouse he had picked up at Rooster's place sat at his feet. He had even extorted a promise from the vet for free shots.

He knocked. Ava came to the door and stared up at him. She was dressed in jeans, two sweaters and pink-and-white athletic shoes. She had a book in her hand.

"Your mom home?"

"She's over at the barn." She pushed her glasses up on her nose with her forefinger.

A puppy yelped and his head popped up, past the rim of the box. "Okay," John said. "I'll go over there."

He turned to leave, but before he reached the edge of the porch, the kid was in front of him, shoving her thin arms into a coat. "I'll show you," she said and headed for the barn. Her eyes kept veering to the squirming bodies inside the box. "What are you doing with those puppies?"

"Nothing much. I just came to show them to your mom."

"Mama doesn't want any hounds. She only likes a few kinds of dogs."

"What kind is that?"

"She likes border collies and shelties. Sometimes she likes Jack Russells, but she says they're useless."

"I see," John said, mentally agreeing with that opinion.

Approaching the barn, John saw new pine poles here and there in the corral fences. He didn't recall seeing them a few days ago when he had come out to investigate the dog shooting. Somebody was making improvements.

Ava and he ducked between the poles of the corral adjoining the big barn and she led him inside. He inhaled a deep breath. Being the son of a cattle rancher, he loved the smell of a barn. The mixed scents of hay, leather and animals were branded on his soul and he missed them. The apartment where he spent his free time smelled like an oil furnace.

He saw Izzy at the far end of the barn mucking out a stall, shoveling soiled hay and shavings and animal droppings into a wheelbarrow. When they reached her, both puppies were straining to crawl out of the box and John set it on the ground.

Izzy stared wide-eyed at the box. She began to shake her head. "No, no—"

"Can we have them, Mama? Please?"

Before John had time to wonder if he had made a huge mistake, a puppy, its tail swinging like a pendulum, climbed out of the box and waddled toward Ava on stubby legs. She picked it up and its tiny pink tongue frantically lapped her face. Giggles bubbled out and John felt his heart lift. The pup that had been left behind in the box began to whine. Ava picked it up, too. Now she had a double armload of squirming, licking puppyflesh and she was laughing nonstop.

No combination was as full of pure happiness as a kid and a puppy. John couldn't keep from grinning.

Izzy gave him a baleful glare and threw her shovel across the muck-filled wheelbarrow. "Don't look so pleased with yourself. They aren't staying."

"Aw, c'mon. Look at your daughter. It's a perfect match."

Peeling off her gloves, Izzy walked over and looked down at the animals in the kid's arms. "What are they?"

John frowned. "Dogs?"

"This isn't funny. I meant what sex." She planted her fists on her hips.

John looked at her, sex leaping into his mind. She had on tight jeans and a green turtleneck sweater that hugged her trim shape. Her breasts weren't huge, but were just right for her build. The outline of peaked nipples showed on the front of her sweater. Chilly temperature. Lord, the sensitivities of a woman's body would fascinate him 'til he died.

She looked solid and strong as any athlete, yet fine-boned and feminine. Memories from high school darted through his head, the hours he had fantasized about touching her. Somehow she seemed even sexier now than back then. With her rosy cheeks, full lips and a storm of hair the color of new pennies, she looked healthy and alive and she was arousing urges he had no business having. "How about one of each?"

She took a puppy from her daughter and examined its underside. "This one's male." She ran her thumb and fingers over a paw. "They're mutts. And they're going to be *big* mutts. Look at the size of these feet."

"A cross between a lab and something, I'd say. Cute, huh? I took one look at them and thought of Ava Bledsoe."

"My name isn't Bledsoe," Ava said. "It's Rondeau."

Confusion muddled John's mind. What was up with these two and names? Had Izzy and Billy not married? Was Ava not Billy's kid? "Oh, sorry."

"I'll take care of them, Mama. They won't be any trouble." A puppy licked Ava's chin and knocked her glasses askew. She quickly righted them. "I'll teach them not to potty on the carpet. Like I did Jack, remember?"

Izzy glared up at him, her jaw tight. "I can't believe you've done this. What kind of a horrible mother would I be if I insisted you take them out of here?"

"I'm going to name the girl dog Jenny," Ava said, "after the girl that got saved by Harry Potter."

Except for having heard the name everywhere, John knew nothing about Harry Potter. "Sounds good. I bet she'll like that."

Izzy heaved a great sigh.

"C'mon," John said to her again. "Don't be grouchy. You're out here all by yourself miles from town. Your neighbor isn't exactly neighborly. You can use a couple of watchdogs. They don't have to be a special kind."

"I'm going to name the boy dog Harry," Ava said.

"Damn," Izzy mumbled, almost but not quite under her breath. "Bring them up to the house."

She stuffed her gloves in her hip pocket and left the barn. Behind her back, John gave Ava a thumbs-up and the girl scrunched her shoulders and giggled. She was a likable kid. They put the puppies back into the box, he picked it up and they caught up with Izzy.

As they walked along the fence, the stud lifted his head from grazing and shuffled toward them. John stopped and waited for him, noticing that he was smaller and lighter than John's rope horse and most ranch horses. Even so, the stallion had the sleek look of an athlete and damn near perfect conformation. A magnificent animal.

And his color was almost blue. A blue roan. John had seen only one other in all his years around horses and livestock.

The stallion craned his neck over the fence and snuffled at the cardboard box. When one of the pups barked, the horse jerked his head up and danced backward, farting and stamping and swishing his tail. Izzy put her hand out to him. "Stop that, you devil, and come here."

The horse approached the fence again. She slipped an arm around his neck and made kissing sounds at him. The horse nuzzled her hair and John had the feeling she had a special bond with him. "You're ornery," she told him softly, as she rubbed the side of his head.

"He's quite a lover," John said on a laugh, smoothing a hand down the stud's neck, enjoying the proximity of a sexy woman and a good horse. "He got a name?"

"Pepto's Blue Dan. I call him Dancer, but Satan would better suit his personality."

John didn't know performance horses by breeding, but he had been around a few highbred horses in rodeos and had heard variations of the Peppy name. "Good breeding, huh?"

"Yep. Goes all the way back to Little Peppy. You know that horse?"

Before John could say he had heard the name everywhere, Ava chimed in. "He was a cutting horse from the King Ranch in Texas. He won a million dollars."

Izzy grinned and pushed strands of hair from Ava's face. "At least a million."

John could see the strength in the stallion's body, the arrogance in his bearing, the intelligence in his eyes. "Cutting horse, huh? You had him in shows?"

"Some futurities in Texas."

"He's got cow," Ava said.

Isabelle chuckled and looked at Ava with obvious affection. "My little expert." She looked back up at John. "He's good with cows, all right, but he's high-spirited. Sometimes he takes some handling. He doesn't mean to be troublesome. His biggest problem is being a five-year-old stud."

John laughed as the two mares ambled up to the corral fence by the big barn on the other side of the driveway and whinnied, no doubt feeling slighted. He turned, walked across the driveway to the fence and gave them a quick once-over. Izzy and her daughter followed. "These are good-looking nags, too."

She cocked her head and looked up at him, squinting from the sunlight. "Get out your checkbook, sheriff. They're for sale."

"They trained for cutting, too?"

"You betcha. That's what Billy and I did in Texas."

John's tongue itched to ask about the state of her and Billy Bledsoe's relationship and how she got her hands on horses like these three, but he restrained himself. "You show them, too?"

"We—I used to. They're too old for futurities, but they're still qualified for some shows."

"Who keeps them in shape?"

"Me. It's what I do. I'm well known for it."

John had spent most of his life in a world of horses. Women were all over it, calling themselves trainers, but he knew of few really successful ones. He looked her in the eye. "You don't say."

"Right now I mostly just want to sell them."

Like hell she wanted to sell them. He could hear that much in the way her voice softened a note when she said it. Still, if that was her story, why had she brought them here? Even with as little knowledge as John had about the cutting-horse community in Idaho, he knew it had to be small compared to the scene in the Southwest. The nearest buyer for a horse like one of these would have to be in Boise, or more likely Texas or California. Anywhere but here.

She spun and marched toward the house. John couldn't keep from thinking her butt still had that twitch he had admired in high school.

When they reached the backyard, he set the box of puppies on the ground. "I brought a doghouse with me and some doggie stuff."

Izzy gave him a flat look. "Doggie stuff?"

He looked right back at her. "Puppies gotta have something to chew on, right?"

He returned to the front porch, picked up the doghouse and the sack of toys and Puppy Chow, then lugged them to the backyard. "Their shots are all arranged. All you have to do is take them by the vet's office."

Izzy stood on the stoop, arms crossed under her breasts while he and Ava located and leveled the doghouse a few feet from the back door, resetting and readjusting it until the installation suited the kid. At the end of it, mud covered his boots and his hands and knees.

"When they're grown," Izzy said, "I doubt if even one of them will fit into that thing, much less two. Does that mean you're going to show up out here with a second doghouse?"

"I could." John walked over to where she stood a couple of steps up on the stoop, pulled his handkerchief from his rear pocket and began to wipe his hands.

"Good thing. I don't have a penny budgeted for doghouses."

Meanwhile, the puppies had climbed out of the box and waddled around the muddy yard, their tails whipping back and forth. "They can sleep on the porch," Ava said, picking them up, one under each arm. She carried them into the house.

Izzy held the door open. "Be sure to clean them up before you turn them loose," she said to Ava. She looked down at him and said, "See what you've done?" But he didn't detect true anger in her tone. "If you want to wash off the mud, you can come in and use the laundry sink."

John stuffed his handkerchief back into his pocket, scraped his boot soles and followed her to a screened-in porch that ran the length of the house in back. A wood-burning cookstove hunkered at the far end. Shelves lined one wall, filled with empty canning jars. He suspected Izzy's mom, like many Callister rural folks, had done canning out here on the porch, using this stove.

Izzy preceded him into a mudroom and pointed out a deep laundry sink. As John folded back his cuffs and began washing his hands, the aroma of something spicy and meaty wafted from somewhere and his mouth watered. Having not eaten since a combination breakfast-lunch hamburger at Betty's Road Kill Café at eleven o'clock, he was hungry. "Sure smells good in here."

"It's beef stew," Ava said, hanging on to both puppies. "Mama cooks it in the Crock-Pot. It takes all day. It's really good. She made some bread, too."

"Homemade stew, homemade bread." John grinned and looked into Izzy's mysterious dark eyes. "Oh, man, it's been a long time since I had home cooking."

She dragged a towel off a rack on the unpainted plywood wall and handed it to him, but didn't extend an invitation to supper. She spoke to Ava. "Sweetie, you can't bring those pups inside the house. They have to stay on the porch."

Damn. He had been dismissed. No home-cooked stew. No chance to learn more about his old schoolmate who, without even trying, had churned up his juices. His hands dry, he rolled down his cuffs and buttoned them. "Well, since we got the pups taken care of, guess I'll get back to town." He lifted his hat and smoothed his hand over hair weeks past needing a trim.

"Hopefully," she said, leading him to the back door, "these dogs won't be grown before that second doghouse shows up. I don't want dogs the size of horses living on my back porch."

# Chapter 6

Isabelle had left Texas with a vow to give up men forever. When she made the pledge she suspected it was a hollow one and meeting John Bradshaw had just confirmed it.

Ladling stew into two bowls, she tried to steer her thoughts away from the image of him standing there at the fence stroking Dancer's neck, one tan boot propped on a rail and Wranglers pulled tight across his bottom. Good Lord, she had even caught herself several times sneaking a look downward from his trophy belt buckle.

Lust. Base animal attraction. It was the only explanation she had for the feeling that had slithered through her. As an animal breeder, she knew more than most about the mysterious, powerful drive in all animals to perpetuate the species. It was called mating. In human beings it was called sex. *Damn.*

Starting her new life in her hometown, she should have made a hospitable gesture and invited the sheriff to supper, but the odd attack of yearning had flustered her, especially when she thought she saw the same yearning in his eyes. Being caught in an unexpected man-woman encounter where sex was an underlying impetus had made her so nervous she could scarcely have a coherent conversation with him, much less share a meal.

In the middle of laying out silverware, Isabelle called Ava to come in from playing with the puppies, wash her hands and sit down to supper. Another of the new leaves she had turned over was putting meals on the table and making sure she and Ava sat and talked about school, about books Ava was reading, about her problems, whatever they were, while they ate. No more grabbing something to eat at separate times in front of the TV.

As she removed butter and milk from the old refrigerator, which had a personality of its own, she thought of how John's eyes slid over her, leaving a little trail of heat everywhere they touched. His gaze had lingered on her breasts. He had definitely stared at her breasts. *Damn.*

*Sex.* How long had it been since she'd had sex? She couldn't put an exact date on the last time, but at least four years had passed. For three of those years, she and Billy slept side by side in the same bed, night after night, month after month, year after year, with little or no physical contact. Then he left.

Oh, hell, water over the dam. Why waste energy thinking about sex? Or John Bradshaw? When it came to women he probably was as bad as Billy. No doubt he had a stable of women younger than the thirty-five she would turn in a few weeks. Buckle bunnies with pierced navels and skinny rear ends. If she knew cowboys—and she did—rodeo groupies were the more likely reason the sheriff was divorced.

Sex, or lack of it, was the least of her worries.

John had left Izzy's house with more aroused than just his appetite for food. And Isabelle Rondeau hadn't been the cause of that particular affliction since he was fifteen years old. Amazing.

What a woman his former schoolmate had become. Teenage Izzy paled in comparison to Isabelle full grown. When he looked at her, all he could think of was fire and earth and sunshine. And sex. Just like when he was a teenager and she had occupied his every thought. Plumb spooky.

He reined in those thoughts. She probably couldn't be trusted any more than any other woman he had met in the horse world.

Besides, he was the sheriff. Or at least he had the title and collected the paycheck, such as it was. He had to file Izzy away in a far corner of his mind, just as he had filed away that soft-looking blond schoolteacher who had moved here from Pocatello and surprised him when she did everything but undress him after hours one night in the courthouse.

Or Rita Mitchell. When he first came back to Callister months back, Rita and her tall, willowy body and long, silky hair had caught his eye. She was pretty and she appeared to be a promising companion. He took her to dinner once at the ski lodge, then another time to a movie in Ontario. Two evenings were enough to show him they had little to talk about. Since becoming single, he had learned something about sex and women and himself: Even if a woman was hell in bed, sooner or later you had to have a conversation.

With Rita, he recognized early on the shortfall in the communication department and he didn't even try to reach her bedroom. Now he was friendly if he ran into her, but he gave her a wide berth except to drop in at her store and buy coffee. She did sell good coffee.

He gave *all* women in Callister a wide berth. Sleeping around didn't seem like a great idea for the county sheriff in a small town that thrived on gossip. And beyond that, he wasn't the dog he had been for a while after Julie and he split. He no longer felt the need to prove it was only his wife who found him offensive enough to reject and replace with another man. He guessed he had grown up a little.

One-night stands, or one-rodeo stands, had brought him a lot of trouble. The last sobering incident with the fairer sex had taken place in Reno, when a pretty little thing whose last name he wasn't sure of to this day tried to drag him off to a wedding chapel. When he balked, a crying, screaming episode erupted, followed by the wanna-be bride ramming her SUV into his horse trailer. She refused to separate a hot night in the sack from love.

Like a glass of ice water in the face, the near-wedding, plus the danger to his horses and the cost of repairing his trailer, had shocked him into spending his nights on the road with a couple of Budweisers and TV reality shows. The alternate choice turned out to be just as bad in a different way, because two Buds became three, then a six-pack, and all of a sudden he found himself on a downhill slide going nowhere but the nearest liquor store.

Deep down, he believed himself to be a one-woman man, even a family man like his dad, despite how that image was at odds with the way he had lived up to this point.

Izzy crept into his thoughts again. A little voice told him he didn't have to worry about her going out of her way to attract his attention. Like porcupine quills, independence stuck out all over her. She had been as standoffish tonight as she was in school, hadn't revealed a significant word about herself or why she had returned to Callister. He could see she had her hands full with a wide-eyed little kid and that rundown place, not to mention those three horses.

At last he reached the highway. A half hour of thinking had shrunk the pressure behind his zipper. A good thing, too. It was Saturday night and he had the bar scene to patrol.

The next morning Isabelle overslept. Now she had to hurry. Her cousin, Nan, had called and offered to pick up Ava and take her to Sunday school with her kids, then to a matinee in Ontario. Isabelle had told Nan her desire to have Ava get acquainted with her family and she was grateful that Nan made the effort. She couldn't offer much in return, but she could teach Nan and Roger's kids to ride if she ever got a couple of good "kid horses."

She had awakened plagued by a jumble of annoyances. Her brief conversation with John about the horses had scrolled through her dreams off and on all night, badgering her about the need to do something about the ownership papers.

She stepped into the shower, absorbed by the problem. Seventeen years of living with Billy had taught her not to trust him in anything to do with money. She had seen too many dollars blown in expensive bars and restaurants and fancy clothing stores, not counting all that had melted away on the craps and blackjack tables when they had worked for a brief time in Nevada.

When he left her and Ava in Weatherford, he said she could have everything—their home, the truck and trailer and the horses. But when confronted with the closing of the sale of their property and the substantial amount of cash from the equity, he reneged and refused to sign his half over. Remembering that put dread in her heart each time she contemplated calling him about the horses.

The antiquated shower in the bathroom was incapable of beating her to life, but it scalded her well, which was equally stimulating. The hot water heater was the only new appliance in the house.

After she dressed in worn jeans and a warm sweater, she cooked a bowl of instant oatmeal in the microwave for Ava's breakfast and made hot chocolate. She sat at the table and sipped coffee while Ava ate, listening to her daughter relate a story she had finished reading about a girl and a horse.

She needed to look for a horse gentle enough for Ava. They'd had one in Texas, but she sold it before they left. Thinking back, she didn't know why. She could have brought it to Callister just as easily as she brought Dancer, Polly and Trixie. A frown tugged between her brows at the reminder of another disappointment she had thoughtlessly added to her daughter's life.

Nan came for Ava and trundled off with her van loaded down with kids. The sky was clear, the sunshine warm. Isabelle snapped leashes onto the puppies' collars and set out on a dog walk around the small pasture nearest the house. The puppies dawdled along on their short little legs, stopping at every plant and rock to either sniff or pee. Damn John Bradshaw anyway. She had no time for puppies. They might be cute now, but she hated thinking how big they would be when they grew up. And they had to be trained. The last thing she wanted was another dog problem with her neighbor.

She felt more energized at the end of the walk. She returned to the kitchen and, armed with a ballpoint, a yellow tablet and her address book, picked up the phone and carried it to the dining table.

She opened the address book to "B" and stared at the Ardmore, Oklahoma, phone number. Billy hadn't given her the number. She had found it written on one of the closing documents when she sold the place in Texas. Knowing him, he wouldn't appreciate her calling him at his girlfriend's house and an argument would probably ensue. Not a good way to start off a conversation where she wanted him to do something for her.

Well, even if it angered him, she had to make the call. She had to. Because spending the money advertising the sale of the horses was a waste unless Billy signed off his interest in them.

She picked up the pen and doodled circles across one line of the blank tablet, remembering a scene in the barn in Texas when, after spending big bucks for semen and an expensive vet to do artificial insemination, they had learned Polly hadn't conceived. Someone popped off and suggested the ten-year-old mare might be sterile. Billy flew into a rage, stormed around the barn ranting that a mare that couldn't breed was worthless. When Isabelle tried to defend Polly, Billy shouted that if she thought a useless horse was so great, she could just have Polly.

Isabelle loved Polly and was glad to claim her. Ambivalent about the mare's ability to have babies, she hadn't pursued tests to verify fertility.

Another worry cropped up. Even if Polly turned out to be sterile, Trixie wasn't; she had given birth to beautiful foals. But with Billy's name on the papers, a foal from Trixie couldn't be registered in only Isabelle's name. And if the foal sold, no doubt Billy would want half the money. *Damn.*

For that matter, even if she were to enter Dancer or Trixie in some local-area shows, their winning money could present another problem with Billy. *Double damn.*

She sighed, took a sip of coffee, picked up the receiver and was poised to dial the Oklahoma number when Paul came through the back door. He walked into the kitchen and poured coffee for himself. "Want some breakfast?" she asked him, unable to resist the diversion from making the call.

"Naw, I ate something at home."

Home to her brother was a thirty-foot travel trailer parked behind a friend's house. She wouldn't venture a guess what he might have eaten for breakfast. He was clean-shaven, she noticed. "You don't look hungover."

He laughed. "Have some faith in me, sister. I was good yesterday. Went snowmobiling up on the other end of Callister Mountain. Had two beers and went to bed early."

Isabelle grinned. "See? That didn't hurt you a bit, did it?"

"Sun's been shining several days now. The barn roof oughtta be dried out. I'm ready to tackle those holes."

The big barn's roof was made of cedar shake shingles that were at least fifty years old. They absorbed moisture like a sponge. She and Paul settled into a conversation about the work to be done and she postponed her call to Billy. Again.

For the rest of the week, between sessions of caring for and teaching the puppies, Isabelle helped Paul with the repairs to the barn. He worked from early morning until dark every day. By Friday the roof shingles had been replaced. A new sheet metal roof was what she really wanted, but that would have to wait until she had an income. Paul had braced and strengthened the stall doors and screwed on new hinges and latches. Now she could pen up a horse and feel confident it would stay put. Paul told her he would start shoring up the roof structure next.

He quit work late in the afternoon and announced he was headed to town for a get-together with Jim Beam. Isabelle tried to persuade him to stay and eat supper with her and Ava, but her invitation fell on deaf ears. She had already pushed him to his limit, she supposed, keeping him busy and sober for a week. She suspected he would be meeting Merle Keeton in town and they would consume a river of whiskey.

After supper, while Ava dressed the puppies in costumes, Isabelle sat down with her budget. She had invested the cash she received from the sale of the Weatherford property in a CD that earned disgustingly low interest. An acquaintance in Texas, an investment planner, had tried to persuade her to put the money into the stock market or some other paper investment. She had refused. She didn't dare risk the only thing she could call hers in a venue about which she knew little. She couldn't even read the stock quotes on the financial pages of the paper. She didn't trust stockbrokers anyway, knowing how they treated their horses.

No, she would take care of her money herself. If she lived frugally and nothing catastrophic happened, she could survive for two years, which should be enough time to get her business going and producing income.

Even with the tightness of her funds, she didn't see how she could avoid hiring help. If she intended to shape up the horses for sale and/or cutting competitions, she had to buy a shipment of eighty to a hundred calves for the horses to work. More animals to feed and look after.

The horses hadn't been ridden more than a few times in recent weeks and part of her dilemma was finding the time to work each of them forty-five minutes or an hour several days a week, along with cleaning the barns, repairing them and the house, advertising her services as a handler and more important, spending time with her daughter. And now, housebreaking dogs.

Though vexed about the expense of hiring help, tomorrow she would call her aunt and her cousin and put out the word she needed a part-time hand. She would ask Nan to help write an ad to put in Callister's newspaper, which was published on Tuesdays and Fridays.

She might even ask Nan to help write a letter to Billy. In the long run, a letter to her ex-partner might be more effective than a phone call.

"Here's a part-time job for you, John T."

Dana leaned against John's office doorjamb reading the local newspaper. It was no secret that John's child support payments kept him strapped. Callister County sheriff's pay wasn't an executive salary. He frequently joked he needed a second job so he could afford to be sheriff.

He peered at her through half-closed eyelids, didn't move his feet off his desktop. "Doing what? Sweeping floors at the Eights and Aces?"

"Izzy Rondeau's advertising for help with her horses."

"The hell." John lifted his hat off his face. His boot heels hit the floor. He sat up and leaned forward. "Lemme see."

Dana passed him the newspaper. He read the ad, then handed the paper back and resumed his relaxed position.

"Doesn't say what she's paying. Has to be minimum wage. She probably wants a grunt."

For the rest of the day he thought about the ad and how long it had been since he had ridden a horse. At four he turned the office over to Rooster and Dana and headed out to Izzy's house.

When he knocked at the front door, her little girl's face popped up behind the glass pane in the upper half of the door. She opened up, the puppies barking and bouncing around her. "Where's your mom?" he asked her.

She held the door wide. "You have to come in. I can't hold the door open 'cause Mama doesn't want bugs to get in the house."

"Oh, okay." John stepped into the living room and felt and heard the creak of the wood floor. He looked around. The room, with its aged pine paneling, looked old but cozy. The furniture looked fairly new—a long leather sofa, a cowhide chair. A huge, draping fern filled one corner and houseplants sat on the windowsills. All of it was spotlessly clean and welcoming.

Ava looked up at him with huge coffee-colored eyes. Plastic clips that looked like little blue bows showed on either side of a part in her red hair. "Can you fix our fire? I know how, but I'm not allowed to if Mama isn't in the house."

John turned his attention to a dying fire flickering in a brick-front fireplace. "Sure." He walked to the fireplace, stepping on layers of cowhides and Navajo rugs covering the floor between the hearth and the sofa. On the thick oak mantel he saw photographs of horses and trophies of various sizes and configurations.

"Those are Mama's prizes," Ava said. "She's won a lot."

"She sure has," John said, impressed. He returned his attention to the fire, found pine rounds in a bin beside the fireplace, then squatted and placed them on the grate.

Ava spoke behind him. "Did you come to check on Harry and Gwendolyn?"

He glanced at her over his shoulder. "Gwendolyn?"

The kid pushed her glasses higher up her nose with the

tips of her fingers and gave him a serious look. "I changed Jenny's name to Gwendolyn. I read this story where someone called his jackass Jenny. Gwendolyn sounds better."

As he reached for the hearth broom and swept stray ash and debris into the fireplace John wondered what book a little girl her age could be reading that had the word "jackass" in it. He stood up and wiped his hands with his handkerchief. "Right. Gwendolyn's a better name. You do a lot of reading?"

She pointed to the lower shelves of a wide bookcase that stretched from floor to ceiling on one side of the fireplace. "These are mine."

The upper shelves were filled with dozens of what John assumed were CDs until he reached for one and examined it. Audiobooks.

"Those are Mama's," the kid said. "She listens all the time. She only looks at horse stuff and vet books, but I read a lot. Sometimes I read to Mama."

"Is that right?" John pushed an audiobook on American history back into its slot.

"Some people wanted Mama to write a book because of all the stuff she knows about horses. I told her I'd help her, but she won't." The little girl sighed, the weight of the world on her narrow shoulders.

Exactly what did Izzy know that would call for writing a book?

The kid picked up a hardback lying on the sofa. "This is *Harry Potter and the Chamber of Secrets.* It's about a boy who can do magic. I've already read it once, but I'm reading it again because we haven't gone to Boise yet to buy the next book."

"I see." John took the book and fanned the pages, thinking of the struggle he and his ex-wife had trying to persuade their older son to focus on reading. "Looks like a good story."

The puppies barked and scampered around his and Ava's feet. She looked at them, then back up at him. "You don't have to worry about Harry and Gwendolyn. I'm very responsible. I sleep with them on the porch."

"You think that's a good idea? Long as they can't get outside, they should be all right out there by themselves."

"But I don't want them to get lonely. And I don't want them to get scared when the coyotes howl. Mama lets me use her big sleeping bag."

"Ah. Guess that makes a difference, huh?" He tilted his head toward the playing puppies. "You think you oughtta have them in here? I'll bet they're not housebroken yet."

The words had no sooner left his mouth than one of them squatted and tinkled at the corner of the tile hearth.

"Harry!" Ava scooped him up and shook her finger at his dark nose. "Bad dog. Now you have to stay on the porch."

"Where's your mom?" John asked again before the girl could escape to the porch with the puppies.

"Over at the big barn. She's painting."

She picked up the second pup and marched away in quick little steps. The word that came to John's mind was one he didn't usually associate with a ten-year-old kid—efficient.

# Chapter 7

John walked toward the massive old barn. Hearing rhythmic hammering, he looked for the sound and saw someone on the steep roof nailing down shingles.

The barn's double doors stood open. Inside, he found Izzy at the top of a twelve-foot aluminum ladder leaned against the tack room wall. Wearing brown padded coveralls, she had a wide paintbrush in her hand. He glanced around. Most of the tack room exterior showed a fresh coat of white paint. But the temperature was in the low fifties, too cold for outside painting.

He thumbed back his hat and went to the foot of the ladder, braced both hands on the side rails and looked up. "You think that'll ever get dry?"

She twisted and looked down. White paint dripped off her brush to the ground, just missing him. "It's barn paint. Not much more than chalky water. What do you want?"

"I saw your ad."

She juggled the paintbrush and a gallon paint bucket into one hand and began to descend the ladder, placing both feet on each rung as she stepped down. When she finally reached the ground, she gave him a shy smile and all he could think of was how soft her full lips looked.

"I'm afraid of high places," she said. "And ladders."

"Then maybe you shouldn't be up there."

She had splotches of white everywhere, even in her hair.
"I just want everything to look better, like there's a live
person here. I'll put good paint on later. You didn't really
come about the job." It was a statement rather than a question.

"Why not? I figure I know as much about horses as anybody. Around here, anyway."

She gave him a narrow-lidded look. "I don't know—"

"Horses like me. You saw. The other day when you introduced me to them."

A stocky, muscular man wearing dirty clothes and a well-
seasoned leather tool belt appeared in the doorway. On a second look, John recognized him as Izzy's kid brother. John
hadn't seen him around town lately. Perhaps Izzy had been
keeping him too busy to frequent the bars. Paul walked over
and John touched his hat to him. "Paul."

"What're you doing way out here, John?" The man's tone
had a wariness to it.

"Nothing official. Talking horses."

Paul grunted and declared he had finished shingling the
roof. Izzy thanked him and hugged him, transferring smears
of white paint from herself and her brush to him, and asked
him to stay for supper.

John's mind spun back to high school, when Izzy had
been her little brother's keeper. And his unfaltering defender.

"No, thanks," Paul said. "If I get hungry, I'll eat at the
café in town."

Isabelle released him. "Thanks again for helping me.
Stay out of trouble, okay?" She stepped aside and he started
toward a silver dually. "I love you, Paul," she called.

He turned back, giving her a big grin. "I love you, too, sis.
And don't be worrying about me. You'll get gray before your
time." He lifted his hand in a wave and continued on his way.

Izzy looked after him with a worried expression. John,
in his role as sheriff, had already become aware that Paul
Rondeau was indeed enough to give a loving sister a gray
hair or two.

After her brother drove away, Izzy turned back and
walked over to a hay bale where the lid to the paint can and a
mallet lay. "Paul's a great carpenter." She pushed the lid onto

the can and pounded it shut with the mallet. "He's helping me out, fixing up the barn and patching the holes in the roof."

"Good for him." John looked up, estimated the barn ceiling to be at least thirty feet high. He gave her a wink. "Being afraid of high places, you'd have a heck of a time up there fixing it yourself."

She laughed and the whole world seemed brighter.

"That's true," she said and carried the brush outside.

John tagged along. The late afternoon's golden sun caught in her hair, turning it the color of fire. "If you need help with the horses, why don't you call on your brother for that, too?"

Copper-colored brows arched. "I said he's a great carpenter. He's terrible with horses."

A faucet stood outside the barn door. She bent over and worked at washing the paintbrush under a stream of water. "You're the sheriff. When would you find the time to fool with my animals?"

"Being sheriff doesn't use up every hour of my day. Lots of days I don't have that much to do."

"From what I've heard, you don't take the job seriously. If you tried, you'd probably be busy all the time."

Well, wasn't she bossy and what the hell had she heard? He shrugged. "Hard to say. What're you paying?"

She grinned. "I only need someone a couple of hours a day, maybe three days a week. Six bucks an hour. That doesn't add up to much."

Mental sigh. That amount of money wouldn't make a pimple-sized dent in his child support payments. "You're right. Six hours a week at six dollars doesn't add up to much."

"I was figuring on a schoolkid."

"You're gonna let a schoolkid loose with horses like yours?"

"Just to feed and do some grunt work. Anything else, I do myself. Unless, of course, I find one with some experience... or talent." She stood up, wiped her wet hands on her coveralls, then started back into the barn. "I appreciate your asking about it, though. So far, you're the only one who has. I imagine kids think the drive out here's too far."

John sensed an air of desperation in Izzy. He weighed the pay against the trip, arguing with himself. Though he missed riding and working with horses, and putting horses like hers through their paces would be a special treat, it made no sense to commit to a thirty-mile round trip three days a week and get paid no more than thirty-six dollars. "I know a few teenagers. I'll ask around."

The corners of her mouth tipped up into another heart-stopping smile. "That would be great."

Warmed with a smile like that, John couldn't make himself say good-bye. "So how're you getting along with the puppies?"

"They're cute."

"Still mad at me for bringing them?"

"I guess not. Ava loves them and they must have been what she needed. She still misses Jack, but—anyway, it was nice of you to think of her."

"Yeah, well, you know. Kids and dogs."

She slid the coveralls off her shoulders. "Just don't forget"—she laughed again—"I'll soon be sending you a bill for carpet cleaning."

She stepped out of the coveralls, carried them to the tack room and hung them on a nail in the wall, then started toward the house. Since she didn't invite him to join her, he debated whether he should follow or just get in the Blazer and go on back to town.

While the question volleyed inside him, he fell in step beside her. "If you're going to the house, I'll just say hi to the dogs," he told her.

They walked along in silence and for the first time John noticed the landscape. Though he had grown up in Callister and had hunted the mountains sandwiching the long valley all his life, he had never been to Frenchie Rondeau's place. The house backed up to snowcapped Callister Mountain. In the late-afternoon sun, the mountaintop shone like gold. The pasture's fledgling green gently rolled uphill to the dark tree line behind the white house and barns. The place was picturesque and had an appeal about it even with the buildings looking old and run-down.

He had never known the size of the Rondeau spread, but the back boundary had to adjoin national forest. "How much land you got here?"

"Not enough. About three hundred acres. Which means once I get calves in, I'll have to buy feed most of the year."

"Calves?"

"For the horses to work with. Cutting horses, remember?"

A flutter beat in Isabelle's stomach as John walked beside her toward the house. Sneaking peeks at him, she saw lashes a woman would kill for and a good profile. She hadn't seen him without a hat, but he wore his brown hair longer than most cowboys. From out of nowhere, this crazy urge cropped up to find a mirror and catch a glimpse of her own unruly hair, which must be flying all over the place.

She found him just as easy to look at today as when he had come out in the rain about Jack. Today, however, it dawned on her that something other than his appearance had seized her attention in the first place. He seemed to own his space, giving off an easy confidence like it came to him naturally. It was something subtle that would have been as foreign to Billy as speaking Russian, something she had rarely seen in men. And it was something she admired, because she engaged in a daily struggle to find her own self-confidence.

Beyond that, the utter maleness that radiated from him grabbed her right where she had no business letting herself be grabbed. John Bradshaw could have his pick of women, even more so than Billy—of that she was certain. Her former partner may have been handsome, but he didn't have John's strong presence.

When they reached the house and she opened the door onto the porch, they were greeted by puppies scampering around their ankles. "Uh-oh," she said. "Ava's banished them to the porch. They must have done something on the carpet. I don't suppose you brought that second doghouse with you?"

"I haven't been down to Boise yet. But I haven't forgotten it. I promise."

She suspected he had done exactly that—forgotten it ten minutes after he dumped off the puppies.

She walked through the porch to the mudroom, pushed up her sweater sleeves and turned on the faucet in the laundry sink, glad to be distracted by washing her hands. He leaned a shoulder on the doorjamb and thumbed back his hat, watching her, which made her too self-conscious to look into his face. "I can't blame you for not wanting to work for what I'm paying, but you must have known it wouldn't be much." She laughed. "That can't really be why you came out."

His shoulder lifted. "I miss being around horses. If you could pay a little more, I could relieve you of the riding."

The offer tempted her. Bradshaws were old-time ranchers in Callister County. John had been around livestock since the day of his birth, but tempting offer or not, she hadn't seen him ride. Her horses were too valuable for an unskilled handler. No way would she hire him without knowing his ability. Nor could she commit to more wages. "Hah. I do the grunt work and you do the riding. Is that the idea?"

He shrugged again. "I'm willing to help you with what needs doing."

She rinsed off soap and shook the excess water into the sink, tore off sheets of paper toweling and dried. "I'd want to see you with the horses and watch you ride."

"No problem. When?"

She pulled a jar of bag balm from the cupboard and scooped out a dollop with the crook of her finger. "The sooner the better. When can you get away?"

As she began rubbing the silky cream onto her hands, he pushed away from the doorjamb, walked over and picked up the jar, the subtle scent of him—something woodsy smelling—overtaking the pleasant fragrance of the bag balm. Her pulse rate surged. Her mind swerved from negotiating his pay to the fact that she hadn't put on perfume since before she left Texas.

The corner of his mouth quirked. Amusement? Well, so what if using udder cream on her hands amused him? It was rich in lanolin. After seeing too many women who worked outdoors with animals let their skin turn tough as leather, she was determined to avoid that happening to her.

He set the jar back on the counter and stuffed his hands

into his jeans pockets. His khaki quilted vest shifted back. A badge hung on the pocket of a tan button-down. She saw the butt of a pistol strapped to his belt, but instead of being uneasy about the unusual circumstance of a man standing in her mudroom wearing a gun, the subject on which her mind settled was how would he look without a shirt?

"If the horses are for sale," he said, "why go to the expense and trouble of keeping them in peak training?"

She concentrated on creaming her forearms. "Would you pay a hundred thousand for a horse that isn't in top shape?"

A few seconds passed. "A hundred thousand? Dollars?"

She suppressed a grin of satisfaction at the astonishment in his voice, having sensed his skepticism all along. She glanced up at him. "No, sheriff. Marbles.... Besides having great breeding, they have winning records."

He looked away, as if he might be embarrassed. "Okay," he said. "Thursday. I could do it Thursday morning."

John now realized Izzy's animals were special. Due to selective breeding and unrelenting training from young ages, they had gone beyond the ordinary cow horse. They had become investments, athletes demonstrating their intelligence and capabilities in cutting contests across the Southwest. Everybody from car dealers to movie stars owned one or more that vied for the generous prizes awarded in cutting-horse performance shows. Her horses could well be worth the number she threw out.

That explained their superior condition and the fancy truck and trailer. What still puzzled him, though, was the contradiction between what she said and what she was doing. If she wanted to sell the horses, bringing them to Callister made no sense. If she intended to show them in competitions, hauling them from Texas to Idaho had been a wrong move. The purses in shows here couldn't come close to those in Texas and Oklahoma.

Well, his questions would have answers eventually. He had never met a woman who could keep secrets for long.

On Thursday morning John headed for Izzy's house, tamping down the guilt he felt for leaving the office to

Rooster. To salve his conscience, he told himself he had worked 24/7 for months and was entitled to a day off.

An excitement buzzed within him. He hadn't been close to a horse in a year. The only rope horse he had left, a big gray gelding named Rowdy, was being used as a cow horse out at his folks' ranch. Since he didn't visit the Lazy B much, he didn't see or ride him.

His gear was there, too. His plan had been to put off riding for Izzy until he picked it up on Sunday when he went out for his mom's birthday, but with riding for Izzy on Thursday, he hadn't had time between now and then to make the trip to the Lazy B.

Izzy had told him she had tack she preferred him to use, anyway. A saddle used for cutting would have different features from the ones he used for steer roping.

When he pulled up beside her big barn, he saw the sorrel mare, Trixie, penned in one paddock and the stud in the other.

Izzy met him with a big smile at the barn door. "Early," she said. "I wasn't sure you'd make it."

He grinned, taken with how pretty she looked with her cheeks and lips even rosier than usual from the chilly morning air. "I always get up early," he said.

Her eyes watered from the cold and looked shiny and alive. She wore a tan jacket and a bright blue turtleneck sweater and the most worn pair of stovepipe boots he had ever seen. Tan chinks covered her jeans. She must be planning to ride with him. Her spurs clinked as she briskly led him to the tack room and showed him the saddle. "You ride Dancer," she said, handing him a pair of spurs. "But I warn you, he can be a challenge."

John couldn't think of a time when he'd had to prove his horsemanship to a woman, but he swallowed his pride and strapped on the spurs.

She patted a saddle mounted on a sawhorse. "You can use this one. It was Billy's. The stirrups should be about right." She dragged a different saddle off a neighboring sawhorse and lugged it outside.

John picked up Billy's saddle and followed. Good God, if

the man didn't take his saddle, he must have left home in a hurry.

When he started across the driveway carrying the tack, Dancer's ears perked up and he watched from a still position. *Uh-oh.* That horse had rodeo on his mind. Though years had gone by since John had last ridden a strong-willed horse, he wasn't frightened. It just called for a little patience.

When John set the saddle on the ground, Dancer lived up to his name and snorted and stamped around the corral, then stopped on the opposite side and stared at him. John stood there, willing the horse to come to him. Minutes later, dark ears pricked forward and the blue devil walked to where John waited. Despite misgivings about hand-feeding a stallion, John dug a couple of carrot pieces from his shirt pocket and offered them. Dancer's attitude softened and finally, with a little neck sawing and a few head tosses, he let himself be haltered.

Munching on the carrot, Dancer accepted the bridle, but sidestepped away from the saddle blanket. John took his time, baby-talking him and letting him smell the wool fabric. After several attempts, the horse stood for the blanket, but he moved every time John started to swing the saddle across his back. Even after he consented to be saddled, he sidestepped when John tried to cinch up. Yep, Fancy Dancer wanted the world to know he had a mind of his own. Izzy had called him ornery. That was a fitting description, but John didn't think him mean.

Meanwhile, Izzy had saddled the sorrel mare, led her over and tied her to a pole rail. "Dancer hasn't been ridden in weeks," she told him with a grin.

*That's just great.* John had no idea what to expect when he climbed aboard the stallion, but he looked him in the eye. "Pal, you and I are gonna be friends whether you like it or not."

The horse snorted.

Izzy tilted her head back and hooted. "He's smarter than both of us."

She left the corral and propped her arms on the top rail. Shit, she intended to watch. Only a lesser man would be intimidated at being set up, then judged by a woman, John told himself, as he stuck his boot in the stirrup.

The moment his butt sank to the saddle seat, he knew he was horseback. Dancer reared on his hind legs, bucked on a dime a few times, blew a few snorts and settled down to a fidget. They circled the corral, warming up, then gradually picked up the pace. Rowdy was fast and smart, but Dancer's stamina and footwork amazed John. The stud's response to subtle signals for flying lead changes, sliding stops and turns on the hindquarters soon had John feeling as if the two of them were one entity. When he wanted to—emphasize *wanted to*—Dancer handled as well as any horse John had ever ridden.

After a half hour of steady work, he reined the horse over to where Izzy stood. "You the one trained this horse?"

She looked up at him, grinning and squinting in the sunshine. "You betcha."

There was no mistaking the pride in the reply. If Dancer was an example of her work, she had plenty to be proud of. "Want me to ride the sorrel?"

"No." She ducked through the pole rails and opened the gate to the large pasture. She mounted the sorrel and rode through with John trailing her. Outside the gate, they rode side by side in an easy walk, letting Dancer cool down in the frosty sunshine.

"This may be the best horse I've ever ridden," John told her. "Like you said, he's ornery, but he's good."

"Thanks."

Isabelle didn't have to be told that much. Among the many horses she had known, she had ridden no better mount than Dancer.

As for John's handling of the rebellious stud, she had seen enough. John had a gentle hand, but a firm hold. His knowledge of horse nature showed and she had seen he had a calm personality himself. Horses were sensitive to human temperament. No way would she allow her babies to be handled by an ill-tempered man.

She looked over at him, cautioning herself not to show too much enthusiasm and jeopardize her chances of cutting a good deal. "I maybe could do something different on the pay."

"I'm listening."

"If I get my asking price for all three horses, it'll be about two or two and a quarter. If you wanted to take a chance and go ahead and work with them, I'd be willing to pay you a percentage when I sell one, or all of them. It's possible I could find one buyer for all three."

She could almost see his brain gears working. A commission on two hundred thousand dollars should make a difference in anyone's thinking.

"What percentage?"

"Two percent, maybe."

He chuckled, showing even white teeth and a twinkle in his green eyes. "C'mon. That doesn't amount to gas money. You gotta do better than that."

She thought he might be teasing her. "Well, I could pay you two percent and let you fill up out of my stand tank."

John laughed. He had a deep male laugh that she liked. "The county buys my gas, even for my own rig."

"Oh. Well, then, guess I'm out of luck. I don't have anything else to offer."

A dare flickered in his eyes. "C'mon, now. I can tell you're an old horse trader, so let's deal. I could be talked into waiting for the pay—if you're willing to double the percentage."

*Damn.* She did a calculation in her head. She had no idea if she would get her asking price for the horses. She gave a little gasp. "You're talking about a healthy chunk of change. And what if the horses never sell? I won't be able to pay you and you'll arrest me or something."

He tilted his head and raised a palm. "Nope. Fair deal. If nobody buys them, I'll just say I worked for fun."

She cast him a dubious look. What was he up to? Probably something she wouldn't like. "I'll have to think about it."

By the time they returned to the corral, the temptation of having him help her won out. She swung out of the saddle and led Trixie outside the corral. John dismounted and began to unsaddle Dancer. She watched a few minutes, debating how best to approach a deal with him and tamping down one of her greatest fears. What if he asked for something in writing? "We don't need to put anything on paper, do we?"

His eyes bored into hers. "I trust you." He walked over

and put out his right hand. "And if all of Callister County trusts me, *you* oughtta be able to."

In spite of her uncertainty, she smiled and shook hands, feeling the warmth and greater strength of his. Calf ropers did have good hands. A strange little shiver traveled through her.

"Okay," she said. "Four percent. I hope I don't regret this."

# Chapter 8

As they carried their gear toward the tack room, Izzy told him she had to go to Ontario and return before Ava came home from school. John glanced at his watch. The small city of Ontario was over an hour away. He volunteered to finish up in the barn.

She told him thanks and headed for her truck, then waved as she rolled down the driveway.

John put away their tack. Leaving the barn, he stopped at the stand faucet beside the barn door, wiped the spigot opening with his shirtsleeve and knelt for a drink of cold, pure well water. He missed having well water to drink. The tap water in his apartment tasted like bleach and slid down his throat like oil.

He missed more than well water. He missed living in the country. He and Julie had owned a hundred-acre place outside Marsing. They'd had half a dozen good horses and a few cows, a new truck, an SUV and a John Deere farm tractor John used for plowing snow when necessary and doing chores in general. All but the truck and the SUV had been sold during the divorce.

Plopping down on a bench in the barn's shadow, he looked around. The sun had burned off the frost and etched the landscape in colors as vivid as a painting. A hawk hovered over the greening pasture, riding a thermal against an azure sky. A thousand birds perched on the bare branches of an oak tree standing at the corner of the barn, all chittering at once. He heard no other sounds. He loved it.

A profound sense of being severed from his world came over him and he pondered how he had come to the point in his life where he had nothing and nobody. He had been valedictorian of his high school class. He had graduated in the top ten percent of his class at Boise State University and come away with a B.B.A. degree. At one time he held standing in the top ten calf ropers in the country and had numerous endorsements from major companies.

He had fathered two healthy, smart children.

Now, here he was, age thirty-two and broke. All he had to his name was a pickup truck, a horse and a trailer and some riding gear and he didn't even have a pasture for the horse. He had no workable plan for his future. He enjoyed the company of his children only for short spurts and only at his ex-wife's whim. And as for productive work in which he could take pride, he filled a chair in the most ridiculous endeavor in which he had ever involved himself.

He steered his thoughts back from the dark side, needing to home in on constructive events. Something positive *had* happened today. Helping Izzy with her horses might not aid him much in making his child support payments, but doing it broke the monotony and bleakness of single life in Callister. He had to not lose sight of it.

He returned to the tack room, unstrapped his chinks and spurs and hung them on a nail on the wall, thinking as he did it about the permanence implied by leaving his chaps here.

On the way back to town he continued to muse on how much he had enjoyed the morning and how the solitude and vastness of the outdoors at Rondeau's place touched so deep a chord within him that it set off the uncharacteristic depression.

A few minutes later he pulled into the driveway of his happy home—a two-bedroom apartment that was half of a duplex two blocks from the courthouse. It wasn't the Ritz, to be sure, but it provided the necessities—a big-screen TV in the living room, a functioning refrigerator in the kitchen, a firm, name-brand mattress in one bedroom and exercise equipment in the other.

"Well, you've hung your hat in worse," he mumbled as he killed the truck engine. In fact, when he had been rodeoing and sending all his money home to Julie and the kids, he lived in or slept in everything from an eight-by-ten motel room to an RV to a horse trailer, depending on where his pursuit of a ProRodeo calf-roping prize took him. He didn't miss the joys of too much fast food, sleeping in unfamiliar beds and waking up hungover, but he did miss the camaraderie of fellow competitors, individuals driven to risk limb and life to be the best at their chosen sport.

And he missed having a willing woman, even one he barely knew by name, heat up and relieve the low ache in his belly.

From out of the blue, he remembered the doghouse he had promised. Anticipating the four walls of his empty apartment felt more dismal than usual and he *had* taken the whole day off. He cranked the engine and pointed his pickup south. Tomorrow he would deliver a new doghouse to Izzy and her little girl.

He returned late afternoon with a fiberglass doghouse to fit a large-sized dog. He hadn't had to go all the way to Boise to buy it after all. He found one at a farm and ranch supply store fifty miles from Callister.

He also found a birthday present for his mother—a pair of silver-and-turquoise earrings he was pretty sure were authentic Zuni. The storeowner's wife had even gift wrapped them. His mom would like them better than the bouquet of flowers he had planned to pick up at Fielder's Mercantile.

He stopped off at the mailbox in front of his apartment before going inside. Though he received little mail, he always checked, just in case one of his sons wrote him. When he pulled out a letter, saw his ex-wife's handwriting and a California return address he didn't recognize, his heart made a happy little leap. At the same time, unease pinched him. She never wrote. She phoned when she wanted something.

John continued to study the letter as he walked into the chilled apartment. He often left the heat off in his absence, so he turned up the thermostat and listened to be sure the antiquated oil furnace clicked on. A few times it had failed and left him shivering through the night.

After what Dancer had put him through, he was stiff. Even working out on his home gym hadn't prepped him for an hour aboard a badass horse. Tomorrow he would be lucky to be able to get out of bed. Damned if he hadn't gotten soft in the past year or two.

He dropped Julie's letter onto the seat of his reclining chair in front of the TV, his memory of their lives together setting off a growing suspicion that the letter held something he wouldn't like. When they were married, he had called her high-strung, a description that gave her the benefit of a doubt and excused some of her more malicious conduct. If someone asked him to describe her now, the words that came to him were "bad temper," "hysteria," "chaos" and "confusion." It was Julie who taught him how much turmoil one small woman could cause.

Without removing his jacket, he put coffee on to drip. While he waited in the kitchen's dull light for the warmth of the coffee and the furnace, he listened to his phone messages. Rooster had been out on a family disturbance call. The other messages were unimportant.

The letter from Julie nagged at him. He sat down with it and a mug of hot coffee. He tore the end off the envelope and pulled out two crisp pages filled with his ex-wife's small, perfectly aligned script. The handwriting style was a reflection of her uptight personality, for sure.

*Dear John,*

*The boys have adjusted to school here and are doing fine. Cody is super smart and making good grades. Trey is struggling with reading like always, but on the whole, they love this place. Carson signed both of them up for Little League when we first got here. They are practicing in a park up the street from our apartment.*

John looked up and stared across the room at pictures in silver frames of his towheaded sons, ages ten and almost nine, trying to imagine them playing baseball in a park or closed up in an apartment somewhere in the sea of humanity that was Los Angeles. When they had lived in Marsing, Trey and Cody had their own horses and John took them on trail rides in the mountains.

He sipped his coffee to ward off the pang that settled in his gut and returned to the letter.

*There is much to like, living here. Southern California is nothing like Idaho, or Washington either. There is so much opportunity and exposure to so many cultures. It will be so good for the boys.*

*I would have called you about this, but I was afraid I might catch you when you couldn't talk or something.*

*She wants more money* was John's first thought.

*I don't know anything else to do but just come right out and say why I'm writing you. I know you don't like people beating around the bush, so here goes. Carson wants to adopt the boys.*

John's fingers began to tremble. He felt a quickness in his chest. Burning moisture rushed to his eyes.

*He's so good with them. He helps Trey with his reading every night, takes them to all the fun stuff to do here. They've already been to Disneyland, Magic Mountain and the other places that kids love. Carson has so many influential friends who can open doors for them and he wants to be able to legitimately call them "his sons." Like he says, if we're going to be a family, then every one of us has to belong to him.*

*I know you, so you're going to say no. But before you do, I hope you'll think of the boys and what a wonderful opportunity this could be for them.*

"No," John said. "Goddammit, no!"

He wadded the letter into a ball and threw it across the room, stopped himself just before the coffee mug followed. He sprang to his feet and stomped outside to his truck, clapping on his hat as he went. He jerked open the door and climbed in, fired the engine, then sat there with it idling.

He had nowhere to go.

A stunning realization came to him. Not so long ago, a bar would have been his destination of choice.

He crossed his arms over the steering wheel and gazed out at the waning day's golden air. Had Julie gone crazy? Did she honestly believe there was a chance on God's green earth he would give his sons over to some panty-ass he had seen once in his life? He loved those kids and she knew it. He was a good father. No damn way would he give up his sons.

He drove the two blocks to town, crept up the deserted main street, looked, but didn't see much action around the three bars. He followed the street on out of town until he came to the Stony Creek Road intersection. Before he knew it, he had turned off the pavement and headed toward Izzy's house. Why not? He had a doghouse to deliver.

He pulled up near the backyard gate, climbed out and lifted the doghouse over the tailgate. Ava ran to meet him, the puppies at her heels. He hoped she had them under control and was teaching them to stay home. Dealing with another dog incident and Art Karadimos was something John didn't relish.

He carried the doghouse across the yard and placed it beside the existing one near the back door. Ava told him she had bedding. As she went inside, Izzy came out, showering him with a dazzling smile. He almost believed she, too, was glad to see him.

Her hair was hanging loose in a mass of curls spiraling from a clip on top of her head and reaching the middle of her back. All the times in his youth he had wanted to bury his hands in that shiny, thick mane came back to him. He didn't feel much like smiling, but she looked so welcoming, he couldn't keep from it.

"I'll bet you thought I'd never get here with this." He tilted his chin toward the doghouse.

She laughed like she was in a good mood. "I'll admit, I did think that, but it isn't a big deal. It wasn't needed. Harry and Gwendolyn have been sleeping inside on the porch. That will probably last a while. There's coyotes all around here."

They stood there a silent minute, watching Ava organize the pups. "I've got a boy her age," John said, for no particular reason other than the fact that his mind was on Trey, with his huge green eyes, his slightly crooked front tooth and hair so blond it looked like he had none.

"You do? I didn't know that. I lost touch with a lot of the kids from school. I don't think I ever heard who you married."

"She wasn't from here. From Seattle."

Izzy cocked her head and both frowned and laughed at the same time. "Seattle? How'd a country boy like you get tangled up with someone from Seattle?"

The words came out with a hint of a twang, sounding more like Texas than Callister, and John chuckled in spite of his bad mood. "Tangled up's the right word for it. I met her in college down in Boise. I've got two boys. Ten and almost nine."

"They live with your ex?"

"Yep." John sighed. "In L.A." He felt his eyes burn again. Shit. What was wrong with him? He needed a change of subject fast, before he turned into a fool.

As if she read his mind, Izzy rescued him. "So you liked working with my babies today?"

"I did."

She ducked her chin and traced something on the ground with the toe of her boot. "I hate selling them, but I have to. I have to get the money out of them." She looked up at him, those doelike eyes surrounding him with warmth and well-being. "Have you eaten? I've got this sort of slumgullion I cooked up—"

"Slum-what?"

"Mama thinks her food is bad," Ava said, coming over and hanging on to a puppy that had almost doubled in size since John brought it. "I always like it a lot. Other people like it, too."

"I'm a menace in the kitchen," Izzy said with a bashful smile, "but you're welcome to eat with us."

John hesitated, trying to figure out how he had lucked into an invitation to supper tonight when she had practically shoved him out the door just a few nights earlier. He didn't know if he was even fit company for supper.

Still, he was hungry and he hadn't had home-cooked food since a month ago when Rooster and his wife had invited him to Sunday dinner. "Okay," he said finally. "That'd be real nice. If you've got enough, that is."

Isabelle entered the porch ahead of John, prattling on like a magpie to ease the tension she felt. "I usually wash up in the laundry sink, but since you're one of our rare guests, I'll show you to the bathroom." She led him through the kitchen, into the hallway. "We've got only the one. It needs remodeling, so try to ignore the chipped sink and the Stone Age plumbing."

She opened the door to the closet-sized bathroom, flattening her back against the jamb and gesturing him inside. He seemed so much bigger in the tight hallway than he had in the barn. He stood there holding his hat, his face only a couple of feet from hers and his emerald eyes focused on her mouth.

"No problem," he said. "It'll be just fine."

She caught herself looking into his eyes and saw a hunger that bordered on raw. She stumbled back. "Oh, let me put your hat in the living room." Before he could offer it, she lifted the gray felt hat from his hands.

As she carried it to the living room, she lectured herself about wanting things she didn't need. *You're an idiot, Isabelle. He's just another horny guy.*

Then, ignoring the lecture like a defiant teenager, she laid his hat on a lamp table beside the sofa and turned on the CD player, letting Norah Jones' seductive voice rise from the speakers and fill the old house's lower floor with mood music.

In the kitchen, supper waited in a large cast-iron skillet. She didn't try to cook dishes that required her to read a complicated recipe. Her culinary reach included what her café-cook mother had taught her hands-on—a fair job at breakfast, fried steak and fried potatoes and, when she felt brave, biscuits and cream gravy.

Tonight she had thrown together a concoction of ground

beef, some onions, carrots and celery, added corn and pasta, then buried the whole mess under tomato sauce and Tex-Mex spices. Among the many lessons she had learned in Texas was that tomato sauce, chili powder and cayenne pepper could conceal a host of cooking catastrophes. She stirred the skillet meal, taste-tested and judged it passable.

While in Ontario, after buying a new washing machine and dryer, she had been unable to make contact with Paul's ex-wife, thus had some spare time. She had used it to shop for groceries. She felt guilty for not supporting Fielder's, sure that the Callister merchant could use every penny's worth of business he could get, but Fielder's produce left much to be desired. Unable to resist Albertson's, she had scoured the supermarket's produce department. Now she pulled out her purchases—fresh spinach, mushrooms, broccoli crowns, a cucumber and a tomato for a salad.

Her guest appeared in the kitchen doorway, looking better than a man had a right to at the end of a workday. His head almost touched the top of the doorframe. He had on a pale blue shirt with a Cinch logo below the pocket. There was just something delectable about a man in Wranglers and a Cinch shirt, especially a man with a body like John Bradshaw's.

The smell of soap and water carried across the room over the spicy food. No cologne or aftershave smelled better than a freshly washed man. She chastised herself for her wicked thoughts and reminded herself he was the age of her little brother.

"Can I help?" he asked, his baritone voice thrumming across the room, almost in tune with the soft bass vibrating from the CD player. He walked into the kitchen, boot heels thudding on the old linoleum-covered floor and stood by the counter, his hands resting on his hips.

She looked up at him, his size and nearness as overwhelming in the small kitchen as it had been in the bathroom doorway. Not only was he a good eight inches taller than she, he was wider. Feeling a breach of her defenses, she took a few seconds to find her tongue. "Uh, no. I think we've got everything under control."

"Good music. Who's singing?"

"Norah Jones. I, uh, usually listen to country, but some-times I like something different."

He smiled. "I like it, too. It's ... quiet."

She could tell having John eat with them thrilled Ava be-cause the ten-year-old had already washed up without a prompt and set the table. "You can sit here, between Mama and me," she said and showed him a chair.

"Great." Another smile tipped the corners of his mouth and he crossed to the table. "Smells good."

*Well, what else would he say?*

"Do you want some tea?" Ava asked him.

"Uh, got any coffee?"

"Coffee. Oh." Isabelle dropped her paring knife into the salad bowl. "Of course. I didn't think—" She moved down the counter, dragged the Mr. Coffee to her and began to as-semble it.

"In Texas, we always drunk tea for supper," Ava said.

"Don't bother with that coffee," he said. "I'll just have what Ava's drinking."

Of course coffee made more sense in the cooler weather of Callister, but iced tea was the most common drink in the South and it had become such a custom, she and Ava drank it without thinking. "But I can make—"

"Really, tea's just fine."

She stopped fiddling with the coffeemaker and returned to her salad making as Ava filled a tall glass with ice and tea.

Accompanied by the super salad and fresh garlic bread also bought in Boise, the dish she had prepared made a sub-stantial meal. John ate two helpings and heaped so many compliments on her cooking, she felt awkward.

As she always did at mealtime, Ava chattered all through supper about everything from dogs to horses to Nancy Drew. Isabelle doubted if John knew anything about Nancy Drew, but he carried on with Ava, asking her questions and causing her to talk that much more. Isabelle appreciated his easy communication with the daughter whose father had treated her as if she didn't exist.

After Ava emptied her plate, she headed for the back porch.

"She's a heck of a kid," John said. "Smart. Bet there's never a dull moment with her around."

"She keeps me on my toes. Half the time I feel like we're in reverse roles."

He reached for his iced tea glass and drained it.

"Are you sure you wouldn't like coffee? It would take me just a minute—"

"Tea's good. Coffee this close to bedtime would keep me awake anyway."

Needing to do something to keep from staring at his very attractive face, Isabelle stood and began to clear the table, "Were you close to your kids?"

"Um, I thought I was. I was just starting to teach Trey to rope when . . . well, when everything blew up." He looked out the bay window into the dark night. "He was coming along good, too."

*Uh-oh.* Pain and disappointment blared like a trumpet in his tone. She remembered what Paul had told her a few days back about John's wife's infidelity. Most people might not want to discuss their former spouses cheating on them, so Isabelle looked for a less intrusive tack. "Your oldest is named Trey?"

"John the third, actually, but we call him Trey. I'm a junior. They call my dad Tom, but his first name's John. We're all three named John Thomas." He ended the explanation with a little laugh.

"Oh," Isabelle said. "I never knew that about your family."

John stood and picked up his dishes. "Trey's the athletic one. Cody's more a thinker."

Isabelle smiled. "Like Ava."

She carried the stack of dishes to the sink, squeezed in some dish soap and turned on the hot water, sending up a cloud of steam and lemony fragrance. She missed having a dishwasher, but only God knew when she would feel comfortable spending the money to buy one. The new washer and dryer had wiped out her budget for appliances. "Nearly nine and ten? Boy, that's close together."

"Yeah, well, we didn't plan it that way. . . . Sometimes you just—" He stopped speaking and shook his head.

She threw a quick glance at him and saw a touch of bitterness in the way his mouth twisted.

"They're fourteen months apart," he said. "That second
go-around, Julie was ready to cut me."

Isabelle hesitated until what he said sank in. Remembering the old saying about little pitchers having big ears, she
glanced toward the porch, to be sure Ava wasn't on her way
back to the kitchen. "Oh, I know all about those accidents. I
remember how stunned I was when I got pregnant. We had
no time and no room for a baby. We weren't even married,
but that's another story."

His head jerked toward her. "Yeah?"

"Sometimes everything goes haywire, you know?" She
quickly rambled on, not wanting to admit aloud, especially to
someone she scarcely knew, that not only had Billy not cared
enough to marry her, but wedlock had been low on her own
list of priorities. "You down too many beers one night or forget to swallow the pill or stop off at the drugstore and next
thing you know, boom. You've stepped in it."

John didn't crack a smile at her attempt at levity. He came
to the sink carrying his dishes. "That how you got Ava?"

Surprised at a question so personal, she tittered like a
nervous ninny. "More or less. I was on the pill, but I'd been
taking antibiotics for a sinus infection. I didn't know antibiotics could make birth control pills ineffective." The expression on his face didn't change as he stood there with his
dishes, so she added, "Don't misunderstand me. I'm not
complaining. Ava's made my life so much better. I can't
imagine what it would be like without her."

"I'm not bitching either. At least not about Trey and
Cody."

She didn't hear a sigh, but she detected one in the ever-
so-slight slump of his wide shoulders. She took the dishes
from his hands and dunked them into the soapy water. "So
you've got kids you didn't plan for. Don't beat yourself up
over it. I'll bet that's how half the kids born come into the
world. It isn't like with horses, where you map things out.
But just because you weren't expecting them doesn't mean
you think any less of them."

John unbuttoned and rolled back his cuffs, exposing muscular forearms dusted with brown hair and for some reason, she thought of his chest and his belly and— "Look, you don't have to help me."

He didn't answer, just picked up a dish towel, the size of his hands dwarfing it, and reached for a rinsed plate. With long, agile fingers, he began to dry. She glued her eyes to the dishes lest he look into her face and somehow see her heart racing.

"You're right," he said. "My boys are great. Even though I didn't plan for them, I've never been sorry."

He was near enough for her to see the late-day stubble on his jaw, the thick brown brows. "When you got married, you must've had some idea about kids. You, for sure, knew what caused them. What *did* you plan for?"

"What I *planned* was becoming a world champion steer roper. But what I became was a father. Then I got married. Everything pretty much went downhill from there. Julie... well, I'll just say there were people she liked better than she liked me." John reached for another plate, dried it and carefully stacked it on top of the one he had just finished. "How about you and Billy? What did you plan for?"

A huff blurted out. Billy couldn't stick to a plan of any kind for more than thirty minutes. "Well, Billy didn't intend to be a father, that's for sure. He didn't even want to be a husband. He hated the whole time I was pregnant. He was at a horse show in Wyoming when I delivered." She laughed, as she always did when she thought about going to the hospital alone and giving birth among total strangers. "Not that I needed him. What could he do except get in the way?" She handed him a rinsed bowl. "I thought in time Ava would grow on him. I mean, how can you not love a little baby? But—"

She stopped herself. Lord, a conversation about her life with Billy could have her wailing all night. "If I had it all to do over, I'd recognize him as a poor choice for a father."

"He doesn't stay in touch with Ava?"

"Heavens, no." Isabelle felt too humiliated to tell him that Ava's father hadn't even helped choose her name.

"Does it bother her, not seeing her dad?"

John's interest seemed intense, so she couched her answer with care. "I don't think so. Even when we lived together, he didn't give her the time of day. Except for how his leaving uprooted our lives, I think she didn't care much." She handed him another rinsed bowl and went back to her dishwater.

Playful barks came from the porch and they both looked in that direction. "I'm glad everything's working out with the dogs. I worried about it. At the time I brought them out here, I didn't think about how pushy it was."

"They make Ava happy. And right now I'm looking for anything that makes her happy."

"Why? Is she a problem?" He started on the silverware.

"Gosh, no. At least not a problem child. She's wonderful. But her life has been turned upside down. She was born in Weatherford. She's never known anywhere else. Add that to the fact that Billy and I weren't model parents to begin with. She's spent so much time with babysitters instead of me. It feels like she doesn't— I'm just trying to make up for all the time I devoted horses that I should have spent with my daughter."

What was she doing? She had no intention of discussing with anybody in Callister her shortcomings as a parent or her unusual relationship with her daughter's father.

"When I first saw her, I wondered if she was Billy's daughter. I couldn't tell by looking. I don't see much of Bledsoes in her. She looks like you."

Isabelle felt her cheeks warm up, the compliment making her self-conscious. "Poor kid."

John's brow creased into a frown. "Why would you say that? You're a pretty woman, Izzy—Isabelle."

"Uh-huh, I call all these freckles beauty marks. And this wild hair? Every day I debate if I should cut it off even with my ears. You'd think I would have at least inherited Pa's orderly black hair, like Paul did."

"Don't put yourself down like that. I guess you never knew, but when we were in high school you were all I thought about. But you turned around and went the other direction every time we ran into each other." His voice turned soft and she sensed his eyes on her. "I had, uh"—he made a low chuckle—"well, I'll put it this way—I dreamed about you damn near every night."

She looked up at him, knowing what he had almost said and feeling both flattered and fearful of what she saw in his earnest expression. "We were kids, John. We were different people."

"Amen to that." He folded the towel into a crooked but neat square and smoothed it out on the counter. His hand came to rest on her shoulder. He lifted a russet ringlet and rubbed the strands between his thumb and finger. "I always wanted to touch your hair," he said. "Don't cut it."

A dozen emotions passed through his expressive eyes. She dropped her gaze to his mouth and his slightly parted lips. She could feel his breath, smell the faint hint of the spices they had eaten. A frisson shot through her. She looked away quickly and cleared her throat, thankful to have her hands immersed in dishwater because she could feel they were trembling.

She didn't reply to his remarks, concentrating instead on washing the last dish. Anything she said could open a conversation for which she wasn't ready. She couldn't guess his thoughts, but hers were all over the place—ranging from wondering about the meaning of his touching her and his comment on why his wife left him to where he lived and, God forgive her, how he would look without his clothes.

"I think it's time for me to hit the road," he said, telling her with his eyes he knew as well as she that something had passed between them, something they might renounce with words but could never erase.

A slutty side of her nudged her to say, *Stay*, but the re-formed parent dried her hands, went to the living room and returned with his hat. She walked behind him toward the mudroom where he had left his jacket. "Thanks for being good to my babies."

"My pleasure. I've got some ideas we could discuss one of these days. About the horses."

"Okay, sure. I'm open to suggestions."

He shrugged into his coat, ran a hand over his hair and set

on his hat. Ava jumped up from playing with the puppies. "Mama cooks supper every night," she said. "We always have a lot."

Isabelle did a mental eye roll. Indeed she did cook every night, but how desperate did it sound having her daughter imply that John should come and eat. "Have you done your homework?" she asked Ava. "Didn't you have geography questions?"

"They only take a minute. I already know all the answers. I learned geography a long time ago."

"I used to be good at geography," John said with an easy grin. "Someday we'll have a contest. See who knows the most."

Ava giggled. Isabelle opened the back door.

"Far as I can tell now," John said, "I won't get back 'til next week. I stick close to town on Friday and Saturday nights."

"Because of the bars?"

"Yep. You never know which sets of drunks are gonna try to kill one another."

Isabelle's thoughts flew to Paul.

# Chapter 9

A houseful of people celebrated John's mother's birthday. His sister, Jessica, and brother-in-law, Richard, had come from Twin Falls for the occasion. Some cousins from Spokane and a few of his parents' friends from town showed up, too.

The home of John's youth was old, roomy and warm from a fire smoldering in a stone fireplace. It was also bright with natural light. No curtains hung on the row of east windows that brightened both the dining room and the great room and none ever had. Katie Bradshaw wanted to look at nature.

With the weather too inclement for a backyard barbecue, John's dad cooked steaks—Bradshaw's own beef—over hot coals on the brick indoor grill in the kitchen. They ate in midafternoon.

After the dishes had been cleaned up, Jessica brought out a large, flat cake and set it on one end of the varnished pine dining table. The confection was big as a saddle blanket and heaped with swirls of colorful frosting. Miniature plastic cows grazed on a sprinkled-green-sugar pasture and plastic bucking broncs reared behind a fence of chocolate strips. The thing looked too pretty to eat. Jessica produced a camera and snapped pictures.

A pile of gifts covered the opposite end of the long

table. As the well-wishers gathered around, Richard pulled bottles of champagne from the refrigerator. John's mother was coaxed to the table by her daughter and listened, her face flushed, while the group toasted her, then sang "Happy Birthday."

Jessica presented a fancy wrapped box from the Bon Marché in Boise. John's mother opened it and lifted out clothes that John thought looked frumpish for a woman who roared around a ranch on an ATV.

The outfit came with a lecture about how she should get out of those jeans and into some feminine clothing now that she was getting older. What in hell did Jessica mean? Their mother was only sixty-three and she still cut a fine figure in a pair of jeans. Mom gushed over the gift John knew she would never wear.

John didn't pretend to understand his sister. With her being ten years older, he felt almost as if they had grown up in different families. She had met Richard in college. Before John reached high school, both she and Richard had graduated from UI with degrees in elementary education and certificates to teach. They had been married nineteen years, had no children. They did have a dachshund they treated like a child and called Adolph. The name fit the demanding little fart. Adolph was the only dog Mom and Dad had ever allowed in the house.

The dachshund and their teaching careers appeared to be his sister and brother-in-law's existence. Neither of them had an interest in ranching or livestock. They sided with the radical environmental groups that believed grazing cattle were a blight on the earth, but, John noticed, they didn't turn down a good steak when it was offered.

At some future point, if his parents didn't sell out, he and his sister would inherit the Lazy B, which encompassed some premium pastureland, a sizeable government grazing allotment and a herd of well-bred cattle and other livestock. When that thought barged into his head, John always set it aside, unprepared to face his parents' passing or the aftermath.

As he knew they would be, the turquoise Zuni earrings he gave his mother were a hit. He and Mom had always understood each other. She put them on immediately. Dad gave her a new watch, which she promptly put on and showed off for all to admire and covet. If John knew his dad, the watch had cost several hundred dollars.

John looked on with something akin to awe as his parents hugged and kissed. There had always been an abundance of expressions of affection between his parents—touching, kissing, hugging. Watching them, he suspected their sex life had been hot and healthy, though try as he might he couldn't imagine his dad as a lover. The testy old guy must have something going for him, though, because even now, at sixty-seven, when he put his hand on Mom's bottom, she sidled closer to him for more.

Growing up, John took for granted that the warm give-and-take between his parents defined married love. That was before he got hitched to Julie, who dashed the illusion in a hurry.

Richard opened champagne, Mom blew out candles and cut the cake. John passed up the champagne for coffee and carried his serving to the sofa near the fireplace. Other than being friendly and making empty talk, he had managed to steer clear of his dad all day. No point ruining Mom's birthday party with a sarcastic exchange between him and Dad. Fortunately, enough people milled through the house to capture and hold the patriarch's attention.

Mom brought her glass of champagne and sat down beside him. "No bubbly?"

John had avoided alcohol since the day he agreed to take on the sheriff's job, believing it tarnished his image as the chief law enforcer in the county. Excessive use of it had damaged him as a man and though he'd seen many a cowboy drown in a lake of booze, some inner force he didn't understand or question had saved him from becoming one of them. He swallowed a sip of coffee and gave his mother a smile. "You never know. I might get a call to go back to town."

She stuck out her arm. "Like my new watch?"

"It's cool. You're a cool lady, Mom."

"Your dad spoils me." She turned and straightened his shirt collar and fondled the shaggy back of his hair that had grown past his collar. "When you were a little boy, those curls were cute, but now—"

"I know, I know. I need a haircut." He grinned, tilting his head away from her fingers, and had another sip of coffee.

"What you need is some doting female to look after you."

Izzy Rondeau's smile and the supper they had shared three nights ago flew into John's mind. He thought about her attempts to elevate his mood, about helping her with the dishes and touching her fragrant hair. The intimacy of hanging his chinks in her tack room. What would his mother make of all that?

"Nadine Flagg," she was saying, "told me you're dating that new teacher who came here from Pocatello."

Callister gossip. John tolerated it because he knew that beneath all the nosing into people's lives, most folks in Callister would do anything they could for you. But tolerating it didn't mean he intended to fan the flames by telling his mom about his meeting with said teacher in the courthouse after hours and how she would have stuck her hand in his pants if he hadn't stopped her. Besides, a man his age *dating* sounded dumb. He chuckled as he sliced off a bite of cake. "Just ran across her accidentally in Betty's Road Kill. And only once, so you and Nadine don't need to get carried away."

"Son, you're thirty-two and you've been divorced over three years now."

"Broke as I am, I can't afford women." He savored a bite of the white cake that tasted as good as it looked.

His mom sighed. "I know you're working for starvation wages. When you finish with this sheriff's thing you've committed to, I wish you'd talk to your dad. Nothing would make him happier than to have you come home and move into the foreman's house. It's just sitting there empty since Warren left us. We could use your help. We aren't getting any younger, you know."

"Mom, you'll be young forever." John didn't like hearing talk about his mother aging. "If Dad wants me closer, it's so he won't have to yell so loud when he chews my ass."

She smacked his knee. "Listen to you. You may not want

to admit it, but you two are just alike. Both hardheaded as bulls."

John winked at her. "It's *you* I get that from."

"Pshaw. What am I going to do with you?" She sipped from her glass and John grinned at her choice of an expletive. If the house weren't full of people, she would have said, "Bullshit."

"Mom, do you remember Isabelle Rondeau?"

"Vaguely. I heard she's back, living on the old place."

"What do you know about her and her family?"

"Not much lately. When she lived here before, she was a shy, good little girl, so self-conscious of her red hair and those freckles. She never gave anyone a minute's trouble. Her mother and I went to Callister High School together. It broke Helen's heart when her only daughter ran off with one of the Bledsoes."

"I'll bet," John mumbled around a bite of cake.

His mother took a sip of champagne. "But Helen accepted it. She told me once she would never try to pick out a man for Isabelle after the bad choice she'd made for herself. Frenchie Rondeau was such a bastard. I suspect that when Isabelle was a girl, she thought Billy Bledsoe was her only chance."

His mom leaned forward, resting her elbows on her thighs, rolling her glass between her palms. Her eyes took on a distant look. John could see she was a little tipsy. "Poor Helen. I always wished I could help her, but I didn't know how. It's bad business to step between a woman and her husband." Mom sighed and sipped again. "She cooked in Betty's 'til the day she collapsed and died."

John had a dim memory of Helen Rondeau cooking at Betty's Road Kill Café, but as a teenager, he had paid no attention to such. "Just like that? What'd she die from?"

"Sudden heart attack. Passed away in the helicopter on the way to Boise. Ten years back, I think. I always figured she died young from living with a mean and hopeless drunk. Paul's headed down the same path as his dad. Don't tell me you've had a run-in with him."

"Art 'Dimos shot Isabelle's dog. I had to go out there. He said some mean things about her. I wondered why."

"Oh, it's probably because Art and Frenchie feuded for so many years. I doubt if Isabelle has done anything bad to Art."

"Okay, you started it, now you're gonna have to tell me the whole story. What'd they feud over?"

"Land, of course. Rondeau's grazing land is some of the best on that side of the county. Art wanted it in the worst way so he could expand his sheep herd. When Frenchie wouldn't sell to him, Art tried to take it by throwing his weight around and bullying the tax assessor."

John's curiosity perked up. Callister County's tax assessor was a nice, grandmotherly lady of sixty-something who had held the office for years. John saw her or someone from her office every day. The idea of anyone bullying her set off a burst of protectiveness in him. "What do you mean? What did he do?"

"Frenchie always struggled to pay his taxes. Art watched like a hawk. He tried to set up a situation where the county would take Rondeau's land for taxes, then if Frenchie couldn't pay up, Art would be able to buy the land cheap for back taxes."

A spark of anger flashed within John. Lately, he kept running headlong into a righteous streak he hadn't known he had. "Why, that old crook."

His mother laughed. "You're too young to remember, but they came to blows a couple of times, downtown in the saloons. Some of us even wondered if one would end up shooting the other."

"Does Art still want the land?"

"I doubt it. Lou leaving took some of the bluster out of his drawers. His thinking's always been screwed up, even when we were young."

"He's got a nice house," John said, picturing the log structure that looked like a picture in a magazine.

"He spent a fortune building it just the way Lou wanted it, but that didn't keep her from leaving him. She'd had all she could take. I don't know why your dad hangs on to his friendship. I don't know what they have in common."

John thought he knew. As far as he was concerned, Tom Bradshaw and Art 'Dimos had similar controlling personalities. His mom frowned and looked at him over her shoulder. "That's something else I hate about you having that sheriff's job. You're bound to have to deal with people like Art. Or Paul Rondeau. You could get yourself shot."

In an abstract way, getting shot had occurred to John, but he wouldn't worry his mother with the thought. "Mom, it's the twenty-first century. People don't shoot the sheriff these days." He popped the last bite of cake into his mouth and scraped the white frosting off the dish with the side of his fork.

"Says you. Policemen get killed every day. I see it on TV all the time in those true crime shows your dad likes. And this is Callister County. There's plenty of misfits around here who might shoot anyone that came in their gunsights." She tipped her head back, drained her glass, then turned to him and patted his knee. "Tell me about my grandbabies."

A part of John wanted to throw his head against his mother's shoulder and weep over the latest turn of events with his sons. "They're doing good. I talked to them on the phone last week and I got a letter from Julie a few days ago."

"California's so far away. But it's not that long 'til summer. I can hardly wait for them to get here. Your dad and I are going to start riding their horses soon as the weather gets better, so they'll be fit for little boys."

The ache inside John's rib cage grew more acute. He had ignored Julie's letter for the past two days, as if it might disintegrate and he wouldn't have to deal with it. Before he could reply to his mother's remarks, to his great relief someone called to her and she rose and left him alone.

As the afternoon turned late, the guests began to depart. His mother had had one glass of champagne too many and his father told her she should go lie down.

John had stayed long enough. If he lingered he might get trapped into conversations about his kids or his ex-wife or his interrupted rodeo career. He had been less than honest with his parents about each of those subjects because he went out of his way to avoid giving his dad a bone to chew on.

As he drove past the corral, he spotted his rope horse. He stopped off and said hello to the big gray. He had always thought of Rowdy as a "man's horse." At sixteen hands he was the perfect mount for John's height and weight. Together, they had been a winning team and Rowdy's power and burst of speed out the gate had been a major factor. John didn't mind giving him the credit he deserved. As the horse snuffled and nuzzled him, John wondered if he would ever again be able to keep him on his own place.

At home, he pried off his boots, picked up the new issue of *Western Horseman* and settled into his chair. He hadn't been there long when the phone warbled. The familiar voice on the other end of the line didn't even say hello. "Didn't you get my letter?"

His stomach knotted. *Chaos and confusion.* "Well, hello to you, too, Julie. Yeah, I got it. How're the boys?"

"Carson took them to the movies. That's why I'm calling you now, so I can talk to you privately."

*Shit.* "Then speak your piece."

"Carson's been to an attorney and discussed the procedure for adoption—"

"Just hold it right there. I'm not going for it. I can't imagine you thinking I would. I miss those kids. They mean everything to me. And to my family. Mom and Dad can't wait for them to get here this summer."

"That's very self-centered of you, John. But then you always did think only of yourself and what *you* wanted." John heard a tremor in her voice—either anger or tears, he wasn't sure which.

"I'm not gonna fight with you," he said. "But I'm telling you, I'm not giving up those kids to your boyfriend."

"He isn't my boyfriend. He's my husband. Damn you, John. Can't you, for once, look at the bigger picture? What can you do for them? You don't even have a decent job. My God, you've been absent more than half their lives."

He had heard the same old accusations a thousand times. He had traveled, sure. But he had not been absent half his kids' lives. Besides, it wasn't like he hadn't begged Julie to go with him and bring the kids.

Before they married, she had been enthusiastic about his rodeo career. After the wedding she refused to even go to a rodeo or to take the boys to one. Every time he tried to discuss it with her, she expounded about cruelty to animals and cowboys being drunks and good-for-nothings. Her rants about his chosen career rankled to this day. "I'm their daddy, Julie, and you can't change that. What I can do is remind them where they came from and be there for them if they need me."

"Given your history, I hardly find that a comfort."

Julie had always gone for the jugular. He let it pass. "So when is school out? I want to get plane tickets—"

"Forget that. My God, with terrorists and child molesters around every corner these days, do you think I'm going to let two young boys get on an airliner and fly across the country alone?"

John rolled his eyes to the ceiling, but he wasn't insensitive to her concerns. "Then I'll come down and get them."

"I don't know. Carson has plans. He's free most of the summer, so he's thinking about an extended vacation—"

"It's my turn, Julie. I didn't raise hell when you got the visitation changed, but I'm telling you now, those kids are spending the summer in Callister. With me and their grandparents. And if it gets to be an issue, dammit, this time, I'll go see that judge myself."

*Clack!* She hung up.

He stood there a few minutes staring at the receiver, wondering how the hell he could feel so strong a bond with children whose mother he barely tolerated.

With his attention fractured, he could no longer concentrate on reading. He punched the TV on and found a movie he hadn't seen, but his mind wandered to Ava Rondeau and Billy Bledsoe. What kind of jerk had no interest in his child, especially when the kid was as cute and smart as Ava?

How could Billy not be there with Izzy when she gave birth? For that matter, how could he walk off and leave her? As unhappy as he had been in his marriage to Julie, he wouldn't have abandoned her.

# Chapter 10

Delayed by a county commissioners' meeting Tuesday morning, John didn't reach Izzy's until afternoon. As he came to a stop, he saw her working a palomino in the corral attached to the big barn. Ava watched, perched on a top fence rail, and John wondered why she wasn't in school. He walked to the fence and rested his forearms on the rail beside her. "What's this?"

"My friend Lindsay's grandpa's gelding," Ava said. "He can't ride him 'cause somebody made him mean. Mama's fixing him. She knows how to make him be nice."

"And how does she do that?"

"She talks to him and tells him she's the boss, but she still treats him nice. That way, when she shows him what to do, he wants to do it and make her happy. She's thinking about getting him some pets."

"Pets?"

"Pets will settle him down and make him feel loved."

John stared at Ava a few seconds, amazed. He had heard unruly horses sometimes calmed when other animals were around as pals. He had never seen the phenomenon, so he had never concerned himself with it. Had Izzy taught her daughter this or had the brainy kid figured it out on her own?

He turned his attention to Izzy, who was standing in the middle of the corral with a longe line hooked to the palomino's halter, moving him in a circle around the corral. She urged him from a walk to a lope and back again with a series of body and hand signals, as if she and the animal had an invisible connection.

"Nice baby, good baby," he heard her softly saying. She dropped her hands and stepped back, letting the palomino take a breather. After a few seconds she walked toward him, holding out her hand, but, John noticed, the horse kept his distance.

Ava was dressed in jeans and boots. "Why aren't you in school today?" John asked her as he watched Izzy and the horse.

"The teachers are having a big meeting and they don't want us kids around."

"Do you know how to ride?"

"In Texas I had a horse, but we didn't bring him."

John thought about the two horses his parents had trained for his sons to ride.

Izzy made some kissing noises and the palomino's ears pricked up. Then she had him moving again. They did several more turns around the pen before she let him stop. Without being led, he followed her to the fence. "Whose horse?" John asked her.

"Jim Fielder's. Isn't he pretty?" She reached up to rub the blaze face, but the horse jerked his head back. Izzy's eyes filled with warmth and affection as she caught his halter. "This is Tarzan," she said in a tender voice. "He doesn't like me touching his face."

"What's his problem?"

"He's been abused."

John looked at the scars on the horse's rump and withers, even on his face. The obvious evidence was bad enough, but no telling what kind of abuse wasn't manifested in visible scarring.

"Because horses are so big," she said, "people who don't take the time to know them think controlling them calls for extreme measures. It's sad. No animal has been more abused and misused by man than horses. Yet they're more loyal than dogs."

Mistreatment of any animal was alien to John's level of understanding. "Damn. I can't believe Jim would—"

"It wasn't Jim who hurt him. Jim rescued him. Bought him at an auction. He's a six-year-old. He has a loving nature, but no one's ever taught him what to do. He's my first student in Callister." She unlatched the gate into the pasture where Trixie and Polly grazed. Tarzan watched her with a wary eye as she removed his halter and spoke to him softly. The golden horse shuddered all over and trotted toward the two mares.

"He likes Polly and Trixie," Ava said. Then as if she were imparting the wisdom of the ages, she added, "It's because he likes having friends. They like him, too, 'cause horses are herd animals."

"Is that right?" John said as she climbed down from the fence rail. "How're you and those pups getting along?"

Ava cocked her head and looked thoughtful. "They're fun, but they aren't as smart as Jack."

Isabelle huffed out a laugh. "There you have it. From the mouths of babes."

The three of them walked into the barn. Isabelle removed her chinks and carried them to the tack room. "I'm going over to the house to finish supper. It's something Italian. You're welcome to stay." She hooked the chinks on a nail and looked down at Ava. "Ready?"

Ava looked up at John and pushed her glasses up on her nose. "You'd better stay. We have pudding. I made it."

"Gosh," John said, winking at Izzy, "I can't turn down a dessert like that."

"It'll be good, I guarantee," Izzy said with a laugh. "This kid's got cooking in her genes."

Ava laughed, too. Something about hearing them laugh made John happy. Izzy held out her hand to the kid.

"I can't stay and visit right now," Ava said, taking her mother's hand. "I have to read the recipe for Mama."

As he watched the two of them walk toward the house, the ten-year-old a smaller version of her mother, he puzzled over the girl's remark.

He rode all three horses until they and he all worked up a

sweat. Dark had descended by the time he made it to the house.

Stepping into the porch, he met Ava feeding and watering the pups. He squatted and helped her with the food while she walked with mincing steps carrying water dishes from the mudroom.

"You still sleeping out here on the porch?" he asked her.

She set down a water bowl and gave him a frown. "No. Mama made me stop. She says they have to learn to sleep by themselves. I worry about them, but—" Her shoulders lifted with a great sigh.

"They'll be all right," he said and patted her shoulder.

He smelled garlic and onions and the tang of cooking tomatoes. He set his hat on the clothes dryer and hung his jacket on a horseshoe hook on the wall, just like he lived here. When he walked into the kitchen, he heard Willie Nelson crooning one his favorites from the living room, "Mamas, Don't Let Your Babies Grow Up to Be Cowboys."

Isabelle looked up from buttering bread slices and smiled when he walked in. An emotion John hadn't felt in years coursed through him and he recognized it as contentment. He hadn't known it many times in his adult life. His imagination took hold of him and would have carried him into dangerous territory if he hadn't reined it in.

"Ava's got the table all set," Isabelle said and slid the bread slices into the oven. "No promises how this tastes. I've never made it before, so you're a guinea pig."

"That's just fine," he told her. "I'm sure I've been subjected to worse."

The "something Italian" turned out to be spaghetti with homemade meat sauce.

"Mama sliced up everything," Ava said, "because I'm only ten years old and I'm too young to slice. But I stirred."

"I could tell," John said, shoveling in bites of spaghetti that tasted as good as any he had ever eaten. "The minute I tasted it, I knew Ava Rondeau had a hand in it."

"My grandmother was a cook," Ava said. "I never saw her, but I'm trying to be like her."

John put down his fork and looked at her, touched by the

fact that the kid had never known her grandmother. Or any grandparents, no doubt. How could she, living two thousand miles away since her birth? His parents, and Julie's too, showered enough affection and attention for a dozen people onto his two sons and he almost felt guilty that Ava had none. "You're doing a good job, kiddo."

"She lived in this town. Did you know her?"

John glanced at Izzy, whose eyes seemed to be glued to her spaghetti. "I sure did," John lied. "She and my mom were the best of friends."

"Eat your supper, Ava," Izzy said, "before it gets cold."

John returned to his meal, stuffing himself with spaghetti, salad and garlic bread. He forced himself to swallow a serving of Ava's pudding, all the while preoccupied with how good a parent Izzy was and what a good kid she was raising, all alone, with no help from anybody.

While the meal had been good, the company was better. Even the old house with its antiquated kitchen and creaking floors cloaked John with satisfaction and he regretted leaving. To show his gratitude for being rescued from another dismal evening in front of the TV, he volunteered to help with the dishes, then brought in some extra log rounds for the fireplace.

While at the fireplace, he asked about some of the trophies on the mantel and Isabelle explained their origins and showed him some trophy belt buckles with embedded gemstones—emeralds and rubies and one with diamonds—that she kept in a locked cabinet. He had seen similar, but not often. So much money surrounded cutting-horse competitions, a buckle of mere sterling silver wasn't enough.

At ten o'clock, not wanting to wear out his welcome, he said he had to go, but he offered to take the dogs out before leaving. Isabelle put on her puffy coat and walked with him while Harry and Gwendolyn relieved themselves. Under an overcast sky, the night was black and cold, but Callister Mountain's snowcap stood out as if substituting for the absentee moon. A few snowflakes floated down.

"How're you gonna train horses in this climate?" John asked her. "At the very least, you need a covered pen."

"What I need is a covered arena and some heat. I was gone from here for so long, I sort of forgot about the weather. I don't know yet how I'm going to work it out."

The lack of conviction in her tone told John she was floundering and he wondered if she might appreciate someone to lean on. He wanted to be that someone, but he didn't know what to say. Who was he to be offering advice when his own life had been one misstep after another? They walked along in silence. Finally, all he could think to do was loop his arm around her shoulder. The encouraging statement that came out was a lame "It'll be okay."

They returned the dogs to the house and John said good night, but he departed with a hunger far removed from the prandial kind. It only grew worse when he reached his gloomy duplex apartment. He couldn't keep from thinking how cool it would be to go to sleep with Izzy at night and wake up with her in the morning.

The next morning, for the entire time it took for Isabelle to French-braid Ava's hair, her daughter talked about John, and continued to talk through breakfast. Isabelle had mixed emotions about Ava becoming attached to John or any man passing through their lives, but she withheld her concerns. For now.

For now, she had a busy day ahead. She had shopping to do in town and a few errands. As soon as Ava boarded the school bus, she put the puppies on leashes and walked them around the pasture, then dressed in clean clothes and drove to town.

She had spent little time in town since returning, so today she moved slower and looked closer as memories of the sidewalks and stores crept back. The town looked much as she remembered it from childhood, except for the Forest Service offices. They had expanded considerably and their buildings, painted a crisp sage green, now filled two full blocks of the main street.

She lingered an hour in the drugstore, which was housed in the same old brick building where it had always been, midblock on the main street. Only the pharmacist had changed in all the years since she had last been in the store. She moved from there to the town's only dress shop. She strolled through and had a conversation with the owner, who remembered her as a little girl.

Callister had one beauty salon and the two hairdressers who owned it had occasionally wrestled her mop of hair when she was a child. That is, when the money could be found in the Rondeau household to pay for the service. She stopped in and said hello. One of the women was now crippled by arthritis. The other had become a widow. The women talked about her mother and how they missed seeing her in the café and Isabelle felt herself pulling away from the conversation.

The visit to town reminded her she had been gone for almost a generation, yet she felt comfortable, as if she had never left. One of the good things about coming home.

The salon's wall clock told her it was after two. Ava would be home by four p.m., so she cut her visit short and hurried to her pickup in the grocery store's parking lot.

When she opened the Sierra's driver's side door, there on the seat, in a glass vase, stood a small bouquet and a clovelike fragrance filled the pickup cab. She blinked and for the briefest of seconds wondered if it had been left in the wrong vehicle. A tiny square envelope was tucked beneath the vase. She pulled out the envelope and read the scrawled note inside.

*Thanks for supper last night. Thanks for rescuing me.*
*John T. Bradshaw.*

Feeling her face flush, she looked around to see who might be watching, then scooted the vase over and climbed into the cab. She sped out of town and didn't slow down until she reached the county road leading to her house. Only then did she stop on the shoulder and reread the note.

*Rescuing him?* Last night's supper had apparently meant more to him than it had to her—or had it? She had been in this strange uplifted mood all day. Otherwise she wouldn't have been wasting valuable time in town.

She fondled the dozen flowers. Carnations, perhaps. She

had some knowledge of houseplants, but scarcely knew one flower from another. Interspersed among the lacy red blossoms were tiny white things she suspected might be baby's breath. The greenery was fern leaves—she did know *that* much—and the red flowers looked pretty against them.

As she read the note again, she felt a grin crawl across her face. In her whole life no one had ever given her a bouquet of flowers. She debated what to do. The proper thing would be to call John and thank him, but did she want to call the sheriff's office, where twenty people might hear the conversation?

Was a phone call even necessary? All she had done was invite him to eat. She hadn't expected a gift of any kind in return. She dithered a few more minutes, then decided to let a thank-you wait until he came out to her house tomorrow to ride the horses.

At home, she placed the bouquet on an antique table in the living room where she could see it every time she passed the doorway. She floated around the house for the rest of the day, doing laundry, helping Ava clean her room, giddy when she thought about the gift. Did all women feel like this when they received flowers from a man?

Don't be silly, she warned herself. He was only saying thank you. Remember, he's a cowboy, which means he's had dozens of women. She hadn't heard about them up to now because she had never gotten on board the gossip train.

He arrived Thursday morning just as she was leaving to take Ava down to catch the school bus, but she waited while he and her daughter had a conversation about school. Feeling panicky and not knowing why, Isabelle stayed out of the way and didn't mention the flowers, hoping to express her thanks in a private moment when she wouldn't be so nervous.

The school bus came late, so by the time she returned, he was already riding Trixie. She busied herself with chores in the house, practicing her thank-you speech and willing herself not to look outside to see what he was doing.

They had agreed he would ride each horse for forty-five minutes or so and he usually rode Dancer last, so after three hours had passed, she let herself look out. Sure enough, he was in the corral attached to the small barn, loosening the cinch on Dancer's saddle. She walked over.

"I found the flowers," she said. "Thanks. They're real pretty." She felt clumsy and stupid at using such an old cliché.

He smiled and said she was welcome.

"It wasn't necessary. I mean, I didn't go out of my way or anything."

"I know. Just letting you know I appreciated you feeding me. Seems like it's hard to find a flock of friends to talk to or spend time with."

She stuffed her hands into her jeans back pockets and looked at the ground. What else could be said about the flowers?

He dragged the saddle off Dancer's back. She helped by taking off the blanket, then the headstall, and together they walked across the driveway to the tack room in the big barn. The morning's panic attack came back and she could feel her pulse swishing in her ears. "How'd it go today?"

"Okay. The blue devil's in a mood. We had a bit of a rodeo at first, but he settled down."

She nodded, tongue-tied, and tried to claw words from the air. Her heart pounded as if she had been the one riding Dancer.

Inside the tack room, he lifted the saddle onto its saw-horse. She watched as he unbuckled his chinks, her gaze settling on the buckle that fit just below the waistband of his jeans. She looked away quickly before he could catch her staring at his fly. The tack room almost seemed too small for the two of them and the electricity humming in the air around them. After he hung the chaps on their nail, he gave her a grin. "I'm thirsty."

He had put a cup in the tack room so he could have a drink of water from the stand faucet just outside the barn door. He picked up the cup, walked outside to the standpipe, rinsed out the cup, then filled it. He tipped it up and drank the whole thing without stopping. She couldn't keep from staring at the muscles working in his throat. When he finished, he wiped his mouth on his flannel shirtsleeve and gave her another big grin. "Good water. I do love well water."

Well, what could she say about that? Who didn't? Tongue-tied again. "If you aren't in a hurry, I could send some home with you. I think I've got an empty jug over at the house."

"Cool," he said.

They walked to the house and she found a plastic milk jug in the mudroom, washed it out in the laundry sink and filled it from the faucet. When she handed it to him, he took it with a big smile. "My morning coffee's gonna taste a whole lot better."

She followed him outside toward his truck. "What's going on in your office today?" she asked him, mostly to make conversation and she liked his company.

"Don't know yet. Haven't talked to Rooster today."

"Ah," she said and nodded.

He opened the driver's side door, set the jug of water inside, then turned back to her. "When are you planning on bringing in those calves?"

"Not until the pasture comes on better. May or June. Why?"

He leaned his bottom against the front fender of his truck and crossed his ankles and his arms, looking like he wanted to talk. "I think the horses are ready. They need more to do."

She leaned against the fender, too, and crossed her arms. "I've been thinking about getting a few head of buffalo instead of calves." She didn't know where that came from. She had thought about it, sure. But not since she had returned to Callister.

He tucked back his chin and blinked at her.

*Uh-oh. He thought it was a dumb idea.* Maybe it was, but she charged on, putting her private musing into words. "If I get calves, I'll have to buy seventy or eighty head, but I could get along with only about a dozen or so buffalo calves."

He looked down, like he was studying his boot toes. "You want the horses to work buffalo instead of cows?"

"The buffalo calves don't get trained to the routine as fast as cows do. You have to replace the cows every couple of months, but you can work the buffalo for a year maybe."

A laugh burst from John and he shook his head. "I've

never seen a horse try to control a buffalo. They're tough animals. Aren't you afraid one of them will challenge the horse?"

"Some of the trainers down in Texas use them. As long as they're no older than yearlings, it doesn't seem to be a problem."

"Aren't they expensive?"

"These days, no more so than cows. I'm just thinking of my pasture. A dozen buffalo will eat a lot less than seven times that many calves."

"Good point."

She nodded. "I'm thinking it's what I should do. I don't need to spend any more money than I have to."

"You'd have to shore up your fences. Four barbed wires doesn't present much of a barrier to a determined buffalo."

"I know, but Paul can do that." She grinned. "He works for free."

John laughed his easy laugh and looked right at her. "Well, it'd be a new experience for me, cutting buffalo calves from a herd. New for these horses, too, I'll bet."

"They can handle it. They'll like the challenge."

He pushed back his hat with his thumb and showered her with a huge smile. "You're something else, Isabelle."

She smiled, too, unable to remember when she had enjoyed a man's company so much. "You are, too."

He glanced at his watch again.

"Gotta go, huh?"

"Not yet. You trying to run me off?"

"No. No, of course not."

"No hurry. I just need to get back soon enough to clean up before I go to the office. Gotta look like the sheriff, you know." He grinned. "I'm pretty low maintenance, so it doesn't take me long."

Low maintenance. She didn't know what he meant by that. "Right," she said, nodding and remembering what Paul had told her about him, which amounted to gossip more than fact.

A pregnant pause, with neither of them talking. "Speaking of being sheriff," she said at last, "I'm curious about something. Did Luke McRae really just up and hire you?"

John laughed. "That's what people think. It wasn't quite that simple. The commissioners were looking for a warm body to fill the seat 'til the election this fall. I was the only one they could find."

"I can't believe you quit ProRodeo to be the temporary sheriff in Callister."

"I'd already quit the rodeo before the sheriff's job came up. I was working at a feedlot in Nampa while I looked for one of those career jobs. I ran into Luke and his wife at a music concert in Boise and the rest, as they say, is history."

"But you said it was the commissioners who hired you."

"After the show, Luke, his wife and I went to dinner. We started talking about college. My degree's in business administration and Luke's wife's got an M.B.A. from one of those rich schools in Texas."

Isabelle had suspected he had gone to college, probably on a rodeo scholarship. What would he think if he knew how dumb she really was? The gap between them grew wider. *Damn.* She looked off and up at the mountain rising behind her house.

"Somewhere in the middle of that evening," he was saying, "from out of the blue, Luke asked me if I'd like to ramrod the sheriff's office for a few months." He looked down and brushed a stone with his boot. "We all had a hell of a laugh."

She giggled, more nervous now than ever. "I can imagine."

"Luke was serious. The commissioners really were looking to hire an interim sheriff. Callister had been without a lawman for over a month. It was a big problem, Luke said, because the sheriff's department has the biggest, most unwieldy budget in the county. The commissioners believed an administrator was more important than a lawman, since there's virtually no crime in Callister. Of course they're wrong about there being no crime, but I didn't know that at the time."

"There was a murder last year." She swung her gaze back to him, wanting to be a part of a conversation she felt was quickly rising over her head.

"A crime of passion. The first murder in this county since 1934. The commissioners think it was a fluke, not

likely to happen again in another seventy years. I lived here
all my life. I know almost everybody in the county, so I
didn't disagree."

"So you said yes."

"I thought about it a while, but I couldn't find much reason to argue against it. I was living from payday to payday,
working at a shitty job. My prospects for the future had me
flummoxed. In the end, I said, 'why not?' I called Luke up
and said I'd meet with the commissioners."

"Wow."

"After they told me what Jim Higgins did, it pissed me off.
I guess it hit a soft spot in me. This is my hometown. All my
family lives here. I want the public officials to be honest and responsible, whether I'm personally a resident or not."

"You're planning on leaving?"

"I have to when this is over. I have to work at something
where I can make enough to support myself and my kids."

Isabelle didn't know why, but that reply left her unsettled.

He glanced at his watch again. "Guess I gotta go," he said
and turned to his truck door.

"Thanks again for the flowers. I really like them."

He nodded again, opened the door and climbed inside.
As he cranked the engine, he looked back at her, squinting in
the sunlight. "I'll see you next Tuesday."

She nodded. He shifted into reverse and the truck inched
backward.

"John?"

He stopped. She swallowed the lump that had grown in
her throat. "I didn't go to college. I didn't finish high school."

His expression softened. "Isabelle, I don't care."

# Chapter 11

Isabelle waved to John as he parked in what had become his spot. He slid out of his truck and ambled toward her, dressed in riding boots, a faded denim shirt and faded jeans. His silver belt buckle shone in the sun.

"Hurry," she called to him, pulling Polly's cinch tight. She had already saddled Trixie.

"What's up?"

"Blue skies. Warm day. Time for a change of pace."

She hadn't seen him or heard from him since Thursday. Five days. *Isabelle, I don't care.* The words had echoed in her head a hundred times since he said them last Thursday.

When he had phoned last night, saying he was taking the whole day off and would come out early, and with a forecast for temperatures in the low sixties, she had made a plan. As soon as she got Ava off to school, she snugged a bill cap on her head and went out to catch Trixie and Polly.

As John neared, she was struck by how much she had looked forward to his arrival this morning, how much she appreciated his laid-back dependability. The very thought delivered an unwelcome blow to her independence. She didn't want to want a man's company, didn't want to rely on a man for anything. She had relied on Billy and look what it got her.

She handed him Trixie's reins, unable to ignore how his

tan canvas jacket set off his eyes and fit in just the right place at his waist. He could be a model in a Western clothing ad.

He gave the deep chuckle she had grown to like too much and rubbed a hand down Trixie's neck. "Sounds good. Where are we going?"

"I figured we'd ride up the mountain. The head of Stony Creek's up near the snow line. I don't know how far we'll get. With the thaw the creek's probably full, but I know a good place for a picnic." She patted a pouch behind Polly's saddle. "I brought us a lunch."

"Cool. I've got all day."

Astride Polly, she led the way, following an evident but seldom used trail that climbed from the back of Rondeau property onto national forest and on up Callister Mountain. They passed through a grove of small evergreens, then broke into a wild grass meadow clear of the trees. The morning sun warmed their faces and shoulders, at odds with the spring air's bite on her cheeks.

When the single-file trail played out, John came up and rode alongside her, softly encouraging Trixie. He was gentle with the horses and she appreciated that. Billy had been rough and impatient.

Mental sigh. She had to stop comparing John and Billy. The Bradshaws and the Bledsoes had never competed in the same arena. John might make flattering comments that made her feel special, but she knew an irrefutable fact. They came from two different worlds—he from Callister's aristocracy, she from the riffraff.

She discarded that depressing thought and turned her attention to the surroundings she loved. A few hardy wildflowers and wild strawberries peeked out from the grass made wet by snowmelt. Small mounds of snow peppered with duff and pine needles still lay in shady spots and shrinking patches of the white stuff glistened like diamonds in the sun. They didn't talk, enjoying instead the call of a bird, the creak of saddle leather, the sounds of shod hoofs striking rock and the soft snorts as the horses cleared their nostrils. The smell of clean, rich earth and new season engulfed them.

They soon reached a rimrock where they stopped and

looked down on the Rondeau and Karadimos spreads. "Art's sheep look like Ping-Pong balls against the hillside," Isabelle said, surprised she could enjoy the sight of something that had caused her so much angst.

"Pretty." John, too, gazed down on the valley greening up and opening itself to spring. The reins hung loose in his hand as he rested his forearm on the saddle horn. He looked right and proper sitting there astride Trixie.

"Paul and I used to hang out here," she told him. "We would pretend we were hiding from outlaws." She turned and looked up the mountain, toward a broad granite face, a place she hadn't been since childhood. "There used to be a miner's cabin up there. It was really old, maybe all the way back to the forty-niners. Paul would go up there and hole up for days when we were kids."

"Hunh," John said. "I didn't know there was a cabin up that high. Where is it?" He reached down and patted Trixie's neck.

"Just below the glacier at the foot of that big granite outcropping. Only accessible on foot or horseback. It's about a day's ride from here. The old thing was rickety, but it had a floor. I remember there was a wood cookstove in it. I used to wonder how they got it up there."

She turned John's way. His eyes were shaded by his hat brim, but she saw something in them that had been there several times now, an appraising look that penetrated her walls and sent a skittishness through her. She quickly switched her attention back to the mountainside. "I mean, it's uphill and steep. And the stove is made of cast iron."

"They did a lot back in those days that makes you wonder."

She didn't dare look him in the face again, didn't want to open a Pandora's box of emotions. Instead, she clucked at Polly and moved ahead, deliberately forcing her mind to a flat limestone ledge on the banks of Stony Creek, where they would lunch.

They rode through burgeoning potentilla and the shadows of lodgepole and bull pine, listening to the creek's susurrus amplify to a roar as they drew nearer its rushing water. After a while they reached the edge of the treeline and she spotted her destination. Bathed in sunshine, the rock ledge the size of a flatcar looked as she remembered it from years ago. She pulled up. "Ever been here before?"

"Nope. New territory to me."

"That big rock's where we're going."

After they dismounted, secured the horses and loosened the cinches, she grabbed the lunch. Along with food, she had brought one of those plaid wool blankets Texans took to football games when they thought the temperature might drop below seventy.

John helped her spread the blanket on the sun-warmed ledge, then she unpacked sandwiches made of tuna salad like her mother always made it, with walnuts and chunks of apple and celery. She had also brought potato chips, bottles of water and a few chocolate chip cookies.

Due to the spring runoff, Stony Creek was full bank to bank. A wall of white water crashed down the ancient glacier gouge that was a trickling brook in the summer. They sat down cross-legged, shoulder to shoulder so they could hear each other talk over the roar of the rushing water. John bit into a sandwich so hungrily she was sure he hadn't eaten breakfast.

"Mmm," he said as soon as he swallowed. "I don't know why you say you can't cook."

He had taken off his hat and the sun caught a few weather-bleached strands of his wavy brown hair. He didn't wear grease on his hair and she liked that.

"My mother was a wonderful cook. She tried to teach me, but I didn't learn. If you'll notice, there isn't much here that was actually cooked by me." She sent him a smile over her shoulder. "All I did was sort of throw it together. Ava baked the cookies from one of those frozen packages."

"Tastes good to me. I don't get much homemade food. If it's not fried potatoes, I'm lost when it comes to cooking."

Beside them, white water threw up a fine mist that showed a rainbow in the sunlight. She looked up at the cloudless blue sky, marred only by a white jet trail thousands of feet above them. The sense of peace she had always found in the mountains seeped into her. "You forget about things, you know? Until I got back here, I didn't realize how much this place was a part of me. Billy and I lived in four states, but the sky doesn't look like that in a one of them."

John looked up, too, squinting from the brightness. "It's God's country, all right. You never came back, not even to visit?"

"Just once. For Mom's funeral. We were in Scottsdale then. I flew into Boise on a red-eye, rented a car, drove up here for the funeral, then left town by dark."

"Why such a hurry?"

"Couldn't stand being here." She felt the tiny pang that always came when she thought of her mother's death. "That was over ten years ago, before Ava was born. At that time I didn't think there was a chance in hell I'd ever come back. Art Karadimos wanted our land and I figured Pa would eventually lose it to him. I didn't give a thought to inheriting it." She looked at him again. "That's why Art hates us, you know. Because of the land."

"My mom told me. But Mom thinks he doesn't want it anymore."

Isabelle shrugged. "That could be true. The great equalizers caught up with him. Age and circumstances beyond his control. He won't be able to bully me and Paul the way he did our parents."

"Scottsdale, huh? I've been there. Cool place. How'd you wind up in Texas?"

"Timing, I guess. We ran into one of those big-shot Texans at a horse show. He had multiple car dealerships and a pile of money. He also had a string of good horses, but they were poorly handled. He knew it. He made us an offer we couldn't refuse, so we trailed along behind him to Weatherford, which, I might add, is a heck of a long way from here."

Her mind struggled to find a comparison between her present surroundings and the flat Texas plains where she had lived for more than ten years. "There isn't a mountain in sight in Weatherford, Texas." Though she had been home only a few weeks, Texas seemed like something she had imagined. She toyed with a potato chip. "We were too busy to think about Callister most of the time, anyway. We handled a lot of horses. Some of those Texas ranches own dozens of cutting horses." She wiped her mouth with a paper napkin. "Weatherford's close to Fort Worth, the be-all, end-all of the cutting world. The NCHA headquarters is there."

"NCHA. That stands for—"

"National Cutting Horse Association."

"I roped in that big rodeo in Fort Worth a few times. Won a little money."

"Did you? I always went to that rodeo. I really liked the animal exhibits. Some of the best-looking cattle I ever saw. I wish I'd run into you."

"I was married then."

His tone had a firmness to it. When she glanced up, he was looking directly at her. She smiled at what he must have assumed. "I only meant, John, that it would have been neat to see someone from home. I felt un-rooted in Texas. With my mountain country ways, I didn't fit into the horse society down there. Those cutting-horse people aren't like the rodeo folks, you know?"

"No, I guess I don't."

"The rodeo's an industry of cowboys. Salt-of-the-earth kind of people. The cutting-horse business is probably more like horse racing than rodeoing. It scares you how much money's involved. Most of the owners are bored and filthy rich. Some are real ranchers, but many don't know much about livestock in general. Some of the owners are celebrities who never got close to a horse until they owned one. Down there, owning a cutting horse is kind of the in thing."

John laughed. "You're right. You don't see too many of those types in rodeos."

"To many of them, the horses are nothing but objects to be used and discarded when they're no longer fun or when they no longer pay off. Assets, they call them, as if the horses aren't living, breathing things. I hated it, but leaving was a hard decision. When you work with animals that are so smart and have so much heart, you can't keep from falling in love with them. It sounds weird, but I kept thinking I was doing the horses a favor by staying around and standing between them and..."

Her voice trailed off as vignettes of her relationships with various horse owners flashed through her mind. The life she had left in Texas, among the rich and famous who indulged their every whim no matter how bizarre, was more than she could describe to someone who hadn't lived it.

"And what? You didn't finish."

"Oh, nothing. It was just another one of my silly ideas. Billy always said I had a head full of them."

"Guess he never had any silly ideas, huh?"

"His ideas couldn't have been called silly, but I could think of a lot of other words."

"So tell me about training a horse to be a cutting champion. Where'd you learn how?"

"There isn't much to tell. I've loved horses for as long as I can remember. I never wanted a dog, but I always wanted a horse. I was lucky enough to hang out with some of the outstanding handlers here and there. I watched and listened and it just came to me." She took a long swig of water. "It's a kind of communication, you know? Almost spiritual. An understanding of something greater than you are."

"Uh-oh. I hope you're not gonna tell me you have one of those secret techniques shrouded in mystery."

"Nothing secret about it. I just think you don't really *train* horses. They already know how to do the things we want them to. They just don't always know when they're supposed to do them. All I do is try to make their lives easier by helping them figure it out.

"You see, horses are prey animals and they know that. We're predators. As much as they fear us, they want to please us." She shook her head. "People and horses don't make sense. Owners pay a lot of money for a high-spirited horse. They take possession and control of an animal that would willingly give its life for them, then they don't go to the trouble to understand it. They blame the horse for their own stupidity."

"Guess the horses are lucky to have someone like you."

"I hope so. I'm on their side. I always made that clear to horse owners I worked for. I always told them up front, if it comes to a choice between you and the horse, I'll take the horse every time. I accept all horses as they are, including the ones people think are crazy. Even the knot-headed ones will do what you want if they just know what that is. Didn't you find that to be true with your rope horses?"

"I guess. They were good and smart, but I bought them already trained. The extent of my work with them was trying not to let them pick up bad habits."

"They can do that, but if they know you aren't pleased, they'll try to change. I can tell you this much. If there's a problem with a horse, it's usually on the people end of the relationship."

He finished off his sandwich and wiped his hands on a napkin. "Want the other half of my sandwich?" she asked him. "I've had enough."

"You don't want it?"

"I ate breakfast." She grinned at him.

He returned a sheepish grin, took the half-sandwich and complimented her again on the tuna salad. When there was nothing left to eat, he lay back, leaned on his elbow and crossed his ankles. Lulled by the warmth and the creek sound, she took off her cap and turned her face up to the sun, relishing the feel of the warmth on her eyelids and pooh-poohing the fact that five thousand new freckles would pop out on her face. She stretched out, too, and closed her eyes, letting her slutty side imagine how it might feel to lie close to her companion.

"I've been wondering why you're not breeding those mares," he said. "Seems to me a foal out of either one of them and Dancer would be a good thing."

She opened her eyes and looked at Trixie and Polly, now snoozing in the sunshine. "We sold a few of their foals."

"What's wrong with doing it again?"

*Damn.* She bit down on half her lower lip, debating how much to tell John about the registration dilemma and at the same time berating herself for not having resolved it. Lord, it had been over a year since Billy left. "A baby's a lot of trouble and expense. A long-term commitment. And if it doesn't sell right away, I've got another horse on my hands to train and feed. And three years before it can compete."

He sighed, an indication that he knew full well the time, effort and money involved with a foal. "Yeah, I know. Horses make expensive pets. I was just trying to think of how you could get some return on your investment."

"I don't think of them that way. Even if I did, I don't have that much invested. We got all three horses free. Polly was given to us as a filly in exchange for care and training. Trixie and Dancer came from horses we used to own, but later sold. Turns out, Polly's the one that's a champion."

"Then she's the one to breed."

"Easier said than done. She might be sterile."

He gave her a look, now more alert. "The hell."

"She's minus an ovary. Tumor. The last time we bred her, Billy wanted to show her that year, so we tried to flush the embryo to transplant in a surrogate. The vet couldn't find a zygote. Besides being expensive, it was traumatic for her and me both. Some horses aren't disturbed by flushing, but it was painful for Polly. I don't like seeing her in pain. Horses like these are our captives from the moment they're born. They have faith that we won't hurt them. I hate letting them down."

"I know a little about horse breeding," he said, "but I don't know much about all this breeding and flushing embryos for money. I'm not sure I even like the sound of it."

She laughed. "Now that the American Quarter Horse Association accepts registration of more than one foal per year from the same mare, it's common practice in highbred quarter horses. It doesn't happen in Thoroughbreds because they have to be bred with live cover."

"What's wrong with live cover?" He sat up, braced on one hand. "Look, it doesn't have to be a big production. If you don't plan to be showing them this year, why don't you turn Dancer out in the pasture with Polly and Trixie and see what happens? Let nature take its course. If they're what you say they are, a good foal could heal up your bank account."

She didn't know what she planned. Part of her frustration was changing her mind every day. Besides the problem with Billy, the horses hadn't worked a cow in months. She shook her head. "Nobody does live cover with horses like these. We tried it a long time ago. Dancer's hard on mares. Besides the

risk of injury to the mare or to him, there's the possibility of
infection. . . . No, if I decided to breed them, artificial insemination's the way I'd go. The mares have a better chance of
getting pregnant."

"Then, until you decide, stand Dancer at stud or sell his
semen. I'm assuming you've done that before."

She nodded.

"So you've got a record of his potency and all that?"

"Oh, yes. He's a super-stud. He could impregnate a
dozen mares with one ejaculation. Maybe more, if I pastured
him with them."

"What's his fee?"

She shrugged. "I don't know. In Texas it was five to eight
thousand. Around here . . ." She shrugged again. "He's never
won any big money. He just has the bloodlines that everybody wants right now." She smiled. "And he's so handsome."

"You're missing the boat," he said. "I know it'd be hard
for you to collect the semen by yourself, but I could help you."

"I don't have a stall or a phantom horse. Or a place to
handle and keep the ejaculate."

"We've got a vet in town who's got that stuff. I know him
pretty well. I could bring my small trailer from Mom and
Dad's and we could haul Dancer over to the vet's barns. Luke
McRae's sort of a horse breeder and he's got a string of good
broodmares. I could talk to him. He might be interested in
foals out of Dancer."

Of course he would. Any sane breeder would jump at the
chance to breed his mares to a sire like Dancer. She *had* to
call Billy or at the very least write him a letter. *Damn.* She
had to call Nan and ask for her help. No way did she want
John, or anybody beyond family, to know how hard it was for
her to compose a simple letter. "I'll think about it."

She rose to her knees and began picking up the lunch
leavings. "Dancer's a unique horse. He's intuitive. He
seemed to know how upset I was when Billy left. I don't
know what I would've done if it hadn't been for Ava and the
horses. Having all of them to take care of every day was what
kept me together. Besides that, teaching horses and taking
care of them is the only thing I've ever been any good at."

"That's not true. You're a good mom. Ava's a great little kid. That has to be because of you."

"I wasn't fishing for compliments. I know my shortcomings as a mother. Ava's spent too much time alone, buried in books, and that's because Billy simply wasn't available, ever, and I was always working with horses. That's why I'm trying to change."

"Can I ask you something personal?"

Oops. That question usually preceded something touchy. She smiled at him. "Sure. I don't guarantee I'll answer, but—"

"What happened to Billy? I never heard."

Isabelle doubted that. Callister citizens took to gossip like a shark to blood in the water. Still, the question came out of left field and startled her. Well, no point in trying to keep secret the facts everyone knew. She let out a bitter laugh, one she couldn't contain no matter how hard she tried. "Nothing happened to him." She averted her eyes, finding it painful even after all these months to admit that Billy had found someone whose company, and whose body, he preferred over hers. "He followed a blonde horse owner to Oklahoma. I guess he's still there."

"So that's why you came back here? Because he left?"

"Not entirely. I want to help my brother. I want Ava to grow up here, around what little family we have. I thought Billy's parents might be interested in knowing their grandchild, but it seems like they don't care about her any more than Billy did. Another one of my foolish ideas."

"I don't understand that. Why didn't he care? And why didn't he marry you and give his kid a legal father?"

She couldn't keep from laughing. "Billy's only capable of caring about this much about anything or anyone." She held up a thumb and finger, showing a distance of an inch. "He isn't the marrying kind. He lives for the moment. Me getting pregnant put him in a terrible bind. Now that I'm over his leaving so suddenly, I know it was for the best. Especially now that I see how much Paul needs someone. Without Sherry and the kids, he's so out there. I worry about him. If Billy hadn't pulled out, I probably wouldn't have come back here to help my brother."

"I agree Paul needs a keeper. I've seen him whooping it up in town a few times."

She would love to question what John had seen Paul do, but decided not to. "Yep, that's Paul."

She got to her feet and carried the lunch trash to the saddlebags, wanting to quash the conversation about the problematic people, all men, in her life. John followed and they led the horses to the stream's edge to drink.

"Speaking of horses," she said, as Polly drank her fill, "did you sell your rope horses?" A picture formed in her mind—John's big body springing off a horse, flanking and hog-tying a calf in seconds.

"I sold two of them to get the money to settle up with Julie. Still got my old favorite, Rowdy. He's out at Mom and Dad's. They're using him to work cattle."

"Ah. He probably likes that. Rope horses are so athletic."

"Yep. He's bigger than these guys." He rubbed Trixie's neck. "He must outweigh Trixie here by a couple hundred pounds and he's stout. It's good he's got a job to do. Otherwise he'd be bored."

"Oh, you're right. Boredom is not good for a smart horse."

They mounted and reined toward home side by side. "So what about your rodeo career? You said you quit?"

He didn't answer right away, as if he might be considering what to tell her. Soon they reached a long flat piece of the trail. "The last year I had my mind on what I was doing," he said, "I collected over a hundred thousand dollars. Had a couple of endorsements and some help from a couple of sponsors on the fees. I still went twenty thousand in the hole."

"Wow," she murmured. "That's a lot."

"From a business angle, it just didn't pay." He stared off at the horizon as if he might be imagining something. "That year I spent more time on the road than I did at home. Hauled my poor ol' horses over fifty thousand miles. Then everything went to hell with Julie. And so on and so forth."

"Umm, yeah. Your personal life does have a way of interfering with all that fun you're having."

He made a noise in his throat, revealing more bitterness than he probably intended to. "Amen."

They rode in silence for a while longer and she waited for him to tell her more about the personal life that had been shattered, apparently by his determination to rodeo. He kept quiet, so she didn't press. The barn came into view. At the pasture fence, he dismounted and opened the gate. On the other side he looked up at her with a devilish grin. "Think you can beat me to the barn?"

She laughed. "You're on, cowboy."

# Chapter 12

Isabelle won the race. No surprise, given her lighter weight and familiarity with her horse. As they walked Polly and Trixie through the round paddock attached to the big barn, John praised both her and her well-behaved animals.

They unsaddled inside the barn, turned the horses out to pasture and carried their gear into the tack room. "That was fun," John said. "Don't think I've ever done it before."

"What, raced?"

"Spent a day in the mountains with a good woman and a good horse."

She turned and looked up at him, struck by the old-fashioned way he expressed himself. His hand was braced on the tack room doorjamb, his gaze fixed on her. Energy shimmered between them. Tongue-tied for a reply and hoping to turn off the tension thrumming inside her, she lowered her eyes to his chest and laughed a little, one of those silly female laughs.

"Julie was scared of horses," he went on. "Scared of the outdoors. She went all to pieces if she saw a frog."

Isabelle couldn't relate. She had ridden a horse as far back as she could remember and she and Paul had spent more time alone in the mountains than anywhere else.

"Let's rest a minute." She ducked under his arm and took two of the partial bottles of water left from lunch to the waist-high stack of hay bales at the end of the barn. She levered herself onto a hay bale and he did, too. He removed his hat and laid it aside, then took the bottle of water she offered, tipped back his head and chugged.

After he had emptied the bottle, he made a growling sound of satisfaction as he screwed the lid on. In the barn's quiet and soft light, they sat there for a time, thigh to thigh, neither his feet nor hers reaching to the ground, swinging their feet, taking in the barn smells and enjoying just being.

"This is a good old barn," he said when he finally spoke. His eyes wandered in a wide circle overhead. "Not in too bad a shape for its age."

"It's coming along." She looked around at the amateur paint job she had done with cheap white paint, the new lumber in the stalls still under construction, then up at the new rafters Paul had nailed up. "When I was a kid, I spent more time here than in the house. That's why I'm a bad housekeeper. I'd rather work in the barn." She braced her hands on the edge of the hay bale, scrunching up her shoulders and remembering slipping out of the house to meet Billy in the barn after her dad had passed out. "We used to sneak in here at night."

A lariat hung within arm's reach over a stall post. John picked it up and deftly tied a crown knot in the end, then a slipknot and made a loop. She liked his able hands and nimble fingers. Both were a necessity for a competition calf roper.

"We who? You and Billy?" He spun the loop over his head a couple of times, threw it out and quick as lightning caught a lone hay bale sitting beside a stall door.

"My mom and dad didn't like him coming around," she said, "so he would park down on the county road after dark and come up on foot. I'd crawl out my bedroom window and meet him here."

John chuckled, whipping the loop loose and pulling it back to him. "Gettin' it on in the haymow, huh?"

She heard cynicism in the question and felt her cheeks flame. Indeed, she had given up her virginity not too many feet from where she now sat. "You know how it is with kids. Gotta experiment."

He threw the loop again and she felt the movement of his

thigh muscle against hers. This time he hooked a pitchfork handle. "It was always just Billy, wasn't it?"

"What do you mean?"

"In high school you never looked at any of us. Me and my buddies had it figured out that Billy was in your pants."

She gasped, insulted and irritated. "That's all men think about, isn't it?"

"At that age, pretty much."

Who was she kidding, being coy or embarrassed over sex? They had just had a conversation about horse sex and she had been an animal breeder for over ten years. She had washed horse penises in the presence of men dozens of times. Still, trading sexy talk with a man who made her pulse race was an unnerving matter. She sniggered and leaned back, braced on her hands. "Didn't you ever make out in the barn?"

His eyes glinted with mischief. "I would've if I'd ever got the chance. I never got any girls to go into the barn with me."

He slid off the hay bale, walked over to the pitchfork and loosened the rope from around the handle, then came back, winding the lariat into a big loop. He hung it in its place on the stall gatepost, turned to her and traced a line with his forefinger along the top of her thigh, ending the trail with a hand on her knee. On a held breath she glanced down at his hand but didn't move her leg.

"So what happens to Isabelle," he asked, "now that her mate's flown the coop?"

The use of "mate" as opposed to "husband" made her wince inside and she didn't know why. Everyone knew she and Billy had never married. She looked away and swept back a sheaf of unruly curls. "She gets along just fine. And she depends on no one except the one person who's dependable."

"Won't work, at least not permanently. Sooner or later everybody needs somebody."

He took back his hand and hitched himself back onto the hay bale, so close their upper arms touched. They were quiet then, until the silence grew uncomfortable. She didn't want him to think he had sent her into a pout, so she sat up and opened another conversation. "Did you and your wife split before or after you quit rodeoing?"

"Before. I roped another year or so after the divorce, but I didn't have much juice for it. I was broke most of the time. Hurt my knee and had doctor bills. Had a sick horse and vet bills. On top of that, with Dad calling me irresponsible every time we talked, following rodeos got to where it quit making sense."

He cupped his hands around the edge of the hay bale and hunkered forward, poised like he might cut and run any minute. "That's partly a lie, Isabelle," he said at last, looking across the barn at the hay bale. "I drank too much. Couldn't keep my shit together. If you want to be a champion at anything, you gotta eat, breathe and live it. I'm sure you know that. I couldn't do it waking up hungover every day. Or singing the blues and chasing women in bars."

*Ah, confession time.* The effort he made to be honest touched her. She had lived her childhood in the household of a man who drank too much. Then for more than half the seventeen years she and Billy had been together, *he* drank too much. She couldn't imagine the John Bradshaw she had come to know with a drinking problem. "Are you an alcoholic?"

"I don't think so. But liquor was a damn tempting direction, so I cut it out."

"Someone told me your wife cheated."

He gave her a hard look and she wished she hadn't made the remark. She opened her palms, making peace. "I'm not judging. Callister grapevine. You know how it is."

"That's the first time I ever heard Callister gossip that made *me* look good." He combed his fingers through his hair and stared down at his knees. "I'm not sure Julie cheated any more than I did. While we were married, I didn't have other women, but I had another life she wanted no part of."

"Rodeoing."

He nodded.

"But you've been performing in rodeos since you were a little boy. She must have known it was in your blood."

"I think she believed, or hoped, I'd grow out of it, but I couldn't. I thought I had a shot at winning. As many years as I'd worked for it, I wasn't ready to give up. Every year I got a little closer, climbed in the standings, won a little more money, but—" He stopped on a sigh. "My dad thinks it would've solved all the problems if I'd got a regular job like she wanted."

Isabelle didn't buy it. She would have stuck by Billy forever, no matter what harebrained dream might have driven him, including following rodeos all over the country if that was what he had wanted. "You're sorry you didn't quit sooner?"

"Nah, not really. Far as the marriage went, even if I'd quit roping, all I would've been doing was postponing the inevitable. Julie and I never should've got married in the first place. If she hadn't been pregnant, we wouldn't have."

"If she'd loved you, she would've supported you. She would've been your partner."

His gaze swung to her face. "Is that what you'd do? Be my partner?"

"That's what I did do. For seventeen years." She looked into his solemn eyes, their faces only inches apart. "I've got a good dry shoulder. You can tell me about it. If you want to."

"No." He leaned toward her. "This is what I want." His hand came up to her jaw and tilted her face up to his and his lips settled on hers.

It was a safe kiss—sweet and earnest, with no pressure. She sat there without moving, letting him caress her lips with his and listening to every sound. She could make herself crazy attempting to analyze what was happening between them, so she threw caution to the wind, turned in to him, slid her hand around his nape and opened her mouth.

He came in, taking what he wanted in a slow dance of tongues. A feeling of the rightness of his mouth on hers stole through her. The barn spun around her as rational thought left her head. The hand that had cradled her face slid down, then closed over her breast. So much time had passed since she had felt a man's hand on her breast and she gave no thought to moving it. Her nipple beneath his palm tightened, pushing against the soft lace of her bra, and the next thing she knew, his hand was under her sweater and his fingers were stroking. A long-missed urgency rose from deep in her belly.

He lifted his mouth from hers. "Oh, shit," he whispered.

She had lain awake nights imagining his touch. She didn't hesitate reaching back under her sweater and releasing her bra hooks. Her bare breast filled his hand. She put space between them to give him access and at the same time, undid his shirt buttons. She collided with a T-shirt, which she pulled free of his belt. She pushed it up, exposing his hairy, rippled middle and his brown nipples. She ducked her head and licked, heard and felt a little grunt escape his chest, felt his hands burrow into her hair. She returned her mouth to his and pressed her bare breasts against his chest, loving the soft keening sound that came from deep in his throat.

"Goddamn," he said gruffly. "You know how long it's been?"

It wasn't a question that required an answer. They kissed more, hands clinging and chests rubbing. He eased her back onto the hay bale, pillowing her neck on his arm, and pushed up her sweater until it and her bra were gathered under her chin. Her nipples stood like stiff little peaks in the cool air and she could feel his eyes, his breath, on her breasts. He bent his head then and made a circle of one nipple with his tongue, setting off a tingling between her legs. She felt hot and liquid and anxious. His hand slid down to the affected place. As she cocked one leg and dug her boot heel into the hay, she wondered if he could tell she was wet.

He thoroughly made love to her one breast, then moved to the other, all the while rubbing between her thighs. She ran her hands over his silky hair, drank in the smell of him up close. His gorgeous agile mouth trailed down her middle until it reached her navel. "You've got an inny," he murmured and blew softly.

A little shiver passed over her. His tongue dipped and as she arched her back, she thought of the school bus. "John," she managed, "what time is it?"

"Hmm?"

His fingers curled into the waistband of her jeans and tugged them down. He licked her belly and muscles up inside her flexed. "John, what time is it?"

He unhooked her belt buckle and unbuttoned her jeans. "I dunno. Does it matter?"

"Look at your watch. Please. Ava—"

He stopped. "Shit." He raised his wrist and frowned at his watch. "Three-forty-five."

She swallowed, feeling her swollen tongue and lips, and sat up. "The school bus gets here at four."

He closed his eyes and covered the bulge below his belt buckle with his hand. "Aw, Jesus—"

"I'm sorry. I didn't think—"

"It's okay," he said, shaky-voiced. "I didn't either." He slid off the hay bale and pulled down his T-shirt, then turned and tugged her to her feet. She struggled to untangle her bra and her sweater, finally succeeded. "Here, let me help you." He hooked her bra with trembling fingers. While she molded her breasts into the cups, he pulled down her sweater and squeezed her shoulders. "I'm gonna go."

A panic darted through her. "John, I—"

"It's best that I go." He picked up his hat and plopped it on. He looked rumpled and sexy with the tails of his white T-shirt and his outer shirt hanging loose. "I'll see you."

He walked out of the barn and left her.

John was in trouble. His brain had ceased to reside under his hat and dropped down to his shorts. He had violated Cardinal Rule #1: Don't get involved in Callister. Though he liked sex and he liked it hot and primitive, holding women, especially local women, at arm's length was a self-imposed discipline after too many misunderstood motives. If a guy didn't keep his libido under control, the next thing he knew, some cute little number with whom he'd had a helluva good time in bed would be talking about commitment and crashing into his horse trailer.

Commitment and Izzy. The combination in one sentence wasn't as jarring as he might have thought a few days or even a few hours ago.

He crept back to town, letting his blood cool. His cock felt like a rail spike. He had to force himself to stop remembering the feel of soft flesh in his hands, nipples that grew firm at his touch and tasted like honey in his mouth.

It wasn't just the kiss in the barn that had sent him over the moon. The whole day had been perfect. Horseback in the mountains and the sunshine in the company of someone with whom he couldn't list all that he had in common. Then, sitting there on that haystack staring at lips that would tempt a preacher and feeling the chemistry boiling between them, he had gone crazy for a few minutes.

To his astonishment, she had been willing. God, had she been willing. She had nearly swallowed him alive. And she had been ready, too. Everything he had dreamed of as a fifteen-year-old had been his for the taking. When he felt the dampness between her legs all he could think of was tearing off their clothes. They would have gone at it right there on the hay bales if it hadn't been for that cussed school bus.

Now he didn't know what to do, didn't know if he could, or should, ever go back to Izzy's house again. After he made such a quick exit, she had to be pissed off, but at the time all he could think of was getting out of there and gathering himself.

At his apartment, he checked his messages. Rooster had called and said they had a prisoner in jail, a speeder on whom he had discovered a hot warrant out of eastern Idaho. Two deputies from Idaho Falls would show up tomorrow to make the pickup.

The sheriff's office business yanked him back on track. If he got through tomorrow without making a total fool of himself in the presence of experienced lawmen, all he had to worry about was what he would do Thursday when he was expected to show up out at Izzy's house again and behave as if they had not practically knocked off a piece in the barn.

Callister County had no jailer other than the sheriff and his deputy. Prisoners were no longer boarded for more than a short stay. The commissioners had realized that the cost and risk in the outdated jail were too great. Consequently, a prisoner slated for a stay overnight meant that either John or Rooster would have to spend the night at the courthouse in the tiny bedroom set up down the hall from the sheriff's office. Since Rooster had been in the office all day, it was only fair that John spend the night. He called the deputy back and made an arrangement to relieve him at eight o'clock.

At least tomorrow would be a busy day. Thank God. Maybe he wouldn't have time to think about crawling between Isabelle Rondeau's thighs.

Isabelle fumbled her way through supper—a new flavor of Hamburger Helper. Ava read her the directions for preparation. She would have never found the concentration to read them herself. It wasn't that she *couldn't* read, but to do it was tedious and slow. The dish turned out a little salty but edible. After supper she and Ava read the latest *Performance Horse* and discussed an ad for a new type of boot to protect a horse's feet and ankles before Ava went to bed. What a blessing to have a child who could read better than most adults.

In the bathroom she filled the claw-footed tub nearly to the top with hot water and bubble bath. She hadn't ridden for a whole day in months and her sore muscles reminded her she was no longer a kid. As she stripped, she thought about the age of her body compared to the age of John Bradshaw's. Three years wasn't a huge age difference and he didn't seem to care, but *she* did. Thinking about the buckle bunnies who hung out around the cowboys at rodeos, she suspected John had never seen or touched a female body as old as hers.

She sank into the warm bubbles and closed her eyes, letting her mind wander where it would. It settled on John and how, at intervals through the day, she hadn't been able to keep from watching him—his incredible expressive eyes, his quick-to-grin mouth and white teeth, his narrow waist and firm butt in tight jeans. She admired the agility and athleticism in his big body, which made her think of all that masculinity pressed around her, against her.

In her.

She lounged in the bubble bath until the water turned cool, then climbed out and dried herself with a thick towel. In front of the mirror over the sink, she studied her thirty-five-year-old self. No discernible wrinkles, no sagging skin, breasts not quite as perky as they had once been but probably still enjoyable to a man's hands. Or mouth.

A cape of freckles draped over her shoulders, upper arms and chest. For some reason, her breasts weren't freckled. They were white and porcelainlike, with vivid rosy nipples. John had stared at her breasts, touched and kissed them all over.

Her belly, the same white color as her breasts, appeared to be as flat as it always had been, except that now there was something different. John's tongue had traced a trail across it just above her pubic hair and sent erotic sensations all through her. As if the line were highlighted in neon, she could still feel it. *Damn.*

What would he think or say the next time they met?

What would *she* say?

She opened the medicine cabinet, took out a jar of sweet-smelling cream and began to rub it over her arms, her elbows and shoulders. What now? If they couldn't move past the temporary insanity in the barn, she would have to find someone else to help her with the horses.

She sat down on a small stool beside the tub and smoothed the soft cream over her feet and ankles, paid particular attention to her heels and the cuticles around her toenails. She moved up to her legs and rubbed her calves and shins and finally, rubbing the silky cream onto her thighs, she thought of John again and his hand between her legs.

She wanted him, more than she dared admit outside this room, more than she had wanted any man since Billy. Would his erection be as his body indicated, long and thick? The old saying came to her about the size of a man's feet. John's boot size must be a twelve or thirteen and a vague visual formed of him standing naked in front of her. In a telephone gossip session, her cousin Nan had told her John had been with a lot of women. Did he have fingers that were good for more than tying a calf in less than ten seconds? Did he have an agile tongue that could make her shudder and cry out as Billy had done?

A profound need gripped her. Her sex began to tingle. She closed her eyes, let her thighs fall wide and gently massaged herself with her fingers. Her belly muscles clenched. Her breath became a pant and she clenched her teeth as intense pleasure took her. When the moment passed, a shiver passed over her.

"Damn, Isabelle," she whispered. "What's wrong with you?"

# Chapter 13

As she made coffee and prepared Ava's breakfast, Isabelle's mind volleyed between the conversation with John about the horses and the memory of their encounter in the barn. She had been so brazen, unhooking her bra herself, then letting him touch her everywhere. When had she become so desperate she couldn't control her urges? Would he think her a slut, as she had been called in high school?

With her history in Callister as a teenager, no one would believe that except for Billy she had no experience with sex. She had never wanted to be with anyone but Billy. When things had been good between them, the sex had been intense and erotic. After he left—well, to be honest, before he left, too—a few men had made passes at her, but she rejected all of them.

Now, after all this time, becoming intimate with any man in Callister reflected something more unsettling than the horse-ownership dilemma. Perhaps she hadn't succeeded in moving past Billy's desertion after all. Maybe it had deeply affected her as a woman. Did the barn incident prove it?

Shoving the scene to the back of her mind, she addressed the easier, more practical need. She called her cousin, Nan Gilbert, and made an arrangement to visit her after Ava left for school.

Since her return from Texas, Isabelle had been to the

Gilbert home only once. The house was old, but its barn-red color and white trim gave it a clean, new look. A tall white fence and a locked gate closed off the front yard, tacitly directing traffic to the back of the frame house.

As soon as Isabelle knocked once, the back door sprang open and her chubby cousin greeted her with a hug and a dimpled smile on a wide, round face. "I'm so glad you came to see me," Nan said.

Compared to Isabelle, in tight jeans and turtleneck shirt, her cousin looked comfortable wearing oversized sweatpants and a huge green ski sweater peppered with a white snowflake design.

Isabelle stepped into an added-on room that was almost the size of the rest of the house. It obviously served a multitude of purposes. A sewing machine, an ironing board and a stack of clothing to be mended or ironed sat in front of a TV. A long table against the wall was covered with Roger's tools and supplies where he reloaded his own ammunition. He was an avid big-game hunter, like most of Callister's males.

In a wood heater, a fire burned and the room felt toasty. Isabelle removed her jacket and Nan held it up, inspecting the rust tapestry fabric decorated with black and brown galloping horses. "Wow," she said. "Great jacket. Expensive, huh?"

Expensive being a relative description, Isabelle laughed off the remark. "Not really."

"I knew you'd have great clothes. Fancy horse people just do."

Isabelle had never classified herself as "fancy horse people," though she knew a few individuals who fit that category.

Nan hung the jacket on a coatrack in the corner. "Want some coffee? There's some left from breakfast."

"Sure." As Isabelle followed her cousin to the kitchen, which smelled of coffee and something baking, she glanced into the dining room and saw a child sleeping under a blanket in a playpen. That would be Amy, the youngest.

Amid an assortment of bowls and pans, Nan poured coffee into a thick ceramic mug and passed it to Isabelle. "Want sugar? Cream?" Nan didn't pour a cup for herself.

"No, thanks. You aren't having any?"

"Coffee's been giving me indigestion." Nan smiled, her brown eyes warm and happy. "I think I'm pregnant. I'm two weeks late."

"Oh," Isabelle said, unsure how to respond. Nan and Roger already had four children and Roger's income from his job as a heavy-equipment operator at the sawmill had to be small. "Congratulations, huh?" She leaned her rear end against the counter and sipped the hot, strong coffee.

Nan gave a jolly laugh. "We weren't expecting it, but when you've got a houseful, what's one more?"

Isabelle glanced at the sleeping child. "You don't use birth control?"

"Oh, sometimes. But when Roger wakes up all hard and ready to go, we aren't always careful." Her lips curled into another smile. "I can tell you the minute it happened this time."

*Sex.* Well, Isabelle thought, that was a topic of which she need not be reminded. "Can't you say no?"

"I can, but I don't." The oven timer went off with a buzz. "Wait. Let me take this cake out of the oven. With six of us, we eat a cake a day around here." She grabbed hot pads and slid two chocolate layers from the oven and set them on trivets on the countertop. "Roger's real good. Know what I mean?" She reached across the stovetop and switched off the oven, then turned to Isabelle, wiggling her dark brows.

Isabelle winced inside, remembering John's fingers stroking between her thighs. Somehow she knew John Bradshaw would be real good, too, and she felt a little flash of heat. Embarrassed, she laughed to cover her discomfort. She didn't have conversations about sex with people she barely knew, even relatives. She could discuss with anyone the mating process between a mare and a stud and their respective reproductive organs, but she had never had girlfriends with whom she discussed sex between humans. "You're such a character, Nan. I hope Roger likes kids."

"He does. But I keep telling him if he doesn't go get cut, we're gonna have a dozen and I'm gonna weigh four hundred pounds. He just laughs and tells me how sorry I'd be if the doc made a mistake and whacked off two inches. And he's right. I'd be sorry." She tilted her head back and cackled.

Isabelle laughed with her, enjoying the wicked female camaraderie that was rare in her life.

"You're probably in a hurry," Nan said. "The computer's in our bedroom. C'mon back." She led the way up a short, tight hallway. "We keep the monster back here so we'll have control of the kids using it."

The bedroom was small, the bed rumpled and unmade, and Isabelle thought of sex again. Nan plopped into a straight-backed chair in front of the monitor and booted up the computer. Isabelle forced her mind to the task for which she had come, handed her cousin the address book and dictated a short, to-the-point letter to Billy Bledsoe. When they were satisfied with the content, Nan printed two copies on plain paper and passed them to her. "Want me to write the address on the envelope for you?"

"Would you? It would take me forever to do it and I don't know if anyone but me could read it."

"Sure." Her cousin reached for a pen and a plain white envelope and wrote the Oklahoma address. "You never did go and take therapy or classes or something, huh?"

"I took some remedial reading classes in Fort Worth." Isabelle folded one copy of the letter, slid it into the envelope and licked the flap. "But I don't know how much good it did." They walked back toward the kitchen. "Thanks for taking the time to do this for me. Ava has a computer, but I couldn't ask her to help me write a letter to Billy. She doesn't even talk about him."

Nan shook her head. "Jerk. I hope he lives to regret what he's done. Hey, I'll bet Ava's a big help now that she's older."

"She is. Me being a poor reader and writer has made her and me both smarter. You'd be amazed at some of the stuff she knows. She reads me technical stuff out of vet books."

In the kitchen, as Nan deftly turned the cooled cake layers out of the pans, Isabelle looked around at the dirty dishes on the counter and in the sink. "Did you make that from scratch?"

"Heavens, yes. We buy groceries in bulk, which eliminates most instant stuff."

"Oh, of course," Isabelle said, thinking of what it must cost to feed a family of six. She picked up her coffee cup, leaned against the counter and sipped, watching. "You do that so easily. I couldn't bake a layer cake from scratch if I was going to be shot. If the directions on cake mixes weren't in pictures, I couldn't even manage one of those."

"Just 'cause your mom was a cook doesn't mean you have to be one. You can do other things. I heard in town you can talk to horses in a way they understand."

"Really. I was wondering what they were saying about me in town. I won't ask what else they're saying." As a Callister native, Isabelle knew better than to wade too deep into the swamp of local gossip.

Nan moved to the refrigerator and disappeared behind the heavy door. "I'll tell you anyway if you won't get mad." She surfaced with a package of butter and a jug of milk and carried them to the counter.

"Do I have a choice?"

"They're saying the sheriff's hanging out at your house, helping you with your fancy horses and Lord knows what else." She set up the mixer and dumped sticks of butter into the bowl.

Isabelle cringed inside, knowing better but wondering anyway if a spy had been hiding in her barn. To throw her cousin off the track, Isabelle gave her a squinty look of disbelief. "He's riding for me. And there is no what else."

"You know people in this town are gonna talk. You're fresh meat and the sheriff ain't just any ol' guy. I think he's hot, myself." Nan laughed as she pulled powdered sugar, cocoa and vanilla extract from the cupboard.

"I guess I hadn't noticed," Isabelle lied. "What're you mixing up?"

"Chocolate frosting. You're kidding, you haven't noticed, right? That cute butt in those tight Wranglers?"

Well, damn. One of the first things Isabelle had noticed about John was how his jeans fit him. "Hmm. Well, inspecting men's bottoms is not something I usually do."

"Oh, c'mon now. All women look at men's bottoms. Just like men look at women, don't you think? Misty Arnold, you remember her. She was in mine and Paul's class in school. She's a checker at Fielder's now. We joke all the time that the whole pattern of grocery buying has changed. Now all the women go shopping around noon so they can be in town to watch when John walks from the courthouse to Betty's Road Kill for lunch."

Isabelle let out a little gasp. "I can't believe that."

Nan measured ingredients into the mixer bowl. "Well, believe it, cousin. You've got every woman in town jealous."

"That's a switch. I don't think anyone's ever been jealous of me before."

"That new lady that opened the fancy coffee shop on Main Street? Can't think of her name now, but she takes phone orders for those crazy coffees and delivers them to the courthouse every day. Three dollars for a cup of coffee. Can you imagine?"

Nan switched on the mixer, then raised her voice to be heard above the whir of the motor. "She's got such a crush on him it's embarrassing. Somebody said she'd dated him or something. After hearing about you, she told Misty she wished she'd opened a stable instead of a coffee shop." Nan cackled again. "Take my word for it, there's a whole herd of women whose beds he could park his boots under if he wanted to."

Isabelle couldn't recall Misty Arnold, but she had seen the coffee shop, Java Junction. She had even intended to drop in. Now she would make it a point to do just that, perhaps buy some kind of specialty coffee to have for John when he came to her house. "Hmm. I'm wondering if I would've been better off opening a coffee shop. I'm losing confidence every day in my plans for a horse-training operation."

On that reflection, she downed the last of the coffee, set the mug on the counter and told Nan she had to go. "Thanks again," she said as her cousin brought her jacket from the coatrack. "As long as we're discussing the local gossips— you won't say anything about this to anyone, will you?"

"What, that you're writing a letter to that asshole Billy?"

Isabelle shrugged into the jacket and tugged her hair free of the collar. "Well, that, and the fact that you had to help me.

I don't want to start talk all over again about how dumb I am. I remember how it used to be when I was a kid."

"Oh, Izzy, people are different now. These days nobody looks at dyslexia as dumb. I think one of my kids has a touch of it. And he's the smartest kid I've got. He can spell words as long as my leg, but he can't spell 'cat.'"

"Really? It's sort of like that, Nan, no kidding."

"Come over someday when you're not in a hurry and let's talk about it."

"Yeah, okay. You understand, though, don't you, why I don't want people gossiping? Ava might hear it. She's such a little fighter, she'd feel like she had to defend me, which could cause her problems."

"Hey, don't worry. I won't even tell Roger." Nan hooked an arm through hers. "I'm so glad you came back to Callister. It's nice to have a girl cousin my age. And you remind me of Aunt Helen." She touched Isabelle's hair. "You've got her hair. Remember how pretty it always was?"

A feeling of being disconnected flitted through Isabelle's mind. The only hairdo she could remember on her mother was a tight bun on the back of her head, a style necessitated by her occupation as a café cook. "Yeah, sure," Isabelle fibbed. "Who's the cook at Betty's now? I wondered who would take that job after Mom dropped dead."

The fun and laughter left Nan's face. "I know you left here with a lot of bitterness, Izzy. My mom's always said Helen was a decent woman. It's just that after she married a good-for-nothing she didn't know what to do about it. She had you two kids and no way to make much money if she left him. Nobody had any idea how bad it was with Frenchie until it was too late."

Isabelle smiled, masking the truth of what her cousin and she both knew. If life in the Rondeau home had been anything other than miserable, Paul might have gone beyond eighth grade and she might not have quit school at seventeen and left town with Billy Bledsoe. "I know. I'm not holding any grudges."

And she didn't. Her life outside Callister had been fun and exciting at times. She had met a host of interesting peo-

ple and acquired a wealth of knowledge of horses. If she had
stayed in Callister, in all likelihood she would have become
Nan, having babies and pinching pennies.

At the front door her cousin threw a heavy arm around
her and hugged her. It *was* nice to have a female relative, and
encouraging. Perhaps a relationship eventually would grow
between Ava and Nan's kids, even Paul's daughters if Sherry
could ever be persuaded to bring them to visit.

All the way to town Isabelle's mind stayed on John
Bradshaw as if he had stamped a brand on her brain that
read s-e-x. She thought about Nan being pregnant and the disheveled bed in her and Roger's bedroom. Isabelle scarcely
remembered sharing a bedroom with a man with whom sex
was a regular occurrence, though once she and Billy had
been that passionate. She could no longer picture Billy naked
and aroused. When he popped into her head, the next visual
was the bottle-blonde, diamond-covered horse owner from
Oklahoma and at that image Isabelle's mind threw up barri-
ers. Lately, the erotic picture that filled her imagination was
the sheriff.

Now she had a new question to consider. Was she one of
that herd of women who wanted his boots parked under her
bed? He had made it plain he was available if she wanted
him. "Don't be insane, Isabelle," she muttered.

At the post office, she took from her purse the three
ownership-transfer forms obtained from the American Quarter Horse Association months ago. She added them to the envelope holding the letter and sealed it. She bought postage,
then carried the letter to the OUTGOING slot. On a deep breath
and a silent prayer, she slid the letter into oblivion.

Then she headed for the coffee shop.

"I can tell you what he likes," a female voice said.

Startled, Isabelle turned from studying a wall of dark coffee beans in fat, squatty jars. Standing just behind her was a
willowy, extremely attractive woman in her twenties who had
eyes so shockingly blue they looked artificial. "Excuse me?"

The woman raised her hand and with long, perfectly

manicured, crimson acrylic nails, swept a long sheaf of raven-black hair behind her ear. "The sheriff. I can tell you which beans he likes."

Caught off guard at a perfect stranger appearing to know personal information about her, Isabelle was dumbfounded. Nan's words filtered back. *Somebody said she'd dated him or something.* In a million years, it wouldn't have occurred to Isabelle that the John Bradshaw she knew would have dated this woman who looked more out of place in Callister than a mule at a horse show. Nor would she have thought John was a custom-ground-coffee-beans kind of man.

She settled a look on the woman she estimated to be, at a minimum, five years younger than herself. "I'm really not interested in—"

"You're that horse woman, aren't you?"

Isabelle heard derision in the question. She drew herself up. "I don't think we've met."

"I'm Rita Mitchell. I own this shop." In a graceful gesture, she pointed to a jar of brown beans. "Traditional Roast. That's what the sheriff likes. I grind them for him every week. Sometimes, when I can persuade him to walk on the wild side, he'll buy French Roast. He's a big-time coffee drinker."

*She's got such a crush on him it's embarrassing.*

Any notion Isabelle had of buying gourmet coffee to please John's palate marched right out Java Junction's front door. "Oh. Well, good for him. And you, too, I suppose."

The woman turned her back and moved behind a counter anchored on one end by a cash register. She had on a form-fitting ankle-length black dress and black ankle-strap wedges. Silver hoops the diameter of beer cans looped through her earlobes. Her hair, shiny and straight as a string, hung past her waist and moved like black water when she turned her head. "Everyone over at the courthouse is wondering," she said, "is it just the horses?" The girl crossed her arms under her breasts. "Or is it something else?" Her red heart-shaped lips curved into such an evil smile that Isabelle thought of a cobra.

Isabelle was as naive at playing head games with women

as with men. All she could think was John must have slept with this woman. Even if he hadn't slept with her, at the very least, he had commerce going on with her. "I guess I don't know what you're talking about."

"I'll pass on something you might find helpful," Rita Mitchell said. "You see, I have this sorting and classifying system for men. I'd file John under 'Type A Taker.' That's one of the most dangerous types. Gives away nothing of himself, but makes you think you're the one who can push his button. Gives you a false impression he has an interest in you." She ran a fingernail along the edge of the counter and Isabelle noticed a tiny white flower painted on it. Isabelle stuffed her hands with their short nails into her jacket pockets. "Then after he's got you tied up tighter than one of those poor calves he used to torture," Rita Mitchell said, "he forgets your phone number."

Panic that had been building since the beginning of this conversation filled Isabelle's chest and she tried to remember what had compelled her to come into this store in the first place. The blended aromas of two dozen flavors of coffee filled her nostrils and she felt nauseated. "Look, it's nice meeting you, but I'm in a hurry. If you'll excuse me, I—"

"Sure you don't want a pound of Traditional Roast?"

Isabelle pasted on a smile, hoping her face didn't crack. "No, thanks. I can't afford it."

Feeling as if she had been ambushed, she tramped to the end of the block where she had parked the Sierra, her boot heels pounding a cadence on the sidewalk. What had she been thinking, allowing herself to be attracted to John? With everyone in town talking, speculating on what was going on between them on the mornings he came to her house, what if someone found out what had happened in the barn on Tuesday? What if Ava started hearing tales about her mother?

What could be more humiliating in a town of six hundred thirty-five than getting involved with a man who had also been involved with who knew how many other women in town? She imagined a pack of clamoring females sitting around a table comparing notes.

She hated to have to find someone else to help her with

the horses, especially since John was so good with them, but she had no intention of succumbing to the charms of the town stud or a Type A Taker.

She imagined him with Rita Mitchell, his hand between her thighs, his lips pressed to those red lips as they had been pressed to hers yesterday in the barn. Why wouldn't he be attracted to Rita? She was beautiful in a Gothic way. She didn't have flyaway red hair and freckles. She was a businesswoman. Maybe she had been to college. In any event, she surely wouldn't have to ask a relative to write a letter for her.

# Chapter 14

The prisoner handoff went without a hitch and by midafternoon the Idaho Falls deputies and their charge were on their way out of town. Though John hadn't slept well on the rollaway bed that stayed in the makeshift bedroom, he remained in the courthouse the rest of the day, catching up on paperwork.

All night and all day he had thought of Izzy and what almost occurred in her barn. The gun-shy man inside him warned him to back off. If he didn't, his good intentions of keeping his pants zipped in Callister would be out the window.

At home, TV movies provided no distraction from the ones going on in his head. At one point, he found himself pacing between his chair and the phone, role-playing phony conversations and offering excuses why he couldn't put in an appearance at Izzy's tomorrow. Christ, he had seen the anxiety in bulls and stallions when they had a female's scent. He didn't like thinking it, but his own behavior wasn't much different.

Thursday morning, having failed to make the decision to tell her he would continue with the horses only until she could find someone else, he put coffee on to brew and took a cup with him to the shower. He consumed another cup while he shaved, the horny part of him planning to bring to a conclusion what had begun in that big old barn.

He drank another cup and returned to the bedroom. He put on his worn-out jeans and well-used riding boots, the responsible adult part of him preparing to ride the horses and work them as usual and perhaps not even see Izzy. By the time he finished dressing, he had consumed the whole pot of coffee and he felt wired.

He climbed into his truck and turned the key, then had a second thought. He slid out and walked back inside to his bedroom, dug in his dresser drawer for the box of Trojan Ultras that had been there untouched since he moved back to Callister. He plucked half a dozen of the foil packets and shoved them in his jeans pocket. What might happen today was anybody's guess, but being prepared did no harm.

The Rondeau place was quiet when he arrived. He saw the palomino, but he didn't see Izzy. He parked in his usual spot between the barn and the house, walked to the back door and gave it a *rap-rap-rap*. She came to the door wearing blue sweatpants and a sweatshirt and looking soft and cuddly.

With trepidation, Isabelle had stood in the window and watched John walk to the back door. After being awake half the night, then going back to sleep after she got Ava on the school bus, she had been in the bathroom drying her hair when she heard his engine. Now, right now, this morning, she had to clarify that the insanity in the barn could never happen again.

"I thought you might not come out this morning," she said, stepping back to allow him entrance onto the porch.

"Why would you think that?"

As he walked past her, she caught a whiff of his shampoo and soap. The scent zoomed straight to her primal center. Following him into the kitchen, even with several feet between them, she sensed that he, too, was drawn tight as a drum. She glanced at the half-full coffeepot. Conversations over coffee seemed to have a better outcome. "There's coffee," she said.

"I don't need any more. I've already drunk a gallon." He removed his hat and set it on the table.

Okay, she could do this without coffee. She stopped beside the counter and faced him. "Tuesday in the barn was a mistake, John. I want you to know I don't blame you. It was my fault. I hope we can put it aside and—"

"Has Ava gone to school?" His green eyes bored into hers.

She felt her face heat under his direct gaze. "Y—Yes, but—"

"Is that what you want, to set it aside?"

She stood there like a dumbbell, her throat working, but no words came out. To her alarm, her nipples seemed to be growing too tight for her skin.

He came to where she stood. His hands came up and grasped her shoulders. "I want you," he said softly and she could see in his expressive eyes that he meant it. "I always have, even years ago. And I kind of feel like you want me, too."

Tears sprang to her eyes. This wasn't fair. No way was she prepared to deal with this. Her lips trembled. "But, John, we—"

His head bent and he kissed her.

She resisted. For about five seconds. Then, as if her traitorous limbs had minds of their own, her arms went up over his shoulders and around his neck and as if her two hands couldn't touch enough of him, she pressed her body against his. He kissed her more, cradling the back of her head with his hand, giving her his tongue and taking hers. His kisses were so good, his mouth so sweet. She drank him in like a victim dying of thirst.

The room began to spin and the next thing she became aware of was his hands under her sweatshirt, making contact with the bare skin of her back. She hadn't taken the time to put on a bra. He leaned away, his fingers at the knit band at the bottom of her sweatshirt. They stared at each other, him waiting for her to confirm the decision that had, in reality, been made Tuesday in the barn.

Unable to endure the dark intensity in his eyes, she looked at the floor, fighting back tears. Desire, want, need, loneliness—all conspired against her determination to not get involved and make her life even harder. Seconds ticked away.

Oh, hell, wasn't it her turn?

*Yes!* her slutty side answered.

She pulled her sweatshirt up and over her head and let it drop to the floor.

"Lord," he choked out, staring at her breasts. He crushed her to him and devoured her mouth with another devastating kiss.

She pulled away, ducked her chin and began to work at his shirt buttons. If she didn't look into his eyes, this would be easier. Her fingers fumbled. No wonder. She was standing here half naked with her nipples sticking out like mountain peaks. "You know we shouldn't be doing this. This is not supposed to happen. I know we'll both be sorry."

He grasped her fingers and kissed them. "Let me, darlin'." As he took over undoing his shirt buttons, she clasped his face and kissed him again, thrusting her tongue into his mouth.

Swearing, he gave up on the buttons and wrapped his arms around her, grasped her bottom and brought her pelvis against his erection. Heat she hadn't felt in years sizzled through her veins and she wriggled against the firm shape of him.

His mouth dragged from hers and trailed down her neck. His ragged breath lay hot and moist on her breasts. She could hear her own breath, shallow and shaky. His hand lifted one breast and he pressed his open mouth to the pillow of flesh.

She closed her eyes and sighed. "Oh, John . . ."

Clutching his hair, she guided him to the swollen nipple that ached for attention. He drew deeply, sucked hard, titillated with his tongue. A maddening tingle began between her thighs. "John . . . John, do . . . do you think you should take your coat off?"

"I can't. . . . I don't want to let you go."

His hands slid beneath the elastic waist of her sweatpants and gripped her bottom, his fingers feeling strong and able pressing into her buttocks. Her pulse throbbed deep in her sex and she thought she might die if he didn't touch her there and relieve the tingle. "John . . .," she whispered, ". . . I need . . . can you . . ." She put space between them and parted her legs.

His hand came around, pushed between her thighs and began to rub her through her panties. "Is this what you want?"

"Oooh . . ." she murmured as unadulterated pleasure coursed through her. "Oh, yesss . . ."

He stopped abruptly. "Shit. I can't stand this."

He shoved both sweatpants and panties past her hips. They fell to her ankles. "Yes!" her slutty side proclaimed again.

She tried to kick the garments off her feet, but they became ensnared by her slippers. He dropped to one knee and began to free her feet. "Step out," he said gruffly, clasping first one ankle, then the other. She watched him lift her feet from the knot of sweatpants and lacy panties.

As he whisked the clothing aside, his head rose. His eyes leveled on the delta where her legs joined her trunk. She held her breath and her stomach began to shake. He swallowed audibly, stayed deathly still for a few seconds. When she did nothing, he leaned in to her and nuzzled.

His breath riffled across her pubic hair. *OhGodohGod.* A part of her brain demanding that she stop him struggled to override the other part that wanted this. "John, you shouldn't..."

His hands clasped her hip bones and gently pushed her back against the counter. His open mouth moved over her belly, murmuring, "I've wanted to do this for eighteen years."

She gripped the counter edge and watched as he parted her gently with his thumbs. The first thrust of his tongue brought a gasp and a shudder. She pushed her pelvis forward, giving him everything. He took, lapping and probing and flicking. She clenched her teeth and endured as sensation suspended her in a purple void of desire. On a whimper that was an undeniable plea, she bent her knees, opening herself wider still. Two fingers worked up into her and her vaginal muscles rejoiced.

Then there was nothing but his fingers and his tongue moving in rhythm with each other. Release hung millimeters away. Her head tilted back, little noises escaped her throat. When she thought she would surely die if he didn't help her, if he didn't *do* something, his mouth gently closed over the sensitive morsel of flesh at the top of her sex and the world exploded. She cried out. Her hips bucked violently. He gripped her buttocks, his hands like a vise, and held her, not missing a beat with his tongue. Pleasure tore through her again and again. When her arms gave away and her knees buckled, he let go and she wilted to the floor whimpering and shaking and clinging to him.

"Oh, God, you're sweet," he whispered and she felt herself being gathered to his chest. He stood up with her in his arms. "Where's your bed?"

"Up the hall," she said in a tiny voice.

She felt weak and helpless as a kitten as he carried her into the dim morning light of her bedroom and laid her on her unmade bed. She grabbed for the sheet, covered herself and stared as he whipped off his coat, then his shirt and T-shirt, his torso appearing inch by inch as each garment fell to the floor.

He dug in his jeans pocket, pulled out packets of condoms and dropped them on her bedside table. For an instant she bristled at his audacity for bringing them, but at the same time she was grateful. She had been off the pill for a long time.

He sank to the edge of the bed and pried off his boots. Her strength returned and when he stood to unbuckle his belt, her slutty side rose to the occasion. She scuttled across the bed and helped him push his jeans and shorts down powerful hairy legs. His erection, as thick and long and eager as she had imagined it would be, jutted from a patch of dark brown curls. "Oooh," she murmured, unable to tear her gaze away. "I knew you'd be beautiful."

"God, Isabelle, just look at me. I've been like this ever since I found out you were back in town."

He peeled his jeans and shorts the rest of the way off, crawled under the covers and stretched alongside her. The mattress sank with his weight and his long arms and legs surrounded her. His mouth devoured hers again and she suckled her own taste from his tongue and lips as they caressed each other everywhere with their hands. Little hums came from his throat, little sighs from hers.

It had been so long since she'd had a naked man at her disposal. She stroked him all over—his fuzzy belly, his hairy scrotum, closed her hand around his thick penis, appreciating the tensile strength.

His thigh thrust between hers, pressing upward, hard against her sex, where she felt hot and empty. The need built again and she pulled back, knees bent and open and begging him to come inside.

He released her long enough to snap on a condom, then moved over her. Jaw clenched, he braced on one hand and his hot penis drove into her. He was big and he stretched her, but no part of her wanted to stop. She came again, arching to him, gripping his biceps with her fingertips and gasping openmouthed.

He kissed her savagely again. She was filled with him, overwhelmed by the strength of him, engulfed by the force of him. His arm held her pelvis tight against him and he began to rock, hard and fast, pressuring the crucial point of contact in a steady rhythm. She dug her heels into the backs of his thighs and hung on until she began to spasm again and she could feel her deep muscles caressing his hot flesh with little sucking contractions. It was coming again, the overpowering wave. "Oh. Oh. Oh, John."

"Come with me," he choked out. He reared back, slid a hand between them and touched the demanding swollen nubbin inside her sex. One touch was all she needed. Her breath caught. Stars burst inside her head. She clung to him as out-of-control sensation hurled her through space and her every cell focused on the agonizing rapture. She barely heard him groan, barely felt him strain, barely was aware he had stopped moving until he collapsed on top of her.

"I told you so," Isabelle's slutty side said. Indeed, she had never known anything quite like what had just happened between her and the naked man crossing her bedroom.

She watched as he came to the bed. Only blindness could keep her eyes from feasting on him. He was a gorgeous man, the epitome of male perfection—long everywhere, with well-defined muscles that showed the physical strength that made her feel small and feminine. He had a few scars and a bit of a tan, which made her wonder where and when he had been exposed to the sun without his clothes.

He slid under the covers, wrapped his brawny arms

around her and pulled her close to his big body. "Cold in here," he said on a shiver.

A half hour earlier, with the fires of passion raging, neither of them had noticed the room temperature. "I haven't opened the vent in here. It's so hot in Texas. One of the things about Callister I missed was nights made for sleeping under warm blankets."

She snuggled closer to his warm skin, tugging the quilt, hand-sewn by her mother somewhere back in time, up to their chins. She pressed her face against his chest and breathed in the earthy smell of him, needing to brand it in her memory. They lay there, belly to belly, drifting in the afterglow of lusty, satisfying sex. "I like sleeping under covers. It makes me feel safe."

"Safe from what? What scares you, Izzy-girl?"

"When I was a little girl, I was afraid of a lot of things. I thought covers would keep someone from grabbing me."

When he didn't reply, she opened her eyes and saw his closed, his long, dark lashes lying against his cheeks; saw his lips slightly parted, swollen and shiny from ardent kissing. She had observed his ability to concentrate fiercely on everything he did. She should have known he would bring the same intensity to lovemaking.

Lovemaking. Was that what had taken place between them or was it something darker and more basic? Scratching an itch they both felt. Whatever it was, it definitely was *not* "safe."

"John?" She spoke just above a whisper, wanting to save the tender moment.

"Hmm?"

"I thought you'd dozed off."

The corners of his mouth turned up in a smile, but his eyes didn't open. "I could. Seeing as thinking about this kept me awake the last two nights..." He kissed her, a languorous, delicious union of lips. "Awesome," he whispered when they parted, his incredible eyes fixed on hers. "You're awesome."

She smiled into those eyes, studied his too-handsome face. "You, too."

The porch roof shaded the bedroom window, making the

room dim even in bright daylight, but a weak sliver of light sneaked through and cast a glint on a few sun-bleached strands of his mussed hair. She reached up and finger-combed them from his forehead. She trailed her fingers over his high cheekbone, down his square jaw. "And I don't mean just... this way. I wonder why I couldn't see that when we were kids."

His hand skimmed over her bottom, caught her thigh and brought it up and across his hip. "You didn't look."

She laughed a little at the truth and shifted to fit herself against his soft penis. "I couldn't. Don't you see? In those days, I thought I was bad because Billy and I... you know, did it. I thought it made me less bad if I steered clear of other boys."

He pressed closer and placed a kiss on her forehead, and she felt the prick of his chest hair on her breasts. "I never thought you were bad. Hell, I was jealous. If I'd been in Billy's shoes, you would've seen me doing handsprings up the hall."

"It's funny how different things look when we grow up. I thought he was so special. I couldn't see him as he really was."

"You'd already been with him a long time when I got to high school. You must've been really young when you and him—"

"I was.... Really young."

Barely fourteen, to be exact. Just a few years older than Ava. She had almost slipped and said it, but a voice in her head stopped her, warned her not to go there. She couldn't bear calling condemnation to herself by confessing to *any-one* that she had been sexually active before her body had fully developed. Nor could she ever openly admit she had en-joyed sex, even when, as a dumb kid, she believed she was doing something wrong.

At this moment the last person she wanted looking down on her was the man now sharing her bed. She reached for his hand and brought it to cover her breast.

"Oh, Isabelle. You're so damned soft." His thumb stroked her nipple and it hardened in instant response. He ducked his head under the quilt and his hot mouth closed around the peaked tip and applied gentle suction. Though she thought her desire had been sated, a deep tingle between her thighs made her shudder.

His head burrowed up from beneath the quilt, his hair askew. He was wearing a bad-boy grin. "You like that?"

She answered with a tiny giggle and he smacked a kiss on her lips. "Want to know how old I was when you stole my heart?"

She felt a shift in his penis and doubted his heart was the organ really on his mind. She moved her hand to touch him again and ran a finger around the tip of him. "How old?"

His eyes closed and a deep hum came from his throat. "Fifteen. You must have been seventeen or eighteen. The older woman."

"Hmm. I'm still the older woman. I just turned thirty-five."

"What? And you didn't tell me you had a birthday?"

She smiled as she felt him growing firmer. "You would've baked me a cake?"

"No baking, but I might've done something else."

She smoothed a finger around the rim at the velvety tip of him. "You would've given me this?"

His eyes were closed, but he grinned again. "Yes, ma'am, if that's what you wanted. Every last inch."

"I love touching you." She closed her hand around his growing erection.

"Ooh, darlin', I love it, too."

"Did you know all about sex when you were fifteen?"

"I knew about sex forever. I grew up on a ranch, remember?...Oh, damn, darlin'. Do that again."

She stroked the velvety tip of him with her thumb. They kissed again and he tenderly bit down on her lower lip. "But just 'cause I knew about it doesn't mean I knew what to do about it. *That* took some teaching. I'll tell you a secret. Back when I spent every day wishing you'd just speak to me? I was a virgin."

She called up memories of an awkward boy with a buzz haircut. "How old were you when—?"

"Sixteen when a woman showed me the ropes."

"Woman? A grown woman?" An unexpected little spurt

of righteousness sparked within Isabelle and she felt empathy with a teenager who had been exposed to adult behavior at a young age. "Who? Someone around here?"

"You don't really want to dig into—"

"Yes, I do. Who?"

"A gal from Twin Falls. Nobody you'd know."

Like a neon sign, RODEO flashed in Isabelle's mind. "I can guess. A rodeo babe."

A deep chuckle came from his throat. "She was that, all right. She came to every show I roped in that summer, including the ones in Utah and Nevada."

"Ah, I see." Isabelle tightened her fingers around him and smiled. "Couldn't get enough of this, huh?"

"I don't know about that. I doubt if I was her only cowboy. I know I sure couldn't get enough."

Feeling a pang of jealousy, she made a little gasp and released him.

"Hey, hey," he said softly as he grasped her hand and returned it to him. "It's a rite of passage, darlin'. All boys go through it. Unless there's something wrong with them. There wasn't anything awful about it."

She resumed stroking, but she couldn't keep from resenting another woman touching him so intimately. Her curiosity wouldn't let her abandon the issue. "How old was she?"

"Twenty-six."

She trailed her finger along the thick vein up the back of his erection lying long and thick against his belly. "And you were sixteen? That's terrible. She was ten years older than you."

"I looked older. I was big for my age." He pushed back the quilt, exposing her breasts. Her nipples stiffened even more in the chill. He began to tease one with his tongue.

She reveled in the delight that sang through her body. "Rodeos and horse shows. They're all the same. They're worse than bars for being pick-up places."

"You never fooled around behind the pens at a horse show?"

He moved to her other breast and sucked at her nipple and an eager muscle moved low in her belly. He did know how to drive her mad with his mouth and tongue. She clasped his head and held him to her breast. "I mostly worked like a dog at horse shows."

"That was a hell of a waste, Miz Rondeau, seeing as how much you like what we're doing."

He moved down and blew a whispery breath on her navel, drawing a different kind of gasp from her. "Now you're making me feel like I'm bad again."

"Nuh-unh. Sexy. A lot of women don't like it. They put up with it, but they don't like it."

His tongue made a pattern around her navel, then dipped inside and she couldn't keep from arching her belly up to him.

"Yes, ma'am, you like it," he said in a rumbly voice. "And that turns me on big time."

She giggled as his mouth moved down and placed a suckling kiss on her lower belly. "John, you'll make a hickey."

He kissed the wet spot left by his mouth. "Something to remember me by."

"As if I could forget."

"You don't really want me to stop, do you?"

His warm lips moved back up, all the way to her neck, then to the sensitive spot behind her ear "Oh," she said, lifting her shoulder as his breath tickled her earlobe. "You're a tease," she said as he sucked on her earlobe. "A terrible tease." She trailed her fingers down the valley of his spine. "Have you known many women who didn't...you know, like it?"

His hand pushed between her legs where she felt wet and wanting again. "You know what, darlin'? We need to change the subject."

She gave in to the desire throbbing anew and opened herself to him. His wicked fingers played and soon had her hips moving against them and her on the verge of begging him again.

He reached across her for a condom and in seconds planted himself inside her. "God," he said hoarsely, and she could feel a tremor in his big body. "All my fantasies of fucking you, Isabelle, don't come close to the real thing."

The bawdy words sent a little thrill through her and she trembled, too. She raised her head and caught his mouth in a deep kiss, drank in the warmth of his lips, the nectar of his mouth. His tongue delved in an erotic rhythm. He brought her leg between his, increasing pressure with his thigh and began to move. Heat rushed through her so hot it threatened to smother her. Her breath hitched. Her deep muscles began to contract. She gave in to another shattering orgasm.

Still shaking, she opened her eyes and stared into his darkened pupils, recognized the moment his release hit him. He thrust hard and deep, strained and grunted as he ground against her. When he finished, he sank on top of her.

"Oh, man," he murmured, breathless, and placed an openmouthed kiss on her shoulder. "You're something else. I'm shaking like a cold dog."

He started to roll to her side, but she stopped him. "Don't you dare move."

He stayed and they lay in the cozy quiet until the storm that had battered them subsided.

In time, they made love again. Soon after, John told her he had to be at the sheriff's office by one o'clock to relieve Rooster. They left the bed and she cajoled him into the shower with her. He wasn't all that reluctant.

"I met your girlfriend," she said as they soaped and washed with honey-almond soap under the warm spray in the crowded fiberglass space.

He stopped soaping her breasts. "What girlfriend?"

"Rita, I believe her name is."

He didn't look at her. He seemed to be concentrating on sluicing soapsuds off her breasts. "She's not my girlfriend."

"Hmm. I'm not sure she knows that. She keeps up with your, um...coffee preferences."

He pulled her against him. "Cut it out," he murmured against her neck. "We went out a couple of times. Nothing else."

Isabelle dropped the conversation, but warned herself to be cautious.

He put forth an effort to make love to her again, but failed. "Give me an hour," he said, excusing himself.

She laughed and told him she would feed him a sandwich for lunch so he could rebuild his strength for the afternoon.

He loitered in the kitchen watching her build ham-and-cheese sandwiches. She put them on plates and pulled a bag of potato chips from the cupboard. "Here I am, slaving in the kitchen again," she said and grinned.

"You're a fine cook."

"I'm no such thing."

His hands went to her waist and he drew her close to him. "And you're a good woman and a fine, sexy lover."

She slid her arms up and around his shoulders. "No, you're the fine, sexy lover."

"It's you. Just being close to you turns me into a wild man. Here I am, can't even get it up again and I'm thinking about crawling back into that bed."

"Callister's criminals are waiting, remember?"

"Shit." With a slap on her bottom, he released her.

She had never liked seeing men slap women on their bottoms, but to her dismay, with John, she liked the possessiveness the swat implied.

When they sat down side by side at the oak table, he placed his hand on her thigh, leaned over and kissed her. "I'm gonna be on cloud nine the rest of the day, darlin'. But what the hell am I gonna do about tomorrow?"

# Chapter 15

John left the office for the day at six, anxious to call Izzy just to hear her voice. An odd but pleasant feeling had drifted within him all afternoon, a quietness. He couldn't explain it or even describe it, but he wanted—no, needed—to hear that the feeling was mutual.

On reaching his apartment, he punched in her number, but didn't get an answer. No big deal. She would be outside at the barn. He thought about driving to her house, but cautioned himself against becoming a pest. He called twice more, at nine and nine thirty, but still didn't get an answer.

At midnight he was still awake, lying in his dark bedroom, wondering where the hell she was at nine thirty at night, especially with a little kid who needed to get a good night's sleep to be ready for school tomorrow.

The morning he had spent in her bed haunted him. Sex had never, ever been better, but that wasn't even the best part of making love with her. He sensed a bond he hadn't felt with another woman, including the mother of his children. With his ex-wife, a longing to be with her again the minute they parted hadn't been present. Was it possible the connection to Izzy he had felt as an immature teenager had been something cosmic, like his instincts telling him she was the woman meant for him?

Nah. Couldn't be. He didn't believe in a bunch of mystical nonsense. He and Izzy didn't even really know each other. What he felt had to be lust, nothing more. He had gone without for a long time. Didn't he have a right to be horny?

Friday started slow, but Dana reminded him that Rocky Mountain Electric was slated to play at the Eights & Aces Saloon both Friday and Saturday nights. Plus, a leg of a darts tournament was scheduled at the Tall Timbers Tavern.

John groaned and swore. Rocky Mountain Electric was a wild and popular country-rock band and dart players had an enormous loyalty to the tournaments that occurred in bars and taverns around the area. Anywhere from a hundred to five hundred strangers could show up to drink, dance and throw darts in Callister. No way would he find the opportunity to sneak out to Izzy's after work.

John called her and explained his schedule, then talked her into meeting him at his apartment for lunch. She was reluctant, fearing someone would see her pickup at his place, but he bribed her with hamburgers he intended to buy at Betty's Road Kill. As soon as she walked into his apartment, they began undressing each other. Everything after that, from the black lacy bra and bikini panties she had on under her sweater and jeans to her clawing orgasm while she straddled him and he was buried all the way up to her heart, was X-rated.

After they gorged on each other, they sat up in bed and ate the carryout hamburgers. "I tried to call you last night," he told her between bites, feigning casualness. "Until nine thirty." He hated himself for sounding like a possessive prick.

"Ava had a thing at school," she said, "and we had tea with some of the teachers afterward. Well, really it was Kool-Aid. It was fun. I haven't done many things with her at school."

He was pleased with himself how he finessed that information without appearing overbearing. He felt better knowing where she had been, but now, instead of worrying about her whereabouts, he worried about what spell she had cast on him. Mind-blowing sex had softened his brain.

Through Friday night and Saturday, exerting epic self-discipline, he did his duty to the county, satisfying himself with phone calls instead of visits to Izzy. He manned the office all day Saturday, which gave Rooster the weekend off. Saturday night he patrolled the unruly crowds congregated in Callister's three bars, making his badge and himself obvious as well as available in case of trouble.

Not one fight occurred and he saw no incident grievous enough to warrant an arrest. He attributed the peace and harmony to the fact that he had no enemies of whom he was aware and most people in the area knew him, as either a hometown boy or a prizewinning rodeoer. Never mind that the latter no longer applied.

He usually held the sheriff's office alone on Sunday afternoon so Rooster could spend Sunday with his family. In the silence of the empty courthouse, John labored over a work schedule.

Since he had been sheriff, he and Rooster hadn't maintained a strict calendar. He kept the office open to the public from nine a.m. to midnight. The budget allowed for a part-time deputy. An ex-deputy retired from a California sheriff's department was available to do the job, but John had rarely called on him. When John first came back to Callister, if he'd had an abundance of anything, it was time. Consequently, he provided seven-days-a-week coverage of the sheriff's office himself. The schedule kept his mind too busy to think about his messy life and his lost kids and his doing double duty saved the county a little money.

He saw the necessity for the schedule to change now that he planned to take an occasional day off and spend time with Izzy and her horses.

Before he left the office Sunday, he called her and she told him she would be waiting for him tomorrow morning after Ava left for school. And he was there, stripping off his clothes, as soon as the school bus departed.

Lost in each other under her warm quilt, she was as shocked as he when they heard footsteps in the kitchen. Neither of them had heard a vehicle's engine.

A male voice called out, "Izzy?"

Her breath caught. "Oh, God, it's Paul."

She vaulted from the bed and grabbed a robe from the back of the only chair in the bedroom. "Stay here," she said, but as soon as she left the room John got to his feet and pulled on his boxers. He felt like a chickenshit, hiding out in the bedroom, but she obviously didn't want her brother to know she had a guest.

"Where's John?" the male voice asked. "I seen his truck, but I didn't spot him with the horses."

"Want some coffee?" Izzy's voice. It sounded unsteady. John heard the clatter of dishes.

"What're you doing in your bathrobe?" Her brother again.

"I, uh, don't feel well. I was up during the night, so I grabbed some extra sleep."

A pause. "What're you up to, Izzy?" Uh-oh. Suspicion in Paul's tone.

A visual of Izzy's clothing they had left on the kitchen floor, including her panties, popped into John's head along with a twinge of concern.

"What, I can't have a down day?" she said.

Another pause. "If I went into your bedroom, I bet I'd find John Bradshaw. And I might even find him with no clothes on."

A longer pause. No doubt Paul had seen the clothing. John puffed his cheeks, blew out a breath and paced in front of the dresser. He picked up a framed photograph of Izzy and her brother as children and studied it, trying to blank the kitchen scene from his mind.

"So what?" Izzy finally asked.

"Jee-zus Christ, Isabelle. I'll tell you this for fuckin' sure. A Rondeau can't be playing hide-the-weenie with a Bradshaw. What'll people say?"

"It's no one's business, Paul. And who're you to suddenly care about what people say?"

"This is the shits, Izzy. I hope you don't believe he thinks you're as good as he is. He's using you."

"Shut up, Paul. It's none of your business. If you can't be civil, just get out of here."

Clomping footsteps. Back door opening. "I'm going. Just see if he still wants to fuck you when he finds out you can't even read and write."

John's fists clenched.

"Paul! Get out of here!"

The door slammed. A minute later John heard an engine. Izzy came back into the bedroom carrying the sweat clothes and panties. "Needless to say, I wasn't expecting him today. He's supposed to be in Boise trying to put his marriage back together."

"Damn, Isabelle, I'm sorry—"

"Oh, to hell with it." She opened dresser drawers, pulled out clothing. "I appreciate you not coming out there, though. Paul can be—well, anyway, I appreciate you staying in here."

She turned to him and slid her arms around his waist. "I'm the one who's sorry. He has to tell only one person about this and it'll spread like a forest fire."

John pulled the tie at her waist loose and slid his hands beneath her robe, clutched her bottom and pulled her close. "I don't like causing you trouble." She looked up at him with those eyes that melted his bones. "What he said isn't true, Isabelle. I'm not using you. I wouldn't hurt you for anything."

"The talk will do you more harm than it will me, John. All I'm doing is living out here in the boondocks taking care of my horses and minding my own business. It doesn't matter what anyone says about me. You're the one who needs to maintain a squeaky-clean reputation."

*Reputation.* All at once John remembered that since he had put on the sheriff's badge, his public image had been a priority. At this moment, the pomposity of it felt silly. "I'm not worried." He bent his head and kissed her. "It's not like I asked anybody for this sheriff job. They came to me. . . . And when I took it on, nobody said I couldn't have a life."

A mysterious little smile quirked the corners of her mouth. Her eyes held a teasing glint. "I just remembered something about you from high school. Something endearing." She raised to her tiptoes and brushed his lips with hers. "You were always high-minded and . . . well, naïve."

"What Paul said about reading and—"

She skirted away from him. "I'm taking a shower. Then I'll fix lunch." She headed for the bathroom. At the doorway she stopped, dropped her robe and threw him a come-hither look. "I dare you to join me."

Blood rushed to his groin. Again. Nothing could distract that demon in his shorts from a dare like that.

They made love in the shower and the tension washed away. So did the conversation John meant to have with her. *Just see if he still wants to fuck you when he finds out you can't even read and write.*

By the time they finished and dried each other, they were able to laugh about the hypocrisy of Paul's indignation.

Since John hadn't ridden the horses, he told her he would come back tomorrow morning.

"There's no need," she replied. "I can get it done before Ava gets home from school."

"That's not the deal we made. I'll be back," he said and kissed her.

*Just see if he still wants to fuck you when he finds out you can't even read and write.* The words ran through Isabelle's mind as she watched John make a left turn onto the county road.

At some point in the near future she would have to explain dyslexia to John. Though she lived with the handicap daily, hourly, she had never learned how to get past feeling pain and embarrassment. The affliction had colored her previous life in Callister, making her the butt of cruel jokes. That, and her hair, her father. Her brother. Now it threatened to do it all over again. The very thought of dealing with the jokes and the "dumb as a rock" remarks almost nauseated her.

John hadn't been gone ten minutes before Paul came into the kitchen, which made Isabelle wonder if he had been parked somewhere watching for the county Blazer to leave. His heavy work boots thudded through the mudroom, into the kitchen.

Not wanting to quarrel with him or drive him away, she smiled. "Hi. I'm glad you came back." She gestured at the tomatoes, lettuce and packages of ham and cheese from which she had made lunch for her and John. "How about a sandwich?"

Her brother didn't return her smile as he came to the counter. He hadn't shaved and he reeked of stale alcohol.

"I guess so. I didn't mean to butt in on you." He hung his head and stared at the floor.

Isabelle's heart ached at his palpable neediness. Now that Sherry and his kids were gone, she was the only caring human contact he had. She hooked her arm with his. "I know. I didn't mean to jump on you, either. I was just surprised." She gave a nervous titter. "And a little embarrassed." She released him and took out bread slices to make him a sandwich. "I meant what I said, though, Paul, about it being no one's business."

He lifted a shoulder. "What you do's up to you. I just think it's dumb. If you gotta fuck around, there's men on our level."

She huffed and rolled her eyes as she dipped mayonnaise from the jar and spread it on the bread slices. She hadn't yet reaccustomed herself to Callister's provincialism. With her brother's lack of education and his only ventures out of Callister County being to work in remote forests, his narrow thinking was to be expected. "And what's our level?"

He lifted his chin and looked her in the eye, his yeasty breath nearly forcing her to back away. "Well, it ain't up there with one o' these snooty ranchers."

"What's any member of the Bradshaw family ever done to you? And they're not snooty." She positioned tomato slices and lettuce on top of ham and cheese slices on the bread. "When we were growing up Mom and John's mother were friends. The Bradshaws are good people."

"But he won't ever care about you, Izzy. He won't take up for you. He'll treat you worse than Billy. Our old man dying drunk in an alley'll always be in his mind."

Despite John's talk about being attracted to her as a teenager, Isabelle feared Paul could be right. And she had to admit Rita Mitchell looked to be more on his social level. "I don't need anyone to take up for me. I take care of myself."

She lifted a plate from the cupboard, placed the sandwich and potato chips on it and handed it to her brother. "Please, Paul. I want you to leave it alone and don't gossip with Merle or in the bars about finding John—" She halted. She had almost said, "in my bed" but couldn't make herself utter the words. "—here," she finished.

Her brother snorted, took the plate and sauntered to the table. "Everybody already knows he's out here fooling with your horses. It don't take somebody smart to figure out he's fooling with you, too."

Precisely what she didn't want. What had she been thinking, not stopping John or herself before they reached her bedroom?

She poured a tall glass full of milk and carried it to the table. "Well, you're right about one thing. What I do is up to me. So I guess if word gets out, it gets out. I'll deal with it then." She took a seat across the table from him. "So tell me what went on between you and Sherry."

He bit into the sandwich and answered with his mouth full. "Nothing. But I know she ain't coming back."

Isabelle felt heaviness in her chest. "She didn't say no, though. Did you promise to quit drinking and disappearing for days at a time?"

"She said she'd think about it. The kids want to come home. They don't like it down in Boise."

Isabelle tried for a hopeful smile. "That's good. Isn't that good?" She reached across the table and placed her hand on his forearm that was covered by the sleeve of a faded flannel shirt. "Oh, I hope she does come back, Paul. She's so good for you. And having your kids home—"

"But I ain't good for her, Izzy. Or them kids, either. I ain't even got a place for 'em to live. That renter don't have to give up my house for six more months."

After Sherry left last year, Paul had leased their home and taken his travel trailer out on a logging job that had lasted all summer. When winter set in, he returned to town and continued to live in the trailer behind another sawyer's house. While she had been enjoying the balmy winter of North Texas, Isabelle hadn't known her brother was spending thirty-below nights in a poorly insulated travel trailer. She marveled he hadn't frozen to death. Just like their father.

"If she says she'll come back, we'll manage, Paul. You can live here until the lease on your place is up. This is a big house and it's half yours, you know."

Isabelle's better judgment shrieked at the proposal. Living with her alcoholic brother and an additional three people would be a nightmare, but the burden would be worthwhile if it saved Paul and his family. "The girls and Ava could double up in Ava's bedroom. You and Sherry could have Mom and Pa's old room."

She hadn't been able to make herself take over her parents' bedroom. She couldn't imagine what went on inside it between her gentle mother and her brutal father. When she came back and moved into the house, she took the bedroom that had been Paul's as a child and her childhood room became Ava's.

"Don't get your hopes up. Sherry's still pissed off."

"She's hurt. She needs to see you're sincere. Maybe she'd be more apt to believe you if you went for some professional help."

"Meaning what?" Paul rose from his chair and picked up his plate. "It's all too fuckin' hard to figure out, Izzy."

He turned up his glass and drained it, then wiped off a milk mustache with his sleeve. Inside, Isabelle winced, realizing how difficult life with Paul would be for any woman. Even so, Sherry must have truly loved him once to have lived with him and given birth to his children. In Isabelle's mind the woman was a saint.

He carried his dishes to the sink. "I'm gonna finish up them stalls today. We just about got that barn whipped."

As he went out the back door, Isabelle sat at the table staring out the window at the sunny spring day, but seeing nothing. If Paul didn't keep his mouth shut about her and John, soon talk would float to the school and Ava would hear it. That prospect caused an even bigger knot in her stomach than the idea of sharing the house with Paul and his family.

# Chapter 16

The next morning John called and reported he had run into Luke McRae at the service station. Some of the Double Deuce's mares hadn't been bred yet and Luke wanted to look at Dancer.

Isabelle gave a breathless laugh as panic surged. She had mailed the ownership-transfer papers to Billy only a few days ago. If he signed and returned them immediately, she could safely discuss breeding Dancer. On the other hand, if Billy balked or if he was traveling, weeks could go by before she heard from him. "I don't think I'm ready for that."

"You don't have to commit to anything."

"I know, but—"

"What's wrong, Isabelle? All he wants is to see the horse. He's anxious 'cause it's getting close to the end of breeding season."

John was right. Most horse owners wanted their mares to foal in the spring and it was already the end of March. Mares bred now would give birth in late February or early March. Maybe there was nothing wrong with showing Dancer off. If Luke had a serious interest, she could make a special effort to reach Billy.

"Tell you what," John said. "I'm holding the fort today, but if you can come to town, I'll buy lunch at Betty's. We can talk about it."

Lunch in a public place. People talking and asking questions. "I don't know, John. Everybody in town eats lunch at
Betty's."

"Isabelle, it's okay for us to have lunch."

"But you're the sheriff."

"Well...only 'til I figure out something else to do. So
come on to town."

She couldn't say no. Memories of him had filled her
every waking moment since he left her house yesterday. Her
desire to spend time with him overrode the onslaught of
doubts about carrying on an affair with the sheriff.

She applied eye makeup and blush. Wanting him to see
her as feminine and desirable, she left her hair hanging down
her back, but she pulled up the sides and secured them at her
crown with a leather barrette.

As she studied her limited wardrobe, she asked herself
just how long it had been since she had dressed to please a
man. She put on a broomstick skirt and a Western-cut blouse,
but decided against it and changed to new Rockies jeans and
a long-sleeved, snap-button shirt. She finally settled on worn,
but not ragged, Wranglers and a blue turtleneck sweater,
over which she would wear the tapestry jacket Nan had liked
so much.

Since the hairdo left her ears showing, she put on little
silver-and-turquoise dangles and added a matching pendant.
And perfume—spritzes of something she had bought in a department store in Fort Worth.

At Betty's Road Kill, she stopped just inside the plate-
glass door, taking in the hum of voices and the good smells
of homemade soup, hamburgers and French fries, chicken-
fried steak and mashed potatoes. The aromas reminded her
of the days when her mother had been the cook. As a kid, she
came here after school and Betty would serve her a dish of
ice cream.

She spotted John in a booth toward the back. Nervous as
a bride, she drew a deep breath and headed in his direction.
As she expected, the eyes of every customer followed her.

Smiling, he stood up and removed his hat when she
neared. She saw approval in his eyes and sensed the current

that passed between them. "You do look pretty, Isabelle," he said softly.

Feeling her cheeks warm, she ducked her chin. "Thanks."

They slid onto vinyl seats opposite each other and she noted he looked handsome himself, even with his hair mussed and flattened where his hat fit. The aura she had come to imagine she saw around him seemed to shimmer as her eyes moved down to his tan-and-green-plaid shirt that showed from beneath a khaki quilted vest. His silver badge was pinned on his vest and she wished she could overcome thinking of her brother every time she saw it. The thought of John and Paul clashing at some point dispelled the aura.

"Our meeting will keep everyone busy for the after-noon," she told him. "I imagine they're speculating on what we're doing together." She cut her eyes toward the dozen other diners within shouting distance of the booth. "They probably think Paul's in some kind of trouble. That's some-thing he doesn't need."

"If they're eavesdropping, all they'll hear is horse talk."

The aged waitress, Lorraine Jones, appeared, coffee carafe in hand, and poured the brew for John.

*He's a big-time coffee drinker.*

Isabelle had always been ambivalent about coffee, but now her cupboards would never be without it. However, she wouldn't be buying it from Java Junction. Dear God, she wondered, would she ever be able to put Rita Mitchell out of her mind?

She ordered a salad, then watched as John ordered the lunch special of meat loaf and mashed potatoes.

"Guess things are quiet over at the courthouse," Lorraine said, peering through her bifocals as she wrote their order.

"Quiet as a church," John answered with a grin. "Get those new boots yet?"

"Not yet. My birthday's still a ways away."

"You be sure you show 'em to me when you get 'em."

"I will, sheriff." Lorraine's mouth tipped into a huge grin. Isabelle could see her glowing at John's attention. He had a gift for relating to people.

The waitress turned to Isabelle. "Betty said you might have some extra manure out at your place. Soon's the ground's good and dry, my nephew wants to work up his garden spot. He likes horse manure. He'd pay you for it."

"Sure," Isabelle answered, "but he doesn't have to pay me. I'm always looking to get rid of it. All he has to do is call me and come get it."

The waitress gave her a wrinkled smile. "I've been meaning to tell you, we're glad you came back."

As Lorraine sailed away, John grinned. "See? Selling manure. There's another financial opportunity for you."

"Don't kid. The way things are looking in the income column, I may have to resort to that."

"That's what we're working on today. Income. When should I tell Luke to come out?"

"I have a problem with that, John." In a voice she hoped was too low for eavesdroppers, she leaned across the table and explained the ownership of the horses. "I'm not sure Billy will sign off," she said in conclusion.

"What's the worst that can happen? He gets half the money. Not a deal you'd like, but not impossible, right?"

"It upsets me to think of Billy getting part of Dancer's standing fees. He didn't like Dancer. He couldn't handle him."

"That blue devil's a handful. I'll be the first to agree."

"It wasn't Dancer's fault. Billy was rough with him. He knew Billy didn't like him, so he threw him many times. Even bit him."

John tilted his head back and laughed and was still laughing when Lorraine brought their lunch. Isabelle waited until she left before continuing. "The reason Billy gave me all three of the horses I have is because he found something wrong with every one of them. He didn't want Trixie because he doesn't like the shape of her head. I've already told you about Polly." She seasoned her salad and speared a tomato slice. "If I hadn't been willing to take the three of them, I don't know what he might've done with them. He doesn't deserve income from them. They're his castoffs."

*Just like me,* she thought, but didn't say it. Seeing how her former partner's attitude blew hot and cold with various horses over the years and even with his own child had given her a premonition that someday he would abandon her, too.

John's hand came up like he might reach across the table and touch her, but she sat back and avoided it.

"Okay, I get it. No touching." He didn't say it angrily, reminding her that his easygoing attitude was what made him so likable. "Let Luke come out," he said. "Can't hurt for him to look. If he's interested, you can take the next step. Besides, Luke's wife's from Texas and she wants to meet you."

Isabelle cocked her head to the side in resignation. She was such a sucker, but she valued John's opinions and had faith in his advice. Unlike her, he was smart and educated.

Now another worry pestered her, something more personal. And something she hadn't intended to discuss with John, at least not yet. If Luke liked Dancer's looks and his pedigree—and what horse breeder wouldn't—an agreement would have to be signed.

She had to go home immediately and find the copies of previous breeding agreements Billy and she had executed over the years. Then she would have to somehow get a new one made and hope no one guessed she had never read a one of them all the way through. Billy always told her what they said, shoved one in front of her and she signed without argument.

They finished lunch and John strolled with her to her truck. The balmy spring day was bright with sunshine and the busyness of people emerging from their winter shells. When she rejected his touch, he bumped her arm with his. They reached her Sierra and he opened the door and helped her up into it. She ducked away when he attempted to kiss her good-bye.

"Oh, no, you don't. You're not gonna escape without kissing me." He took off his hat, darted his head through the open window and planted a quick kiss on her cheek.

She giggled like a silly girl. "John, you're going to get us in trouble."

"So, Miz Rondeau," he said, drawing back from her window and resetting his hat, "what kind of a story am I supposed to tell if somebody asks me what's going on between me and Isabelle?"

She smiled, masking her apprehension about the subject. "You're supposed to say, 'Isabelle Who?'"

John was still standing there grinning like a goose as she put the truck in reverse and drove away. Damn his cowboy charm anyway.

Back in his office, the date circled on the calendar caught John's attention. April 1, a day past the mental deadline he had set to hear from Julie about travel arrangements for his sons' impending visit. Since he had reminded her that he expected her to live up to the agreement she had made, he had heard nothing. Imagine that. April Fool.

In California it would be two thirty. Julie should be home. He sat for a few minutes, drumming a pencil on the desk blotter, working past the dread of calling her. When he thought he had readied himself, he stood up and closed his office door, then dug her phone number from his wallet.

"I don't know yet," she said when John questioned her about preparations for Trey and Cody to travel. "Carson hasn't said."

"Julie, this isn't up to Carson. And this is the only phone call I'm gonna make."

"Are you threatening me?"

Her voice sounded giddy and uptight and John couldn't figure out why. When had she ever been afraid of him?

"Nope. Just telling you the facts and giving you time to get their stuff ready. School's out the end of May. I'll be there on June first."

"That could be a big mistake, John. Carson still hasn't gotten over what you did—"

"Cut it out, Julie. I'm coming to get my kids on June first."

John arranged an appointment for Luke McRae and his wife to come on Thursday afternoon to look at Dancer and Isabelle worked herself into a frenzy. She had dealt with a multitude of millionaire horse owners and breeders and not been nervous. In the Texas cutting-horse world, Isabelle Rondeau was a horse handler who could correct the seem-

ingly uncorrectable in the unruliest of animals. Knowing her
name meant something gave her boundless confidence.

This was different. In Callister, Idaho, she was an im-
moral runaway and the redheaded, freckle-faced, dumb-as-a-
fence-post daughter of a drunk. The locals couldn't care less
what she had accomplished two thousand miles away.

John showed up early to help her. He seemed to sense her
anxiety and as they curried Dancer he tried to calm her with
overblown but reassuring words—what good shape the
horses were in, how well trained they were, how impressed
Luke would be when he saw Dancer. The efforts were
clumsy, but they endeared him to her all the more.

As for Dancer, he seemed to know he was the horse of
the hour. He strutted and stamped around the corral.

Luke came soon after lunch, accompanied by the woman
Isabelle had heard the Callister grapevine discuss as the
brainy half-Asian beauty from Texas who had put a halter on
the elusive Luke McRae. According to gossip in Betty's
Road Kill, Dahlia's entrance into the McRae clan had
changed all of them as much as it had changed Luke. Claire
McRae, Luke's mother and the Double Deuce's matriarch,
had stepped down and totally turned management over to
Luke and his new wife. That fact alone gave Dahlia revered
status among Callister's citizens.

The thought of meeting this perfect, powerful woman
made Isabelle as anxious as having Luke come to look at
Dancer.

Luke parked in John's usual place, walked around to his
truck's passenger door and held his wife's arm as she scooted
out. "Careful, now," he cautioned as her feet touched the
ground, his tone gentle and solicitous. It appeared that
Dahlia had turned the edgy Luke McRae into a kinder, gen-
tler man.

She smiled up at him, then moved from behind the truck
door. She looked ten months pregnant.

"This is my wife, Dahlia," he said.

Isabelle hadn't seen Luke since school. When she was a
sophomore, he had been a senior. Still, in a high school population that totaled fewer than a hundred, she had known him.

Rich, good-looking and reckless was the description that
came to her mind. She had forgotten that he, too, had red hair
and freckles.

He looped his arm around his wife's shoulder and looked
down at her with pride and an affection that seemed to have a
life of its own. He placed a large hand on her huge stomach
and said, "And this is Corazon."

Dahlia laughed and covered his hand with hers. "Corazon Matilda McRae. An interesting mix of cultures, don't
you think?"

Everyone laughed with her. Isabelle felt an immediate
affinity with the black-haired woman. They had to be
roughly the same age. "Are those family names?"

"My mother's name. She was Filipino. And Luke's paternal great-great-grandmother's. We're going to call her Cory."

"My daughter and I are both named for grandmothers,"
Isabelle said. "French-Canadian. When are you due?"

"Next week, but I look like it could be any minute. That's
why I wanted to come and meet you while I have the chance.
I heard you've been living in West Texas. I'm from a little
town named Loretta. My best friend still lives there."

"Oh, I've heard of it. Do you miss it?"

"I miss a few of the people, but living at the Double
Deuce makes me feel like I've come home after a long jour-
ney. It's strange. I have a hard time explaining it."

As John led Luke toward the corral, a conversation en-
sued between Isabelle and Dahlia about Texas places and
people. Taken by the warmth and gentleness she sensed in
the woman, Isabelle asked her if she, too, wanted to look at
Dancer.

"Of course," Dahlia said. "John told us he's blue."

"Well, he is, sort of. He's a blue roan, which is a rare
color. Really, the color is a deep gray, but it's mixed with
white, which gives a blue tint." They strolled toward the paddock where Dancer had been penned.

"Why, he's beautiful," Dahlia said on a caught breath.

Isabelle put her hand on Dahlia's arm. "Are you all right?"

"I'm fine." Dahlia's hand splayed on her stomach. "There
almost isn't enough room for this baby and my lungs."

"If she doesn't come next week, will they induce?"

"Oh, she'll make it. If she doesn't, Luke's promised to take me for a ride on a rough road. And Granny McRae wants to feed me castor oil."

"*Blech*," Isabelle said and they laughed together.

"Is this a Texas horse?" Dahlia asked, peering through the pole rails at Dancer.

"Yes. I've had him since he was born. He's a love. He's one of my best friends."

"John says you have a gift with horses, that you can communicate with them."

Isabelle had wondered what John might tell others about her skill and occupation. She gave Dahlia a look. "Really? He said that?"

"That's what he told Luke."

Isabelle couldn't stop a huge smile. "He's probably partial."

"You and John are together?"

Words escaped Isabelle for a moment, but she bolstered her courage. "Well . . . yes, I suppose we are."

"You look like you fit."

Isabelle smiled again, feeling a tiny pride in saying John Bradshaw was her man. "I guess that's good, looking like you fit with someone."

"I think so. I think I fit with Luke. We're both tall and sort of lanky. He's light and I'm dark, so we contrast. We made a very handsome son. Luke calls him a good cross."

Isabelle laughed. "Like in cattle, huh?"

"The first time I heard Luke say that, I was insulted, but later I realized, coming from him, it was a compliment."

"John didn't mention that you and Luke have a son."

"We have a houseful of kids. Luke's three from his former marriage, then our son, Joe. He's a three-year-old magpie."

Dahlia's openness made Isabelle feel even more at ease.

"Oh, look. He's impressed," Dahlia said, catching her breath again and veering her attention to her husband. They watched Luke make a circle around the stallion.

"How can you tell?"

"See how he's pinching his lower lip with his thumb and

finger? He does that when he's either really interested in something or worried about it."

Isabelle lifted her chin. "Ah, I see. Well, I'm glad he's interested."

As Luke moved around the corral, Dahlia's eyes followed him. "You knew my husband when he was a teenager, didn't you?"

"Not very well. He was a couple of years ahead of me. I remember, though, he always seemed to be in charge of things."

A laugh burst from Dahlia. "I can well imagine. He's that kind of person." As Luke and John walked toward them, Dahlia's gaze lingered on her husband. "He's so strong and so smart."

"Wow," Isabelle said, realizing she could say the same about John. "What nice things to say about him."

"Isabelle," Luke said, approaching them, "that's a helluva horse. Go ahead and hit me with it. How much are you gonna want?"

Isabelle's horse-trading experience kicked in and she began to talk breeding fees with Luke. He wasn't interested in paying for artificial insemination at first, but Isabelle stood her ground. He listened to her arguments and relented, said he would deliver four mares to the vet's office. The conversation ended with a handshake and Isabelle assured him she would follow up with written agreements to be signed.

As Luke's arm slid around Dahlia's shoulder again, a gesture obviously meant to be both protective and possessive, she said to Isabelle, "After the baby comes, let's get together. I'll come to town one day and we can have lunch and talk about Texas."

Isabelle agreed. She had observed that no matter where Texans were placed or misplaced, they always wanted to talk about Texas.

As they drove away, Isabelle looked after them with an unexpected yearning. "They're really in love, aren't they?"

John's arm came around her waist and she looked up at him. For a few seconds his eyes locked on hers. She was sure she saw the same emotion in his eyes she had just seen in Luke's when he looked at Dahlia.

"Isabelle," John started, but she stopped him.

"Don't say anything, John. We aren't there."

His expression changed. What had almost fallen from his lips, what she saw in his face and what dangled unresolved within her was commitment.

"Then where are we?" he asked.

Fearing conversation could unweld the glue, she hedged. "I don't know, but this whole thing scares me. It's good between us right now. Let's leave it be."

He continued to look at her for a few beats and she couldn't turn away, either. Finally he picked up her hand and kissed the back of it. And just like that, a distant sense of a pact sealed came to rest within her.

# Chapter 17

As they walked toward the house, Isabelle reached for John's hand. He interlocked their fingers and she relaxed in the warmth and security of being near him. "Thank you for helping me today."

"You don't have to thank me. I liked doing it. Just remind me to never get into a negotiation with you over money. I can't think of half a dozen people who could have squeezed that much out of Luke McRae for stud fees, especially when he started out not wanting to do AI."

"You probably can't think of half a dozen people who're as desperate as I am or who need it more than I do, either."

He planted a kiss on her lips. "Define 'it.'"

"Money, John. Money."

"Oh. I thought you were talking about something else." He grinned.

She punched him on the arm. "That, too."

He ducked down and kissed her again. "When's Ava coming home? I want to take you and her out for a steak dinner, up at the ski lodge. To celebrate a bunch of new foals sired by . . . what's his real name?"

"Pepto's Blue Dan. What if someone sees us?"

"What if someone does? Isabelle, it's okay for me to take a woman out to dinner."

"But people will talk."

He slapped her bottom. "Let 'em."

"I'm not as fearless as you."

He stopped her at the back door, his eyes catching hers. "You're wrong, Izzy-girl. You're a lot braver than I am."

In the kitchen Isabelle pulled coffee mugs from the kitchen cupboard. She had made a decision she wanted to share. Since the day she and John rode in the mountains, she had been mulling over breeding the mares. "I've been thinking about Trixie and Polly."

He grinned like an imp. No doubt he knew he had planted an irresistible idea in her head. "And?"

"Polly's coming in heat. Trixie will be soon." She filled the coffeepot reservoir. "I'm thinking I should try to breed Polly again. Since I've gone this far and I'll be hauling Dancer to the vet's clinic anyway, it would be convenient."

He came and leaned on his elbows on the counter, his arm touching hers as she measured the coffee. "You don't want to consider hand-breeding or just turning Dancer and Polly into the corral together?"

"No. I don't want to risk either of them getting hurt."

"Poor ol' Dancer. So good-looking. Full of piss and vinegar and he never gets any."

Isabelle laughed and clicked the ON switch. "It's his own fault. He shouldn't be so wild and crazy."

"That's the way us super-studs are. Wild and crazy."

She bumped his hip with hers and slid her hand along his belt. "I know. It's more than I can resist."

"What made you change your mind?"

"Reality. I could go broke before I ever get a horse training business going here and if my horses won every show in Idaho it still wouldn't be enough money to keep me afloat."

"But what about the long-term commitment of a foal?"

"I think Ava would love watching foals grow up. The last time I had one, she was too young to enjoy him—and I'm not going anywhere anyway."

He straightened, hooked an arm around her neck and drew her up to him. "That, lady, is the best news I've heard all day. And what about Billy?"

"I'll have to make that call to Oklahoma. My horses can't be producing foals I can't register."

One more thing she had been dreading for days had to be done. She flattened her hand on his stomach. "You're so good at favors. I need another one."

He bent his head and kissed her. She turned in his arms, raised on her tiptoes and savored his soft, sweet-tasting mouth. In time, he lifted his lips from hers and brushed the tip of her nose with his. "You could talk me into just about anything," he said softly. "Name it."

She leaned back and looked into his eyes, wanting to be taken into the magic of his space. A word for how she felt about him had so far eluded her. "The old breeding agreements Billy and I used are up in the attic. I need you to help me find one."

She had already been into the attic bedroom and found the file box in which the agreements were stored, but attempting to sort one from the other and from various other filed documents became such a jumble of undecipherable words, she had given up on the task. A puzzled expression crossed John's face and the obvious question—why did she need help for *that*?

"Remember when we were in bed and Paul came into the house?"

"Hmm. I doubt if I'll forget that." He bent and teased her earlobe with his tongue. "You know, we've got an hour before Ava gets home."

"You're distracting me." She closed her eyes and tilted her head for more of his warm mouth on her skin, a sensation that made her jittery. "Remember what he said about reading and writing?"

"Who, Paul?" His mouth moved down her neck and he gave it a gentle bite.

"It's true. I can only do it with a great struggle."

"Do what?" His head moved back up and he placed a kiss at the side of her nose. "All this talk about breeding must have made me horny." He reached for her hand and placed it on his firm fly.

She smiled as she rubbed his erection. "You're always horny."

"Cool, huh?"

"I should tell you something before we get too far into this. My period started this morning."

"Not a problem for me. You?"

"Yes," she said and smiled again.

"Damn, you're tough." On a sigh, he released her. "Okay, why do we need to find the agreements?" He picked up the carafe of hot coffee and poured both cups full.

"I want to copy one of them. I've never read them. I know what Billy said they say, but I haven't *read* them." She paused, shoring herself up for what she wanted to say. "I can't, John. . . . I'm dyslexic."

She waited for his reaction—a gasp, a facial expression, something.

He set his mug on the counter and placed his hands on her waist, pulled her tightly against his big body. He tipped up her chin with his knuckle and looked into her eyes. "So what? I'm left-handed."

Hoping he had hidden how Isabelle's revelation had stunned him, John followed her to an attic bedroom lit by bars of sunlight shining through a small octagonal window. There was an antique oak dresser, a tall stand-alone mirror in a frame and an iron bed covered with a homemade quilt.

A dozen stacked cardboard boxes stood in one corner, tucked between the exposed roof joists. Isabelle handed him several file folders and he thumbed through them. The breeding agreements were legibly signed on the top line by William R. Bledsoe, but Isabelle's signature beneath his was childlike and often had missing letters.

"I just need you to tell me what they say so I can pick the one to use," she told him.

A lump formed in John's throat and stayed there through the perusal of the documents. They sat side by side on the edge of the bed and she kept her head lowered while he scanned them, then told her what each said. The agreements were simple, no ten-dollar words, no complicated lawyer jargon. After he read and explained the last one, she made her choice.

He caught her chin with his thumb and finger and lifted her face to his, saw her eyes shiny. "This reading thing doesn't make any difference to me." He kissed her, hoping to prove it. "Why didn't you tell me sooner?"

She sniffed and smiled. "It isn't something I brag about."

"But this is me. You can tell me anything. I'll never criticize you."

"It's hard. I didn't want you to think I'm dumb." She picked up the loose file folders and walked over to return them to the box. "I guess it's okay to go ahead. As far as the breeding fees go, we aren't talking about enough money for me and Billy to fight over. If he gets half of it, I'm sure he won't mind going along."

She raised her head and stared out the octagonal window. "On the other hand, if I breed Trixie and Polly, the money from their foals could be substantial." She sighed. "I hate to bring up my finances, but I could really use that money. I've had to spend more here than I anticipated and the only paying customer I have so far is Mr. Fielder with his palomino. I'd really hate to have to share so much with Billy."

*And why should she,* John thought as he sorted through other folders related to Isabelle's career. The sonofabitch deserted her. He felt a small twinge of guilt for pushing her in this direction. Still, maybe breeding the mares would spur her to settle up with Billy once and for all.

John landed on one file folder holding copies of articles that had appeared in various trade magazines and newspapers about the Bledsoe-Rondeau training operation. Each article named Billy as the "trainer" and "handler," with no mention of Izzy. "I don't remember Billy being especially good with horses," he said.

She smiled. "Well, he isn't that great. He's too impatient, especially working with the ones that are hard to handle. He's best at hanging out in the bars and BSing with the high rollers."

"Your name is hardly mentioned in these articles."

"When they were written it wasn't that important. Billy needed the boost to his reputation and that was okay with me." She lifted her shoulders in a shrug, telling him she had willingly accepted the second-place role. "I mean, we were partners and partners should support each other. Most of the owners knew who really did the important work with the horses. Some of them wrote me letters."

She plucked another folder from the box. It held a dozen letters from grateful horse owners praising her skills.

"Here's your leverage with Billy," John said, scanning the letters. "If he thought you might spill what a phony he is, he'd be glad to cooperate on signing the horses over to you."

"Isn't that a little like blackmail?"

"I don't see it that way. He had no conscience about shutting you out of the praise for the work done or about leaving you and his kid high and dry. He already said you could have the horses. And he already proved he didn't want them. All you'd be doing is reminding him of his commitments."

"I don't know, John. I'm not good at being tough."

"You don't have to be. You still know cutting-horse people. I know a few in the AQHA. They all like to gossip. A few well-placed words and Billy's reputation would be history. Under the circumstances, I see no harm in pointing that out to him. A prick shouldn't win every battle."

Isabelle waited until after Ava left for school the next morning to place the call to Ardmore, Oklahoma. With the time difference, she hoped to catch Billy before he left the house. She sat down at the kitchen table with the phone, her pad and pen and a fresh cup of coffee. Before keying in the number she lectured herself on being cordial but businesslike. She no longer cared about him in the way she once had, so there was no reason for melodrama. No quarreling.

A Hispanic woman answered the phone—Isabelle assumed she was a maid—and asked her to wait. Soon Billy came on the line. He sounded surprised, but relaxed, even friendly, which was a relief, since she knew his mood swings.

Before she could say why she called, he launched a long

story about how well one of his horses had done in a show somewhere, how successful his breeding program was and how much money his assets were returning.

Isabelle cringed at the terminology. She hadn't heard that kind of talk about horses since she left Texas. Still, hearing him speak of doing so well gave her confidence and she asked if he had gotten her letter.

"Yeah, I got it," he said. "Who helped you write it?"

She ignored the barb. "I need you to sign those papers and get them back to me. I'm stuck without clearing up the registration."

"I don't see why. You can do whatever you want to, sweet thing. If you make any money, just send me my half. I trust you, Izzy-darlin'."

Her jaw tightened. He had always called her that when he talked down to her. "You washed your hands of these horses, Billy. You gave them to me." Drawing a deep breath, she built a mental picture of John standing behind her. "I expect you to keep your word."

A few seconds of silence. "I don't know what you're talking about. Why would I give away my interest in good horses?"

Anger began to grow as she recalled his stubborn stonewalling when she sold the place in Texas. John's image nudged her and she found courage she hadn't had when she dealt with her ex-partner before.

She talked about a few mutual friends, including some who knew his Oklahoma girlfriend and a freelance writer who regularly contributed to *Performance Horse* magazine. She followed up by reminding him he had never paid a penny in child support and in the same breath she mentioned a mad-dog lawyer whose horse she alone had taken to a hefty cash prize. She concluded by telling him she wanted the signed transfer papers back via overnight mail.

Billy argued, accused her of blackmail and hung up in her ear, but she wasn't put off. He wasn't a terribly fearless guy. She believed he would finally sign, would be afraid not to. He would bluster and cuss and call her names, whine to his bar buddies for a day or two, but faced with her threats, which he had never had to face before, he would sign. He knew she could make his life one long embarrassing moment and he had ample respect for the mad-dog lawyer, who had always liked her.

Why she hadn't tried this tactic before she didn't know. "No guts," she mumbled as she sat there staring at the phone, still skeptical that he would actually send the papers. Getting his cooperation had been almost too easy.

Two days later the signed ownership-transfer documents arrived and she wasted no time taking them to the court-house. Using the fax machine in his office, John sent them to AQHA headquarters in Amarillo. Now the horses were hers. She was free to breed the mares and/or sell Dancer's semen.

# Chapter 18

John had no experience with artificial insemination in horses. On his parents' ranch, horses bred naturally. As a practical matter, he could see the advantages to AI that Isabelle had pointed out and he supposed if somebody owned a horse worth six digits, he would take every measure to keep it safe from injury and free of infection.

When Isabelle called and said Luke's hired man had delivered a mare to the clinic, John dropped everything and went to help her. He had already picked up his two-horse trailer from the Lazy B and taken it to her to be used for transporting Dancer to the vet's clinic. At the clinic, he found she had hauled Dancer and Polly both.

The McRae mare was a rare grulla color and she was beautiful. Luke's man explained the mare had been bought from a horse farm in Montana that bred for the unique blue-gray color as well as for conformation and performance. Her name was Smokey Jane, but they called her "Janie." She had foaled once.

Excitement glowed like a bright light around Isabelle. Anybody could see she was in her element.

When they collected semen from Dancer, John saw that the stud could be hard on a mare. They used Janie to tease him into readiness and by the time he reared and mounted the dummy, he was ready to tear up the barn. John had seen well-seasoned mares abused by an anxious stallion, so an in-experienced mare like Janie might indeed kick and injure a stud as aggressive as Dancer.

The whole process, from semen collection from Dancer to insemination of both mares, was completed by noon. The vet expressed his belief that pregnancy would result. That breeding Polly was a long shot went undiscussed.

Even with the vet's positive attitude, an inexplicable sadness welled within John. Something was missing. All of it was so sterile and artificial. It was possible a valuable stud like Dancer could spend his entire life siring foals and never physically touch a mare. John couldn't get past feeling that the horses were treated like machines, though he knew that notion was unfounded in Isabelle's case. She loved her horses and would allow only what was best for them.

Still, animals as beautiful as Dancer and Janie and Polly should be able to mate and procreate the way Mother Nature intended.

*I can't, John. . . . I'm dyslexic.*

For the next few days, when he had free time in the office, he logged on to various Web sites and read about Isabelle's handicap. He couldn't remember hearing the word "dyslexic" when they were kids, but he could remember talk of Izzy being dumb.

She was the least dumb person he could think of. Besides being some kind of wizard with horses, she was a loving, responsible mother and the most interesting companion he'd had.

And she was articulate. John marveled at how well spoken she was and how she had been able to function so successfully despite a limited ability to read and write. Now he had the explanation for the bookcase filled with audiobooks, the explanation for Ava's puzzling remarks about reading to her mother.

He didn't know how he could admire Izzy more, but knowing the impediment she lived with and overcame daily and the effort she had invested through the years to become knowledgeable of words and books only elevated her in his eyes.

And, he feared, in his heart.

He couldn't remember being happier. Thoughts of her used so much space in his head, they left no room for him to worry over his uncertain future or his lack of money.

He walked around in a perpetual state of sexual awareness. Sex flowed like a deep, swift current between them, punctuating and underlying even simple conversation, though they managed to maintain a dispassionate facade in Ava's presence. John wondered if, as smart as that kid was, she had her mother's relationship with him figured out.

Today, he felt horny as a billy goat. Isabelle had been having her period for nearly a week. Six days. It was too weird, considering that until her, he had gone without sex for a long time. He went to sleep Wednesday night wondering if he would be spending the next morning in her bed or working her horses.

A call from her awakened him early. "It's over," she said.

A prayer answered. He couldn't stop a wicked laugh. "Is this a come-on?"

"What do you think?"

"It'll take me about twenty minutes to shower and shave."

"Don't," she said. "Come as you are. I'm waiting."

He threw on his clothes, left his apartment with a hard-on and drove like a madman all the way to her house. She answered his knock on the back door, naked as the day she was born.

A burst of pure testosterone shot through his blood. His dick turned to steel.

As he shed his jacket she took hold of his waistband and tugged him into the mudroom. Giggling, she unhooked his belt buckle and undid his jeans.

Laughing with her, he threw his jacket on top of the washing machine. His pulse pounded in his dick and he gave the washer and dryer a second look. The top of the washing machine was good, just the right height.

"Don't even think about it," she said, as if she read his mind. She pulled him on into the kitchen and pressed her bare body against his, wound her arms around his neck and kissed him, shoving her tongue all the way to his tonsils.

He peeled her off him, laughing and swearing. "Damn you, woman."

She giggled more, sliding both her hands into his shorts and grasping his straining erection. "Hmm, I knew you'd be glad to see me."

"Oh, Jesus, don't pump."

She didn't, but she stroked with her fingers. "I've been thinking about this all night," she said huskily.

Too late to go slow. He groaned and shuddered and kissed her again. When they stopped for breath, he gripped her ass, lifted her feet off the floor, half stumbled and half carried her up to the hall to the bedroom, kicked open the door and tumbled her onto the bed.

Still laughing, she scuttled backward, up to the headboard, and flopped back against the blue pillows. For a moment he just looked at her, stopped by how he loved seeing her. Flaming hair draped over the pillow like a beckoning hot fire, rosy nipples, peaked and ready for his mouth, perched at the tips of perfect round breasts. A glint of a gold earring peeked from beneath her flurry of hair. His gaze moved down to her smooth, flat belly, to the triangle of red curls at her groin.

"Christ, Isabelle," he choked out, "you take my breath." He bent over and pried off his boot, hopping on one foot while he kept his eyes on her.

Her mouth curved into a lazy smile. She raised her arms and gripped the headboard, cocked her legs and let her knees fall open, exposing the pink petals of her sex, glistening with moisture.

*Oh, Jesus.*

He hopped on the other foot, tugging at the second boot, nearly losing his balance.

"Watch," she said, running her hands over her breasts. She plucked at her nipples with her fingers. While one hand continued to play with one nipple, the other moved down her belly. Her palm covered her mound, her middle finger pushed into her opening and he thought his brain might explode. With a sly smile, she withdrew her finger and began to rub herself.

Christ, he was shaking all over. He shucked his jeans and shorts in one motion, didn't take time to tear off his shirt or his socks. He crawled onto the bed, between her knees and crouched over her. "I'm not gonna last a minute," he said.

Her hands fisted in his hair and she pushed his head down. *Oh, yeah.* He slid his hands under her ass, lifted her to his mouth and plunged his tongue into her silky sweetness.

"Oh!" Her body arched up and she pushed herself against his face. "Oh, John ..."

Before his blood pressure burst his skull, he forced himself to calm down to a slow tongue-fuck, suckling and titillating, deliberately teasing her, deliberately avoiding the magic button.

She whimpered and squirmed against his mouth. "John ... please ..."

He was too lost in delicious pursuit to reply. He knew what she wanted, but he clutched her hips and thwarted her attempts to relocate his mouth until she began to beg in earnest. Only then did he slide his tongue upward and answer her plea. She came long and hard, sobbing and clawing his shoulders. He hung on the painful edge, his balls drawn clear up in his belly.

Then her hands were pulling at him, urging him upward. "Inside me," she panted. "Hurry!"

He climbed her body, frantically trying to lick and touch her everywhere at once. When he reached her mouth, he kissed her savagely and she matched his ardor.

Then, all at once he was there, hovering above her, braced on his elbows, his cock throbbing and ready. And she was wet and slick and open and lifting herself to him. Her hands reached between them and steered him into her. Her lazy-lidded eyes locked onto his and all he had to do was push.

He barely glided into her before her hot flesh tightened and swallowed him. Searing pressure swelled in his belly. *Rubber! Shit!*

She came again, panting and humping him hard, her muscles milking his cock.

He gritted his teeth and tried to pull out, but her legs were locked around him. "Izzy, let me—I'm not wearing—"

Release charged through him like a mad bull. He held his breath and tried to fight it, but lost the battle. On their own, his hips pumped once, twice and on a guttural cry, he plunged and spurted every drop of his essence inside her.

His trembling arms gave way and he dropped on top of her, gasping in short bursts against her shoulder. "Oh, shit. . . . Oh, God, Isabelle. I'm sorry. . . . I didn't intend—"

"Oooh, John. . . . That was sooo good."

Their bodies were slick with sweat. He could feel her breath hot against his neck, her legs still wrapped around his hips.

Her hands smoothed over his shoulders and down his back. "You're sooo good. I feel like lightning struck me."

"Izzy, you didn't let me—I couldn't pull out." Breaking free, he rolled off her, still struggling for oxygen. He threw the back of his hand against his damp forehead. Shit, what had he done?

She curled to her side and began unbuttoning his shirt. "You've got too many clothes on." She grasped his arm and urged him to a sitting position.

Spent of energy and strength, he allowed her to slip his shirt off, then his T-shirt.

"Isabelle, we have to—"

"Shh." She placed fingertips that smelled sexy and earthy on his lips, then moved down and stripped off his socks. "Come into this bed"—she scooted between the covers and opened them into a tent—"and put your arms around me."

He did as she ordered, stretched along the length of her and drew her close, placing his wet, sticky, flaccid penis against her wet, sticky belly. The scent of sex ballooned from beneath the covers. He gave a deep sigh. He was home. "Damn, Isabelle. You turn me into a crazy man."

She buried her face against his armpit and inhaled deeply.

"I love how you smell," she whispered. "That's why I didn't want you to shower." She brushed his mouth with her lips, then settled into a long, slow kiss with lots of tongue. He didn't participate as much as he might have if he hadn't been sick with concern.

"Stop worrying," she said softly. "It's okay. It's only the seventh day."

As a man who had fathered two unplanned children, the information gave him no comfort. "Hah."

"My cycle's very regular."

Years had gone by since he'd had sex without a rubber. He had even been sheathed in latex when Cody was conceived. He had always heard careless foreplay could be as risky as penetration and the conception of his second child proved it. "I should have had more sense."

"I'd rather hear you say you were insane with desire." She ran her tongue around one of his nipples.

"I did say that. My God, Isabelle, I am.... And you're doing it again." He couldn't believe, after what had just happened, that he already wanted her again. "I don't know what I'm gonna do. I think about you day and night. I went without for over a year, didn't even want it. Now, I walk around with a hard-on half the time."

She smiled with rosy and swollen lips, laid her cheek on his chest and covered his swelling penis with her hand. "I sort of like you, too."

He looked down at her tousled curls draping his chest astonished at how quickly life-altering events occurred. At this very moment, his little swimmers could be penetrating one of her eggs. As fraught with difficulties as the prospect was, some macho part of him was having trouble not being thrilled by that. "You're a brat." He cupped her head with his hand. "If you get pregnant, Isabelle"—he drew a deep breath—"you don't have to worry. It's not a problem."

A total lie. He could scarcely feed himself and pay his child support, much less provide for a wife and another child. But at the same time, the notion of a part of him growing inside Isabelle didn't scare him. Nor did taking on responsibility for her and Ava.

"It'd be a huge problem. I'm not going to get pregnant. But even if I did, I'd deal with it."

*What the hell did that mean?* "No. *We'd* deal with it. The two of us. Promise me, Isabelle. No sudden moves."

"I promise."

\* \* \*

Isabelle nuked leftover tuna casserole for lunch. They were quiet as they sat side by side at the table and ate. He was upset, she knew, over the risk they had taken. With her consent and even at her encouragement, they had made love a second time without protection. Long and slow and wonderful. With his hot, bare flesh melded with hers, it had ended with a tangle of heat and profound emotion, each intensifying the other to a point that bordered on pain and she had wept in his arms. Something between them had changed.

"My mom and dad," he said, "have a couple of 'kid' horses they're getting in shape for when Trey and Cody come for the summer."

The announcement blindsided her. "Your sons are coming for the summer?"

"It's part of the revised custody agreement I made with Julie when she moved them to California."

Isabelle's mind spun backward, trying to recall when she had last heard him mention his family. "Wow. You haven't said much about your sons. Or your ex-wife."

Without a word, he put down his fork, reached back and brought forth a brown leather billfold, as if doing it was something dreaded but inevitable. He opened the billfold to two yellowed acetate sleeves holding what looked like school pictures of two handsome boys. The older child had white-blond hair and green eyes with a striking resemblance to the father. The younger boy, with hair more golden, had dark brown eyes.

Isabelle looked at him. "Was your ex brown-eyed?"

He nodded and returned to his food, leaving her pondering if his marrying a brown-eyed woman was nothing more than a coincidence or if it had some significant Zen meaning that went all the way back to the teenage crush he'd had on brown-eyed Isabelle Rondeau.

When he offered no words to carry the subject of his children or his ex-wife further, an unexpected pang pierced her. Though it was none of her business, she wanted to know the true "why" his ex had cheated. But looking into his face, all she could see was a shutter closing. She rose and gathered her dishes. "They look like great kids."

"I thought Ava would like to go riding," he said, still sitting at the table and looking across the room at her as she rinsed her plate under the faucet.

Clever how smoothly he skimmed past discussing his family. Isabelle dredged a smile from the emotions that had begun piling up inside her like debris from a storm. "I'm sure she'd love it."

He stood then and brought his plate to her. "Since Rooster's taking the early shift Saturday, we could go out to Mom and Dad's, as long as I get back to town by six."

How he had ignored a conversation about his family as if she hadn't said anything was enough to make her dizzy. "Okay, I guess." She took the plate from him and placed it in the sink.

"It's a plan, then. I'll tell Mom and Dad."

Isabelle nodded.

"Walk me out," he said.

She dried her hands, slipped her arm around his hip and hooked her thumb in his waistband. He looped his arm around her shoulder and they moved through the living room to the front door. There, he held her against his chest for what seemed like a long while. She could hear his heart beating against his sternum. Until a few minutes ago she had felt that strong heart belonged to her. Now she wondered. If he cared about her, wouldn't he have discussed something like his children coming for the summer?

A minute later he kissed her good-bye and left with nothing more than an "I'll call you." He hadn't departed so abruptly since the first time they had kissed in the barn, weeks back. She watched from the living room windows as he made his way down her long driveway.

Anxiety danced inside her. Sometimes her slutty side raised its uninhibited head and she just gave in to it. Her good-little-girl side berated her for putting John in this predicament. He would have been more responsible if she hadn't teased him and egged him on.

Still, her slutty side refused to regret. Just the opposite.

She had thoroughly enjoyed herself and she had enjoyed John. In truth, they had enjoyed each other. He had been as unbridled as she, which was very unbridled indeed.

. The pleasure she took from sex went deeper than satisfying a biological urge. It had been one of the few areas of her life where her appearance or her intelligence hadn't made so much difference. For a girl who grew up believing herself an ugly duckling, who had drawn the short straw on parents and whose peers called her dumb, sex had leveled the playing field. Firsthand knowledge made her feel wiser and more sophisticated than classmates who looked down on her because of her grades or her wild hair. Or her family.

Knowing that Billy Bledsoe—all the girls called him "hunk" or "stud" or something like that—wanted her body without criticism or condition had been a boost to her short supply of self-esteem. Naturally they all said the only reason Billy hung out with her was because she put out.

Now that she was older, she knew the real reason Billy hung out with her. He was weak; she was strong. He had needed her strength. It was that simple. The human community wasn't so different from animal communities. There was always a dominant member, usually the strongest and smartest animal, the alpha male or female. It was part of the mating process.

*If you get pregnant*... The possibility of motherhood had been absent from her life for so long, she couldn't drum herself into hysterics over it now. Nor could she feel that a baby with a man like John would be a disaster—except, of course, for how it would affect Ava and the fact that they now lived in a town where every citizen inserted himself into every other citizen's life, invited or not.

She disliked causing John worry. He was the best man she had ever known. Not only was he handsome and a wonderful, considerate lover, he had a rare, quiet strength she revered. Her feeling for him had grown to something deeper than she had expected.

Or wanted.

Until now, that is.

# Chapter 19

Failing to use protection on Thursday had been a mistake, but John left Izzy's house sensing that wasn't the only error he had made. Her attitude when he picked her and Ava up on Saturday morning confirmed his concern. She was almost as standoffish as she had been the first day he saw her when he went out to check into the dog shooting.

Not that she was mean or hateful—just bristly.

The horseback ride turned out great. What could go wrong on a sunny day in the mountains? They rode along the shoulders of Sterling Mountain through a landscape of new spring growth and endless blue sky. He insisted Isabelle ride his rope horse, Rowdy, and teased her about "riding a good horse for a change."

She didn't so much as grin.

The horse his mom assigned to Ava—a bay gelding named Pancho—was a dream horse for a kid. As they rode, she went into a long explanation of the differences between Western saddles and the smaller English equipment. Where a ten-year-old got all the information that floated around Ava Rondeau's head, John didn't know.

After the ride, John volunteered to haul Pancho to Isabelle's for Ava to ride at will, but Isabelle declined the offer, telling him that keeping a man's horse in her corral was a little like giving the guy a permanent place at the table. *Ouch.*

John's mother spread joy all over them. He hadn't brought a woman to visit since before he married Julie. Mom met them at the barn on their return and invited Isabelle and Ava into the house for a Coke or coffee while John unsaddled.

His mother's welcome didn't come as a surprise, nor did his dad's noticeable absence. John was unsaddling when his dad came into the barn.

"Good ride?"

"Great. Grass up in the foothills looks good."

Dad nodded and hung his elbow on a stall door. Something was stuck in his craw, for sure. It didn't take a genius to know it was Isabelle. "You might as well say it and get it over with," John told him.

"Well... I'm just wondering what you're doing with that Rondeau woman."

His dad knew the relationship with Isabelle was more than casual or he wouldn't have brought up the subject. He pulled Isabelle's saddle off Rowdy's back. "That's between her and me."

"Art's already had a falling-out with her."

Still irritated when he thought about the incident that had taken him to Isabelle's house the first time, John turned, resting a hand on Rowdy's back. "I don't know what Art told you, Dad, but he shot her dog. It was a pretty little border collie. If there had been something I could've done about that, I would have. It tore the little girl up."

His dad looked away. He had border collies himself and it would have been out of character for him to wish ill on a kid. "Well... Art gets carried away sometimes.... But he's not wrong about that Rondeau bunch. Paul Rondeau—"

"I'm not seeing Paul."

"An apple doesn't fall far from the tree, son. Just don't forget that."

John puffed his cheeks, blowing out a breath. "We done?"

"That's all I'm gonna say. I promised your mother." His dad walked out of the barn.

Unfazed, John watched him walk away. In truth, his dad had thought no better of Julie, had considered her a gold digger from the first. Perhaps he hadn't been wrong about Julie, but he was way off base with his negative opinion of Isabelle. The only things Julie and Isabelle had in common were they were both female and they both had brown eyes.

Only a clone of Katie Bradshaw, John suspected, would please his dad. It dawned on John that Isabelle came close.

By the time he retrieved Isabelle and Ava from his mom's kitchen and started the drive home, Isabelle had grown even more distant. They reached her house and he began to help her take her gear to the tack room. "I don't need your help. I can do it," she told him.

His mom had given Ava some books and a couple of videos. To John's relief, she took them and skedaddled to the house, giving him an opportunity to corner Isabelle in the tack room. "What's wrong, Isabelle?"

She whirled to face him, fury burning in her eyes. "I'll tell you what's wrong. Why don't you want me to meet your kids? You think I'm not good enough?"

Shocked, John blinked and tucked back his chin. "Where'd you get *that* idea?"

"You didn't even tell me you'll be spending your time with them all summer."

He shook his head. "I wasn't ready to discuss it."

"You intended to hide me under a rock for three months?"

"No. I want you to meet them. When it's right."

"I wonder if you've been honest with me, John."

"I haven't lied to you. About anything."

"By omission, John. By omission. I saw how your dad behaved toward us. I should've known better than to go to his house. I know he's always been friends with Art Karadimos." Her eyes teared up, but she sniffed and dashed them with her sleeve.

Lord, he hated to see her cry. Bewildered, he moved closer to her. "What do you think I haven't told you?"

"What you're planning with your kids, how you feel about your divorce. Any of it."

"I haven't discussed my divorce with anybody, Isabelle. I'm still sorting through it."

She began to pace the tack room. "What's to sort through? If it's over, then it's over. That's what I'm talking about."

Was she jealous? Did she think he harbored hidden feelings for his ex-wife? He put his hands on her shoulders and stopped her pacing. "Isabelle, isn't it enough that I don't have anything to do with Julie except for the kids?"

"It isn't her. It's me. I don't want to be walked out on ever again. Getting past it took too damn long. It was too damn hard." She stepped away from his hands. "I'd rather be alone for the rest of my life than go through that again."

"Don't you think the same applies to me? Hell, I didn't even know my wife had a boyfriend until I walked into my own house and found the sonofabitch in my bed."

She stopped pacing and stared at him, wide-eyed. He hadn't intended to blurt out that information, but now that he had, he felt compelled to continue. "I came home a day early from the show in Pendleton and—" He stopped, his explanation overcome by the memory of walking up the hall and seeing the bedroom door that wasn't usually closed tightly shut, then opening it and seeing a man he didn't know scrabbling for his pants. He had tried for a time to drown the memory in alcohol. To this day, when it came back to him, self-doubt assailed him.

"You loved her, then."

"I don't know. I just believe when a woman gives birth to your kids, it has to mean something. . . . Then again, maybe not. It sure didn't mean as much to her as it did to me."

She crossed her arms and looked at the tack room floor. "I'm sorry. I don't know what came over me. I shouldn't have—" She straightened and started for the door, but stopped and looked at him over her shoulder. "Just to satisfy my curiosity, what did you, um . . . do?"

"Well, not what I wanted to, 'cause I couldn't see spending the rest of my life in jail. I punched the wimpy sonofabitch in the jaw and threw his naked ass outside."

Isabelle blinked. "You're kidding."

He saw mirth in her eyes. He couldn't share in the humor, but he guessed the scene did have its funny side. "Julie gathered up his clothes and took them to him."

"Where were your kids?"

"At her sister's. When I cooled off and came to my senses, I figured out the guy had been at my house all weekend and that wasn't the first time he'd been in my bed. Hell, for all I know, he used my toothpaste and my spare razor. The signs were there. I was just too preoccupied to see them."

"So you got a divorce."

"Not right away. We went to marriage counseling."

Isabelle's eyes questioned him.

"Nope, didn't work. What she *said* she wanted was for me to quit rodeoing. But what she really wanted was that dude she'd brought into my bed. The counselor figured that out in two visits. Deep down, I already knew it, too. Julie always believed she was a cut above the rodeo crowd."

Isabelle closed her eyes, frowned and pinched the bridge of her nose. "Damn," she said under her breath, then looked up at him. "Come on over to the house. I'll cook supper."

Confused, he cocked his head and gave her a narrow-lidded look. "I don't know. Are you mad?"

"No. But I will be if you don't stay and eat supper.... And if I don't get to meet your kids."

*Women.* If he lived to be a hundred, he would never understand them. As they walked, he looped his arm around her shoulder and tucked her close to his side. "Don't be mad at me, okay? I'm the only member of my family to ever get a divorce. I'm still coming to terms with the whole mess. As for my kids, they'll be lucky to get to spend time with you."

Isabelle cooked her mother's chicken-fried steak recipe for supper, one she knew from memory. Along with canned green beans, frozen biscuits and cream gravy she made from scratch, the meal turned out edible. Or, at least it appeared so because John ate until he was stuffed and had no room for the brownies Ava had made. Ava wrapped some up for him to take home.

They cleared off the table and played Trivial Pursuit, where John's competitive nature manifested itself. Ava challenged him with a vengeance and he barely defeated her. Isabelle's daughter had a competitive streak almost as fierce as her mother's. Isabelle was lost in a game like Trivial Pursuit, so she mostly worked at providing refreshments and participated as an "also-ran."

After John left, she lay awake under the blue patchwork quilt staring out at the three-quarter moon that looked like she could reach up and pluck it from the star-dusted sky. The visual of a furious John throwing a naked man out of his house made her grin in the dark. John was over six feet tall, must weigh two-ten or two-twenty and was solid as a rock. He was so easygoing she couldn't imagine him in a temper fit, but she could imagine it would be a terrifying sight.

As a caring, sensitive man, he must have been crushed by his ex-wife cheating on him, especially if he loved her.

Cheating spouses. She could never have cheated on Billy and they weren't even married. She'd had chances, though. The bored, rich horse crowd was notorious for its swinging lifestyle. More than one millionaire had made her an offer many sane and practical women couldn't and didn't refuse.

It would have served Billy right if she had taken up with someone else, but that kind of disloyalty didn't live within her soul. Even after his being a player became common knowledge, she still couldn't turn her back on him. He was the father of her only child and they had been together since she was fourteen years old. His presence had been as much a part of her as one of her limbs. She had foolishly thought that at some point he would wake up and come to his senses. Stupid. And a waste of time.

Now that the shock of his leaving had passed and the fear for her and Ava's welfare consumed only half her waking moments instead of all of them, she knew at the ripe old age of thirty-five that she hadn't been in love with Billy. Oh, she had cared about him, but more than anything he had been a means to an end. She didn't like thinking of herself as having used him, but if she hadn't had him to take her away from Callister, she couldn't guess what might have been her fate. Even if she hadn't loved him in a bells-ringing, heavens-opening kind of way, she owed him gratitude for rescuing her.

What she felt for John Bradshaw was different. Just seeing him striding across the corral, his chaps flapping, his spurs clinking, filled her heart to its brim. His very touch turned her into one of those silly, giggling females who had always revolted her. And sex. He was hot and skilled and earthy in all the ways she liked. And gentle and loving and sensitive in all the ways any woman would like.

She had stepped out on a long limb. After swearing to stay as far away from men as possible, and cowboys especially, here she was, bowled over and knocked flat by the ultimate cowboy...

... Who was also the county sheriff.

And that fact might be the most vexing. The law and the Rondeaus had always had a borderline relationship.

Her thoughts veered to Paul. She hadn't seen him in two weeks, but his boat was missing from its parking place beside his travel trailer. She presumed he was fishing, which was a good thing. He had always found himself—or lost himself— in the vastness of the outdoors.

John spent a busy week. He settled two domestic disputes, investigated a horse-neglect case, accompanied the fire truck to fight a house fire. Plus, he had gone out to the vet's clinic and assisted the vet and Izzy in breeding two more of Luke's mares and Trixie. Come next spring, blue horses would be popping up all over the county. He and Isabelle had also managed to sneak in a lunchtime quickie in his apartment.

As usual, he ended his workday Sunday with the calendar, making up a work schedule. He had put a small red mark on the twenty-seventh, the day he calculated Izzy would get her next period. Not that he expected her not to.

Only ten days had passed since they had been so careless. Nine more days to wait and worry.

They hadn't discussed the "what if" once. She didn't seem the least bit anxious. He tried to let her casual attitude seep into him, but the possibility of her being pregnant did more than give him pause. It forced him to give serious consideration to what he wanted for the rest of his life.

His feeling for Julie had been all tangled up with devotion to the two kids they brought into the world. While he loved the kids, the emotion with Julie had no solid seat in his soul. The feeling he had for Isabelle was as pure as it had been when he was fifteen, a part of him, like the marrow in his bones. Isabelle had been the one from the first day he started paying attention to the differences between boys and girls. Without knowing it, she had been the first to teach him that plumbing so different from his brought a passel of pain as well as pleasure.

He tried to visualize a child he and Izzy would produce. Would he or she be athletic and competitive like him and Izzy? Or brainy like Ava? All that intelligence in Ava's head had to come from Izzy. None of the Bledsoes had ever been especially smart. Would his and Izzy's kid have a mop of wild red hair and coffee-colored eyes or would they be tow-headed like his boys?

He wouldn't call himself a romantic, but some things were meant to be. And if it was meant for him and Isabelle to be together, then it could also be meant for them to have kids. He couldn't quarrel with the possibility.

# Chapter 20

The warble of the phone brought John awake from a sound sleep. His clock radio showed eleven thirty and caller ID showed the Eights & Aces Saloon. John groaned and answered. The bartender on the other end of the line reported a loud disturbance and a fight brewing.

Still half asleep, John got to his feet and pulled on the clothes he had removed earlier, strapped on his pistol and grabbed a jacket. As a last-minute thought, he plucked a pair of handcuffs he had rarely used off the coatrack by the back door. If the bartender thought things were bad enough to call him at nearly midnight, somebody could be going to jail.

He headed out, thinking about his own drinking days. Since yow-yowing and fighting hadn't been his style, he hadn't realized how much trouble drunks could be.

He reached the bar in a matter of minutes, but too late to prevent the fight. Elbowing through the throng of onlookers and agitators, he saw the two combatants on the wooden floor, grunting, flailing fists and tearing at each other's clothing. To John's dismay, he recognized one of them as Izzy's little brother. The opponent was a stranger.

On a surge of adrenaline, John waded into the fray, gripped a fistful of the back of Paul's shirt and hauled him to his feet. The tree-faller blindly threw a fist. John ducked, but the wild blow glanced off his jaw.

*Fuck!* John flung him against the bar. "Paul! Cool it!"

John swerved his attention to the other man, whose nose was gushing blood, making a bib pattern on the front of his light-colored shirt. The guy teetered on his feet, his arms hanging as if disconnected from his shoulders.

"You need a doctor?" John asked him.

The stranger staggered to the edge of the bar and the bartender thrust a towel across the bartop. The injured man used it to cover his nose and dragged himself to the far end of the bar. Anybody could see he had lost the will to fight and he was outmatched. Paul wasn't a big guy, but his body was compact and muscular. Years of wielding a heavy chain saw and wrestling behemoth trees had made him strong as a Titan and John had always suspected the guy had rattlesnake blood in his veins.

A cut on Paul's cheek was bleeding slightly. He swiped it with the back of his hand, smearing a crimson stain across his face. "Just 'cause you're fuckin' my sister," he cried, "don't mean you can push me around."

*Jee-zus Christ!* Paul was shit-faced drunk. John restrained himself from punching his mouth. He gripped his shirt in his fist, shoved him down onto a barstool and pressed him back against the bar's edge. "Goddammit, I said cool it!" John turned to the other man. "What's your na—?"

"John! Look out!"

The shout came from behind the bar. John whirled just in time to get a glimpse of a blade in Paul's hand. He jerked backward, but not far enough or quick enough. The knife swiped across his midsection, caught his shirt and scraped his stomach.

Anger turned to rage, mixing with the dose of adrenaline already buzzing in his system. He grabbed Paul's wrist and forced the smaller man to the floor with sheer brute strength, breaking his grip on the knife handle. He reached behind himself for the handcuffs, locked Paul's hands behind his back and hauled him to his feet.

Now slumped on a barstool, Paul's opponent sat holding the towel to his nose.

"What's your name?" John barked.

The man mumbled through the towel, "Larry . . . Atkins."

"You're not from around here."

Atkins shook his head. "Come to see my sister."

"Who's your sister?"

"JoAnn Howard."

John knew the woman's husband. He turned to the bartender. "Call Bob Howard. Tell him I said come get his brother-in-law and take him over to the hospital to see the doc." He turned back to Atkins. "You don't move 'til Bob gets here."

A line of pain stung John's stomach on his left side. He looked down and saw a ragged tear in his shirt. *Fuck!* He stooped and picked up the knife, a heavy hunting type. Paul had sat down on a barstool again. John yanked the little fucker to his feet by the shirt. "C'mon, loudmouth. You're spending the night in a cell."

After John locked Paul into one of the two cells in the courthouse basement, he stamped to his office, his whole body abuzz. His stomach burned like a bitch. His jaw ached. Bloodstains showed at the ragged tear on his shirt a few inches above and to the left of his belt buckle, but he felt energized and loaded for bear, euphoric even.

Amazing substance, adrenaline. He had felt the rush many times, poised on the back of a charged-up horse behind a barrier in a narrow chute, waiting for a calf to cut loose. As much as anything, the high that lingered long after his seven-to-ten-second run under the bright lights had driven him to soak the letdown in a fifth of Crown Royal.

For blood to have soaked through both his T-shirt and his outer shirt, he must be bleeding heavily. He shucked the jacket and threw it on the desk chair, plopped his hat on top of the filing cabinet, then went to the small storeroom where medical supplies were kept. On a shelf near the first-aid kit lay a bulletproof vest he had put on once for size. He admonished himself. If he had worn it tonight he could have avoided being cut by a drunk's knife.

He unholstered his .45, removed his belt and whipped off the outer shirt. A damp football-shaped bloodstain had blossomed around a tear on his white T-shirt. He pulled the T-shirt over his head and examined a clean five-inch laceration just above his waist. The cut wasn't deep enough to need stitches, though it was more than a scratch.

He knew first aid, had helped a fair share of rodeo cowboys patch themselves up after injuries. Inside the storage cabinet, he found some gauze pads and a bottle of peroxide. He soaked a wad of gauze with peroxide and swabbed away blood, wincing and gritting his teeth as the peroxide set fire to the wound. Even after he cleaned the injury, blood still oozed, so he pawed through the supplies until he found a tube of antibiotic ointment. He made a long thick bandage from a few of the gauze pads, squeezed on a line of antibiotic and taped it onto his stomach, mumbling and cussing the whole time. Hell, it was a wonder he hadn't been killed.

He trashed the T-shirt and put on his outer shirt, then took a close look in the mirror. As poor as the single overhead light was in the bathroom, he could see a red patch showing on his jaw. He couldn't tell if it would be followed by a bruise.

After working his jaw and determining he had no loose teeth or broken bone, he returned to his desk where he had dropped Paul's knife on the blotter. He picked up the weapon and turned it over on his palm. It looked to be a custom-made job. He ran his thumb along the blade. Jesus Christ, it was sharp as a razor. No wonder it had cut through both his shirt and his T-shirt. Fortunately, only the tip of the blade had caught him. He threw the knife into his bottom desk drawer and locked it, then leaned back in his chair and just sat there, summoning calm.

As his heartbeat slowed, he thought of Izzy. *Christ.* Her own brother had smeared her reputation in front of a dozen or more onlookers and he, John, had been unable to do a damn thing to prevent it. He didn't have the heart to tell her.

But he had to tell her he had jailed Paul. She worried over the little fucker day and night.

For the first time in a year, John wished he had a drink.


"You what?" A shot of fear ripped through Isabelle's heart. She stared at the clock. Twelve forty-five a.m. "Who—who was he fighting with?" She hadn't seen her brother since the day he had walked in on her with John.

"I dunno. Some kid from out of town."

She lunged to her feet and stumbled to the dresser, tearing off the T-shirt she slept in as she went. She jerked open a drawer and reached for underwear. "Was he hurt?"

"Who, Paul? You couldn't hurt him with an axe handle." Propping the phone under her chin, she pulled on panties. "The other person?"

"Paul beat the shit out of him. I sent him to the ER with his brother-in-law."

Isabelle closed her eyes and drew a deep breath. She knew too well that Paul could be a loose cannon, and more times than not there had been no one but her to take his side. Big-sisterly need to come to his defense surged within her. She grabbed the jeans she had been wearing earlier off a chair back and stuffed her legs into them. "You arrested Paul, but not the other person?"

"He took a swipe at me with a knife, Isabelle."

"What kind of knife?" She pictured the scabbard she had often seen attached to Paul's belt. She should have come back to Callister long ago, when perhaps she could have made a difference in her brother's attitude and behavior.

"He had a hunting knife a foot long."

She had never looked closely at the knife. "That's nothing. It probably wouldn't cut butter."

"Oh, it'd cut butter all right. Fact is, it cut me pretty good."

Isabelle's heart yo-yoed to her knees and back. "You? . . . Wh-where?"

"My stomach. But don't worry about it. It's no big deal."

She fought back a sob. "Oh, John, I'm sorry."

"Isabelle," he said softly, "don't be upset. I said it's no big deal. I fixed it up with a bandage. It's okay."

Relieved to hear he wasn't seriously hurt, her mind jumped to a picture of her brother behind bars. "Well . . . well, you have to let him out, John."

"I can't. He's got too many priors. I'm gonna have to leave it up to the judge."

Paul had had run-ins with the law through the years, but she had no idea how serious they had been or what might be on his record. Panic closed in. Wounding the sheriff with a knife had to be more than a simple matter. If John charged him... "But you know he's harmless. He just drank too much."

"Taking a swipe at me with a knife isn't the act of a harmless individual. I could've maybe let it slide if all he'd done was get into a drunk fight, but the knife adds a new dimension. It's assault and battery. A felony. He assaulted an officer of the law, Isabelle."

Too many times, Isabelle had heard John belittle the job he held. She felt her hackles rise as the need to stand up for her little brother pushed her. "Officer of the law. Who are you trying to kid, John Bradshaw? You don't know any more about the law than I do. I'm coming to town to pick him up."

"Isabelle, don't. Please don't. I can't release him. Not for you or anybody. It's my job."

"You don't even care about the damn job. You're waiting for it to end so you can go on to something else."

"I know it may look that way and I may have even said it, but I have to do what I have to do. Sometimes I think Paul's a scary guy, Isabelle."

"Oh, really? And what do you think of me? Do you think I'm scary, too? When you lie down beside me, do you fear you're in bed with some kind of crazy?"

"This has nothing to do with you and—"

"Oh, but it does. It puts the differences between the Rondeaus and the Bradshaws nicely into perspective. As if your dad hadn't done that already."

"Jesus, Isabelle, that's not fair."

"You know what I think? I think reality has finally dropped on both of us. Just tell me when I can come and get my brother."

"It's the middle of the night. I'll have to run down a judge first thing in the morning. I can ask him to do a bail hearing on the phone. If Paul's got the money, he can probably post bail."

"Well... if he doesn't have it, I do."

"Isabelle, you shouldn't—"

"I know what you're going to say and I don't want to hear it. I'll be there in the morning. Just tell me what time."

"I don't know. On a Saturday, I'll have to catch a judge at home. I guess you'll have to wait for me to call you."

Panic and frustration beat in her chest. How could she deal with her brother getting drunk and injuring a man she cared about? How could she deal with that same man intent on locking up her brother? She couldn't abandon her brother. She couldn't help him and continue to see John. Their relationship was too difficult. It had to end. "Just make sure that you do."

*Click!* She hung up in his ear. Shit.

Suddenly John felt exhausted. The rollaway bed in the horse stall of a bedroom up the hall seemed a mile away. He forced himself to his feet and managed to make it to the tiny room carrying his pistol. He didn't expect a jailbreak, but under the circumstances and considering where he would lay his head, only a fool wouldn't keep his gun handy.

In the courthouse basement, with no windows, the room was dark enough to scare a bat. He left the door ajar so he could hear noise from the office or jail cells and so the light from the office would steal up the hall and into the bedroom.

His stomach hurt, his jaw hurt. Izzy was pissed off at him. He pried off his boots, then tucked the .45 under an extra pillow. He lay back with a groan and pulled the bed's one blanket over himself. The idea that he should see a doctor flitted past. No telling what Paul had last cut with that knife.

He closed his eyes, but sleep eluded him. His memory kept jumping back to childhood, a rare occurrence until hooking up with Izzy. He thought of the times he had seen Paul Rondeau come to school in ragged, hand-me-down clothes that didn't fit. He often had bruises. It was common talk that his dad whipped him hard, but no one ever said why. Back then, John couldn't relate. His dad had never struck him. His parents had loved him and provided everything they could afford.

A sullen, troublesome little kid, Paul made mostly failing grades, but no teacher who had ever had him in a classroom wanted to retain him. The system moved him on, like a conveyor belt in a warehouse. Social promotion, they called it these days. After eighth grade, Paul quit school altogether and went to work fixing flats at the Exxon station and John lost all but occasional track of him.

A vague memory of Paul and Izzy's dad formed in John's mind, a swarthy, burly man felling trees in the summer months, then through the winter sweeping up after hours in various businesses in town. And drinking up his wages in Tall Timbers or the Eights & Aces.

*Izzy.* In those days, if Paul had been getting beat up by his dad, what had been happening to Izzy?

The next sound he heard was Rooster's voice. "John T., you okay?"

Startled, John sprang to his feet, his mind addled by a deep sleep. His head spun and the stomach injury nailed him with a stinging bite. He sank back to the thin mattress and braced an elbow on one knee, dropped his forehead into his palm. "Yeah, I'm okay."

"What's going on?"

"Nothing much. Just a fight." John glanced at his watch. Nine o'clock. "You make any coffee?"

"Pot's on." Rooster tilted his head toward the cell area. "I see Paul Rondeau back there. Snoring like a buzz saw when I came in. Who was he fighting?"

"Kid from out of town."

"Who got hurt?"

"Hurt?"

"The bathroom trash is full of bloody gauze. And a T-shirt. Who bled?"

As the cobwebs cleared from John's mind, he rubbed a palm over his morning stubble and sore jaw. He gave a humorless chuckle. "Would you believe it was me?"

The deputy's eyes grew wide. "No shit? What happened?"

John recounted the previous evening's incident. The deputy listened transfixed. "Man, oh, man. Ol' Paul's up a tree with a grizzly this time, ain't he?"

"I don't know about that, but he's damn sure crossways with me."

Rooster's eyes moved to the bloodstained tear in John's shirt. "You better have Doc Thornton take a look at that."

John shook his head. "I doctored it. It'll be all right." He pushed himself to his feet, feeling as stiff and achy as if he had been bucked off an ornery bronc. "Keep all this under your hat, Rooster, especially about the knife. I haven't figured out how to handle it yet."

Rooster peered up at him, uncertainty on his face. "You can hide that cut, John T., but what're you gonna tell the folks about the bruise on your jaw?"

John shot him a look.

The deputy lifted his shoulders in a shrug. "Just asking."

After he relieved himself, John checked his jaw in the tiny mirror on the front of the medicine cabinet and saw a faint half-dollar-sized bruise. Maybe nobody would spot it if he didn't shave. He worked his mouth sidewise, then open and closed it. Satisfied for the second time that all he had was a bruise, he went to the office and poured a mug of coffee.

Last night he hadn't filled out an arrest report and this morning he was glad. He had been on the job long enough to learn a county sheriff had broad leeway in the charges he brought against those he arrested. A decision, black as the hot coffee, brewed in his mind, but he wouldn't settle on it until he went home, showered and changed clothes.

He finished his coffee and set the empty mug in the bathroom sink. "If Isabelle calls before I get back," he said to Rooster, "tell her I'm at home."

The phone in his apartment didn't ring. He wasn't surprised.

He returned to the office clean and freshly bandaged, but unshaven. If folks saw through his whiskers and asked him about the bruise on his jaw, he would tell them it was none of their damn business.

Rooster reported that Paul had been fed breakfast from Betty's Road Kill. Knowing Paul, a café breakfast could have been the best meal he had eaten in a week.

As John approached the barred front of the cell, Paul, sitting on the cot, looked up at him with dark eyes so much like

Izzy's. Several days' growth of black whiskers showed on his jaw.

John opened the cell door and sat down beside his prisoner, who reeked of body odor and yeast. "I'm dropping the charge to disturbing the peace. I'm letting you out on your own recognizance."

"What's that mean?"

"The judge'll be up from Boise on Wednesday. It means I'm trusting you to show up in court at ten o'clock."

Paul's palms rested on his knees. He looked down at the dried bloodstains that covered his fingers. "You'd do that for me?"

John nodded. "If you don't show, I promise I'll hunt you down, Paul. Hope you've got some money. Since Judge Morrison's seen you before, he'll probably fine you heavy."

One side of Paul's mouth tipped up in a crooked grin. "You doing this 'cause you're fuckin' Izzy?"

In no mood for bullshit, John ignored the insult. His conscience and his duty had warred within him all morning. "I'm giving you a break. I don't need a reason."

Paul looked across the room at the gray concrete wall. "What about my knife?"

John couldn't believe he had heard right. The guy either had nothing under his hat but hair or he had more balls than anybody John had ever met. "What about it?"

Paul shrugged. "I need it. And it cost me a lot of money. Buck Brown made it."

"The knife's gone, buddy." John got to his feet, out of patience. "This is your last chance on my watch, Paul. Don't fuck it up. Clean up your act. You got a sister that cares about you. Do it for her sake as well as your own." John turned his back and stepped to the cell door. "Rooster'll do the paperwork to get you out of here."

"John?"

John stopped in the cell's doorway. "What?"

"I didn't get you with that knife, did I?"

John's jaw clenched. "No."

A soft *heh-heh-heh* came from Paul. "Well, that's good, I guess. Things is a little fuzzy. I thought I'd cut you."

A shiver ran all the way up and down John's spine. He didn't know if the man was relieved to hear he hadn't done serious bodily harm or was lamenting the fact that he had failed to. Was it a dangerous mistake letting a man as squirrely as Paul Rondeau off the hook?

# Chapter 21

John walked from the courthouse to Betty's Road Kill for breakfast. With a stiff body, a sore stomach and little sleep, he didn't feel up to facing Callister's citizens, but he didn't feel like hanging out in his dismal apartment either. Later, after Izzy had time to cool off, he would drive out to her house and discuss Paul.

When he returned to the sheriff's office after breakfast, Rooster had already cleaned up the empty cell. No sign of the prisoner remained. "Come on into the office," John told him. John shrugged out of his jacket, then unlocked his bottom drawer, removed Paul's knife and laid it on the desk blotter. "Take a look at this."

Rooster picked up the knife and turned it over in his hand, gripped it by the handle, tested it for weight, then gave a low whistle. "This is a Buck Brown knife." He handed the knife back to John and pointed out two *B*s engraved on the hilt.

"Paul said the same thing. Who's Buck Brown?"

"An old hippie up on Cabin Creek. He gets a pretty penny for his knives. Never could afford one myself."

"Yeah?" Curiosity aroused, John took back the knife and looked at it closer, hefted the weight of it. "From now on, it stays in the gun safe. You could gut an elk with it."

Rooster grinned. "Guess that's what Paul uses it for. In

hunting season or out." The deputy started for the door, but turned back. "You know ol' Paul pretty well, don't you?"

"We were in the same grade in school 'til he quit. Why?"

The deputy looked at the floor and shook his head. "Something about that little dude makes me twitchy."

*Twitchy.* Good description for how Paul affected John, too. "He drinks too much. Otherwise, I think he's all right."

As the words left his mouth, John wondered if they were a belief or a prayer.

"Guess so." Rooster gave up the discussion and left the office.

John hadn't had time to pick up the phone and call Izzy before he heard her voice in the anteroom. He walked out to where she stood hanging on to Ava's hand in front of Rooster's desk.

"Hey, Isa—"

"Where is he?" she demanded by way of greeting.

She was on edge. She wore no makeup and her face looked drawn and tired, like she had been awake since his midnight phone call. He wished he could take her in his arms and comfort her, but with her attitude about public displays of affection, he didn't want to embarrass her. Nor did he want to aggravate the already touchy situation.

Rooster spoke. "He didn't exactly draw us a map."

Her hot brown glare roasted the deputy, then swung to John. "You released him and you don't even know where he went?"

John clasped her elbow and urged her toward his office, speaking over his shoulder to Ava. "Wait out here for just a minute, okay?"

Rooster stood up and offered the kid a candy bar.

As John closed the office door, eager to explain Paul's circumstances, Isabelle yanked her arm free. "Don't man-handle me. This is the craziest thing I've ever heard."

"Tell me about it," John said, surprised at her ferocity. "Look, Paul's facing minor charges, nothing more. I could've—"

"What charges?"

"Misdemeanor drinking and disturbing the peace." He

met her eyes, hoping that when she heard Paul was in less trouble than he could have been, she would become less angry. Wrong. She continued to glare at him.

"What I started to say, Isabelle, is I could've charged him with something more serious. It's not right for me to make this personal, but it's hard not to when I'm . . . well, when I'm with you and when I've known him my whole life. And I feel for him."

When she didn't reply after a few beats he pushed on. "This isn't the first scrape he's been in. When he's drunk, he's mean and dangerous. He could kill some—"

"My brother isn't mean. Nor is he dangerous."

Her eyes and body might teem with defiance, but John recognized bravado when he saw it. As smart as Izzy was, she had to be scared for her brother. John ached to comfort her. "Okay, maybe he's not mean. But he's got the worst judgment I've ever seen in a grown man and he drinks too much."

She lifted her nose and crossed her arms over her chest. "I guess you should know about drinking too much."

John had heard the accusation many times, but coming from her, it hit a nerve. "Low blow, Isabelle. You've never seen me take a drink."

In an attempt to regain control of the conversation, he moved behind his desk and planted his fists on his belt, hoping he appeared authoritative. "I may not be a hotdog peace officer, but at the moment law and order in this town and this county are up to me." He offered a palm to accompany a forewarning. "I'll tell you the same thing I told Paul. He fucked up bad last night. If he does it again, I won't be able to cut him any slack. I won't have a choice."

Her eyes grew shiny as lumps of coal, her chin trembled. "This is my brother, John. My family. Don't you see? He's never had a chance."

Anger he could deal with. Tears were hard. He ducked her gaze, picked up Paul's thick file from his desk blotter and fanned through it. "He's had a lot of chances. All you have to do is look at his record. The law in this town has been turning a blind eye and giving him another chance since he was a kid."

She looked away. A pulse throbbed in her neck. "Wha-what happens now?"

John dropped the file back onto the blotter. "Nothing much if he shows up in court Wednesday. He'll probably pay a fine and that'll be the end of it. I'm not mentioning the knife to the judge. I figure to keep that between Paul and me."

She bit down on her lower lip. A tear slid down one side of her nose.

To hell with her attitude about a public display. He stepped toward her, intending to take her in his arms. "Isabelle, listen—"

She stopped him by backing away. "Leave me alone, John. I wish I'd never gotten involved with you."

"What're you talking about?"

"The facts," she said in a stage whisper, her voice filled with pain. "You've always been on a different level from me. From us. As crazy as Paul acts sometimes, he knew that much. I'm the one who's been living in some kind of dream world."

Her words stunned him. He could think of nothing he had ever done to make her feel she was beneath him in any way. "Isabelle, we need to talk. Rooster's gonna do the bar patrol tonight. I'll be able to get out of here in a few hours. I'll come out and we'll—"

She shook her head. "No. I'm going to look for my brother. When I find him, I'm taking him home with me. I may have been gone when he needed someone in the past, but I'm here now." She took a step toward the door, then stopped and turned to face him. "You're not welcome, John. You can't be around him because of your job. I know that. . . . Besides, you don't like him."

"What?" He gave her a look and tucked back his chin. "Isabelle, I didn't say that."

"And I don't like *you* much anymore. I don't want to see you again." She walked out of his office and slammed the door.

He rounded the end of the desk, following her. When he opened the door to the anteroom, she had Ava by the hand and they were already marching up the stairs. His heartbeat took off. "Isabelle, listen to me—"

She kept climbing, pulling Ava along. The kid turned her head toward him, her small brows drawn into a frown over teary eyes. "'Bye, John," she said in a tiny voice.

He wanted to break into tears himself.

He became aware of Rooster's watchful gaze and faced his deputy.

"My mama always said blood's thicker than water, John T. . . . And I'm pretty sure it runs deeper than screwin'."

Her hand clenched around Ava's, Isabelle lectured herself all the way up the stairs. Sleeping with John had been a mistake from the beginning. Carrying on an affair with the county's sheriff and trying to reform a brother who was one of the county's outlaws presented crushing conflict. Didn't she already have enough on her plate just surviving and working toward the goals she had set for herself? What kind of person had she become? What kind of example had she set for her daughter?

Outside, said daughter wrenched her hand away, stomped to the passenger side of the Sierra and climbed in.

As Isabelle scooted onto the driver's seat, Ava sat with her arms crossed over her thin chest, her lower lip protruding. The ten-year-old jerked to face her, magnified eyes snapping with anger. "What did you say to him? You said something bad, didn't you? Now he won't come to see us and ride the horses anymore."

"Ava, his helping me with the horses was always temporary. He was an employee."

"He was not. He was my friend." Tears leaked from the corners of her eyes. She threw her shoulder against the passenger door. "When I get grown, I'm leaving here. I hate it here."

Emotion swelled in Isabelle's throat as she turned the key in the ignition. Not only had she been dumb letting herself get involved in an affair with John, she had been foolish letting Ava build a relationship with him. The last thing her daughter needed was to see another father figure disappear from her life.

Well, she couldn't think about that at this moment. Paul

was somewhere alone and depressed. As she backed in a loop in the courthouse parking lot, her mind ran down the list of places she might find him. "We'll talk about it when we get home, okay?"

Her angry little girl didn't reply.

It wasn't eleven o'clock, so Isabelle doubted Paul had hit the bar yet. Her second choice was the travel trailer where he lived.

As she drove the unpaved streets of Callister, disjointed thoughts careened through her head. Every waking day had become a reminder of just how out of place she was in this town and how the life she had cultivated since leaving Callister all those years back had separated her from what she thought she wanted in her small hometown.

An idea had been growing in the recesses of her mind, one as irrational as the one that had driven her back to Callister in the first place. She had to return to Texas, where she could make a living the only way she knew how and where she could associate with people and groups with whom she had something in common. Good grief, what insanity had made her pull up stakes from an area where one out of every fifteen cutting-horse owners in the whole United States lived?

Why hadn't she put it all together before she sold the place in Texas, before she moved back here lock, stock and barrel, before she had two mares in foal? And before she let herself fall into an affair.

She had been kidding herself thinking she had something worth hanging on to with John Bradshaw or any other man she might meet in Callister.

Even before she arrived at the sawyer's house behind which Paul lived, she saw her brother's boat parked beside his travel trailer. Being an ardent fisherman and white-water river runner, he owned a modified sledboat with an engine powerful enough to take him from here to Portland. The boat was bigger than the travel trailer.

She came to a stop behind it as Paul picked up a plump roll Isabelle recognized as a sleeping bag and tossed it over the side onto the deck. "Stay in the truck, Ava."

She slid out of the Sierra and approached him. "Are you taking the boat out?"

"They're catching some good ones down on the Snake."

"That's eighty miles away." She threw a pointed look at the sleeping bag. "You'll be back by Wednesday, right?"

He stopped and looked at her, his expression dark and insolent. "Maybe. Maybe not."

"Paul! Don't say that. You have to be back."

"I don't *have* to do anything, Izzy."

She almost screamed in frustration. A memory rushed at her—all the times she had seen Paul, even when he was no older than fourteen, stand toe-to-toe with their father. He'd had a rebellious streak from the day he was born and he feared nothing he could see. The tormentors he couldn't see were another story.

"Okay." She threw a hand in the air. "Be an ass. Make life hard on everybody. I don't blame Sherry for not wanting to come back to you."

He came to where she stood, his eyes red and tearing. "Izzy, I gotta get outta here. Don't you see that? It's all falling in on me." He released a sob and wiped his eyes on his shirtsleeve. "I ain't no good in town. Don't you see? I gotta get on that river where there ain't nobody but me and that black water."

She thought of the times she had followed him into the forest and found him in a cave or curled in sleep under a tree. Perhaps, in his adult life, the boat and the river had replaced the dark woods as an escape from a pain greater than he could manage. She swallowed the tears that had been pressuring her throat all morning. "I understand, Paul. Honest, I do.... Look, a travel trailer is no place to call home. When you get back, I want you to come to the house. Be with me and Ava. John says you only have to pay a fine. I can cover it, then we'll work on putting your life on track. We'll find a counselor and we'll talk to Sherry. Together, Paul. We'll work it out together."

He hefted a Styrofoam cooler over the side of the boat.

"We're family, Paul.... We're family." Even she heard the desperation in her voice.

He wiped his eyes again. "I can pay the fine, Izzy. I got money. You go on home and don't worry. I'll be back in time."

She let out a held breath. He seemed to be more in control of himself. Of course he could pay the fine. He made good money when he worked. "Okay, good." She started to walk backward toward the Sierra. "You bring us a big fish and we'll cook it. I'll make fried potatoes like Mom used to."

"Izzy?"

She stopped. "What?"

"I'm sorry. I didn't mean to get between you and somebody you care about. I just ain't good for—"

"That isn't true, Paul. The only people I care about are you and Ava. You just come home. Ava and I'll be waiting for you."

He turned and lifted his tackle box over the side of the boat. "I'll see."

More words would fall on deaf ears. Her brother had a stubborn streak that ran as deep as his penchant for self-destruction. She climbed behind the Sierra's steering wheel and lowered the window. "We'll be waiting, okay? Don't let us down."

# Chapter 22

By law, the sheriff acted as bailiff in Wednesday court. John half expected Paul to ditch his court date, but the guy showed up on time—sober, scrubbed and shaved and wearing pressed clothes. So Izzy had honed him into good shape for his appearance before Judge Morrison.

She accompanied her brother. The minute John saw her pass through the old courtroom's tall double doors, his heart pitched into a jitterbug. He hadn't seen her or talked to her since Saturday morning in his office.

Duty-bound to stick close to the judge, he had no opportunity to speak to her. From the corner of his eye, all through the hearing, he watched her sitting alone on the long front bench. She ducked her head and dabbed at a tear with her fingertip as the judge delivered a stern warning to Paul, levied a heavy fine, then released him. It could have gone a lot worse.

Though Paul fared well with the judge, John still felt a stricture in his chest knowing and seeing firsthand just how much Izzy had been hurt by her brother's latest stunt.

After the hearing she followed Paul out of the courtroom but didn't so much as nod to John. With two more cases slated to be heard, John couldn't break away. At the end of court Judge Morrison called him into chambers to discuss pending issues, which consumed another hour.

When he finally escaped the prosecution process, John

stopped by the clerk's office and was told Paul's fine had been paid. He only hoped the payer wasn't Izzy. Not wanting to add to gossip, he didn't ask.

Back in his office, the state of affairs with Izzy and her brother continued to peck at him. Surely, as soon as she worked past her anger and embarrassment, she would call and thank him for what he had done for Paul. She had to know his decision not to charge him with a felony had saved his ass from a fate far more serious than a fine.

For the rest of the week John waited for the call that didn't come. Misery weighed on him like a heavy cloak. He had lost his taste for food, thus his belt fit a little looser. The red mark he had made on the calendar glared back at him. She should get her period any day. He fought to keep from calling her.

On Sunday, a week later, the person who did call was Luke McRae, reporting that Smokey Jane was pregnant.

The news brought both joy and sadness. Izzy would be thrilled. John longed to be a part of her happiness and felt disappointment she hadn't been the one who called and told him.

At the same time he celebrated the prospect of a new foal, he wondered if Izzy, too, was pregnant.

*Nah.* Why was he worried? Maybe she wouldn't call him and tell him about a horse being in foal, but she would call and discuss herself, wouldn't she? She had promised.

At the beginning of the third week, John felt he was on the road to recovery. He began to accept the facts. The romance was over. Like a man who had been trapped underwater, he struggled to the surface and appreciated the breath of fresh air. Kicking the Izzy habit made him feel as triumphant as when he gave up booze.

A serious relationship with any female was pointless anyway. He didn't make enough money to be squiring a woman around and soon he wouldn't have the time. In a few weeks he would be going to Los Angeles and bringing back his sons for the summer.

He approached the role of sheriff with new resolve. It had taken more than three months to penetrate his psyche, but he now realized the scope of the job of a county sheriff, the complicated function of the only law enforcement agency in a large rural county. He wasn't just another administrator of a government bureaucracy as he had originally—and erroneously—believed. He was everything—the department's operation and finances manager, the server of warrants and subpoenas, the guardian of the county's prisoners and their transporter between Callister County and other jurisdictions. And he was an officer of the court, a role in which he took some pride.

And most important of all, he was the county's only policeman and jailer, the last bulwark between anarchy and Callister County's thirty-five hundred citizens. Daunting as the responsibility was, he had discovered he liked the challenge.

Other than perfunctory supervision by the county commissioners, he answered only to himself. He could see the possibilities for rampant corruption if a man—or woman—was dishonest. If he had a notion to continue in the job—which he didn't—he would press the commissioners to understand that if they desired an ethical, trustworthy individual filling the office of sheriff for a lengthy span of time, they would have to vote in a decent salary. If he knew the commissioners, that wasn't going to happen.

Saturday rolled in wet and gray. After the weather had teased them with spring, a squall had sent the temperature plunging all the way down to the low forties again, but the forecast for Boise was for sunshine.

Rooster would be coming in at three and taking the Saturday night patrol. For his night off, John decided to wander down south to Boise, call up an old friend, have dinner in a good restaurant, maybe go to a movie. A change of scenery and an evening away from the TV would boost his morale.

Betty's was still crowded when he took a break for a late lunch. Sitting alone at a table near his usual seat in a booth in the back corner of the spacious dining room was Rita Mitchell. He was almost glad to see her, wondered if she would like to go to a movie in Boise.

*Hell, why not?* he said to himself and ambled to where she sat. "Care if I sit down?" he asked her.

She looked up at him and smiled. "Please do."

Lorraine scuffed over. "You almost missed the special. Betty cooked fried chicken and mashed potatoes. There's still some left. She made Emeril's apple pie. He's that TV cook."

"Great," John said. "I'll have some of all of it."

"Got my new boots." Lorraine stepped back, placing her feet precisely together for him to look. Her jeans were stuffed into the tops of bright turquoise-blue boots with fancy white stitching around tooled red leaves.

"Hey, those are cool, Lorraine. I haven't seen boots that fancy since I left the rodeo circuit."

"I doubt that. I've heard those cutting-horse people all wear fancy clothes."

John managed a laugh at the obvious reference to Izzy. "I've heard something like that, too. Which son sent the boots?"

Lorraine pulled a pencil from her helmet of blue hair and wrote his order on a pad. "The one in Portland. When I told him I wanted new boots for my birthday, I never expected fancy ones."

John watched as she shuffled away with his lunch order. Lorraine was a widow who lived alone. Her kids had moved away to Portland and Seattle. She stubbornly hung on in Callister because she knew nothing else and her family had been here since 1840. She had to be over seventy, yet she came to work every day waiting tables in Betty's Road Kill Café.

In the introspective mood that had settled on him today, John thought about the fact that Lorraine and others like her were the citizens he had sworn to protect. Only this week he had come to realize he would do anything it took, including risking his life, to meet the obligation.

"*Does* she have fancy clothes?"

Rita's words brought his attention back to her. "What?"

"I asked if she has fancy clothes?" She picked up her cup and sipped, looking at him across her cup rim with blue eyes he had always thought were pretty. Today they reminded him of ice.

"Who?"

She set down the cup, smiling. "You know perfectly well

who I'm talking about. The reason you haven't been in to see me lately." She pulled two fingers with talonlike nails through a two-foot-long fall of black hair. "I tried to tell her what kind of coffee you like, but she didn't buy it from me. She must have gotten it somewhere else, hmm?"

The confrontation caught him off guard. John squirmed. Nope. Not only would he be making a mistake asking her to a movie, he had already made one sitting down at her table. "Guess I don't know what you're talking about, Rita."

He picked up his cup and sipped and dodged the look in her eye. Lorraine brought his lunch and he had just tucked into it when he glanced up and saw Izzy and Ava come through the front door. *Shit.* His lunch companion visibly stiffened and the smile fell from her face.

Izzy had on faded jeans and a barn coat. Ava was wearing clean jeans, boots and a puffy nylon coat. She carried a little purple satchel. Confusing emotions beleaguered John. On the one hand, he hoped they wouldn't see him sitting with Rita, but a more perverse part of him hoped they would.

"Is that an example of her fancy clothes?"

John shot his lunch companion a look. Yep, taking her *anywhere* would be a big mistake. She picked up her check, stood up and looked down at him with a smile he couldn't describe. "If you ever get tired of those barn smells, sheriff, you know where I am. My shop smells much better."

She sauntered toward the door, speaking to someone as she went past. Yep, he was glad he had stopped going into Java Junction. He cut a look toward Izzy, sure she had seen him and Rita sitting together.

He watched her chat with Lorraine. Ava set her satchel on the floor and climbed up on a stool at the yellow Formica-topped counter. Soon came a drink in a tall cup. He couldn't hear her conversation, but he could see she was talking ninety miles an hour, as usual.

Anguish built within John. He missed that kid and her nonstop talk and unfettered opinions about any subject you could name. Seeing Isabelle reminded him how her and her daughter's absence had left a ragged hole in the very fabric of his life.

Soon a heavyset woman he recognized as Nan Gilbert
came in. John hadn't seen her since high school when she
was a good fifty pounds lighter. With her were two dark-
haired girls who looked to be near Ava's age.

The girls sat down beside Ava and they talked and giggled. Nan leaned on the counter, laughing with Izzy and Lorraine. Soon Nan adjusted her purse on her shoulder and told
the girls in a loud voice she was ready to go. They all hugged,
Ava picked up the satchel and left the café with Nan and the
two girls. John surmised Ava was going somewhere for the
night.

John hadn't talked to Izzy once since the morning after
Paul's arrest. He watched as she paid at the cash register.
When he saw her walk out, a longing besieged him and the
progress he had made putting her out of his mind deserted
him. He pushed aside his slice of the TV cook's apple pie,
left the table and paid for his lunch, then followed behind her.

When he reached the sidewalk, she was climbing into her
truck at the end of the block. She drove away before he could
get her attention.

Though he usually walked from the courthouse to
Betty's, today, with the inclement weather, he had come in
the Blazer. By the time he reached the rig, Izzy's Sierra was
out of sight. He tore through town and turned onto the county
road, attempting to catch up with her. When he saw her truck
again, she was turning into her driveway. He had come this
far, so he followed it all the way to the house and stopped behind it.

She slid out and waited for him beside the driver's door
as he dismounted and walked to her, squinting his eyes and
hunching his shoulders against a fine cold mist. "Just wanted
to say hi," he said and wondered just how pathetic he
sounded.

She started walking toward the back door, her head
down. "Okay, hi. . . . How was lunch?"

He walked beside her, stuffing his hands into his coat
pockets for warmth and passing over the pointed question.
"How you been?"

"Okay."

Encouraged that she hadn't told him to get lost, John tried for an engaging smile. "Don't suppose you've got a cup of coffee."

She looked up at him. "I think there's some left from this morning." She opened the back door. "If you can stand it, you're welcome to it. I *didn't* have it specially ground at Java Junction."

"C'mon now. I haven't been in that coffee shop in weeks and you know it." John followed her into the porch and was met by Harry and Gwendolyn, their toenails clicking on the plywood floor as their tails lashed his boot tops. "They're getting big." He bent down and scruffed their heads with his knuckles.

"They keep Ava busy." She unhooked a slicker from an iron horseshoe hook on the mudroom wall and threw it around her shoulders. Then she reached for two leashes and snapped them onto the pups' collars. "You can stay indoors where it's dry. Help yourself to the coffee. Heat it in the microwave."

"I'll just walk with you." John followed her outside, shoving his hands into his pockets as he walked beside her.

"So you've gone back to fooling around with Rita Mitchell," she said. "That's good. You need—"

"I've never fooled around with Rita Mitchell, so I haven't gone back to anything."

The speech she had made in the sheriff's office the morning after Paul's arrest had come back to John a hundred times and left him wondering if she had indeed taken her brother into her house to live. Even with Callister's gossip gazette, he hadn't heard yes or no. "Paul moved in with you?"

"No. He isn't in town. I don't know where he is."

That could be good news or bad. "I see."

She gave him a sharp look across her shoulder. "I'm sure he's fishing or something. You don't have to worry about him."

"I wasn't worried. I saw in court he can be responsible. I believed him when he told Judge Morrison he'd shape up."

In spite of his upbeat words, John still had a vivid visual of the heavy-bladed knife lying on the bottom shelf of the sheriff's office safe. And every time he removed his clothes, he saw a red scar on his stomach that reminded him of Paul Rondeau.

"I was proud of Paul that morning," she said.

"Yeah, he did okay. The judge thought so, too, or things could've gone south."

"Did you speak for him to the judge? I'm sure you were asked for your opinion."

"To be honest, no. But I didn't speak against him either."

"That's fair, I guess."

"Yeah, well, fair is what I'm supposed to be."

John didn't want to discuss Paul. She seemed to want to hear praise for the guy and John had none to offer. "Listen, I saw Ava leave the café with Nan Gilbert. I didn't know her and Roger had kids Ava's age."

"That was Paul's daughters, Emily and Olivia. One of Nan's kids is having a birthday, so she's giving a party."

"That was something you wanted, wasn't it? To get Paul's daughters to come up?"

"Yes. I told Nan and Paul's wife I'd teach the kids to ride. The weather's too nasty for it, so Nan put together the party."

They completed a wide circle around the pasture and returned the dogs to the porch. She retrieved a towel from the mudroom cabinets and began wiping their feet. Ignoring his own feet, which felt like frozen stumps, John helped her.

Wearing a slicker and all-weather boots, Izzy had stayed dry, but John's canvas coat felt wet and heavy and the saturated grass had soaked his street boots and his jeans all the way past his knees.

As she stood up and peeled her slicker off, her gaze fell on his boots. "There's a fire in the fireplace if you want to take those off."

He pried off his boots. His socks were wet, too. "If you wouldn't mind, I'll just set these on the hearth to dry out for a few minutes."

"Sure," she said. She braced a hand against the mudroom door, pulled her own boots off and slid her feet into slippers.

Feeling chilled through and through, John carried his boots to the living room and warmth. The mantel clock struck two, but the drizzly day made the room gray and dim.

A low fire in the fireplace cast the red-brick hearth in a soft amber light. He sat down on the hearth, pulled off his socks and hung them across his boot tops.

A few minutes later, she brought steaming mugs from the kitchen, handed him one, then sank cross-legged onto the rugs in front of the fireplace. "Everything feels so damp," she said and sipped. "I'm having some of Ava's hot chocolate."

He sipped the coffee, but it didn't do much to warm up his feet. "I was thinking, we've never gone out, just the two of us. Want to drive up to the ski lodge for supper? I could go back to my apartment and get some dry clothes and—"

"It's so cozy here, I hate to leave. You can't afford supper at the ski lodge anyway. I'm sure asking me out to dinner isn't why you came."

"I just now thought of it. Something to do, a place to sit and talk."

She smiled up at him and some of the weight lifted from his heart. "We've had some of our best conversations right here," she said. "What do you want to talk about?"

As if she didn't know. He looked down at the dark liquid in his mug. "I miss you like hell, Isabelle. I don't like my life without you in it."

"Don't say that, John. I've been thinking ever since that day in your office. We *can't* keep on like we were. It causes too much trouble for all of us, you most of all. We both should have known better. We can be friends. We can't be lovers."

He looked up, across his shoulder, and to his dismay, saw not just sadness, but sincerity in her expression. A kink began to form in his gut. He didn't want to be *friends*. No relationship as close or as hot and passionate as theirs could fall in the "friendship" category. "I'm your friend, if that's what you mean," he said, as if her words hadn't sliced into him deeper than her brother's knife. "I always have been."

"I believe that." She ducked her chin and stared at the contents of her mug. The dampness had caused her hair to frizz. The firelight reflected in it, making a fiery aura around her head. He loved her hair, loved how the thick curls fell halfway down her back, loved how it smelled, loved burrowing his hands in it. His throat constricted at the thought of losing that.

"And I hope you'll continue to be," she went on. "I just think I need to concentrate on what I'm supposed to be doing, which is building a horse business and making a good life for me and Ava. I have too much to lose here to be behaving in an irresponsible way that reflects badly on me. Or doing things that don't have a future. After your agreement with the county commissioners is done, you're moving on, remember?"

The future. For sure, they hadn't discussed the future. The truth was he had been too engrossed in the here and now to consider the tomorrow and next year. He couldn't read her today, but he could see she wasn't leveling with him. Something was bothering her, but it wasn't her reputation or concern for his honorable intentions.

"If it's gossip that's worrying you, everybody in town knows about us. No one thinks we're doing something wrong."

"I don't care what they think, not really. I mean, I do, but it's a small thing."

"Since when?" He bent his head to make eye contact. "Up to now it's been a big thing. If it's gotten small all of a sudden, then why don't you tell me the other big thing that's a problem?"

# Chapter 23

Isabelle could see the emotion in John's eyes. Why didn't he leave well enough alone? Except for Ava's surly attitude, the past two weeks had been almost a relief, a reprieve from looking forward to and waiting for his arrival on Tuesday and Thursday mornings. She drew in a deep breath. "It's too hard to overcome who I am, who my brother is."

How could she explain that she would let nothing, including what she felt for John, prevent her from having a relationship with or defending her brother?

"We all grew up together. Don't you think I already know who you are, who your brother is? I don't hate him, Isabelle."

"I don't think you could hate anyone, John. You know he's one of the reasons I came back here. It's true I didn't realize how bad things had gotten with him, but I won't forsake him. It isn't fair for me to impose such a conflict of interest on you."

"Can't *I* decide what's fair for me?"

She smiled. "You sometimes have impractical expectations. Just like when we were kids."

"Impractical expectations are the foundations of hope, Isabelle. That's what put me on the Wrangler rodeo team, what took me to the finals in professional rodeo. If we didn't have hope, how could we look forward to anything?"

She couldn't keep from smiling. She had never known

anyone with more ideals or a more positive attitude than John Bradshaw. "That's exactly what I'm talking about. You're a half-full-glass kind of guy."

"And that's a bad thing?"

"No. It's something I admire about you. I tend to be the opposite."

He set his mug on the hearth, moved down and sat beside her on the rug, hip to hip. He braced himself on one hand and cocked his knee, placing one pale bare foot on the floor in front of them. His feet were long and high-arched, narrow for a man's, like his hands and fingers. They had to be freezing after being wet for so long, but he wasn't a complainer. "At least there's something you can admire," he said.

She could feel her resolve slipping away. How could she be just friends with a man who had touched every part of her body and soul?

Knowing she was inviting trouble, she set her mug on the hearth beside his, picked up his foot and began to rub it between her palms, like she sometimes rubbed Ava's. "Your feet are cold," she said.

"Isabelle, listen to me." His voice came low and soft and warm as the fire. He ran the backs of his fingers up and down her arm. "I'm an ordinary guy who's done more wrong than right, but I know this much and it has nothing to do with philosophy. The way it is with us doesn't come along every day."

True enough. In her most far-fetched dreams, she hadn't anticipated encountering in *any* man what she had found in John. She missed his good company, his easy laugh, from some level deeper than she understood, the sense of connection to another human being. She smiled into his eyes. "Okay, I admit it."

He picked up one of her hands and lifted it to his warm lips. "I don't have wise answers to anything, but I believe people who care about each other can work through whatever happens. That would include your brother."

"You make it sound a lot simpler than it is."

"What's so hard? You just get up every day and do the best you can with what comes. I'm open-minded. As long as he doesn't break any laws I have to enforce, everything's cool."

"That's the challenge. He's so unpredictable."

She looked down at her small hand inside his large one. "You know what I thought that morning after we—well, when you left here so worried about me getting pregnant?"

A half-smile quirked a corner of his mouth. "Are you? Pregnant?"

She grinned at the expectation in his expression. "No. Don't you think I would've told you?"

"I know that's what you said, but . . ."

Hearing his voice trail off, she knew he *had* thought she would be that spiteful and a little pang pinched her. A frown tugged between her eyes and she cocked her head. "Did you want me to be?"

"I don't know. Maybe. What I mean is, I wouldn't have minded. . . . Would you? . . . Mind?"

She wasn't prepared to answer that question. With his eyes locked with hers so intensely she had to look away. "I want you to know I felt bad after what I did that day. When I watched you driving down the driveway, I was thinking, here you are, honest and loyal, and I'd done something that worried you."

"It wasn't really worry, but it made me stop and think. Made me realize we'd been treating this thing between us too casual."

"But me being Frenchie Rondeau's daughter, my getting pregnant could damage you in this town, John. I don't want to ever do anything to damage you."

"Darlin', a tiny little baby never damaged anybody. Anyway, you're taking too much of the blame. The way I remember it, you weren't all by yourself that morning." He grinned and winked. "I had a real good time." He leaned forward and began to kiss her face, her nose, her cheeks. "Sometimes fun has results you didn't expect, but it's still fun."

The tip of his tongue tickled her earlobe and she tilted her head for more. Lord, she did love his touch.

His fingers came beneath her chin and he turned her face to him. His eyes leveled on hers, his lips only inches away.

"The only way you could damage me is if we don't take up where we left off. That would seriously damage my heart."

He was so close she could smell his cologne, smell the coffee on his breath, hear the soft lisp of his tongue when he spoke. "In a roundabout way," she said, "it's Paul I'm talking about. How me being his sister could damage you."

"I'd rather talk about how sweet your lips are."

"You're a Pied Piper, John Bradshaw. It isn't fair I'm such a soft touch."

"Hmm. . . . Thank God for that."

Her misgivings dissolved like candy in the warmth of his sweet mouth. She couldn't refuse to kiss him back. His hand slipped under her sweater and in one quick movement unhooked her bra. The same hand closed over her breast as his tongue played with hers. His thumb brushed her nipple and a familiar urgency called out from a deep place in her belly.

He cupped her shoulder, eased her back and pushed his knee between her thighs. She was such a slut. Already she had grown hot and swollen and damp. "You really are a devil," she whispered when they stopped to breathe.

"I almost went crazy when I thought I'd lost you," he murmured. "Don't you know I need you?"

She sniffed away gathering tears. "You had lunch with Rita Mitchell."

"Not lunch. Not even a full cup of coffee."

His deft fingers moved down and undid her jeans, pushed them down her hips. "Lift up," he said and she lifted her bottom for him to slide her jeans and panties past her hips. He slipped them off one leg, then undid his fly.

His erection made a tent in his boxers. She opened the fly, freeing him. His penis, swollen and roped with full veins, stood like a monument bronzed by the firelight, visibly throbbing, and it was all hers. She closed her hand around him, sat up and took the bulbous head into her mouth, ran her tongue over the velvety cleft, tasted his salty moisture.

A grunt, low and deep, came from his chest and his body stiffened. "I don't know if I can stand that," he choked out. His hands closed on her shoulders and he pulled her up. "It's been too long since it was inside you."

He wrapped his arms around her and rolled her to her back. In no time, through a tangle of arms and legs and denim fabric and with her help, he slid his boxers down and rolled a condom onto his turgid shaft. He pushed into her and the utter bliss of him filling her made her gasp.

His head lifted and eyes dark with passion looked into hers. "Okay?"

Oh, she was so okay words eluded her. She sniffled and nodded.

"Then stay with me," he whispered. He clutched her bottom, pressed her closer and seated himself. She lifted her knees and took him deeper. A guttural response came from the back of his throat and thrilled her. He braced himself over her, hooked his forearms behind her knees, spreading them wide. She lay helpless beneath him, his long, thick erection buried to the hilt, but she wasn't afraid. He would never hurt her and delicious sensations were rushing through her. She would do anything to please him.

For a few seconds, he held himself motionless, looking into her eyes. "I love you."

She thought her heart might burst with joy. How could she have ever believed she could be happy without him? The tears that had been hovering trailed from the corners of her eyes, past her temples. "I love you more."

"Not possible." He began to move, in and out with a slow, steady rhythm, the tip of him touching her deepest place with each stroke. Their souls met and she felt the moment they became a unit. She lost count of his thrusts, lost touch with time, could think of nothing but the incredible friction as the root of him drove against her again and again. She wanted to squirm, her hips wanted to pump, but couldn't, pinned as she was. Lightning began to skitter inside her, sending fire everywhere, pushing her to the edge of a steep cliff. His mouth moved over her face, her throat. His voice murmured sexy words in her ear, whispered how much he loved making love to her.

Her head spun as she teetered on the edge, panting and desperate. "John . . . oh, please . . ."

His pace picked up. His chest heaved, his breath rasped

in her ear. He thrust harder and she began to spasm. She dug her fingers into his biceps and hung on as he flung her into a great abyss and she cried his name as she fell.

Then she was floating in a mindless purple haze. She felt his body turn rigid, felt him buck, heard him shout out, caught him as he sprawled on top of her.

They lay for quiet minutes, until the last embers of the fire within them died, until the last contraction made him shiver. She loved knowing they had come to this moment together.

"Godalmighty," he mumbled. He slipped to her side and took her with him, cocooning her in the nest of his arms. "Christ." His chest heaved for several breaths. "Want to know what I think?"

"I want to know *everything* you think."

"This feels a lot better in bed without our clothes. . . . Not that it felt bad."

She giggled and nuzzled his chest, inhaling the scent of him in his clothes. A pulse thumped in the hollow at the base of his throat, just above the neck of his T-shirt. "Want to know what *I* think?"

He grunted.

"I think you're right. We should try it again. Ava won't be home until after church tomorrow. Do you want to stay the night?"

"I thought you'd never ask. I've had dreams about waking up with you."

"I'm a witch in the morning."

"Haven't I ever told you how good I am at witchhandling? I'm as good with witches as I am with horses."

"Are you hungry?"

"For food?"

"Soup? It's homemade."

"Sounds good. I might need the energy later. 'Cause I intend to fuck you 'til you beg me to stop."

She smiled and ran her hand through his soft hair. "Never happen, cowboy."

They gathered themselves and while Isabelle went to the kitchen to reheat the soup she had made the day before, John added logs and stoked the fire in the fireplace.

The rain had increased in intensity and beat in a roar on the house's tin roof. They ate on the sofa in front of the fireplace, then stretched out their legs, placing their bare feet in front of the flames.

"I can't think of a thing to do but go to bed," John said.

She laughed. "I can. I have to take the dogs out."

He groaned. "Awww, shit. I'll do it."

"I should let you since it's your fault they're here, but your clothes are still damp. I don't want you to take pneumonia. I'll only be a minute. You can warm up the cold sheets."

While she took the dogs out, John cleared away their dishes and put them in the sink. Then he wiped the counter and straightened the clutter they had left in the kitchen, the whole time his mind on the coming hours. Lord, if sex with Isabelle got any better, he would end up so pussy-whipped he couldn't function.

In her bedroom, he picked up the picture of her and Paul as children, rubbing the scar on his stomach as he studied it. Five weeks had passed since the bar fight. Enough time for a wound to heal up and hair over, but John hadn't forgotten how close the knife slash had come to being serious. As he looked at the picture of Paul this time, he saw him from a different perspective.

He began to undress. He wanted to be in bed when she returned so he could watch her take off her clothes.

He had just pulled off his T-shirt when she came into the room. Her eyes landed on the scar, still red, on his abdomen.

She came to him and placed her palm on it. "Oh, John. I had no idea.... When you said he cut you, you made it sound like a scratch."

He picked up her hand and kissed it. "It's well now."

She looked up at him, her eyes glistening. "This is what I mean? How can we—"

"Shh. One step at a time, remember?"

They crawled under the blue quilt and he wrapped his arms around her. She kissed his shoulder. "Paul really isn't a bad person," she said.

John's feelings about Paul Rondeau spanned a wide spectrum. "Tell me something. I know he's your brother, but he's a grown man. Why do you feel so responsible for him? Other than patching up the barn, I can't see that he does much for you. I'd like to understand your feelings."

"I owe him, John. Pa was so mean to him and no one ever helped him."

"If he was mean to Paul, wasn't he mean to you, too?"

"Not in the same way. He beat Paul. He used to say he was teaching Paul to be a man, but what he was really doing was destroying my brother's future."

She turned her back, but he kept her close against him, his arm around her waist, his knees fitted against the backs of hers. At least he wasn't hearing what he feared he might about Izzy and her father.

"My mother always took up for me," she went on, "but she just sort of abandoned Paul. Fortunately, he was tough. By the time he was about fourteen, he was a match for Pa. One day in the barn, Pa went at him over something, probably something that happened in the bar that had nothing to do with Paul. The next thing I knew, Paul had hit him with a shovel. Pa staggered backward against the stall. Paul had just come back from hunting and had his rifle with him. I was terrified. I thought Paul was going to shoot him."

John frowned. Even as bad as the story sounded, it didn't seem enough to warrant the kind of devotion Isabelle had for her brother. "What else?"

"What was so bad was Paul had no way to get away from him. In the summer he could run off into the forest, but in the winter he was trapped."

Her voice became a dull monotone. "It was such a nightmare in the house. Pa would come in from the woods around November or December and it was nothing but hell until he went back in June. School was the only place we could escape to. Neither Paul or I had a car. He had no friends except Merle Keeton, who did have a car. And I had no one but Billy."

"Child abuse has been against the law for years. Why didn't you go to the sheriff?"

"John, I didn't even know who the sheriff was. And whoever he was, in Callister there was no telling how he might have handled a child-abuse complaint. Besides, Rondeaus didn't hang out around the sheriff's office."

John's imagination didn't stretch far enough to picture Izzy's childhood. He couldn't imagine a man being mean to his kids, though as sheriff he had seen it firsthand. He had been out on a couple of domestic-abuse calls, one where a grown man had severely beat his wife and kids. He felt the same emotions tonight as he had felt then, disgust and frustration.

"So you see, neither one of us could stay home. I had terrible grades in school and no one believed I would ever graduate. I started nagging at Billy about leaving Callister. Everyone thinks it was Billy who lured me away, but that isn't true. He left here because I wanted to. His life at home wasn't great either."

"You were kids. I don't know how you survived."

"Billy wasn't. He was twenty. We went to Nevada and looked for ranch work. We had it figured out that we'd get jobs on some spread about as remote as it could possibly be. You can get completely lost on some of those desert ranches. It could have been dangerous for him because I was underage. After I turned eighteen, we left Nevada and went to Arizona, then Southern California, then back to Arizona. Finally ended up in Texas."

"Training horses?"

"Yes. I loved it and Billy followed along. In those days he always followed along. We didn't have this great romance, but we sort of occupied the same cage and we depended on each other.

"I was so grateful to him I tolerated worse treatment from him than I should have and stayed with him too long. Maybe things could have been okay if he had been able to resist all that we found ourselves exposed to. Once we got to Texas, a world I never dreamed I would be a part of became our livelihood. More money than you can imagine, plus booze and drugs. Billy jumped into that huge mud hole with both feet. It's funny how life comes full circle. By the time Billy left me, he behaved a lot like Pa."

"He wasn't mean to Ava—"

"No. He didn't have that much interest in Ava."

She paused again and John heard her sniffle. "So that's my sad tale. If Billy hadn't become such a problem, I wouldn't have lost touch with Paul. I didn't even come back here when he and Sherry got married because Pa was still alive then. I hated the idea of seeing him."

"I remember when Paul and Sherry got married," John said. "I was in college, but I was home for the summer."

"Paul seemed to be getting his act together as long as he had Sherry and his kids. When she left him, he became a real mess. He's always been a maverick, but never mean. I can't desert him. He deserves to be saved. He deserves to be loved by someone in his family."

He drew her against his body, wrapped her with his arms and legs, and buried his face against her neck, as if he could shield her from hurt with his body. "It's a good thing your old man's already dead. I'd have to kill the sonofabitch."

# Chapter 24

John's week began with him in high spirits. Today as he made coffee on top of the filing cabinet in the corner, he was happier than he had been in months, maybe years, maybe ever. Saturday night he and Izzy had spoken their feelings aloud for the first time. In a matter of a weekend his life had made a sea change.

He finally understood Isabelle's devotion to her brother and now knew that if a man wanted her, Paul came with her. He could learn to live with that. Paul wasn't hopeless.

Typically, Mondays were spent preparing cases to be heard by Judge Morrison when he came up from Boise on Wednesday. John had an organized, disciplined mind, which had taken him to good grades in high school and college, even while being distracted by rodeoing. The same discipline and organization skills had earned Judge Morrison's respect and John did all he could to sustain that status. This week there was one domestic-abuse and one burglary case to be cleared. While he waited for the coffee, he opened the file folders and glanced through them, sorting and planning.

Disciplined or not, he couldn't keep his thoughts from drifting back to the weekend. After making love and talking for hours Saturday night, he and Isabelle had awakened together and stayed in bed 'til noon, dozing and making love more until the threat of Ava coming home from Nan Gilbert's house forced them to get up and dress.

When Ava returned, the three of them had gone to Boise, where they watched *Finding Nemo*, a movie that, along with Ava's long explanation, gave him a new perspective on fish.

While he worked on the case files, a serious plan for his future cooked in his head. Election of a real sheriff would take place in the fall. He had only a few months to find a career at which he would make enough money to pay his child support and provide for a family of three. He needed the increase in income because he couldn't imagine his future without Izzy and Ava in it. He intended to approach her with a proposal of marriage. He wanted to be able to assure her that he could take care of her and Ava.

Promising opportunities were available to him. One position in particular interested him—sales for a lariat manufacturing company, with the possibility of early promotion to management. An old friend from his rodeo days had told him the company execs were chomping at the bit at the chance to hire an ex-rodeoer who had placed in the money. If he took the job, some travel would be required, but there was a good chance he could continue to live in Callister. That would work out just fine. Izzy could continue with her horses.

As he planned, a possessiveness about the sheriff's job niggled at him and he worried about who would replace him. Even with his fumbling inexperience in law enforcement, he had done some things for the office he deemed worthwhile. He had implemented a dependable 9-1-1 service—key word, "dependable."

On a few occasions, he had been able to truly help some folks and they had shown emotional displays of gratitude. A few times someone had thanked him by baking him something and one elderly woman had knitted him a wool scarf. He wasn't supposed to take gifts and he knew that, but how could a man who lived on café food refuse one of Georgia Plunkett's chocolate cakes or a plate of Merry Jordan's chocolate oatmeal cookies? No one with any sense could view simple gifts of that type as bribes.

Beyond helping people, he liked being the voice of sanity

in an often insane world. He believed he had built goodwill and earned the confidence of the local people. If he ran for the office, he might win.

*Forget it,* he told himself. Callister County was poorer than a Third World country and almost as backward. No way would the county ever pay the sheriff a salary that could be called a decent living. The low pay was the major reason few wanted the office.

He had tried unsuccessfully to convince the commissioners if they wanted a sheriff who had some smarts and who didn't take money under the table like Jim Higgins had done, they had to pay a living wage. But, with the exception of Luke McRae, the commissioners were mossbacks determined to fend off the outside world and its customs. With no crime of great consequence in Callister, they reasoned, why did they need a professional lawman to be the sheriff?

He kept his old friend's phone number and the scant information he had about the sales job in a file in his desk drawer. Finding out the salary and more details about the job was, at the moment, more enticing than studying the case of a wife beater or a petty thief, so he set aside the court case files and began to punch in his friend's phone number.

He heard the distinctive sound of the metal door from the outside open and someone came into the anteroom whistling a tune. Rooster coming to work.

As he listened through the receiver to the burr on the opposite end of the phone line, the deputy appeared in the doorway and leaned a shoulder against the jamb as he usually did when he had something to say. His face looked more dolorous than usual. "Mornin', John T."

Getting no answer to his phone call, John hung up and slipped the folder labeled JOB FILE into his middle desk drawer. "Mornin', Rooster." He walked over to the farthest filing cabinet and filled his mug with coffee. "What's up?"

"Thought I'd better tell you Mae Hamlin came in yesterday. She's worried about Frank."

Frank Hamlin, the local Fish & Game officer. John hadn't seen much of him of late, but had known him for years. Frank had moved to Callister before John left home for college. "What's he done?" John sipped, the coffee warming him from the inside out.

"She ain't seen nor heard of him since Thursday. Says it ain't like him to go off for four days and not say when he's gonna be back or even call her."

John returned to the desk chair and tilted backward, a dangerous move given his size and the age of the chair. "Did she call up Fish and Game? They must know where he is."

"She talked to somebody, but they told her not to worry. They said with steelhead season going on, he could be laying out looking for illegal fishermen."

"Well, there you go. Where'd she say he's supposed to be?"

"She don't know. But she's afraid he's lost or hurt."

John had been in the law enforcement community long enough to know that cops didn't rush headlong into a search for reported missing persons because a majority of them turned out not to be missing at all. Still, something tickled the hairs on the back of his neck. Frank Hamlin was a dedicated conservation officer who, in his effort to protect Idaho's wildlife and enforce the state's game laws, sometimes traveled bad roads in country only mountain goats could love. John couldn't imagine any corner of Idaho where an outdoorsman like Hamlin would get lost, but it was conceivable he could roll his truck off a grade and be injured or stranded.

"Knowing Frank, if he's prowling the river checking fishing tags, he likely lost track of time." John didn't believe it, but thinking it made him feel more comfortable.

"Humph. Mae ain't the best-looking woman I ever met," Rooster muttered, "and she's a bit of a pinch-mouth, but I can't believe Frank'd forget where home is."

John recognized the deputy's call for him to take action. "Tell you what," he said, standing up. He unhooked his jacket from the coatrack and shrugged into it, then picked up his hat. "I'll drive over to the boat landing and see if I can find him."

\* \* \*

Swollen by the spring thaw, the Payette River zoomed like a bullet through the northern part of Callister County on its way to Hells Canyon. There it dumped its glacial contents into the Snake River. The ice-cold white water attracted sport fishermen from every state, even foreign countries. To accommodate anglers, the state and county had built boat landings along the banks at random intervals, the nearest being forty miles from town. John drove there first and met several men launching a sledboat. He learned nothing from them, so he proceeded to other boat landings, stopping and talking to cold but hopeful trout fishermen when he saw them.

Having no luck with boaters and fishermen, he left the rugged riverbanks and followed the narrow and steep back roads that paralleled the river. Along the way he dropped into the scattered stores that sold groceries and fishing gear and asked questions of owners and employees. Stopping for food in a mom-and-pop café, he asked more questions. Nobody had seen Frank Hamlin.

On the way back to town, as he mulled over his day, an urgency began to stew within him. He must have talked to dozens of people in twenty different locations. It made no sense that in the middle of the intensely monitored steelhead trout season, nobody along the Payette River had seen the game warden.

The Fish & Game Department offices in Boise were already closed when he reached the courthouse, but he made a mental note to call them first thing in the morning.

He called Izzy before going out to tour the streets of Callister. With Ava doing homework at the kitchen table, they kept their conversation respectable, at least on Izzy's end. She talked about Ava's day in school and the state of the horses. From his end, he teased her with naughty remarks, told her he couldn't wait to see her naked tomorrow morning and to crawl under what had become his favorite blue quilt.

He hung up on a chuckle and left the office for the Exxon service station. Sooner or later, every citizen of Callister went to the Exxon station, if for no other reason than to rent movies. The owner, Holt Johnson, reported he hadn't seen the Fish & Game pickup or its driver since Frank had filled his gas tank a week earlier.

Before going out to Izzy's the next morning, John called Fish & Game in Boise and asked after Frank. He netted no more information than he had learned along the river the day before. No one in the state office knew Frank's exact where-abouts, but none of his fellow COs appeared to be worried about him. John said thanks and hung up without discussion. No sense in unduly alarming a higher-up in Boise. Frank might come in today.

When he returned from Izzy's after lunch, Mrs. Hamlin had been into the office and talked to Rooster again and John felt the return of that prickle on the back of his neck.

The Snake River bordered Callister County on one side, separating Idaho from Oregon. Though it was not the ideal steelhead fishing river, fishermen nevertheless flocked to it. Leaving Rooster to mind the office, John drove the sixty miles to check it out and followed the same procedure as the day before on the Payette—asking questions of fishermen and merchants, driving the back roads along the river.

Nothing.

He gave up at dark and turned the Blazer toward Callis-ter. As he drove, a feeling of helplessness and inadequacy washed over him, reminding him of his lack of qualifications for the job he had committed to do. Two weeks of sheriff's school did not a detective make. Oh, sure, he could run the office and play the politics with his hands tied behind his back, but that wasn't police work. Yep, he had to take that job with the rope manufacturing company and leave law enforce-ment to the qualified.

Rooster was working at his computer when John arrived at the office early Wednesday morning. "Any luck on Frank?" the deputy wanted to know first thing.

John shook his head, fearing his voice would reveal the concern growing inside him. Court would convene at ten and having spent two days on two rivers, he wasn't pre-pared. Embarrassing himself with Judge Morrison went be-yond annoying.

Rooster left his desk and followed John into his office.

"Well, the Fish and Game Department might not be worried about Frank, but that ain't true about Mae. She came in again after you left yesterday. She looks like she ain't slept in a week. I told her you were checking on him. I tried not to upset her any more than she already is."

John plopped his hat on top of the filing cabinet behind his desk and sank into his chair. In the last two days he had done more than check on Frank. He had covered miles of remote territory. And in the mountains of Idaho, "remote" wasn't an adequate word to describe the isolation and wildness of Callister County's pristine geography that was inhabited mostly by wildlife. "Where the hell could he be, Rooster? I've looked in every canyon I could drive to along the rivers."

"I don't know, John, but being out of touch six days is a long time, even for a man who's used to doing it."

As John contemplated his own question, someone entered the office and Rooster walked out to meet the visitor, closing the door behind him. A few minutes later he came back. "John T?"

John looked up. Instead of leaning his shoulder on the doorjamb where he usually posted himself, the deputy was standing in front of the desk, his face bleached white. A dart of anxiety stabbed John's stomach. "What is it?"

The deputy glanced back toward the outer office and whispered, "There's a guy out here says he found a body."

For a few seconds John drew a total blank. "As in dead?"

Rooster nodded.

A thud in his chest drove John to his feet. "Shit. Get him in here."

The short, stout man who followed Rooster into John's office could be thirty-five to forty-five and his face, like Rooster's, showed an ashen tint. John put out his right hand. "Sheriff John Bradshaw. You say you found a body?"

The stranger shook hands. "George Powell. It's buried except for a hand and a foot. I didn't touch anything."

Suddenly the room seemed colder despite the rustle of the antiquated furnace. John hiked up his pants in an effort to look like a man who knew what to do next. "Where'd you find it?"

"Me and my brother were fishing on the Snake. He stumbled across it upriver from that big concrete boat launch."

A quick picture of the county geography flashed in John's mind. He had been at the big boat launch just yesterday. He stalled, waiting for the next question he needed to ask to come to him. "Uh, can you be more specific?"

"About ten miles above the dam. My brother went up into the trees to take a leak and—"

John stopped him, grabbed a note pad and pen and handed them to the stranger. "Draw me a picture."

The stranger took the pen and pad, but hesitated. "I don't think I can draw a map, but I can take you back there. My brother stayed, watching out."

John shot a glance toward Rooster. The deputy's eyebrows were drawn into a woeful tent and his teeth were clamped down on his lower lip. "We'll meet you outside," he told the stranger.

As soon as Powell left his office, John turned to Rooster. "Get your hat and coat."

He yelled for Dana. The dispatcher came into the office pale-faced and wide-eyed. Of course she had been eavesdropping. "Rooster and I are going out," John told her. "We might be out of touch, so get that retired guy to come in and man the office."

He didn't have to say the retired guy was the backup deputy. She nodded. "And Dana—this is not yet public information." She nodded again. Despite the admonition, John knew that by the end of the day everybody in Callister County would know the sheriff's office was investigating a dead body.

Outside, the stranger strode to a battered Dodge Caravan where a dark German shepherd the size of a yearling filled the passenger seat. It went on alert, fidgeting as John passed. Flatlanders. No dedicated fisherman would take a big dog on a fishing trip.

He and Rooster climbed into the Blazer and followed the Caravan out of the courthouse parking lot. As the Dodge raced up the highway at over eighty miles an hour, John pushed the old Blazer to keep up. From the corner of his eye,

John could see Rooster pressed into the corner, hanging on to the dash with one hand and the seat back with the other.

"Who do you think it is, John T?"

"No clue," John answered, but that strange tickle wouldn't leave the back of his neck.

# Chapter 25

Seventy miles of crooked highway at high speed was enough to shut Rooster's mouth for the rest of the trip. Finally, the maroon Caravan turned off onto a dirt two-track and continued on, traveling too fast for the rugged road. The county's aged Blazer rattled behind it, bouncing over small boulders and climbing out of erosion ditches that had cut furrows across the dirt surface.

They soon saw a man John assumed to be Powell's brother. The Caravan slowed and stopped. John brought the Blazer to a halt behind the Dodge. His stomach kinked as he anticipated the coming minutes. They all climbed out into the sunshine, but John shivered.

Powell introduced his brother, Weldon, then hauled the German shepherd out of the van and hooked a leash onto its collar. Rooster walked a wary circle around the energetic dog.

"Show me the body," John said, unable to divert his attention to anything else, even the dog.

As George Powell and his brother set out uphill, John unsnapped the strap that secured the pistol he had fired at uncountable paper targets but never in the line of duty. He didn't expect to need it, but it seemed like a good idea to keep it handy as possible.

They hiked in a straight line up a thirty percent grade. The German shepherd lunged ahead against the leash. For two short men, the Powell brothers covered a lot of ground in a hurry. John had to hustle to keep up. With every stride a sense of dread built in his chest.

Rooster tagged behind, audibly struggling for breath. "Lord, John T., I've got a bad feeling about this."

The mother of all understatement. John didn't reply.

The trek took them to a four-strand barbed wire fence that had been cut, and to trespassing on the Double Deuce Ranch. Drawing a welcome deep breath after the fast uphill hike, John glared at the brother named Weldon. "You cut this fence?"

"I found it like that," he answered defensively, then added, "I didn't touch anything."

As they approached a stand of fir, a distinct septic odor permeated the air, masking all other smells. John recognized it instantly as a dead-animal smell.

The shepherd went nuts, whimpering and barking and pulling at the leash. Powell yanked it back and they moved forward. Fifty feet inside the trees, the man stopped and pointed. "It's over there."

John's gaze traveled forward from the end of the stranger's finger to the toe of a black boot and bloated human fingers protruding from the loose soil. Along with a breathtaking odor, the silence hummed with a million flies swarming the area and covering the fingers. "Jesus Christ," John mumbled as an icicle skittered up his spine.

Rooster backed up and buried his head behind a syringa bush, retching and choking.

John's mind darted everywhere at once. Unbidden, Frank Hamlin's wife leaped to the forefront. Grappling for composure, he pointed at the excited dog. "Get that thing outta here."

George Powell dragged his dog over to an out-of-the-way bush and tied it.

From the looks of the torn-up ground, a digging varmint had exposed the boot and fingers, then got scared off—or dragged off. "Your dog been up here?" he asked George Powell.

"Hell, no," the stranger said from behind him. "When we're out like this, I keep her on a leash."

John made a mental note of that lie as Rooster came up

for air, eyes tearing, face red. A wet stain showed on the front of his shirt. Both Powell brothers leveled a look at the deputy that was somewhere between confusion and contempt.

John remembered even less than usual of what he had learned in sheriff's school. Not expecting to ever use most of the information that had been imparted, he hadn't paid close attention in the first place. But he did recall it was his duty to protect a crime scene. Deep down he wondered if any evidence present was already tainted beyond use.

"Rooster," John said, "go on back to the rig and—"

Before John finished, the deputy started down the hill.

"Find some of that yellow ribbon," John yelled, "and bring it back." He hoped Rooster had watched as many TV crime shows as he, John, had and knew what yellow ribbon he meant.

The Powell brothers watched them with eagle eyes.

John thumbed his hat back. At the moment, the two brothers were his only suspects. He questioned them at length, learned they lived in Boise and were employed by Hewlett-Packard.

Before he finished his questions, Rooster returned, panting and carrying a thick roll of inch-wide, hot-pink fluorescent ribbon. Surveyor's tape.

"This is all I could find, John. There ain't any of that yellow stuff."

John grabbed the roll. Muttering some of his most creative expletives, he set about marking a perimeter around the crude grave, looping the ribbon around trees and tying it to bushes.

"Aren't you supposed to rope off two perimeters?"

John gave Powell an arch look.

Powell lifted a shoulder. "I saw it on TV."

The guy could be right, for all John remembered, but he didn't have enough ribbon to span that far anyway, so he ignored him. He ended the task when he ran out of ribbon.

He also knew he had to get the coroner on the scene. He unclipped his cell phone, but was met with a NO SERVICE message. Shit. "Rooster, I'm going down to the Blazer to use the radio. You stay here. Don't touch anything inside that tape. And I mean *nothing*." Feeling more in control, he looked at the stranger. "You, Mister Powell, take that dog outta here and you and your brother stay in your van 'til I tell you different."

Powell pursed his mouth, jerked the German shepherd's leash from the branch where he had tied it and he and his brother stalked down the hill.

"You sure you don't want me to do the radioing, John?"

That he didn't want, so he ignored the deputy and headed for the Blazer.

"You think whoever done this could still be around here?" Rooster called from behind him.

"Keep it together, Rooster," John yelled without breaking his stride. *Forgodsake, keep it together.* "Whoever did this is in Canada by now."

*Or Mexico. Or, hell, maybe Europe.*

As John reached the Blazer, it came to him he should be taking notes and photographing evidence. He had seen a Polaroid camera in the Blazer's cargo hold once. He rummaged, came up with it and discovered it actually had film. In the jockey box, he found a pocket-sized spiral notepad. Beyond that, all he could think of was calling for help.

Walter Thornton, one of the two doctors in town, served as coroner. John radioed the sheriff's office and instructed Dana to call Dr. Thornton and tell him to come out to the south edge of McRae's place just up from the Snake, off Windy Ridge Road. He disliked telling Dana they had found a body, but he had no choice.

John looked at the sun. Noon. He hoped the doc didn't get lost.

The Double Deuce Ranch's headquarters was located a few miles on up the mountain, on Sterling Creek. Cattle could be grazing nearby and soon milling through the crime scene. John sent Rooster to the ranch to inform Luke McRae that his fence had been cut and a murder victim had been discovered on his property. And to ask for the use of some shovels.

Within the hour Luke arrived with tools, barbed wire and two hired men and John asked them instead of repairing the cut fence and returning it to its original location to fence off the crime scene to protect it from wandering livestock.

While he waited for the doctor, John asked more questions of the two fishermen. They had come up from Boise to spend the day on the river. They had no boat. They gave permission for John to look inside the Caravan. He did, but found nothing incriminating. He wrote every scrap of information he could think of about the Powell brothers in the spiral notebook, then sent them on their way with instructions to keep themselves available.

He returned to the crime scene and looked around outside the perimeter of pink ribbon. The grave was located several feet from a massive evergreen. Overhead, a canopy of limbs so thick that sunlight barely filtered through made the area dark and eerie and colder than the sunlit pasture leading up to the trees. Thick duff and soil had been disturbed in a ten-foot circle around the grave. John saw nothing he could identify as a clue to the victim's identity or the killer. Finding a footprint would be a miracle. He tied his handkerchief around his nose and mouth and began to work his way in a methodical circle inside the pink ribbon, picking up and saving every item that showed promise, marking and photographing where he found it.

When he had finally worked around to the protruding fingers, fighting off swarming flies, he squatted and looked closer. Though before he took the sheriff's job John had never seen a corpse outside a funeral service or a funeral home, in the past few months he had witnessed two—one, an auto accident victim, and the other an elderly woman who had died in her sleep. He might not be familiar with dead people, but living most of his life on a cattle ranch he had seen any number of dead animals. He had more than the average person's knowledge of the decomposition process. Whoever this poor sucker was, he couldn't have been here more than a few days.

Mae Hamlin had expected to hear from her husband on Thursday, six days ago. "Fuck," John muttered.

He saw no indication the corpse had been dragged to its burial site and he speculated it must have been carried here from somewhere else by someone on foot. Either the killer was a big, strong dude or he'd had help.

Another hour passed before Dr. Thornton arrived, followed by a crew of EMTs in Callister's only ambulance. John and Rooster had snapped pictures and combed every inch of the area around the grave. They turned it over to Dr. Thornton. He examined what he could see, then asked that the body be uncovered.

John, Rooster and Luke McRae tied bandanas around their faces and picked up shovels. They had scarcely turned over soil before a khaki-colored sleeve appeared and John knew, as he had suspected since he first saw the fingers, Frank Hamlin was no longer missing.

When the EMTs were able at last to lift the corpse from the shallow grave, they saw two dark, dirt-encrusted stains on Hamlin's uniform shirt in the middle of his chest. Gunshot wounds.

The group stood staring in brittle silence as Dr. Thornton went about his work. Every man present was acquainted with Hamlin at some level. Rooster, who went to the same church, broke into tears. One of the Double Deuce's hired hands had been childhood friends with Hamlin's son and was too distraught to speak.

Rooster being the better acquainted with Mrs. Hamlin, John dispatched him in the Blazer to bear the message that her husband had been found.

"It'll be dark before long," John said to the remaining men, battling the lump in his own throat. "It's a long shot, but look around for shell casings or bullet fragments in one of these tree trunks." He didn't expect them to find any, but he issued the order to give them something to do, something to distract them from the grisly sight of the decaying body.

John walked around the area snapping more pictures. Close to and nearly behind the tree trunk, a chunk of metal caught his eye. He snapped a picture, then gingerly pulled a heavy steel knife from the duff. Double Bs stood out clearly on the hilt.

John's focus zoomed to the night he had locked Paul Rondeau's similar knife in the safe in the sheriff's office storeroom. John hadn't looked at it since. Was it still there? Or had it somehow made its way out of the safe? Had he just now picked it from beneath the pine needles at the head of Frank Hamlin's grave?

When Dr. Thornton finished, the EMTs loaded the corpse into the ambulance and headed for St. Alphonsus Hospital in Boise for the autopsy.

John rode back to town with the doctor. "How long before we'll know about the gun?"

"Not long."

The doctor remained quiet, which was okay with John. Like an old silent movie, the events of the past few days streamed behind his eyes, swerved repeatedly back to the hunting knife and the morning he had released Paul Rondeau from jail, charged with nothing more than drinking and disturbing the peace.

Something else had been gnawing at him all day. It came to him as the doctor pulled into the courthouse parking lot and John saw the sheriff's department's white Blazer. Where was the Fish & Game Department vehicle that Hamlin drove? John had seen no trace of it. He had been so shaken by the crime and so preoccupied with the body, he hadn't thought of Hamlin's truck.

He went into his office intent on accomplishing one task. He opened the safe and saw that the knife he had taken from Paul Rondeau was still there, lying on the bottom shelf where he had put it. He hadn't thought it wouldn't be, not really. But he had to check.

He took the knife back to his desk and compared it to the one he had found at the crime scene. They were identical. The possibilities that fact opened were mind-boggling.

John reached his apartment after ten thirty. Izzy had left a voice mail message. He wanted to curl up in her soft arms and let her whispery voice drive away the horror of what he had seen, but it was too late to call her, much less see her.

His heart, having been in race mode all day, felt like a dead weight in his chest. It pounded like a bass drum. He had never felt more lost. He fell into bed exhausted, but lay awake, too keyed up to drop off.

The last time he had seen Frank Hamlin haunted him.

They'd had breakfast together months ago in Betty's Road Kill and Frank had been bragging and brandishing pictures of his new grandson.

At eleven the phone rang. Anticipating news, he answered in his official voice.

"John?"

*Julie?* His thoughts flew to his kids and his heart flip-flopped. "Yeah, what's up?"

"Did I wake you?"

"That's okay. Something wrong?"

"I'm, uh, in Boise. You couldn't come down here, could you?"

John frowned. "When?"

"Now. I've got a flight back to L.A. booked at six. I need to be on it. . . . John, I need you to take the kids."

That statement brought John to a sitting position. "What? Where the hell are you?"

"I said I'm in Boise. I can't keep them, John. They're causing trouble between Carson and me. He doesn't want them. I want to leave them with you."

John stood up. "Where are you?" he asked again.

"I'm at this big truck stop on the Ontario side of the freeway. Can you come?"

John knew the one, near the Oregon state line. He grabbed his jeans. "You know it'll take me three hours to get there."

"This place is open all night. Just hurry, okay?"

John dressed in minutes. He put a pot of coffee on to brew while he pulled on his boots and combed his hair. If anything had happened to those kids, he would never forgive Julie and that overeducated sonofabitch she had married.

He filled a thermal cup with hot coffee, grabbed his jacket and hat and headed for Boise. He shaved twenty minutes off the three-hour trip. By the time he saw the truck stop, two dozen scenarios involving his kids and Julie's husband—none of them pretty—had played out in his head.

He hadn't seen his ex-wife since she moved the kids to California over a year ago, but he recognized her sitting in a booth working a crossword puzzle. Emotion swept through

him when he saw both his boys asleep—Trey on the seat opposite her and Cody with his head on her lap. John crossed
the room and scooted in beside Trey, jostling him to make
room. The ten-year-old mumbled and didn't awaken, which
kept John from crushing him in a hug. Julie rolled her crossword puzzle book into a tube and stuffed it into her purse.

She was a pretty woman who had always had her share of
vanity. In the artificially cheery restaurant lighting, she
looked worse than he had ever seen her. Her long brown hair
was pulled back in a collapsed ponytail, loose strands hanging. Against her pale face, her dark eyes looked swollen and
red, with smudges of black makeup beneath them.

"Jesus Christ, Julie, you look like hell. What's going on?"

"Thanks a lot. You don't look great either."

The exchange was nothing more than an extension of the
animosity that had existed between them for years now.

"I've brought you the kids," she said, "so that should
make you happy."

"I'm glad to take 'em, but I still want to know why."

A weary-looking waitress came with a coffee carafe and
filled a mug for John. He blew on the surface of the hot liquid, then sipped, waiting for another charge of caffeine.

"I didn't know what else to do. Carson doesn't want to
raise another man's children. If he could have adopted them,
perhaps it would have been different—"

"What kind of a damn nut is he?" John shot her a
squint-eyed look as a new concern flew at him. "Has he
mistreated 'em?"

She frowned. "No, no, no. Nothing like that. You always
think the worst."

"Well, I don't get it. One day he wants to adopt them and
the next he's kicking them out of his house?"

"John, please, let's don't argue." Her eyes grew shiny
with tears. "I'm under a lot of pressure. I've brought them to
you. They're yours as much as they're mine. They wanted to
be with you anyway. Trey and Carson have been getting on
each other's nerves really bad."

The words in the letter she had written just a few weeks
ago came back to him. He wanted to ask what had happened

to all the great stuff in Southern California, but what would be the point? "Don't talk to me about pressure. I've got this murder that cropped up—"

"Murder. In Callister?" A silly grin crossed her mouth. "That's too ironic. What do *you* know about solving a murder?"

"Not as much as I'll know next week. I've got to get back. Did you bring suitcases or something?"

"Outside. I've got a rental car."

"Then let's get on with it."

He roused Trey, who was too sleepy to say much of a hello, then picked Cody up from his mother's lap. Carrying Cody and leading a groggy Trey by the hand, he followed Julie out to the parking lot.

Her good-bye to their sons was short and weepy. The boys were too sleepy to notice. He stood by, trying to piece together what had gone wrong between her and his kids. A conversation needed to be had about the future, but not tonight.

The sky was turning from deep blue to steely gray when he reached Callister's city limits for the second time in a twelve-hour span. Knowing his parents would be up, he called them. His dad answered the phone. "I've got my kids with me," John told him. "I can't explain why and I don't want to make a big production of it right now, but I need you and Mom to look after them. I'm sure you've heard about Frank Hamlin."

Twenty-four hours had passed. Everybody in Idaho had probably heard about Frank.

"Who do you suspect?" his dad asked, his speech revved up with excitement.

"I can't talk about it. It's under investigation."

"You don't have to worry. We'll take care of those kids."

John helped his sons shower and get dressed in clothing he took from their suitcases. Why had Julie dragged them away from their home with nothing more than two small suitcases? She must have left in a hurry.

"Mom's gonna ship our clothes," Trey said in explanation. "We're not going back," he added defiantly. "Mom's husband's a jerk."

John stared at him, stumped for a reply. The sudden change in his and his kids' lives refused to mesh with everything else going on in his mind.

He had nothing but a loaf of bread in his kitchen, so he made toast for their breakfast. It wasn't adequate, but his mom and dad would prepare a feast for them. Before they finished eating, his parents' truck pulled to a stop outside.

As he walked his sons to the truck, Cody looked up at him with big brown eyes. "You want us, don't you, Dad?"

"Of course I do." John felt like crying. It was only five a.m., the day hadn't even started and he was already faced with one more crisis he didn't know how to handle.

# Chapter 26

Like a truckload of rocks, the onerous responsibility that had fallen to him settled on John's shoulders in the shower. What faced him now was no rodeo, where the stakes were nothing more than a fat cash prize and a fancy belt buckle. A good, honest man had lost his life. What could be the reason, other than pure evil?

John's past, his present and his future formed a pyramid in his mind and atop it sat justice. Everything of value in his life—including the woman he loved—rode on how he handled events in the coming days. He couldn't even let himself be distracted by celebrating the reunion with his children.

The heavy hunting knife with two *B*s engraved on the hilt loomed in his mind. He had to know, besides the one in the safe and the one he had found at Hamlin's grave, how many others this recluse Buck Brown had crafted.

Phone service didn't exist in isolated mountain pockets, so of course the knife maker had no phone. That would be too easy. John had no choice but to make a personal visit. Rooster had given him directions to where Brown lived on Cabin Creek.

The phone warbled as he shaved. When he picked up, Isabelle was on the line. A clear memory from the morning John had released her brother from jail fixed itself as firmly as a granite boulder in his mind. "Are you okay? I've been worried. I heard about the game warden."

"I'm okay, which is more than I can say for poor old Frank."

"It's so awful. I don't think I ever met him."

"Nice guy. You'd already left Callister by the time he came to town."

"Do you have any idea who's responsible?"

"Not yet, but I expect to know more today."

"I'll be thinking of you. Is there anything I can do?"

"I don't think so. I'll be in touch as soon as I can."

"I love you, John."

"I love you, too, Isabelle." Emotion swelled in his chest. He wanted to tell her about his boys, but he didn't have time.

They said good-bye and John glanced at the clock. He had been awake twenty-four hours and more than a day's work awaited him. He felt like a zombie, but he didn't feel tired.

Before he left for Cabin Creek, he had one more call to make. From the beginning of John's tenure as the sheriff of Callister County, he had been adopted as a quasi protégé by the sheriff of a neighboring county. Walt Cassidy had spent a lifetime in a law enforcement career that spanned three states. He had been everything from a big-city homicide detective to a chief of police in a small town. "I like you," he had told John. "You've got guts and you show promise."

At the time John had laughed and replied, "Don't get to liking me too much because I'm strictly temporary."

Most of the time John muddled through legal procedure on his own, having discovered that much of it was plain old horse sense. This morning he didn't want to make a procedural mistake that could cost a conviction. He wasn't too proud to call for help from a man more experienced than he. Cassidy told him he had already heard about Hamlin and would leave at once for Callister, which gave John time to go to Cabin Creek and come back before the older sheriff arrived.

The trip to Buck Brown's was a half-hour ordeal up a rugged road. John had never met Brown and hadn't heard of his artistry until Rooster told him. Indeed, the scraggly-bearded craftsman was what the deputy had said. A recluse. An old hippie. A throwback to the seventies.

When John showed him the pictures of the knife he had found at the gravesite, Brown said he had made only two like it, confirmed that a few weeks earlier he had sold them to Paul Rondeau and Merle Keeton at a bargain price.

"Do you put your initials on every knife you make?" John asked him.

"Ever' one. I do it in a way nobody can copy. I'm an artist."

Creeping down the mountain from Brown's shack, visions of knives and incredible coincidences swirled in John's mind. Paul Rondeau and Merle Keeton owned twin knives. Now John had both in his possession. What were the odds of that?

While he knew the location of the knives, he didn't know where to find either owner. They could be anywhere.

Both Rondeau and Keeton had a long history of run-ins with the Fish & Game Department, most of the incidents with Frank Hamlin. Both men, over the years, had paid fines at various times for poaching big game, fishing out of season and illegal trapping and were, even now, at risk of permanently losing their licenses to hunt, fish and trap in Idaho.

Frank Hamlin must have weighed around one-ninety. John believed his body had been carried to its grave. It would have taken two men.

When John reached his office, Cassidy waited for him. The old lawman had to have driven a hundred miles an hour to reach Callister so soon. They wasted no time going to the crime scene.

The Fish & Game pickup truck had been on John's mind at various times all night. He and Cassidy had no luck locating it. After several hours of searching and questioning, they stood on the big concrete boat landing and wondered if the green Ford rested at the bottom of Hells Canyon Reservoir, a hundred feet down.

"Looks like I'm gonna have to call in a diver," John said.

"Looks like," Cassidy agreed.

At the grave, they searched for more clues, picking up and labeling items John and Dr. Thornton had overlooked the day before. John showed Cassidy where he had found the knife and related the encounter with Paul weeks back and the morning's meeting with Buck Brown.

"Then there's your suspects," Cassidy said.

"It's not that simple. I've got this conflict of interest." John didn't say so, but that was what really weighed on his mind. Determining the suspects had been easy.

"Like what?" The older lawman gave him a look, his laser-blue eyes almost hidden in a squint.

"I don't know Rondeau real well these days, but I went to school with him. We're the same age. Keeton's a little older. I've got something going on with Paul's sister. The fact is, we're kinda serious."

"In a small town, when it comes to a crime committed by the locals, you'll usually have a conflict of interest, John." Cassidy walked to the edge of the trees and looked out over the sunlit landscape. A quarter mile away they could see the Snake River shining like a silver ribbon. He smoothed his hand over his thick mustache. "You can't let a woman, or anything, come between you and the badge. If you do, you won't like yourself and it'll be a mark against you for the rest of your life."

"I already figured that out, Walt, but knowing it doesn't make things any easier."

"I can advise you about your case, but I'm not arrogant enough to try to help you in the romance department. Hell, I'm on my fourth wife."

John cut the sheriff a look. He had never heard a word of Cassidy's personal life. "Don't worry. I'll do what I have to."

"I know you will, John, because you're that kind of man. I can tell you this much. Being the only peace officer in a big county is hard on a man. And it's hard on wives and girlfriends."

"But I'm not really a peace officer."

"Yeah, you are. Even if you didn't think you were before, you're one now."

"There's still those two goofy fishermen from Boise to consider. Maybe my thinking is wrong. Maybe Paul and Merle didn't have anything to do with this."

"And maybe they did. You know where they're at?"

"I know where Paul lives. Finding out where Merle lives shouldn't take more than ten minutes in Callister."

"Then we can pick up these bastards and clear this whole messy business."

Back in town John wasn't surprised when they failed to find Merle where Rooster told him he lived or Paul at the travel trailer where John knew he lived, though Paul's boat was there. The tree-faller's wife who lived in the house told them Paul had been gone over a week.

John left her standing on the front porch and climbed into the Blazer. He sat for a minute and looked over the mountains that surrounded him. Though inhabited by only thirty-five hundred people, Callister County encompassed over five thousand square miles, an area larger than the state of Connecticut. Most of the topography was steep and rugged. Two major mountain peaks and two major rivers framed the valley. The east side bordered a federal wilderness area where no motorized vehicle was allowed to travel. A man savvy to the outdoors could hide out and elude being found for a long time, years even.

"You know," John said to Cassidy, "Paul Rondeau's even more well known for his survival skills than for drinking and hell-raising. I've heard stories about him spending weeks in the woods hunting. Sleeping on the ground, living on hard cheese and dried bread or wild onions and berries and what game he could kill."

Cassidy nodded and John knew they were on the same wavelength. "I expect his friend's no different."

While John sat pondering, a frantic Rooster came on the radio. "John! You gotta get back here! I gotta tell you something big."

John sped to the courthouse, where he found Rooster pacing and trembling. He shut himself into his office with his deputy and Walt Cassidy.

"Paul called," Rooster reported. "He said to tell you he

heard the shot when Merle Keeton killed Frank. And he
helped Merle bury him."

The hair on the back of John's neck didn't prickle; it
stood straight up. "Where was he? Where's Merle?"

"He wouldn't say where he was. I asked him about Merle.
He says he don't know where he went." John muttered curses,
wishing he could be in two places at one time. "I wrote down
the time," Rooster said. "It was thirty minutes ago."

A rap came at the door. When John opened it, Dana
handed him a faxed report from St. Alphonsus Hospital's
pathology department. Hamlin had been shot at close range.
Two 9 mm slugs had been removed from his corpse. John
had already learned that Hamlin went out armed with a 9 mm
semiautomatic. More than likely he had been shot with his
own gun. John felt something heavy drop in his stomach and
his hand automatically went to the .45 he wore.

By late morning, a drama he couldn't have envisioned on
his most imaginative days had started unfolding. Like a
spark in the forest on a July day, word spread that Paul Rondeau and Merle Keeton murdered Frank Hamlin and were
hiding out in the mountains. Fish & Game employees from
other parts of the state filtered into the sheriff's office and
took up the chairs, waiting for John to organize a manhunt.
Even local Forest Service employees came.

An Idaho State Police captain appeared, outraged that
some asshole had dared to murder a game warden. He introduced himself as Dan O'Neal and touted his background in,
first, the military police, then years as an investigator with
the ISP. He came close but didn't quite insist the investigation be turned over to him.

Not far behind were reporters and choppers from Boise's
TV stations, adding cameras and dazzling lights to the small
anteroom outside John's office. After John made a brief
statement, the reporters joined the throng of volunteer
searchers, filming and interviewing anybody who would talk.
And in Callister, that was almost everybody.

To John's dismay, but not totally unexpected, Izzy came,
too. She'd had no sleep and had been crying. John cleared
out his office and guided her to a chair.

"They're saying Paul did it. Is it true? You talked to him?"

"He called and left a message with Rooster. He said Merle fired the shots," John said gently, as if her brother's not being the trigger man somehow exonerated him.

"Shots?"

"Two shots to the chest. Paul was there, Isabelle. We don't know what role he played."

She bit down on her lower lip. Her head shook slowly. "I can't believe it. I know he drinks too much, but—" She sank to the chair seat, staring at nothing. "He wouldn't kill someone."

"Isabelle—"

"What are you going to do?" she asked, her voice breathless. She looked up at him and the pain he saw in her eyes hurt his heart. "All those men out there. What are they going to do?"

"Darlin', do you know where he is?"

"No. I told you, I haven't seen him in days. I'd have to think back when I last saw him."

"He'll have to come in. Or be brought in—"

A sob burst out and her hand flew to cover her mouth. She sprang to her feet. "They won't bring him in! They'll kill him! Isn't the game warden a cop? That's how it is when a cop gets killed, isn't it?"

"They can't do that, Isabelle."

"Out in the mountains all by themselves? They can do anything they want to. Who'll stop them?"

"They're officers of the law, darlin'. They have ethics and morals."

"Oh yeah? Well, I happen to think a lot of them are as bad as the criminals they chase."

"Look, if he gets in touch with you, you'll have to tell me—"

Her fists clenched. "You stay away from me, John. I won't help you and those maniacs out there kill my brother."

She lunged toward the door. John grabbed for her arm, but she was too quick. She pushed her way through the throng of assorted volunteers who were yammering and drinking coffee and milling like a bunch of cattle in the office. As she raced up the stairs, reporters followed hot on her heels. John started after her, too, but was stopped by Walt Cassidy's gravelly voice.

He turned and saw the old sheriff standing in his office doorway motioning to him with a tilt of his chin.

"Fuckin' reporters," John muttered, returning to his office.

Cassidy closed the door. "That the sister?"

"Yeah." John's heart thumped in his ears. Izzy was too distraught to have to deal with a bunch of vultures. He stared at the door as if he expected her to run back to him for sanctuary, though he knew better.

"She'll go to him if she can."

The fear that Cassidy could be right set off a new panic within John. "I don't want her in the middle of this, Walt."

"You can't stop her. The best you can do is keep an eye on her. Meanwhile, let's give that mob outside this door something to do. Might as well take advantage of all this manpower."

"Yeah, I guess you're right." John reached for the doorknob.

Cassidy stopped him again. "Let me say one more thing, John. Just remember Callister is your county, your jurisdiction. This is *your* investigation. You take the lead and don't let the big boys run over you. You're capable of doing as good a job as anybody and you've got an advantage."

John made a sarcastic huff. "In what way?"

"You know the terrain and you know the perps."

Unconvinced that Cassidy's opinion was well founded, John could only stare at the old lawman. He had never been a control freak, but he had to become one now.

He couldn't be more unprepared for what lay ahead.

Isabelle raced to Paul's travel trailer. Though his boat was parked in its usual place, when she banged on the trailer door and called Paul's name no response came. Having no key, she moved around the outside, peering through the windows.

The owner of the house behind which the trailer was parked came out into the backyard and told her the sheriff had already been there but Paul hadn't been in the trailer in days.

At home, Isabelle skidded to a stop by the barn and practically fell out her truck door before the engine died. She ran inside the barn calling Paul's name. Getting no response, she dashed to the house and tramped through the rooms, calling to her brother. She even climbed the stairs to the attic room.

She returned to the kitchen, trying to remember the last conversation she and Paul had had. After the court hearing, he had told her he intended to spend the days remaining before he went back to work in the woods fishing for steelhead. So his boat, instead of being parked, should be on a river somewhere.

"Get a grip," she mumbled, stopping in the kitchen. She ran a glass of water from the tap and drank it. As her thoughts assembled, they traveled back to childhood and all at once she knew where to find her little brother.

She set down her glass, returned to the Sierra and drove to the far end of Dancer's pasture, where a copse of evergreens and thick brush grew.

And there she discovered Paul's silver truck dually parked, so well hidden in the brush no one would ever find it.

The door was unlocked and the keys were in the ignition as if he expected *her* to find it. She searched the interior for a note, some kind of sign, but found nothing that told her his whereabouts or how long his pickup had been parked there.

She looked up, above the tall pines, at the gray precipice toward the top of Callister Mountain and knew—knew without a doubt—where her brother was.

She was in no shape to make the ten-mile climb on foot, but she could ride the distance easily. She returned to the house, put on long underwear, old jeans and her riding boots, packed enough food to last a couple of days. She called Nan Gilbert and asked her to pick up Ava at school and keep her overnight.

Then she went to the barn and saddled Dancer. With any luck she could be at the miner's cabin by dark.

# Chapter 27

John and Cassidy organized the volunteers into teams, out-fitted them with maps and Cassidy lectured them on "go-ing by the book." No shoot-outs, no unnecessary heroics. The teams set out on foot and in four-wheel-drive vehicles, armed to the teeth and itching to be challenged. What John knew that they didn't grasp was that if Rondeau and Keeton didn't want to be found, most likely they wouldn't be.

After the searchers and reporters cleared out of the court-house, Cassidy left town to see to his own county. Taking ad-vantage of the first calm and quiet he had known in twenty-four hours, John sat down at his desk with his notes. He set Dana to looking up recent photographs of Paul and Keeton and working on getting a flyer out to other county sheriffs' offices.

A loud argument erupted in the anteroom and John thought he recognized Art Karadimos' voice. He got to his feet and made for the door, saw Rooster with his hand pressed against the sheepman's chest and a TV cameraman standing on a chair filming.

When Art saw John in the doorway, he pushed Rooster aside and strode in John's direction. He carried a rifle and had a pistol strapped on his belt. The cameraman came right behind him.

A new adrenaline rush streaked through John's body. A

visual of Isabelle's border collie lying in the bed of her pickup flashed in his memory. Without a second thought he grabbed Karadimos' rifle with one hand, his collar with the other and shoved him through his office doorway. The cameraman attempted to follow, but John slammed the door in his face. Karadimos stumbled across the room and landed against the desk.

"What the hell are you doing?" John shouted.

The sheepman drew himself up to his full five feet eight inches. "I know how to deal with those fuckers," he shouted back. "That Rondeau outfit's nothing but vermin. It's time somebody cleaned 'em out for good."

"Rooster," John yelled.

The deputy appeared in the doorway.

John handed the rifle behind himself, glaring into Karadimos' eyes. "Rooster, take these goddamn guns and lock 'em up."

The deputy grabbed the rifle and John began to yank Art's belt loose. The older man fought John's hands, but John had his belt and pistol off before he could defend himself. John handed the pistol, too, back to Rooster.

"I oughtta lock your ass in one of those cells," he said to Karadimos.

The sheepman crossed his arms over his chest as if John had stripped him of clothing. He backed away. "Your dad says—"

"Shut up!" John loomed over him. "You don't know what my dad says. And if I ever see you again with any kind of a gun in your hands, you're toast. Got it?"

Karadimos tucked back his chin. His eye twitched at the corner. "You can't take my guns! I'll get my lawyer. I'll—"

"Go home! And don't even come out for food 'til this is over."

Art stomped out of the office muttering and swearing. John flopped in his chair, his pulse pounding, his head buzzing.

A reporter appeared in the doorway. "Do you have a statement, sheriff?"

"Get outta here," John shouted.

Rooster and Dana rushed into the office and Rooster hustled the reporter back to the anteroom. Dana stood in front of the desk, wide-eyed. John drew his hands down his face, aware that neither Rooster nor Dana had ever seen him have such an outburst.

"Want me to get you a cup of coffee?" Dana asked.

"No. Thanks, Dana, but no." He leaned forward and rubbed his scratchy eyes. "Christ, I'm wore out."

"You should go home, John, and get some rest."

"Yeah. I will. Soon."

He spent the next couple of hours calling pilots he knew who owned airplanes and asking if they would fly the valley and search the vast mountainsides and hidden vales from overhead. He found only a few who were willing. The siege mentality that had always existed in Callister had kicked in. Already the citizens were choosing sides.

John didn't have much confidence in flying the landscape, anyway. His thoughts kept drifting back to the immensity of Callister County's two mountains, the density of the forests and the memory of a crashed small plane that had been lost for four years before a hunter stumbled onto the wreckage.

And he recalled the old saying about looking for a needle in a haystack.

By late afternoon, Isabelle could see the old cabin in the distance. She spotted smoke, so she knew the woodstove inside still functioned. Snow lay in patches in shady spots and under trees, but the south side of the mountain was mostly bare, though wet. Still, she knew the temperature was cold because her breath and Dancer's made little puffs of vapor. Dancer had carried her well, considering his hooves had never before touched mountainous terrain.

Then Isabelle saw him waiting for her, standing in front of the cabin, his hair disheveled and shaggy, his jaws whiskery, his hands stuffed into the pockets of a ragged coat. Childhood memories flooded into her brain and it was all she could do not to break into tears.

"What're you doing here?" he asked, reaching for

Dancer's headstall as she swung out of the saddle. "What'd you bring that horse up here for?"

Relieved to see him, she pressed her head against his hard shoulder. Words gushed out. "Oh, Paul. You have to go back. Please. It'll be so awful if you don't. There must be a hundred people from everywhere searching for you and Merle."

"What makes you think it won't be awful if I do go back?"

She remembered a small corral attached to the back of the cabin and led Dancer to it. "I've brought food. Have you eaten?" She unlashed her sleeping bag from behind her saddle and swept her saddlebags from Dancer's back.

"I've got a little," he said and helped her as she began unsaddling.

"You have to trust John, Paul. He's the only chance you've got." She didn't add *of staying alive*, though she thought it.

"I didn't do nothin', Izzy. I was sober and everything. But Merle—hell, I think he's gone crazy."

"Dancer needs water. Is the spring still flowing? I hope it isn't frozen."

"That's where I've been getting my drinking water." Paul walked with her as she led Dancer to the water.

An old trough sat near the spring at the base of a huge granite boulder some hundred feet away.

"What happened? And if you didn't do anything, why did you run away?"

"That crazy bastard Merle. He threatened to kill me, Izzy, after I've knowed him all my life and all we've been through together. I didn't know but what he might do it. That's how come I come up here. I don't think he knows where this place is."

"I heard in town Frank was shot with his own gun."

Paul nodded. "I don't know how Merle got his hands on it. Frank must have drawn, but I was back at the truck. I didn't see what happened."

They reached the spring and Dancer drank. "But why did Merle shoot him? Was he drunk? Were you drunk?"

Her brother shook his head. "I wasn't. Merle had been drinking a little beer maybe. I had it made up with him to meet him at the boat launch with some food and whiskey. When I got there, Frank was there, too, and him and Merle was arguing over Merle hooking a sturgeon."

"Paul, you know that's illegal."

"I wasn't in on it, Izzy. Frank was talking about giving Merle a big ticket. I didn't want Frank to think I had something to do with it and give me a ticket, too, so I left. My truck was parked up on the road. I went back up to get the cooler. That's when I heard two shots. I run back down to the boat launch. Frank was laying on the ground and Merle had a pistol in his hand. I knew Frank was dead without even looking close. Hell, smoke was coming out of his chest."

"Oh my God," she whispered, suddenly realizing she had been holding her breath. "Paul, that's terrible."

His eyes teared. "I didn't know what to do, Izzy. Hell, I've argued with Frank a hundred times, but I never thought he deserved killing. I started shaking all over. I backed up, thinking I'd just leave, but Merle told me we had to get rid of Frank, like I'd somehow helped him shoot him." Paul's voice broke and he wiped his eyes on his sleeve. "I wasn't sure what he meant, Izzy. For a minute, I was scared he meant we had to quarter him."

"Oh, Paul—"

"Then Merle decided we ought to bury him and he started talking to me about where. I didn't know where, so I didn't even say nothin'. He said it would be smarter to bury him on private ground than on state or Forest Service land. I didn't care. All I wanted to do was get out of there alive."

Dancer raised his head and snorted and Isabelle started leading him back to the corral. "You have to tell John what happened. It's too late to go back down tonight. I'll stay with you. We'll go first thing in the morning."

"I can't, Izzy. You know how it is for me. Even before this, everybody already thought I was a damn criminal."

"What else can you do? You can't live here in this cabin, you can't run away. If you're innocent, you have to clear yourself."

They penned Dancer and Isabelle spotted a rusted frying pan on the ground. She dumped oats into it from the little sack she had brought for the horse, then picked up her sleeping bag and her saddlebags. "Where are you sleeping?"

"I got my old laying-out outfit with me."

Isabelle followed her brother into the cabin. Paul's camping equipment and some clothing lay around the floor of the single room. A fire burned in the woodstove, but the dilapidated cabin was no better than a barn. To stay warm, they had to huddle around the stove. "This place still looks the way I remember it," she said, looking around. "How long have you been here?"

"I don't know. A week maybe. I lost track of time."

They ate the cheese, meat and bread Isabelle had brought, then began to bed down for the night. Isabelle was tired. A four-hour horseback ride uphill had been taxing.

John tried Izzy's number one more time. He had called all afternoon, but got only her answering machine. He dared not drive out to her house, lest one of the overzealous volunteers or a hungry reporter follow him.

At dusk the searchers straggled back into town empty-handed and filled up the only motel and all the barstools in Callister's three bars.

John had now been without sleep over twenty-four hours. His head spun, his eyes felt as if they were full of sand and he could scarcely put one foot in front of the other. He gave up, but before he left the office, he called one more person. Nan Gilbert told him she hadn't heard from Izzy. John didn't believe her, but it would have to wait 'til tomorrow.

He drove to his parents' house to spend the night with his family and try to get reacquainted with his sons. He barely made it through supper.

At four a.m., in the bed he had occupied as a boy and with Cody asleep on his shoulder, his eyes sprang open. Like a vision in the dark, he saw an old cabin at the base of the rock face on Callister Mountain.

*They won't bring him in. They'll kill him.*

Izzy could tell him how to find it.

By six o'clock he was dressed, fed and out the door.

Though the Lazy B and Isabelle's home were on opposite ends of the valley, John reached her place in half an hour. Plowing up the driveway, he looked for the faint trail of smoke that usually came from the chimney, but saw none. He braked in his usual parking place and dashed to the back door. No one answered his knock or his call. Peeking through the porch windows, he saw Harry and Gwendolyn asleep in their beds. He walked around to the front door and knocked. No response.

From the front porch, he looked down on the pasture. Polly and Trixie grazed peacefully in their ordinary world.

He stamped back to the Blazer and scooted in, taking one more look around the deserted farmstead. Both Izzy's fancy horse trailer and his lowly two-horse rig were parked in their respective spots beside the big barn. Easing on down the driveway, he peered into the barns, then the pasture where Dancer stayed. The blue horse was nowhere to be seen.

A light clicked on in John's head. *"Fuck!"*

He twisted in his seat and stared up Callister Mountain. He could barely spot the rock face Izzy had pointed out the day they picnicked. It looked to be fifty miles away, but John remembered her saying it was ten or twelve miles from the limestone ledge beside Stony Creek. "Lord, Lord, Izzy," he mumbled. "What have you got yourself into?"

He stared hard at Polly and Trixie. Did he dare ride one of them up the rugged face of Callister Mountain? Both mares were strong and in good shape, but both were pregnant and he had no idea how they would handle a hard ride.

He threw the transmission into gear and punched the accelerator. Roaring down the driveway, he jerked his cell phone from his belt and thumbed in a "saved" number. His dad answered on the second ring.

"Dad, I need your help again. Get Rowdy up and saddled. I'm coming to get him."

"What's going on, son?"

"I'll tell you when I get there. And Dad, I need one more thing. I need to borrow your horse trailer."

He disconnected and called Information, got Nan

Gilbert's phone number. When Nan came on the line, he asked her for the second time if she knew Izzy's whereabouts. The hesitation before she answered was all John needed to hear.

By the time he finished his conversation with Nan, he had reached his apartment. He changed clothes—put on silk long johns usually saved for extreme weather and traded his jacket for a shearling-lined parka. Last, he pulled on his riding boots and dug his down sleeping bag out of a closet. He left the Blazer parked and climbed into his personal pickup that had a trailer hitch he knew would fit his dad's horse trailer.

On the way to the Lazy B, he called Rooster and told him where he was headed and to keep it quiet, told him to pick up the county's Blazer at his apartment. He ordered him to maintain control of the manhunt, which would surely restart early.

After all of that, he still had enough time before reaching his parents' house to worry.

As unpredictable and headstrong as Dancer was, a rider could get in trouble with him on a mountain trail. Any number of things or beings in the mountains could spook even a calm-natured horse. Dancer was anything but calm-natured. John had never seen Izzy lose control of a mount, but he had never seen her ride Dancer in the mountains either.

Paul and Keeton, wherever they were, would be armed. John didn't believe Paul would hurt his sister, but he didn't know what Merle Keeton might do. Desperation drove ordinary people to extraordinary behavior.

When he reached the Lazy B, he saw Rowdy saddled and tied to the corral fence.

"I'll go with you," his dad volunteered as they hooked the horse trailer onto John's truck bumper.

"I'll have more luck alone."

His dad went into the barn and came back carrying his deer rifle. "I mean it. I'll go with you, son," he said again.

"No, Dad. It'll go better if I'm alone."

"But they're two armed men."

"I don't know that Paul and Keeton are together. If what

Paul said on the phone can be believed, they aren't." John placed his hand on his .45. "Besides, I'm armed, too."

"Wait," his dad said and trotted to the barn again. He returned with a saddle scabbard, which he tied onto the left side of John's saddle. He checked the load in the rifle and shoved it into the scabbard.

John looked at the 30.06, then at his dad. "I don't need a big rifle."

"It doesn't hurt to take it. You may be glad you've got it."

This was no time for an argument. John gave in. Maybe his dad was right. A rifle powerful enough to down an elk with one shot might be useful. He put out his hand and Dad laid a handful of extra ammo on his palm.

John slipped the shells into his coat pocket as he walked over to the fence and said hello to his old friend. The horse nickered and snuffled at him. John untied him and led him to the trailer. "I'll need a nose bag and some oats," he said to his dad, "and hobbles, in case I have to sleep out."

"Right." His dad loped back to the barn.

John urged Rowdy into the trailer. The horse had been loaded and unloaded a thousand times. The old boy remembered the routine and walked right in with no trouble. He seemed glad to have something different to do. Maybe he thought he was headed for a rodeo.

John slammed the trailer gate as his dad came out of the barn carrying an armload of items—everything John had requested, plus saddlebags. "Your mother put together some food." His dad patted the saddlebags and threw them behind the saddle. "If you don't want me to go, then get Walt Cassidy."

John shook his head. "I'm gonna be moving fast. Walt's too old to get around."

"It can't be the right procedure for you to be doing this alone."

Dad was probably right, but John didn't know the proper procedure exactly.

*They won't bring him in. They'll kill him.*

For all he knew, Izzy could be right, too. For all he knew, the volunteer posse of strangers was no better than a lynch mob. No way was he going to direct them to where he believed Paul and Izzy to be. He looked his dad in the eye. "Try to understand, Dad. I have to do this my way. I have to do it for Isabelle."

His dad opened his mouth to speak, but must have thought better of it because he closed it.

"Don't worry," John said. "I've got surprise on my side and I know these people. Rooster knows where I'll be. If I'm not back by tomorrow night, then he and Walt can come looking for me."

"You gonna say 'bye to your boys?"

John shook his head. "I don't want to scare them. They've been through enough already. I don't know what's been going on with them and Julie's husband, but I'll deal with it later." John climbed into his truck and lowered the window.

"You be careful," Dad said. "You'll be in our prayers."

John glanced up to the ranch house. His mother and his two sons stood on the long porch. A knot leaped into his throat. He put up a hand to them as he gave them a last long look, swallowing the fact that it was possible he would never see them again. "Whatever happens, Dad, take care of my boys."

"We will, son. That's what family's for, helping out each other."

"Yeah," John mumbled as his grim thoughts swung to Isabelle and her brother.

# Chapter 28

At the gate in the fence along the backside of the pasture that separated the Rondeau property from national forest, John picked up the trail he and Izzy had followed the day they picnicked. He soon reached the limestone ledge beside Stony Creek. From here, he had a clear view of the rock face marking where Paul had hidden out as a child in an old miner's cabin. Callister Mountain was a twelve-thousand-foot ancient volcanic peak. The rock precipice loomed maybe a quarter of the way down from the snowcap. He reined Rowdy in that direction.

Rowdy performed like a champion, but John knew better than to push him too hard traveling uphill in cold, thin air. As they climbed, the trail grew fainter and more rugged, the timber thicker, causing John to duck low-growing limbs. At times he was forced to dismount to cross rockslides and coulees. He reached patches of snow and began to feel the chill. He dismounted and untied his shearling-lined coat from behind the saddle and shrugged into it, then wrapped a wool scarf around his neck.

He was no tracker, but occasionally he saw fresh horse tracks. They had to be Dancer's. In the solitude that surrounded him questions assailed him. Could Paul be believed? Was Merle Keeton with him? How much danger was Izzy in?

Where would her loyalty lie if or when it came to a show-down with her brother?

The air became cooler yet and he encountered more snow. The sun began to lose heat and he checked his watch. Soon it would be too dark to travel in the thick timber. He didn't know the precise location of the cabin, but he kept climbing toward the rock face, believing that at its base he would find what he sought.

All at once he topped out in a small opening and saw in the distance a pass over the ridge of a drainage he had been paralleling. He rode toward it, keeping the rock face in sight.

On the other side of the pass, he dropped into a small valley flatter and more open than the heavy timber through which he had just ridden. In the pure mountain air the distinct smell of wood smoke touched his nostrils.

Excited, he broke his binoculars out of his poke and scanned the surroundings. In the far distance he saw something foreign to the natural landscape. He urged Rowdy to a trot on the almost flat ground and rode toward it, at the same time keeping undercover near the tree line at the edge of the vale.

After a short time, he stopped and homed in on the object. Damned if it wasn't a cabin and a faint trail of smoke drifted from its chimney. It could be no more than half a mile away.

His pulse kicked up. He scanned with the binoculars again, looking for Dancer, but didn't see him. If the horse wasn't there, was Izzy? Concern nagged at him as he ran down the list of reasons the horse wasn't visible, not the smallest of which was that he, John, had played a wrong hunch and wasted a day.

He dismounted and led Rowdy into the thick trees. The last thing he wanted was to be discovered. He debated whether to take the cabin occupants now and have to deal with them in custody and camped out all night or wait until daylight when it would be easier and safer to get down the mountain.

He tied Rowdy and fed him oats from the nose bag. Once he was satisfied the horse was secure, he took the binoculars and made his way on foot closer to the cabin and spotted

Dancer in a small lean-to attached to one side of the structure. He was almost as glad to see Dancer as he would be to see Izzy. At least he knew she had arrived.

He assessed the structure, which was nothing more than a primitively thrown together room on the verge of collapse, backed up to an enormous granite outcropping. John had seen many such huts and hovels in out-of-the-way places in the mountains and he knew the old thing would have only one door. He made a half circle around the building, sneaking among rocks and downed trees, being cautious to stay hidden and downwind from Dancer.

Head-on appeared to be the only way to approach the cabin.

John had never faced a life-threatening situation. He had sometimes wondered how he would handle it. What he felt wasn't fear exactly, more like a peculiar high, more like a stranger had seized control of his body. He didn't care, as long as the stranger knew what the hell to do.

He returned to where he had left Rowdy and made a cold camp, having decided to make his move at daybreak. Through the night, he awoke several times and checked his watch.

He came awake for no good reason and felt a presence, felt something against his head.

"Time to get up, sheriff," a gravelly voice said.

John's eyes popped open. He turned his head and found himself staring into the business end of a pistol. He blinked, wide awake. His hand wanted to grab for the .45 tucked under the edge of the sleeping bag, but he checked himself.

"Come outta there on your hands and knees, sheriff."

John peeled the sleeping bag back and complied. In the steely gray of first light, he looked up at Merle Keeton. His thoughts flew to his sons and he wished he had chosen to hug them good-bye.

"Gimme that pistol," Keeton said, beckoning with his finger. "Butt first."

John handed the .45 up to his captor, then reached for his boots. He sneaked a glance toward his saddle and saw the 30.06 safely tucked into the scabbard. In the dim early-morning light, possibly Keeton hadn't seen it.

"Now, get to your feet real slow. I already shot me a game warden. I figger adding on a sheriff won't make much difference."

Awake now and on his feet, John could think. If Keeton intended to kill him, why hadn't he simply pulled the trigger while John slept?

His captor chuckled. "'Course I never figgered you was a real sheriff, John. That's why it didn't scare me none to walk up on you like this." Keeton's chin hitched in the direction of the cabin. "Let's get up to that cabin. I see they got a fire going. I been freezing my ass off all night out here in these woods."

"My horse," John said.

"To hell with him. For all I care he's cougar bait."

John clenched his jaw and looked Keeton in the eye. "If I go, the horse goes. Otherwise, you can shoot me right here."

When Keeton stamped over to where Rowdy was tied and untied him with one hand, John's confidence lifted a notch. Keeton didn't have the nerve to look him in the face and pull the trigger. And he still hadn't spotted the rifle.

"The horse goes with me," Keeton said. "You walk ahead."

How the hell had Keeton happened upon him on the side of a vast mountain? John wondered as they walked. And what was he doing here? "Where'd you come from, Keeton?"

"Here and there. I been on this mountain a few days, lookin' for that cabin. I figgered ol' Paul'd go there. Then I heard your horse. Don't know if you know it, John, but a horse tromping through the woods ain't real quiet. When I saw it was you riding him, I knew I'd found that stinkin' rat Paul."

So it was Paul that Keeton was after. And after he found him, then what? John swore mentally, disgusted that he had let himself be caught and forced to lead Keeton to the cabin.

Isabelle awoke shivering from the cold. The wood cookstove's narrow firebox simply wouldn't hold a large enough

log or enough small pieces of wood to burn all night. The dilapidated cabin's walls and roof were full of holes and
cracks. Paul awoke, too, and stuffed small pine splits into the
firebox. They huddled around it and shivered, waiting for the
flames to take off.

Soon as she got warm, she would help Paul pack and together they would head down the mountain. If he was with
her, surely he would be safe.

He had a coffeepot and coffee. Isabelle had just set it on
the rusted stove's cast-iron surface to brew when she heard
Dancer whicker. She opened the door to go outside and
check on him and her stomach lurched.

There stood Merle Keeton holding a pistol on John.

He pushed John into the cabin and followed. "Guess you
thought I wouldn't find this place," Merle said to Paul.

John's heart beat like a snare drum as he surveyed the
cabin's dim interior. One room, two windows, one door. He
saw two rifles standing in the corner. They would be Paul's.

"Okay, so you found me," Paul said to Keeton. "So
what?"

John angled his eyes at Paul as it dawned on him Paul
had come here to hide out from Keeton, not the law.

"You, Red"—Keeton pointed the pistol at Izzy—"get
over there and get me them rifles."

Izzy stared up at John, terror in her eyes, and at that moment, he made a vow. Merle Keeton would never see Callister again if he hurt Isabelle. "Do what he says," John told her.
*That is, 'til I come up with something.*

Izzy brought the two rifles from the corner of the room.

Keeton gestured her to prop them beside the door and ordered John and Paul back toward the cookstove. "Now," he
said to Izzy, "I figger you must have something to eat up
here."

"Nothing but lunch meat and bread."

"That'll do. Get me a cup o' that coffee."

John's gaze swerved to the steaming coffeepot on the
cookstove and suddenly he found a plan.

Izzy looked up at him again. She had more guts than any

woman he knew. He only hoped she didn't waver now. He held her gaze, formed a ring with his thumb and forefinger and barely tipped his hand.

He saw in her eyes she understood and braced himself to grab Keeton's gun. Paul's eyes darted everywhere and John could see he had a scheme of his own.

"The handle's hot," Izzy said in a quavery voice.

A flannel shirt lay on top of a pile of clothing on the floor. "Get her that shirt," John said to Keeton. "She hasn't done anything to you. Why make her burn herself?"

Keeton sidled over to the shirt. Eyes glued to the three of them, he bent, picked up the shirt and threw it at Izzy.

Her hand trembled as she wrapped the shirt around the coffeepot handle. She poured the tin cup full, then lifted it using the shirt as a pot holder. She walked the four steps to where Keeton stood and, just as John hoped, dumped the steaming cup of coffee onto Keeton's gun hand.

He let out a howl and fired the pistol on reflex. *Blam!*

Paul cried out, stumbled backward and fell.

John grabbed Keeton's wrist with his left hand and buried his right fist in the man's gut. Merle doubled over with an *oomph!* but managed to fire the pistol again. John twisted the wrist until he felt it snap. The .45 hit the floor and to John's horror, Paul went for it, crawling across the floor, his arm extended, his fingers clutching.

John lunged toward the rifles, grabbed one and popped the safety. "Don't do it, Paul."

"John, no," Izzy cried, in tears now and kneeling on the floor beside her brother.

The .45 lay there, only inches from Paul's fingers. "I mean it, Paul. I'll shoot you."

Izzy reached out and shoved the .45 beyond Paul's grasp. "He wasn't going to shoot."

"John, I was gonna help you," Paul said, getting to his feet, favoring his left shoulder.

John didn't know if he believed that. He didn't dare take a chance. A moan came from Keeton, who lay in a fetal position. John grabbed him by the coat and hefted him to his knees. "Put your hands behind your back," he ordered.

Keeton did as he was told. He had lost his starch. John reached behind himself for the handcuffs attached to his belt loop and cuffed him.

"My arm's broke," Keeton whined, in tears. "I'm burned. Them cuffs is tight."

John picked up his .45 and leveled it at Paul as he propped the rifle by the front door. "Paul, I've got only one pair of cuffs. Give me trouble and I won't think twice about blowing your ass off."

"He's hurt," Izzy cried, stepping in front of her brother. "He's innocent. He can tell you, John."

John caught her arm and drew her away from her brother. "You okay?" he asked her and pulled her closer to his side. "You scared the shit right out of me."

"It wasn't me that shot Frank," Paul said, standing with his shoulder angled.

"How bad are you hurt?"

"I'm okay. Just burns a little."

"Paul didn't do it," Izzy said, her voice breaking. "You have to listen to him, John." She went back to her brother and began working his wounded arm out of his coat sleeve.

John looked into Paul's face as Izzy wrapped the dirty flannel shirt around his bleeding arm. "What makes you think you're innocent, Paul? You were there. You helped bury Frank. You said so."

"I was trapped. If I hadn't, Merle would've shot me, too."

John didn't know if he believed that, either. Paul and Keeton had been friends for years.

Izzy had done the best she could bandaging her brother's wound. "Let's get Dancer saddled," John told her, then turned his attention to Paul. "You help her."

John picked up the coffeepot and used the remaining liquid to douse the fire in the woodstove, then directed all of them outside. Paul followed Isabelle to the corral.

"Goddammit, John," Keeton said, in tears, "don't do this to me. You've knowed me all your life. I got rights—"

*Miranda. Shit.* John had never memorized the Miranda declaration. "Shut up, Keeton."

John pulled his wallet where he kept the statement out of

his back pocket. By the time he read Keeton his rights, Izzy and Paul had Dancer saddled.

"Anything in that cabin you need?" he asked her.

"Paul's gear and there's some food."

"Get it and let's go," John said as he unloaded Paul's guns.

She came out carrying a gunnysack. He prodded Keeton to his feet, hefted the rifles under one arm and told Isabelle to mount up. He pointed the direction and trailed behind, leading Rowdy as they returned to his camp.

He rolled his sleeping bag and tied it behind his saddle, found a pigging string in his poke and used it to tie the rifles onto his saddlehorn. "I'm gonna tell you something," he said to his prisoner. "You stay twenty feet in front of me. If that distance varies an inch, you're in deep shit." He unsnapped the strap holding his pistol. "I *always* hit where I aim. That goes for you, too, Paul."

"Paul can ride double with me," Isabelle said.

"No. That's dangerous."

"It's at least ten miles," she argued. "He's wounded. He can't walk—"

"Isabelle. He walked up here. He can walk back. He's not that bad off. I intend to get all of us off this mountain with nobody else getting hurt."

At the limestone ledge, John unclipped his cell phone and tried for service. To his relief, the phone worked. He called the office and Rooster answered. John told him to meet him in the Blazer at Isabelle's house.

An hour later, an armada of vehicles met them in Isabelle's driveway. She stood back as John loaded Paul and Keeton into the Blazer. Walt Cassidy and Dan O'Neal approached.

"Thank God," Cassidy said and patted John's shoulder.

"Good job, Bradshaw." O'Neal stuck out his hand. "Proper procedure would have been for you to have notified the right people and gone in with enough assets to prevent injury."

"Not enough time. I knew where I was going and what I was doing." He would probably never tell O'Neal about Keeton getting the drop on him.

"I'm a little pissed off," the ISP investigator said with a laugh, "that I didn't get a piece of this. Nothing would've made me happier than to surprise those fuckers in a deserted cabin."

John glanced over at Izzy, who was standing at her back door, chewing on her lip. Rooster waited in the Blazer's driver's seat. John slapped the roof a couple of times. "Go to town, Rooster. I'll be right behind you."

The caravan members all seemed to crank their engines at once and headed down the driveway like a parade. When they had gone, he walked over to Izzy. Every inch of her appeared to be in agony, but she was dry-eyed. He took off his hat. "You're a brave heart, Isabelle."

"He's so easily influenced by the wrong people," she said, wiping away a tear that had sneaked out. "I always wanted him to find someone besides Merle to be friends with."

John nodded, surprised that he had come to a similar conclusion himself.

"Thank you for saving him, John. They would have killed him. You heard that one guy."

He enclosed her in his embrace. "No, they wouldn't have, darlin'. They're professionals. That's just adrenaline and ego talking. All bullshit." He set her away. "I have to go. You'll have to come to town and make a statement. Take your time, but come as soon as you can."

"Okay," she said in a tiny voice. "He's hurt. What about his wound?"

"You don't have to worry. He and Merle both will get any medical treatment they need. I'll see to it."

She gave a big sniff. "I know. I trust you, John."

"Everything will turn out okay. You'll see." He cupped the back of her head and placed a soft kiss on her forehead. "I love you," he said softly. "Don't ever forget that."

"I won't."

He drew back with a kiss on the back of her hand and put on his hat. "Can Rowdy stay here 'til I can come back and get him?"

She nodded. "I'll unsaddle him and put him in the barn with Polly and Trixie."

"You don't have to—"

"I want to." She gave him a hint of a smile. "What, you think I can't take care of a horse?"

He walked toward his truck, turning back to gaze at her again before he climbed in. He had never seen anyone look more forlorn. Heart aching, he walked back to where she stood and took her hand. "He needs a lawyer. Get somebody good from Boise."

He dredged up a smile, too, remembering what she had said the night she told him why she felt so much loyalty to her brother. "I'm responsible for him as much as I am for everybody else, Isabelle. I'll look out for him."

# Chapter 29

"Helluva thing," Walt Cassidy said, setting his coffee mug on the corner of John's desk. "After Keeton had already offed one official, I'll always wonder why he didn't shoot you, too."

Court had ended minutes earlier. Keeton had been arraigned and denied bail. Cassidy would be transporting him to his larger, more secure jail. John had offered to deliver Keeton, but Cassidy had wanted to come to the court hearing.

Represented by a pit bull defense lawyer Izzy had hired, Paul had been released on bail, for which he had the money, and restricted against leaving Callister. Fate had smiled on him. God help him if he screwed up because he wouldn't have a supporter left anywhere.

A week had passed since John's trip up Callister Mountain to the miner's cabin. Since then his every hour had been filled. He had seen Izzy once since the day she came to the courthouse and gave her statement. They had talked on the phone but had not had a detailed discussion about her brother.

In his off hours, John had been telling his sons about his relationship with Izzy and her daughter. His mom had been talking to them, too.

"I've known Merle Keeton my whole life," John said to Cassidy. "It's hard to think of him as a killer. I always looked at him and Paul both as nothing more threatening than dumb bastards who get drunk and don't think."

The veteran lawman chuckled and smoothed his mustache. "All criminals are dumb, John, or they wouldn't get in the messes they do in the first place. Some are just dumber than others."

John stood and walked over to the coffeepot for a refill. He brought the carafe back and poured another cup for Cassidy."You believe Paul's story?"

"Yeah, I think I do. Most of it anyway. More important, ISP's polygraphist believes it. I don't doubt Rondeau was scared after he saw that his buddy had shot Frank. I'm sure he was afraid *not* to help bury the body. Keeton himself admitted Rondeau was no hand with a pistol and that was the only weapon in play."

"You're satisfied then that Keeton just accidentally dropped the knife in the process of burying Frank."

Cassidy nodded. "My only question is if Rondeau's lying when he says he didn't see Keeton fire the shots."

"I've heard a lot of things about Paul, but I've never heard him called a liar."

"Well, no matter. A lie's hard to maintain over time. In the coming months, Paul'll have to repeat his story a dozen times. If he's lying, at some point he'll trip himself up."

"How do you think Merle got Frank's gun? You suppose Frank really drew on him over a fishing violation?"

Cassidy shook his head and sipped his coffee. "No. But we might as well face it, John. Some things we'll never know for sure. That's the way it is in criminal investigations."

"Think Paul'll do time?"

"I don't know. He sung like a canary, seemed eager to help out. Him making that call to your office brought the whole thing to a head and he supported you up at that cabin. If he's willing to be a witness in court, well, who knows? Judge Morrison seems to like him. He must believe he's redeemable."

"One thing's for sure," John said, "I'll be keeping an eye on him. Isabelle's gonna put him to work. She told me his wife is coming back and bringing his kids and that'll make a difference in his behavior."

"A family in the picture is usually a good thing."

"I feel Paul's got a decent streak. But he needs some order in his life."

"Who doesn't? My ex-wives would tell you the same thing about me." Cassidy drained his cup, rose and reached for his hat. "If you need Keeton, he'll be locked up safe and sound in my jail."

"Thanks for everything, Walt. I don't know how I would've handled all of this without you."

"You'd have done just fine, sheriff. Just fine. A little bird told me the county commissioners are going to have a meeting about raising the sheriff's pay and pumping up the budget for the office. With two murders in three years, maybe they see they need a real sheriff after all." The old lawman looked at him with a twinkle in his eye. "Maybe you'll stick around. Maybe you'll run for the office."

John grinned. Luke McRae had all but promised him a raise in pay if he would just run. And Dan O'Neal had left town calling him "Sheriff" instead of "Bradshaw." For the last few days John had been secretly thinking he might contact the ISP about taking a few classes in their peace officer training school.

After Cassidy left with Merle Keeton in his custody, John sat for a few minutes contemplating irresponsibility and bad judgment and the catastrophic result. Fishing for sturgeon was forbidden in Idaho waters. Everybody knew it, including Paul and Keeton, but they did it anyway, for fun. The penalty was a heavy fine and possible restrictions on fishing licenses, but it didn't compare to the punishment for murder. And it sure wasn't worth the loss of a man's life. The whole episode made John shudder.

He shrugged into his jacket and put on his hat and told Rooster and Dana he was going home. He walked outside and looked up at the azure sky. Spring in the mountains. The sun had some warmth to it. The earth smelled fresh. He had two healthy sons of whom he would soon have sole legal custody. A lawyer in Boise was handling the matter now. He owned a good horse and a good woman loved him. What more could a man ask for?

His boys were still with his folks. His horse and saddle and his horse trailer were at Isabelle's. His clothes, his TV and his king-sized bed were sitting in his duplex apartment. What he needed to do now was have a long talk with his boys, then organize and consolidate.

He drove to the Lazy B, where his family welcomed him with smiles and open arms. Whatever the thing was that had hung between him and his dad for the past few years seemed to have vanished and they were returning to the warm relationship of long ago. John guessed his dad no longer thought him an irresponsible screwup who gave no thought to his actions.

He spent a good evening with his sons, telling them his plans for his future and theirs. They liked the idea of living in the country again, in a household where horses and dogs were part of everyday life. They didn't even mind that a girl came along with it.

The next morning, while he showered and put on a dress shirt, his mom helped his boys into the new jeans and boots she and his dad had bought them. After John finished dressing, they stood straight as arrows in front of him for his inspection. They seemed to be excited about making a good impression.

His parents came into the living room. "Here's the ring, son." His dad handed him an antique wedding ring. "I'm not convinced this move you're about to make is for the best, but—"

"Hush up, Tom," Katie Bradshaw said. "It's none of your business. This is John's life, not yours." She came to John. "It can be resized if necessary. I had it cleaned and had the stone tightened."

The ring had belonged to John's paternal great-grandmother. John's mother had worn it when she married his father. As stones went, the emerald was small, but its symbolism wasn't. Four generations of solid marriages and families stood behind it.

"Are you sure you're finished with it?" John asked his mom.

She laughed and hugged him, then looked up at his dad. "I haven't worn it since your dad bought me this marble-sized rock. It's for good luck, John. Someday you'll pass it on to one of your children for the same reason. I know you've found the right one this time. I can't wait to welcome Isabelle and her daughter into our family."

"Dad, is our new mom gonna let us have our own horse again?" his nine-year-old asked.

John had called Isabelle earlier and told her he would be dropping by to introduce her and his sons. "Son, she'll even teach you how to talk to him."

He and the boys stopped off at Fielder's Mercantile to buy a bouquet. Fielder's didn't have roses, so Trey said he thought the red carnations were pretty. John thought so, too, remembering the day he had bought Izzy a bouquet of carnations and placed it on the seat of her truck. Izzy wouldn't care what kind of flowers they were. She would care more about the sentiment.

As he came to a stop in his usual place near the barn, Izzy and Ava came outside. With the sun shining on her hair, Izzy looked beautiful. He and his sons climbed out of the truck.

Izzy eyed the bouquet and grinned. "What's that?"

"It's flowers," he said.

She laughed. "I can see that."

He urged Trey and Cody forward. "This is Trey and Cody." Solemn-faced, both boys put out their right hands and John hid a grin. Isabelle smiled, shook their hands and introduced Ava.

Before the moment could become awkward, he dug the ring from his shirt pocket, then sank to one knee and prodded his sons to do the same. He thrust the ring and the flowers out to her. "Isabelle, we came to ask you and Ava to marry us."

She gave a little gasp. "You are *crazy*, John Bradshaw." She turned her head and covered her face with her hand.

"How about it? Since you've already got my horse and my saddle and my heart, I'm hoping you'll take me and my kids, too."

Ava looked up at her mother and grabbed for her free hand. "Mama! Say yes."

But Isabelle was wiping her eyes with the tail of her shirt.

John cocked his head. "Isabelle?"

Ava stepped up. "We will."